To Jeanett

Love & best w...

Dilli Ashleu.
&x

the last chorus

a warrior creek novel

When the last chorus ends get ready to sing a new song.

NIKKI ASHTON

dedication

For George

Good friends are hard to find
Harder to lose
Impossible to forget

Warrior Creek Statement

It was confirmed today that the band, Warrior Creek, are to split. This comes six months after the tragic loss of Beau Bradley's wife and three-year-old son in a car accident.

The group's front man, Beau, hasn't been seen in public since that day. It's believed that bass guitarist Elliot Andrews stepped in as lead singer to complete the final songs for their upcoming album, *'Lay Down Your Arms'*.

Ali Bennet, the band's manager, said that working with the boys had been six years of pure joy, but the time had come for them to go their separate ways. She then continued to read a brief statement.

"After a Grammy, two Brits and two platinum albums the time has come for us to lay down our instruments and say goodbye.

Since the awful loss of Cassie and Bobby, continuing with the band is inconceivable for Beau. He wishes to honour their memory. To do that he needs some quiet time to think of them and to contemplate his future. The rest of us cannot see ourselves performing without him. He is our brother, and we respect the time he needs. That is why, with great sadness, we have made the decision to split.

Beau, Elliot, Joey and Ronnie would like to thank you, the fans, for all your support over the years and they hope that you understand how difficult this time has been for them. Our love and respect also go to Brit Arts UK, our management company, and our label Tenfold Music. Specifically, we want to thank Ali Bennet who has not only been a great manager, but a treasured friend."

Miss Bennet refused to answer any questions and looking physically distressed she left the press conference.

While the heart-breaking death of Bradley's family appears to be the catalyst for the split of the tight-knit band, for those in the industry it comes as no surprise. Before the accident Bradley had already recorded some solo material. It is also well known that Joey Farrow, the band's drummer, shows a talent for acting. He recently appeared in the Netflix Original show, *"Backstage Pass"*, as the brother of a teenage rock star.

one

Beau

I rolled over and burrowed my face into the pillow wishing that it still smelled of her. I was desperate to still feel her there. In that bed with me. Wrapped in my arms. Tangled together. Her smelling of flowers and sunshine and me worshipping every inch, every bone, and every hair on her head.

My arms felt empty. My heart felt lifeless.

Death had stolen the beauty and purity of my wife and replaced it with loneliness and pain.

We weren't perfect, not as people or as a couple, but we loved each other. I fucking adored her and the life we led. A life that was full of everything, sadness, tears, pain, love, joy, happiness. We were fractured at times, but we were us. Me, Cassie, and Bobby.

Bobby, my gorgeous golden-haired boy with his perfect smile and infectious giggle. Our little surprise who, from the minute he was born, had me wrapped around his finger.

Now they were gone, and the house was silent, cold, and empty. My life, meaningless. Not even music brought me any semblance of comfort. My band, filled with the three men I thought of as brothers, couldn't help me any longer. The songs didn't fill my veins with adrenalin, performing didn't give me a buzz. The only thing existing inside of me was a crumbling ache of nothingness.

A deep breath helped to loosen my chest from the pressure of grief, and I moved onto my back. The room was dark despite it being two in the afternoon. The curtains and blackout blinds hadn't been opened for God knew how long. I barely left the bed or the room and had only been out of the house once in a year and that had been for their funeral. A funeral where I'd disrespected them both by getting shitfaced at the wake. Falling all over the place and sobbing like a baby, Ronnie had tried to get me to leave but I wouldn't listen. In the end he and Ali turned my mother on me. My tiny little Ma, who stood a little less than five feet and four inches.

"You want them to be ashamed of you?" she'd asked as I lolled in my seat. "Because they would be. That beautiful girl and that sweet boy would be embarrassed and humiliated that you're behaving like a drunken animal."

"But they're not here, are they?" I curled my lip and tried desperately to stay upright.

Ma drew in a shaky breath and shook her head. "No, they're not but it doesn't mean you disrespect them by acting like your damn father."

That shocked me almost to become sober. "I am nothing like him. I know how to handle my drink. That man had no damn clue."

"Prove it then," she'd hissed. "Drink some coffee, sober up and behave like Cassie would expect you to."

I did as she asked and the remaining guests had seen me pull myself together. Once I was home, I decided I was going to grieve in whatever way I wanted, even if that was drinking myself sick on alcohol. I didn't, I chose to lie in my bed for weeks, barely eating and only talking to the other lads or my ma via text. Even my little sister was ignored, and she was my third favourite person in the world.

At that thought, I laughed emptily. Belle was now my *first* favourite person.

My stomach rumbled and I groaned. Food was something I needed to think about but that would mean not thinking about *them* for a few minutes and that was a few minutes *too* long. My hand reached across the creased duvet and landed on the soft wool of Bobby's blanky. Lifting it up to look at it, my heart sank. I couldn't remember his smell. No matter how much I tried, or how hard I concentrated, I couldn't remember. That was almost as heart-breaking as knowing he would never run into our room again dragging the blue wool behind him.

When another gurgle came from my gut, I heaved a sigh and rolled up into a seated position. A stench of sweat and grime hit me. Not only was it time I ate something but took a shower too. I was pretty sure I'd only had three or four in the last few months. As for food I could go days without it.

As I contemplated whether maybe today was the day that I showered and ate, my phone rang out on the set of drawers next to my side of the bed... it had been Cassie's side, but now it was mine.

"Fuck."

It was Elliot, our Lead Guitarist and the only man who could make me see sense about most things in life and I'd avoided his calls more than anyone else's. I didn't want to be persuaded to get out of bed and start to live my life without them.

Watching the phone jump about, I gripped hold of Bobby's blanky and waited for the ringing to stop and Elliot to get the hint that today was another day I didn't want to talk; especially today.

Finally, it stopped, and I breathed out slowly waiting for his text to come through, which was what he usually did.

The ringing started again almost immediately. Elliot and I completed the same routine until the sixth time when I snatched up the phone.

"Do you ever get the hint?" I snapped.

"No. Are you getting out of your fucking pit today?" I heard a door shut on the other end of the line. "I get what you're going through, but it's time you stopped being a total wanker and actually start speaking to people. Everyone is worried about you. It's gone on long enough."

"Is that it?" I asked. "Can I go now?"

Elliot sighed. "Beau, mate. You have to carry on with your life at some point. We've all been pretty patient and given you long enough to grieve but it's time."

"Time for what, Elliot. To move on from my wife and child. Shall I get myself on Tinder and see if I can grab a quick shag for tonight?"

"Don't be a dick. That isn't what I was saying. Your ma called and—"

"Oh, I might know she was behind this. Well, you can call my ma back and tell her 'not today, Sylvie'."

"Do you think that—"

I interrupted him again. "*Do not fucking say it.* Don't you dare ask if I think Cassie would want this. Of course, she fucking wouldn't. If she had a choice neither she nor Bobby would be dead. So, no, of course she wouldn't want me to be like this. She'd get hold of my ear and drag me from this fucking bed and tell me I was being a dick head and to man the fuck up. She's not here though is she, Elliot. She's fucking dead, or have you forgotten that."

Breathing heavily, I pushed the heel of my hand against my eyes. The walls felt as though they were closing in. Suddenly it was too dark. Getting up from the bed, with my phone still pressed to my ear, I went over to the curtains and dragged them open to pull up the blind. The wintery light made me wince with its harshness. I threw my arm over my eyes and blew out a breath.

"What do you want, Elliot?"

"You know what I want, Beau. I want you to get out of bed. I want you to shower and eat. I want you to be ready for when we come over in a couple of hours."

Bracing my back against the wall, I slid down it and dropped my head back. "Who are we?" As if I didn't know.

"Me, Ronnie and Joey. We're coming over."

"What the hell for? I don't want you here. Not today."

Elliot was quiet and I thought that maybe he'd finally got the message, but then he sighed.

"You're a wanker, Beau. Don't you think we're grieving as well? Cassie was my oldest friend. We were all Bobby's godfathers. She was the one who helped get Joey off drugs when he wouldn't go into rehab. Bobby was Ronnie's best friend because basically they had the same mental age."

I laughed at that. He was right. Ronnie and Bobby would play together for hours. I never even minded that Bobby had thought Ronnie was a better guitarist than I was a singer.

"I know Cassie and Bobby were important to you all," I replied, feeling the blood in my veins starting to heat up. "But I just don't want company, El."

"Too fucking bad. Today of all days we need to be with you. We'll be there in two hours."

The line went dead, and I knew I had no choice. Elliot meant what he said. They would be there in exactly two hours because aside from everything else he was an anally attentive fucker when it came to time keeping.

two

Beau

"What the fuck have you done to yourself?" A voice exclaimed.

I pulled up short, surprised to see my band mates—former bandmates, I corrected myself—sitting in my lounge, drinking what I guessed were mugs of tea. We'd always drunk gallons of it.

"How the fuck did you get in?" I padded over to the armchair and gingerly lowered myself into it. Months of doing nothing except walking to the bathroom or downstairs to get a drink of water and the occasional meal seemed to have taken its toll on me. My legs were like jelly. My arms had just about managed to reach up and wash my hair in the shower.

"Your mum gave us a key for intervention purposes," Joey replied.

"I don't need an *intervention*," I complained. "And *she* shouldn't have given it to you."

"And I repeat," Joey sighed. "What the fuck have you done to yourself?"

"Nothing." I rubbed my fist against my breastbone and the constant pain.

"Exactly." Elliot leaned forward and placed his mug on the coffee table. "Put it on a coaster, Cassie will…"

Cassie wouldn't be complaining about mug rings on the wood, or that one of them had trailed mud in on their shoes, or that I'd left clippings from my shaver all over the bathroom floor.

Joey cleared his throat and picked up Elliot's mug and placed it on a Take That coaster. Cassie had got them for me one Christmas mainly because she thought she was fucking hilarious. I hated the band but loved those damn coasters.

"You look like shit," Ronnie announced, breaking the heavy silence. "When was the last time you had a shave?"

I shrugged. "I'm going for the sexy lumberjack look."

"Well, it's not working," Ronnie replied. "You look more vagrant than lumberjack."

"A vagrant who hasn't eaten in weeks." Elliot got up from the sofa, took off his leather jacket and threw it over the arm. "I'm going to make you something. What about you two?"

"Depends on what you're cooking," Joey replied with a curl of his top lip. "I'm trying to stay off meat."

Elliot rolled his eyes but remained silent. Whatever Joey tried to do to get clean and stay clean we put up with. No one wanted to risk him going back on the toot; not that a fucking pork chop could send him over the edge.

"Omelette, so you want one or not."

"Yeah, go on then."

"I'll have one as well then," Ronnie replied.

"I don't want one." I rested my head back against the chair and took a deep breath. "Not sure I've even got any eggs."

"Yeah, you do," Elliot said as he left the room. "I brought a load of food with me."

"Fuck," I groaned. "I knew I should have pissed off somewhere remote."

"He'd have tracked you down, you know that, right." Joey gave me a smile that made me want to punch him. I didn't want their sympathy; I just wanted my wife and boy back.

***

My stomach felt much better for having food inside of it, not that I planned to admit it. I'd fought the three of them about eating until Ronnie and Joey threatened to hold me down while Elliot forked some in. I figured I may as well give up at that point and eat the omelette and bread and butter put in front of me.

"Thanks, Elliot." I pushed my almost empty plate away. "Just can't eat that last piece of bread."

Ronnie leaned forward and snaffled it from my plate and then wiped it around his own, mopping up the tomato ketchup he'd almost drowned his food in.

"You really need to start and look after yourself," Joey said, resting his elbows on the granite top of the kitchen island. "Staying locked up isn't good for you."

"So, you didn't call just for a social visit then?"

"Beau," Elliot warned. "Of course, we'd come today. It's been a year, so what did you expect us to do?"

My stool scraped across the tiles as I pushed it back and picked up my plate taking it over to the dishwasher. When I pulled open the door, the sharp edge hit me in the thigh. It hurt like hell, but I remained silent. The pain was nothing compared to the one I'd had in my chest for the last three hundred and sixty-five days.

"Beau."

I winced at the sound of Elliot's soothing voice. "What I expect you to do, Elliot, is let me be alone to grieve or maybe fucking kill myself, because at this point the latter seems the better option."

Three different responses sounded out. A gasp, a curse and a slam of a mug.

"You don't mean that," Ronnie said. "Tell me you don't."

Ronnie Dwyer the little kid in the man's body. The one who wanted everyone to be friends. The one who hated arguments. The one who wanted everything to stay the same. The one who wanted to live in a land of unicorns and rainbows—well guess fucking what, Ronnie, life is shit, nothing stays the same and people you love die. They take the car out in the damn snow because their stupid, fucking, selfish, cunt of a husband ate the last of the bread before he left for the studio mid-afternoon, knowing that his three-year-old son liked a piece of toast before he went to bed at night.

I slammed the dishwasher door closed. "Yeah, Ron, I don't mean it." There was a distinct lack of conviction in my voice, but I couldn't give a shit.

"Beau, stop it. You know he'll be fucking worried sick about you now."

While Ronnie was the man-child, Elliot was the grown up. The caregiver, the sensible one. He was the leader of the band. It was *his* band, yet he was so full of fucking goodness he didn't care that I was the one who got all the attention as the singer. He was happy that his best friend forever fell for me and was stupid enough to marry me. He was our best man; he was always the fucking best of men and it pissed me off.

"Well sorry for upsetting you, Ron," I jibed. "It must be awful for you."

Elliot ran a hand down his face and pushed away from the island. He stood up and gathered all the plates, carrying them over and handing them to me. Breathing heavily through flared nostrils, I opened the dishwasher door again, this time missing my leg, and practically threw the plates in.

"We want to talk to you." Elliot leaned back against the counter; his arms crossed over his broad chest.

"No way, that's a surprise. I thought you just wanted to feed me and drink my tea and celebrate the anniversary of my family's death."

"Don't be a twat, Beau," Joey said and then turned to Ronnie who was staring into his mug. "He's not going to kill himself."

Ronnie looked up at me, his green eyes searching my face for some sign that I might.

"I'm not, Ron," I sighed and ran a hand through my too long hair. It was usually a scruffy mess, but perfectly styled that way, now it was almost to my shoulders with a hint of a curl. The same curls that Bobby had.

There was that pain again.

"Don't," Ronnie replied, "you're a pain in the arse, but that doesn't mean I don't want you around. We knew you'd feel bad today."

"No worse than any other day," I muttered, and my shoulders sagged. "Okay, what do you want to talk about other than the obvious."

They all shared a look and I waited for Elliot to speak. I knew it would be him.

"We think we were hasty in putting the statement out that we've split," he said and scratched his cheek. "Instead, we want you to think about taking another six months out and then getting back together. We're still officially signed with Tenfold for another year."

I shook my head. "No. Made my mind up."

"It was a knee jerk reaction and we all agreed because we were grieving too," he replied, pushing off the counter. "Having had the last few months to think about it. Having talked about it, we think it'd be better for you to just take a break for a while. You can still do your solo stuff either in the meantime or when we get back together, it's up to you. It was working before, us all doing solo material as well as Warrior Creek music, so it could work again. Joey's still doing a little bit of acting but he wants to go again, don't you, Joey?"

Joey nodded. "I got asked to try for a guest role in another Netflix show, but I'd be free in six months. In time for us to start making music again."

"No." I shook my head again and again and again. "I don't want to. I was doing it for my family and now I don't have a fucking family, so…" I shrugged.

"You were doing it before you even got with Cassie, so that's bullshit," Joey said. "You were doing it for you. You just liked that it gave Cassie this big fucking house and Bobby a fancy nursery school."

I rushed towards him and pointed my finger, only inches from his face. "Don't tell me what I did or didn't do for my family. You have no fucking idea what goes on in my head." I used the same finger to stab at the side of my head, practically spitting the words at Joey. "You don't fucking know."

The breath I took was painful and when Elliot placed his hand on my back, my throat tightened and burned. I would not cry in front of them over an argument about the band. My tears were for Cassie and Bobby, not damn music.

"Calm down," Elliot said soothingly. "Calm down. We didn't want to upset you, but it's been a year and maybe with a little more time you might change your mind. So, all we're saying is *if* you do, don't be afraid to say. We'd definitely be open to starting up again."

"I won't regret it." I moved to the other side of the kitchen. My teeth clenched and my hands fisted as I dared them to say anything else.

"Beau—"

"No Ronnie," I blasted at him. "I won't fucking regret it. I lost my family, or have you forgotten that?"

"Of course we haven't," Ronnie replied. "We all lost them."

"No, no, no," I hissed, rushing at him and halting toe to toe. "You do not get to piggyback on my fucking grief. They were *my* family. *My* wife. *My* son. What don't you understand about the fact that music will never ever make up for them?"

"Beau, calm down," Elliot said, holding out a hand to me as I whirled away from Ronnie.

I smacked it away. "Saint-fucking-Elliot. Smoothing the waters as usual. Well, I don't want you here. I don't want any of you here. I don't want to get the band back together. I just want Cassie and Bobby back." My chest heaved with the effort it took to yell at them through the ball of anger nestled in my chest. Tears and great crashing sobs were moments from spilling over as panic, loneliness and pity hit me.

Joey slapped his hand down on the counter and leaned forward. "You have no right to treat us like shit, Beau. We weren't the ones who made it snow. We weren't the ones who hadn't gritted the road. Losing them wasn't down to us. All we've ever done is try and be there for you."

He was right. It wasn't their fault. If anyone was to blame it was me for eating the last of the bread. Cassie would never have got in the car and driven to the shop if I hadn't been so selfish. Knowing that though didn't mean that I cared what the three men in front of me wanted or thought.

"I fucking know that."

Joey took a breath. "I'm sorry, Beau. We obviously got this all wrong, but maybe in time it's something—"

"Fucking hell, Joey, take a hint." I slammed both my hands on the counter next to his and yelled into his face. "Just fuck off and leave me to wallow in my own self-pity and grief!"

Ronnie quickly moved next to me. He was almost allergic to confrontation. We all knew his childhood hadn't been great, but that had only been because he'd lost his parents at a young age and had to live with his auntie Mo, who was one of the loveliest women I'd ever met.

"Beau, mate," he whispered. "We're sorry okay, really sorry. But remember everything we do comes from a good place."

I knew Ronnie was right, they *were* trying to come from a good place. If they'd been any other men, or we'd been any other band I might have thought they'd suggest getting back together for selfish reasons, for the money, or the fame. I knew them though. We'd been together as a band for eight years, since we were eighteen; we were brothers. They were doing what they thought was right for me. But I just wanted them gone.

I let out a long breath and closed my eyes.

"If it makes you feel better and it also gets you to fuck off out of my house, I promise that if I change my mind, I'll tell you." The words were forced and ground out, but I knew that they wouldn't leave otherwise.

"Okay," Elliot replied. "That's all we can ask." He nodded and the other two moved towards the door. "We'll go and leave you be. If you decide you don't want to be alone today, we can come straight back."

That was Elliot. He always knew what the right thing to do was. If they stayed any longer things might be said that I'd regret more than those I'd already yelled at them. Elliot was more than aware of that.

Each one silently slapped me on the back and then left, the only noise the click of the front door.

Ten minutes later as I sat on the kitchen floor and took my phone from my pocket, I realised I hadn't asked for my key back. Yet, when I pressed play it was no longer important. All I cared about was the blonde beauty on the screen, holding the cute little boy with my curls and her colouring.

"Bobby, say hi to Daddy. Go on, say hi Daddy, we miss you."

"Miss you Daddy. Wuv you."

"You're such a good boy." Cassie blew a kiss to the camera. "Love you babe, can't wait until you're back home. Bye for now."

As tears dripped onto the screen, I hit play again and felt my chest crack open once more.

"Bobby, say hi to Daddy…"

three

Beau

The anniversary of Cassie and Bobby's death kind of became a turning point for me. There was no major revelation or decision made to live a normal life again, but at least now I was showering and eating regularly. Funny that the second worst day of my life was the one that kicked me up the arse.

Standing at the floor to ceiling windows at the back of the house, I looked over the garden; all clean and tidy, ready for Spring. Alex, my gardener, had been visiting regularly as had Diane the cleaner. They both had keys so over the last year they had done what they had to do without bothering me too much. Cassie had arranged for them both to be paid via our accountant, like proper employees, so it wasn't like I even had to see them to hand over any cash. All I did was move from the bedroom for Diane to clean it and then move back again once she'd finished. For the first four months I hadn't let her in there. I'd needed to be able to smell Cassie for as long as possible. Eventually though, once my stench of grime and sweat were the only things invading my nostrils, I gave in and let her change the sheets and do a bit of dusting and vacuuming.

Drinking down my coffee I looked over to the corner of the room where one of my three guitars stood. It hadn't moved for a year. I'd not been inclined to play or sing so the guy's idea to start up again in six months' time was ridiculous. I wasn't even sure I had a singing voice anymore. I'd certainly not used my voice much for anything, seeing as I'd avoided everyone and relied on text messages to confirm that I was still breathing—just.

With a sigh my gaze went back to the garden, and I watched as a couple of pigeons landed on the bird table and started to peck at the food. There we were in the countryside and the only birds we got in the garden were flying fucking rats. It seemed that since Cassie had gone, all those pretty birds with different coloured feathers that she and Bobby liked to watch had decided I wasn't worth the effort. Couldn't say I blamed them.

"Oh, Beau, I didn't realise you were down here."

I turned to see Diane coming in with a duster and can of polish.

"Hey, Di. Yeah, thought I'd actually have breakfast today." I lifted the mug of coffee in my hand.

"Coffee is not breakfast. You want me to make you some toast?" she asked.

"It's fine," I replied. "I can make it. It's not your job to cook for me too."

"It's toast, Beau," she called from the utility room. "Hardly cooking."

I knew if I didn't eat something that she'd keep on at me. "I'll make it. You want some or a cup of tea."

Diane poked her head around the doorway. "Tea would be lovely, but just put the kettle on. I'll make it, your tea is bloody awful."

I rolled my eyes. There was nothing wrong with my tea. It was nice and strong, nothing like the piss weak stuff that she liked to drink.

Once I'd filled the kettle, I pulled a mug from the cupboard for her and dropped in a teabag. While I waited for the water to boil my eyes were drawn back to the garden. There was a ball in the middle of the lawn that hadn't been there before. My immediate thought was Bobby must be cold out there… I'll take him his hat and scarf… but then my heart sank as realisation dawned.

"Di," I called.

"Yes."

"Stupid question, but do you know if that ball has been outside since…" My voice trailed off and I inhaled deeply.

She joined me at the island and followed my gaze. A cool hand landed on my forearm. "Sweetheart, that's not Bobby's. His balls and outside toys are all in boxes in the garage. Alex did it."

I moved away from her, closer to the window to stare outside at the blue and black ball. It was nothing yet the sight of it brought a huge fucking lump to my throat. All I could think about was the fact that my boy should have been out there running and jumping around getting fresh air into his lungs.

"New people have moved in next door," Diane said hesitantly. "Maybe they have kids and one of them has kicked it over."

I turned back to face her. "Di, I'm not going to break down because you mention kids or families."

"I'm sorry, Beau. It's just that…well, you've not been handling things well and I didn't know whether it would upset you."

"Well, it won't," I snapped.

Immediately I felt guilty. She'd only tried to be sympathetic, but I wanted to scream at her to stop being nice and fuck off out of my house.

The kettle clicked off and I heard Diane pouring the water into her mug. A few seconds later there was the clink of the spoon against the china and then the scraping of a stool. The ball outside rolled a little as the wind caught it and at the same time the pigeons flew away. My shoulders sagged.

"I'm sorry, Di. I know you are only trying to be nice."

"It's alright, sweetheart. I know it's been awful for you. Devastating. But it's hard to know what to say." She laughed softly. "You haven't actually spoken more than a dozen words in the last year so I'm probably out of practice."

I turned and smiled. "It's been shit, but I'm trying to take small steps to get better."

"You actually getting out of bed for the last two weeks is a start." She took a sip of her tea and gave a satisfied smile. "Lovely. Much better than yours."

Another eye roll from me.. I turned back to look out of the window, and almost missed him. A small, brown-haired boy dressed in jeans, red anorak and blue wellies. With the ball under his arm he was disappearing through my hedge. I leaned closer to the window and saw that there was a small gap, just big enough for a little kid to get through. Mystery solved.

"You were right, Di," I said, still watching the garden. "There's a family moved in. One of the kids just came in and got his ball back."

She didn't answer, or if she did, I didn't hear her as I was concentrating too hard on not puking up the coffee I'd drunk.

***

Most of my morning had been spent aimlessly wandering around the house, having no damn clue what to do. My skin itched with boredom and frustration—frustration because I was bored, even though I knew that there were plenty of things I could have been getting on with. Sorting through Cassie and Bobby's clothes and stuff, organising the memorial that I should have organised for their anniversary, or even contacting my solicitor to check all Cassie's affairs were sorted. There'd been no way I was up to even talking about her to anyone else, never mind hanging on a telephone line listening to shit music for ages just to tell someone she'd died and no I didn't know her fucking password. So, there were plenty of things that I could have done with my day but had no desire to do.

Flopping down onto the sofa, I turned on the TV and flicked through the channels. Nothing caught my attention and I switched it off again before throwing the remote down.

The lounge also had windows that overlooked the garden so when I caught movement out of the corner of my eye, I leaned forward. The ball was back again. That meant the kid would be back. I moved over to the chair by the window and sank down so I wouldn't be seen from the garden. Something ached inside of me to see a kid in the garden again. I didn't care that he probably shouldn't be pushing through my hedge, I just needed to see him. I knew it would sound fucking weird to anyone else, but the kid wasn't tainted by the shit in my life. He was innocent and hopefully happy and if I just got to watch him collect his ball again, I thought it might bring a tiny bit of brightness to my blackened heart.

It took him ten minutes to appear, his leg pushing through first followed by his body. He was small, I guessed about four or five. His brown hair was cut short, not like Bobby's which was fairly long. He screamed blue murder if we ever suggested we got it cut.

"No. Want my hair like Daddy's."

The memory made my chest ache. Bobby idolised me and I'd spent his whole life being everything I could to him. Fatherhood had been the best thing to ever happen to me. We hadn't been planning on having kids so soon after we got married but once we knew he was on his way, Cassie and I couldn't wait. The moment Bobby was put into my arms, I vowed that I'd protect him and love him better than anyone. He'd never want for anything. The fucking irony being that he died because I couldn't provide him with bread for his fucking toast.

Steadying my breathing to push away the panic of my grief, I moved my concentration back to the garden. Instead of picking up his ball, the boy ran past it to the small pond that had plenty of plants in it but no fish because in the two years we'd lived in the house, we'd never got around to it. I straightened up and watched. I knew he was in no danger of falling in because we'd had a grill put over it but when he started to try and climb onto the small wall that surrounded it, my breath caught.

I was out of the patio doors and running across the lawn within seconds.

"Hey there," I called, not wanting to startle him. "Did you come for your ball?"

He stopped, one knee on the wall, his other leg poised to get into the same position and turned his head to look up at me with big brown eyes.

"I'm Beau," I said and held out my hand.

You'd never know I'd been a father for three years. Who offered a kid that age a handshake?

"What's your name?" Withdrawing my hand, I crouched down in front of him.

He stared silently at me, his mouth slightly open and his eyes getting wider with each passing second. There was no real danger for him, other than maybe falling back onto the grass or forward and landing on the grid. Either way the slightest movement and I'd catch him and stop it happening. I still felt anxious though and would feel better once he had two feet on the ground.

"You don't want to tell me?" I asked.

He still didn't speak but understood that I didn't want him climbing onto the pond because he scrambled down. Once both feet were on the floor, he turned to face me and shoved his hands into the pockets of his anorak. It was then that I remembered I was only dressed in sweats and a t-shirt. I didn't have anything on my feet except a pair of socks that were now damp from the grass.

When I shivered, the little kid looked down at my arms which were covered in goosebumps.

"I saw you come through the hedge," I said, glancing over at his ball. "To come and get your ball. Do you want to get it now so you can go back and play?"

He nodded but didn't move, his gaze never veering from mine. When I ran my hand through my hair, I realised that I probably looked like some kind of hairy giant. My beard was pretty unkempt as well, no wonder the poor kid looked terrified.

"Would you like me to get it for you?" I asked.

This time he shook his head and ran to the ball. As he picked it up and sprinted for the hedge, disappointment washed over me. I watched as he scrambled through it without looking back. His rejection felt like a punch to the stomach. I didn't care that at that very moment he was probably telling his parents about the strange bloke next door who wanted to know what his name was. No doubt I'd be getting a knock on the door asking me why I'd been weirding their kid out.

When my phone started shrilling in the pocket of my sweatpants my breath caught, stupidly thinking it might be the police wanting to know why I'd been talking to small boys. Shaking my head with the absurdity of the idea, I pulled out my phone and answered it without looking.

"Beau, love, are you okay?"

It was my Ma. God, of all the people I didn't want to talk to, she had to be top of my list. I loved her dearly, but she was interfering at the best of times but two weeks after the anniversary of her daughter-in-law and grandson's death, she was bound to be more interfering than usual.

"Hey, Ma. I'm fine, why?"

"Because you actually answered my call. For a long time, we've just communicated via text and if I have spoken to you, it's after calling you about ten times. So, you'll understand if I think there's something wrong with you."

Shivering I rose to my full height and ran back to the house, once inside slamming the door behind me.

"Maybe I've decided to come out of hiding," I replied. "You've all been telling me for months to get on with my life."

"True, just didn't actually believe you would. So," she said with a sigh. "You are alright then?"

My heart softened a little at the worry in her voice. Me and Belle were everything to her, and despite the fact she'd given us a ridiculous pair of names, we loved her just as much. We were happy to give her dad's share of our love too.

"I'm as good as can be expected, Ma. What about you? How're you?"

"Apart from a few aches and pains I'm dandy, love. Your sister isn't so good though."

"What's wrong with Belle?" I asked, the guilt of not speaking to her in almost a year hitting me like a ton of bricks.

"Oh, just a broken heart. It's complicated but top and bottom of it is that the lad she was seeing turned out to be a wrong 'un."

"What lad?" I flopped onto the chair and pulled off my damp socks.

"Of course, you won't know, not having spoken to her in so long."

Immediately my hackles rose. That was why I tried to limit my conversations and the time spent with her. She had a fucking amazing ability to piss me off despite how much I loved her.

"Tell Belle I'll call her sometime this week," I replied, wincing at the lie.

"Hmm whatever. Anyway, seeing as you're up and about I'll come and stay for a few days."

"What?" My heart thudded at the thought of her being in my space. With no parents of her own, Cassie used to love having her to stay. I could take or leave her visits. "Ma, I'm not ready for—."

"Too late, you said you were feeling better so I'm coming to stay. I'll bring Belle too; it'll do her good to get away for a bit. I'll let you know what train we'll be getting in on so you can either pick us up or send someone for us."

There she went telling what to do. You wouldn't think I was a twenty-six-year-old man who hadn't lived at home since I was eighteen. A twenty-six-year-old man who had numerous music awards and a few million quid in the bank. A man who'd had his own family.

"Ma, I don't want you to come," I said, voice a childish whine. "You don't need to come."

She sighed heavily. "I haven't seen you since the day of the funeral. Of course I'm coming. You may not need to see *me* son. But *I need* to see you."

And that was it. It was decided because she'd used the 'emotional blackmail' trick.

"Okay, just let me know when you'll be here."

We only spoke for a few more minutes before she told me that her potatoes were boiling over and she needed to save them.

The thought of her spending time in my space gave me a headache, so I decided my bed was the best place for me. I was almost at the stairs when there was a knock at the front door. I turned and hesitated. It had been a long time since anyone had knocked at that door but also it was something that Cassie had taken great pride in choosing. She'd said if this was our forever home, she wanted to pick a front door that was worthy of us walking through it for the rest of our lives. Stupid though it was, opening it without her being there felt like I was being disloyal. When another knock sounded out, I inhaled a shaky breath. I was supposed to be starting my life again and being frightened to open a door wasn't doing that.

With three shaky steps I reached for the lock and pulled open the door— reminding myself it was just *a fucking door*. As soon as I did, the cool air smacked me in the face, and I saw a petite dark-haired woman standing on the doorstep.

"Hi," she said, her arms wrapping a cardigan, thick and sloppy, around her body. "I'm Simone Addison from next door." Her eyes widened and it was obvious that she recognised me. "I believe you've met my son, Ethan. He's been in your garden."

four

Simone

Oh, my buggering hell. Beau Bradley was standing in front of me. *The* Beau Bradley. I had no idea he was my neighbour. To be honest in the three months since we'd moved in, I'd thought the house next door was empty. Not that you could see a great deal with the huge wall and hedge that surrounded it.

The neighbourhood was classy and expensive so I shouldn't have been surprised to find someone famous lived in the quiet, leafy road. Never in a month of Sundays would I have expected it to be the man whose music I loved. Seeing him there almost took my voice away with shock but I just about managed to push out the words.

"Hi, I'm Simone Addison from next door. I believe you've met my son, Ethan. He's been in your garden."

Beau didn't speak but just nodded. His face remained a blank canvas so I'd no idea what he was thinking about me going round and knocking on his door. If I'd known that he was our neighbour, I wouldn't have gone. It'd been widely reported in the press that he'd pretty much become a recluse since his wife and son had died. His band had split up and he'd lost his family. It was highly likely he was pissed that I'd called just to apologise for Ethan pushing through his hedge.

"I'm so sorry I disturbed you." I wrapped my arms tighter around me against the cold and the enormity of my embarrassment. "I just wanted to apologise for Ethan, he's my son. God, sorry, I've already said that. He's been coming through the hedge to get his ball and I didn't realise until he said he'd seen you in the garden. I asked him how and he told me about his ball and—"

"Hey." Beau held up his hand. "It's fine. It's not a problem."

My knees literally gave way as I stared up at him and I reached out to the door frame for support. I hated confrontation and while he hadn't bitten my head off, he wasn't exactly giving off a friendly vibe either.

"I'll tell him not to do it again," I offered.

"If he needs to get his ball back, it's no problem. I'll get my gardener to maybe cut the hedge back a bit."

"God, no!" I cried. "You don't need to do that. I can easily get him another ball, or you can throw it back."

A small smile cracked and it almost knocked me off my feet. His whole face changed even though a lot of it was covered by a shaggy beard. Beau Bradley wasn't heart-stoppingly beautiful like Elliot Andrews, the band's lead guitarist, but there was something about him that garnered him all the attention. Maybe it was a frontman thing, or that he always appeared to be so humble. It was obvious he adored his wife. I had no clue what it was, all I did know was that standing in front of me with a half-smile, looking as hairy as a yeti, he had to be the sexiest man I'd ever shared air space with.

"Like I said, it's not a problem. Tell him to come in any time."

I sucked my bottom lip into my mouth and nodded, unable to think of anything else to say without sounding even more of a bumbling idiot.

"Okay then," Beau said, leaning the top half of his body forward and arching his brows. When I still didn't speak, he cleared his throat. "Thanks for calling but it wasn't necessary."

I startled realising he wanted me to leave. "S-s-sorry. Yes. I'll get going. My brother is with Ethan so I should get going. He doesn't live with me, he lives in London, he's been here for the weekend and is leaving in..." I glanced down at the big, silver watch on my wrist. "Oh shit, now, he's leaving now. He has to get a train. Sorry, I'd better go."

Beau gave me a smile that said 'yes, go you crazy woman' and stepped back from the doorway and started to push it closed.

"Nice to meet you…"

"Simone," I replied. "Simone Addison. Right. Yes, nice to meet you too." I gave him a wave of my hand and half-turned to leave and before I'd even taken a step, I heard the door behind me click shut.

***

"Sorry," I called as I stepped into my hallway. "I'm here now so you can go."

Marcus, my brother came into view, his rucksack over his shoulder. "It's fine. My cab is about five minutes away." He pulled me into his side and kissed my head. "Was he okay? Didn't growl at you and tell you to keep your pesky kid off his land?"

I shook my head and pulled free of his hug, an itch spreading over my skin.

"Sorry," he said, holding up his hands. "Forgot you 'don't do affection'."

He was right, I didn't particularly, but he didn't know why. He barely knew me at all really. We probably only kept in touch because we only had each other and that had only got worse after I'd felt he'd let me down one night five years ago—a night that had changed my life. That was why Marcus even visiting had been a surprise, but I was sure it was more to do with the fact that I lived close to some of his old friends, so could visit them at the same time.

"I do," I protested, a little heat on my cheeks. "I'm just hot, that's all."

Marcus raised his eyebrows and put a hand to my cold face. "Whatever. Anyway, tell me about the guy next door. Did he tell you not to darken his doorstep again?"

"No. He was really nice about it, actually. Said he'd get his gardener to cut the hedge back."

"He has a gardener, eh. Must have some money."

Like you wouldn't believe… I chose not to say. I was pretty sure Beau

Bradley wouldn't want me spreading it around that he was my neighbour.

"Not surprised though," Marcus added. "Living on this road. I'd still like to know your friend who's rented this place to you for next to nothing. Does she have any properties like this in London that she'd like to help your big brother out with?"

I smiled and felt a little bad for him. Ethan and I were rattling around in a huge house while he paid a fortune for a one-bedroomed flat in Islington where he worked as a teacher.

"No, I don't think so." I rolled up on my toes and kissed his cheek. "Thanks for coming this weekend. Ethan's loved seeing you. We both have." Until another year passes.

"Loved being here, sis. Ethan's in his room. He was reading when I left him."

"He was okay?" I asked, glancing towards the staircase. "I take it he didn't speak to you."

Marcus shook his head. "No, sorry. I tried but nothing. He was smiling the whole time and seemed happy when I read him a story."

"That's a positive, right?"

Marcus nodded sagely; his brow furrowed. "Yeah, definitely. A real positive."

"Did you try and get him to talk?" I asked.

He nodded. "Yeah, yeah, but nothing."

I could tell by the thin line of his lips that his smile was hiding something. If even he, someone who taught kids, couldn't get Ethan to talk then there wasn't a great deal positive about the situation. For all of his five years, Ethan had only ever spoken to me. When he did, his speech was strong, maybe a little quiet, but his vocabulary was great for his age; he simply chose not to share it with anyone but me. Not even his uncle.

A car horn dragged me back to the present and I was back in my brother's arms for a much quicker hug this time.

"Ring me when you get home," I said as I led Marcus to the front door.

"I will, I promise. And, Simmy, please don't worry too much about Ethan. When he's ready he'll talk and then you'll never shut him up."

Then with a quick kiss to my cheek he was off, running down the drive to the taxi waiting for him.

When I closed the door, I leaned my forehead against it, wishing as I always did that, I had someone else who could tell me everything would be okay. Someone else to share the burden of a little boy who was broken.

five

Beau

I breathed out heavily and placed both palms against the front door. Just talking to another human being, someone outside of my circle, was damn tiring. I felt bone weary, like I'd just done a two-hour gig, not had a three-minute conversation with my neighbour. I couldn't believe how hard my heart had been beating the whole time. Thudding beats and sweaty palms all because I'd had to open the door to a stranger.

"What the hell is wrong with you?" I muttered to myself and banged my head against the door three times. "Stupid fucking idiot."

Taking another calming breath, I shuffled through to the kitchen and pulled open the fridge door. On the top shelf was a bottle of Patron and next to that a bar of Fruit & Nut—thank God for Di. I picked up both and thought about my options. Get hammered or stuff myself with chocolate, which I hadn't eaten in almost a year. Either way I was likely to puke.

"Damn it, Cassie, I could fucking kill you right now."

I slammed the door on the booze and chocolate and stared out toward the garden lit by the external lights that Cassie had insisted be put on a timer.

There was no ball, no little kid just a whole load of fucking nothing. A few trees and bushes blowing in the March wind and that was it. Just like my life, empty. I had nothing. No wife, no son, no music, totally devoid of any fucking joy. What was the point of me staying around?

I thought back to the conversation I'd had with the boys; the way Ronnie had reacted to the idea that I might kill myself. He was a little kid at heart, and he'd be the one something like that would hit the most. Apart from the fact that I couldn't do it to him, I didn't really have the nerve. The bone aching pain of losing Cassie and Bobby was constant but still wasn't enough to make me end my life; no matter how lonely and crap. I was enjoying the misery too much. I also had no idea whether there was life after death but if it led to more nothing, I couldn't stand that. At least this nothing gave me time to think about the two people I loved most. If I ended up in the ground with zilch after it, how the hell would I remember them? I wouldn't be able to look at their pictures, watch videos of Bobby telling me he loved me, get into my bed and remember nights where Cass and I had got lost in each other in it.

"Death is even more fucking miserable than life," I muttered and moved up to the window and stared out, my eyes searching. "What the hell are you even looking for, Beau?" I blinked and then smacked myself on the forehead. "And don't talk to yourself in the first person you prick."

That was the sort of thing that Dick Gregory, our label exec, would do. Because he *was* a prick. I could be a prick occasionally, but not generally. Talking to myself in the first person moved the prickishness from occasional to general.

Looking over towards the hedge, an image of my neighbour slipped into my head. She'd looked scared to death as soon as she set eyes on me. I knew she'd clocked who I was. She had that wide-eyed stare of a fan who didn't want to act like a fan but was quietly pissing her knickers with excitement.

It struck me that apart from Diane, the neighbour was the only woman I'd spoken to face to face in a year. I really hoped that she wouldn't find reasons to keep popping round. I'd meant it about the kid, he could come and get his ball anytime, but I didn't want his mum knocking on my door every day.

"God." I closed my eyes and dropped my forehead against the glass. "When did I turn into this fucking miserable twat who doesn't want perfectly nice neighbours calling around."

When my life was taken away from me.

The knock at the front door, startled and pissed me off at the same time. It had already started. She knew I lived here and was probably going to use any excuse possible to come and knock on my door.

Ignoring it, I held my breath. The next knock was louder.

"Go away," I muttered.

"Beau, open the door."

Fucking Elliot—again! *Not* the perfectly nice neighbour.

I chewed on the corner of my lip, contemplating hiding in the cupboard under the stairs. Knowing that if I did that, he'd only let himself in with my damn key anyway. Pinching the bridge of my nose I decided to let him in. At least I might then have a chance of persuading him to fuck off.

"Again?" I asked as I yanked open the door.

"Yep." He pushed past me.

"And no key"

"Key entry is intervention only, remember." He flashed me a sarcastic smile. "So, thought it best to be invited in."

"What are you a vampire all of a sudden?" I closed the door and watched as Elliot wandered through into the lounge.

"No idea what you're talking about," he called over his shoulder.

I shook my head and gave an empty laugh remembering it was another of mine and Cassie's things—The Vampire Diaries. Well, it was Cassie's thing, I just watched it with her because it meant she'd be curled up at my side. I got into it as well, not that I'd ever admit that to anyone, although Joey did catch me watching it on the tour bus once. I had to pretend I wasn't really taking much notice of it, not sure he believed me though, especially as I winced when Damon took a drink of bourbon laced with vervain.

"What are you doing here, Elliot?"

He was already on my sofa, his hands linked behind his head. Looking far more relaxed than he should have been having landed on me unannounced. I wanted to feel irritated by him being in my space, but something had shifted because I offered him a mug of tea instead.

"A biscuit would be good too," he replied.

Five minutes later and we were both dunking digestives into big mugs of strong tea.

"What do you want?" I asked. "I only saw you a couple of weeks ago."

"There was a time when we spent every day together, Beau. Now I'm limited to once a fortnight."

"Once a month would be fine. Now answer my question." I said and reached for another biscuit from the packet.

Elliot looked at me over the top of his mug and though I could barely see his face, the way his brows knitted together showed me he was anxious. Whatever he had come to see me about had him feeling jumpy.

"Elliot, you have to tell me otherwise we could end up sitting here all night just staring at each other over mugs of tea."

"Ali called me last night," he said, leaning forward and putting his mug down on top of a Take That coaster.

My heart stuttered and the sadness engulfed me again. I must have flinched or something because he inhaled sharply, and his gaze went down to the coffee table.

"And what did she want?" I asked, clearing my throat.

He didn't say anything but slowly looked up at me and then back to the table. The colour slowly drained from his face, and he ran a hand over his head.

"Fuck I miss them," he breathed out. "So damn much."

My throat constricted and my grip tightened around my mug.

He missed them! How the hell did he think I felt?

Elliot always one to spot everything, always the good guy, cursed.

"Shit, I'm sorry, Beau." The pain in his eyes made me almost feel guilty for being grief stricken. "They were your entire existence, I know that. I feel like such a dick."

Then it was my turn to feel like shit. "They meant a lot to you too. Grief isn't exactly selfish you know. It likes to spread itself around."

"I know but—"

"El, seriously man, it's okay to be sad. To be heartbroken. You knew

Cassie before I did. She was your friend."

Elliot nodded and blew out slowly. "She was my *oldest* friend. She was the one I told when I lost my virginity to Scarlett Dolan on the school trip to see Romeo & Juliet in Stratford."

"You lost your virginity at a play?" I asked, incredulously.

Elliot grinned. "It was on the backseat of the coach on the way home. For a first time it was pretty epic but then Scarlett had already been shagging Jack Rogers for most of the year. I think he must have taught her a thing or two. She was straddling me, and people just thought we were making out."

"Did Cassie make a heaving noise and stick her fingers in her ears when you told her?"

"Yeah," he replied with a short laugh. "She did. She never changed, did she?"

"Nope, never." I was so glad she hadn't. No amount of fancy designer clothes or fuck-off diamonds changed my Cassie. She still ate peanut butter out of a jar, with her finger, thought that M&S sold the best bras and Primark the best knickers, she cut the blue bits off slabs of cheese if the rest of it was okay, and she always insisted we wore pyjamas all day on a Sunday if we were home. She also gave me shit if I acted like a big star, yet she still loved me with every bone in her body.

"It's fucking shit man," Elliot said, breath shaky and uneven. "You were so damn good together. You two were… what the hell does my sister call them…" He looked up to the ceiling and then clicked his fingers, snapping his gaze back onto me. "Couples' goals. Yeah, that's it. You were couples' goals. So, I get why you just wanted to hole yourself up here for the last year. I barely get through a day without thinking about her and Bobby. It must be a thousand times worse for you."

"But?" I asked, knowing that there was most definitely one coming—he had that look.

Elliot swallowed and sat forward, resting his forearms on his knees. "You know what's helped me?"

I rolled my eyes. "Yeah, I think I know. And we already talked about it. Two weeks ago, I told you no, El. Nothing has changed in the last fourteen days."

Nothing unless you counted my ma barging her way into my misery, or me finding a kid in my garden and his mum calling around

"Since we talked though, Beau, I've felt better about things." As soon as he said it, he winced.

"Really, Elliot?" I asked, nodding twice, very slowly. "Two weeks of thinking about making music has wiped memories of your best friend, my wife, from your head?" Okay, so that wasn't exactly true. I knew how much it had broken Elliot's heart losing his best friend of forever. I just couldn't bring myself to care though, so defaulted to wanker mode.

"No, fucking hell no," he cried, flashing me a look that said *I* was the insensitive twat. "All I'm saying is that it's helped keep me occupied. Kept my mind occupied and maybe it could do the same for you too."

I widened my gaze and leaned forward. "Shit, Elliot why don't you set up a counselling service. You're amazing at this. Why the fuck didn't I think of that for the last year of not being able to breathe and my chest feeling like it was cracking open. If I'd played a little guitar or maybe even got my old school recorder out and I'd have gotten over my grief a lot sooner. Or maybe I should have given Diane a few months off and taken up cleaning. Perhaps that would have had the same affect."

"Now you're just being a fucking cunt. That isn't what I meant, and you know it." He pushed up from the sofa and walked to the window that I'd spent a large part of the day looking through. "All I'm saying is having something else to concentrate on has helped me. It hasn't made the pain or me missing them go away but it has eased it. I've had something else to think about." He turned to look through the window. "There's a football in your garden."

It was like being on a rollercoaster the way my stomach dropped. I felt my pulse speed up and little beads of sweat formed on my forehead as I wondered why I felt side-swiped by a football on my lawn. "It must belong to the kid next door."

"Y-you have a kid next door?" His shoulders and back tensed.

"Yes, and I'm not going to crack up because of it." I dragged an agitated hand through my hair, feeling exactly like I was going to crack up. My neighbour had a child and the thought of it made my gut wrench with jealousy.

"You sure?"

"Yeah," I muttered.

"As long as you're sure." After a short pause, Elliot turned back to me. "Listen, I told you Ali called, right?"

Tuning him out, my gaze went over his shoulder to the window. All I could concentrate on was the kid's football and I had to grip the edges of the leather cushion to stop myself from getting up to stare at it.

"Beau," Elliot snapped, bringing my attention back to him. "What do you think?"

"I said I would think about it. I told you that two weeks ago," I replied, my eyes still concentrating on the garden.

"No, the interview with String Magazine. The one that Ali suggested."

I looked back at him and shook the fuzz from my brain. "What?"

"The interview with String. They want to do a six-page spread on us. You know, how we're doing being apart, memories from the years together."

"I don't want to do music because I lost my family," I replied, standing up, "but I'll do an interview on how I've been feeling since my wife and kid died. *Fucking no!*" I stalked towards him. "Fucking no, Elliot. How could you think I would do it? Music is one thing but talking about my grief, it's not happening."

"It wouldn't have to be about that, but I already told her it'd probably be a no," he protested with his hands up in surrender. "I just thought it was an option if you didn't want to do the music thing. I'm sorry I mentioned it. I'll tell Ali it's a definite no."

"Yeah, too fucking right you'll tell her no. I can't believe you even…"

"I didn't." He strode up in front of me and took hold of my shoulders. "I just want to help you. I'm fucking scared that I'm losing you too and I can't stand the thought of it. You're so lost Beau and I get it, we all do, but we need you to come back because you're just going deeper and deeper. What happens if you get so deep that we can't get you back? All I'm trying to do is find something to help you get back."

The pain was back in his eyes and his fingers were gripping my shoulders tight to the point of hurting me.

"Elliot, I'm just not ready. I need you to understand that," I pleaded. "I don't want anything to do with music or the industry at all. In fact, I don't want anything to do with the outside world full stop. I want you to go home and fucking leave me alone. I don't want to see you or the guys until I call you. Until I'm ready."

He breathed out heavily and pinched the bridge of his nose. "Yeah, well that's going to be difficult since Sylvie invited us all for dinner next week."

"What?" I pushed him away and stamped both my feet. "She can't do that."

"Yeah, well she did. She called to say she and Belle were coming to stay and wanted us all to get together. I thought you knew."

"Why the fuck would I want you all to come for dinner? I can barely get out of bed of a morning." I dropped my head to my hands and groaned. "Just go, Elliot. I can't talk to you right now."

Dinner would definitely be happening. When she was determined my ma got whatever she wanted. Didn't mean I had to like it. It also didn't mean that I had to talk to Elliot.

"Beau please, mate. We're just fucking scared. We worry about you every single day. We love you, please don't make us lose you too."

He slapped my shoulder and, running a hand through his usually perfect hair, left. As soon as I heard the door close, I moved over to the window and watched a football on my lawn for God knew how long.

six

Simone

Watching Ethan eat his breakfast I couldn't help my mind wandering to my neighbour. It was *Beau bloody Bradley*. I couldn't say I'd ever had his posters on my bedroom wall. When they first started out, I was seventeen and studying hard for my A-levels because I was so desperate to get to university. Listening to music would have meant time away from my textbooks. Once the dream of getting a degree died though and I had time on my hands, that was when I started to listen to Warrior Creek. They got me through some hard times not least a thirty-six-hour labour. Weird to think that my neighbour had been in the delivery room when I'd pushed my son into the world.

Breathing out heavily, I just about managed to flash Ethan a smile. "Okay, baby?"

He nodded and my heart sank. Apparently, today was a day of no words. I watched carefully as he pushed his Coco-Pops around his bowl, his spoon chasing the last few floating around. His usual routine was to then lift the bowl and drink the chocolate milk which would leave a dark milky moustache. Then he'd grin at me like it was the best thing ever.

I just wished he'd speak more. The times I'd prayed for him to just say one word, to say no when I asked him to go and clean his teeth, or to ask for sweets when we visited the supermarket, but he never did. The times that Ethan spoke were of his choosing as were the number of words that he used. If he didn't want to speak there was nothing I could do or, ironically, say, to persuade him otherwise.

I looked at the clock on the fancy cooker I barely used. My heart sank. The hours were going to crawl along slowly, I could tell.

"You want to play in the garden today?" I asked, glancing out to check it wasn't raining.

Another nod—this one accompanied with a smile. He was generally a happy child anyway, but the days when he didn't speak if he smiled it made things a little easier.

"Okay then, go and brush your teeth and wash your face and we can go outside."

Once he'd finished up that was exactly what he did, leaving me to clear up the breakfast dishes. I could hear him banging around upstairs when my phone started ringing from its place on the kitchen island. Quickly drying my soapy hands, I snatched it up and groaned when I saw who it was calling.

"Vanessa." I snapped out the name.

"Hello, Miss Addison, how are you today?"

"Fine." I fought the urge to roll my eyes. I always got the feeling that Vanessa could see exactly what I was doing even on the other end of a telephone line and almost two-hundred miles away.

"Mr Richard wanted you to be aware that he has organised for a gardener to visit today."

"What?" I closed my eyes and left my head tip back on a silent groan.

"A gardener, Miss Addison. He will arrive today and is called Alex Monroe. He does a lot of other gardens in the area."

"I can do the garden," I protested, even though I'd been dreading having to tackle it. It was bloody huge. "You don't need to ask anyone else. Please can you ask *Mr* Richard to cancel him." I hated how she bowed down to him and called him *Mr* Richard. It was like living back in the dark ages.

Vanessa made a strange noise which sounded like it was coming from the back of her throat. I'd never met her but had a picture in my head of a Miss Trunchbull lookalike. She certainly tried to boss me around like she looked like that. I got a call from her generally once a month, usually to snap some sort of order at me or to tell me something her boss had done that would affect me.

"Mr Monroe will be with you today. At, I believe…" She paused for a few seconds, and I heard a sound like she was tapping on a keyboard. "Nine-thirty. He has all his own equipment including a lawn mower."

"Nine-thirty?" My gaze snapped to the clock again. It was almost nine-fifteen. "Could you not have told me earlier? Yesterday, maybe?"

"I am extremely busy, Miss Addison. Checking up on you isn't the only thing on my to do list. I have a lot of responsibilities."

"Just some more warning would have been nice, that's all I'm saying."

Vanessa was silent and I was sure she was blinking rapidly and waiting for me to get over what she'd see as a tantrum.

"Mr Richard would also like to ask if there is anything that you need?"

I fought the desire to gag. "Nothing."

"I'll speak to you in a few weeks."

That was it, she was gone. No other questions, or orders. Just that I needed to be ready for some bloke to come in and sort out the bloody garden.

I was dressed, but sweats, no bra and a vest were probably not right for greeting him, so decided to go and throw something over the top. I also needed to tell my little boy he wouldn't be allowed to play in the garden.

***

"You do most of the gardens around here?" I asked as I passed Alex a mug of tea.

He took it from me looking grateful for some warmth. The March wind was blowing ice cold and he'd been working in it for the last two hours.

"A few," he replied lifting the mug to his mouth. "Mrs Devonshire at number nineteen, The Carlisle's at thirty and then Mr Bradley next door."

My heart skipped a little beat at the mention of Beau, and it didn't escape my notice that Alex had only referred to him as Mr Bradley. I guessed he'd probably signed an NDA or something.

"I met him yesterday," I offered.

Over the rim of the mug, I noticed a raised brow as Alex took a drink.

"I think he thought I was a stalker." I giggled. "I wasn't. I swear. Ethan, my son has been sneaking through the hedge to get his ball, so I felt I should apologise."

"I know," Alex said, lowering the mug and scratching at his beard. "I found the hole."

"God, I'm so sorry. He just loves playing football and he'd take that ball to bed with him if I said it was okay."

Alex shook his head. "It's fine, Miss Addison, honestly. Beau is cool about it."

"He is? Are you sure?" I wrapped my arms around myself, trying to keep warm despite the huge hoody that I was wearing. "And please, it's Simone."

He smiled and nodded. "Okay. But yeah, Beau is fine. He even mentioned about maybe putting a gate in or cutting it back."

"He said that to me too," I replied. "About, cutting it back. I just thought he was being nice."

"He was. He's a good guy but he was being serious." He went back to drinking his tea and I suddenly felt a little conscious of hanging around.

"I'd better go in." I shuffled around to face the back door. "I left Ethan watching TV so he could be doing anything by now."

I knew he'd still be exactly where I'd left him. Ethan rarely did anything he wasn't supposed to. I think I said it because part of me wanted him to sound like every other child who disobeyed their parents from time to time. I wasn't ashamed of him, not by any stretch, but it was hard to explain to strangers what Ethan was like. People thought the fact that he didn't speak or act up made him weird. My boy wasn't weird, he was amazing, he just didn't like talking and not everyone got that. Even his therapist had used the word 'normal'. We didn't visit her again.

"He seems like a nice kid," Alex replied.

My eyes went wide. "You've spoken to him?" I knew it wasn't possible, but I had to ask.

"Well, he waved at me through the patio door." Alex grinned. "I'm lucky if I get a grunt from my kids, so a smile and a wave make me think he's great."

"Oh, okay," I breathed out, a little disappointed but also glad. As much as I wanted my son to talk more, it would sting him speaking to the new gardener on a day that he had no words for me.

"Okay," Alex said, nodding in the direction of the lawn. "I'll get on. I'll put the mug just inside the kitchen door when I've finished. Won't trail my muddy boots over your floor."

"It's fine." I waved him away. Mopping the floor would give me something to do at least.

When I turned to leave, I heard a text message beep. Pulling up to a stop, I took my phone from my pocket to check it.

"It's me," Alex said and looked down at his phone. "Talk of the devil. It's Beau."

"Oh, okay," I replied, hesitating between staying to find out what Beau Bradley had to say and disappearing back into the house so that I didn't appear nosey.

"There you go. Told you." Alex held his screen for me to read.

Beau: Alex, might have to nip out later. If I don't see you, can you do what we discussed and make a decent sized hole in the hedge for the little kid next door. Want him to be able to get his ball whenever he wants to. Cheers.

Wow, Beau Bradley was a really nice man, and I couldn't help but feel thankful that he was looking out for my boy. Rushing a goodbye to Alex, I went inside and wiped the tears from my cheeks.

seven

Beau

I seriously needed to grow some balls. I was twenty-six-years of age and still afraid of my mother. She'd told me that she was coming to stay, and I'd said nothing. She told me that I had to pick her up and I was now in my car driving back from the station while she wittered on. She hadn't shut up from the minute I'd picked up her and Bella's cases to put into the boot of my car.

It was all a load of shit as well. I really didn't care whether Debbie Blake's husband was shagging around, or that Mr Wrench, Ma's neighbour, was getting unsteady on his legs. He was a nice bloke from what I knew but I didn't give a fuck if his daughter wanted him to go and live with her or not.

Her chatting non-stop did hide the awkwardness that a year of silence with my sister brought. Belle and I had always been close. I adored her and after Cassie and Bobby I could honestly say I loved her the most. After they were killed in the crash though, I just pushed her away. I only spoke to Ma because I had to—she'd have turned up on my doorstep otherwise. Belle, though, well I should have given her the time. She'd struggled with self-confidence most of her life, and although she'd got better as she got older, I knew she still needed a pep talk from time to time. Ma tended to talk at her, just like she did everyone, whereas I listened and then told her how amazing she was. And she was. I might have been biased but Belle was the kindest, sweetest person I knew. She'd help anyone and her working in a nursing home wasn't a surprise to me. Ma told her she could do better for herself than wiping old folk's arses, but Belle loved it. Personally, I thought she could had done modelling, but she'd have never had survived in such a cut-throat business—she was too fucking nice.

"Is the house in a mess?" Ma asked. "Do I need to clean as soon as we get there?"

"No," I sighed out, glancing in the rear-view mirror at Belle in the back seat. "Diane our cleaner has been coming in."

My throat constricted and I rubbed at my breastbone. She was just *my* cleaner now.

"Oh, so you let the cleaner in, but I haven't seen you in a year. Your sister hasn't seen you in a year. But the cleaner that's okay."

"Ma," Belle said looking out of the side window. "Leave it. There was nothing stopping you getting on a train before now."

I raised my eyebrows and smirked. She'd got some sass from somewhere.

"If you're wondering, she's been like that since she broke it off with that idiot," Ma replied. "All bossy and opinionated."

"Can you read minds or something?" I asked.

"Yours and hers I can. You're my kids, I gave birth to you both. I know exactly what you're both thinking at any given time, and *you* are wondering where *she* got her mouth from."

"I was hardly being mouthy, or opinionated, Ma." Belle sat back and sighed, going back into her shell no doubt.

Apparently, my mother was still a domineering pain in the arse. Losing her daughter-in-law and only grandchild hadn't softened her in any way.

"As for saying I could have got on a train before now," Ma said, never one to let anything drop. "He wouldn't have let me in. Three hours on a train to be turned away isn't my idea of fun."

I inhaled sharply. She was right, I would have turned her away. Still, I was grieving, and I was her son. She should have tried. But that was her, she only ever interfered and never did anything that would be helpful.

"I've asked you to move here loads of times." I'd promised myself I'd keep the peace with her for once but couldn't help myself. "You're the one who wants to stay in Leicester."

"There's nothing for me in bloody Cheshire," she complained.

"You could live close to the city. There's loads to do there." My hands gripped the steering wheel tightly as I recalled the arguments that we'd had eight years ago. I'd told her that me and the lads were leaving Leicester to live near the studios we'd been signed to in Manchester and she'd gone ballistic. Told me I was selfish for leaving her and Belle for a career that would probably never take off. Yeah, who had the last laugh on that one?

"Well, I fully expected you to be back in a year," she grunted.

I glanced in the rear-view again and caught Belle's gaze. She didn't smile and her eyes were cold, none of the usual sparkle of mischief and joy. Yep, she was mad at me.

"Offer still stands," I said, more to Belle than Ma, hoping it would be an olive branch. "I'll get you a place here."

Belle's head moved; a movement so small and quick that I almost missed it. She was listening and thinking about my words. I made a mental note to be talk to her about it. I doubted Ma would make the move, but I would try and get my sister to.

Silence fell in the car as we continued down the country lanes towards the house. As we got closer, I started to feel sick. It would be the first time anyone had ever visited without Cassie or Bobby being there too. The first visitors that I'd be having on my own. There'd be no cake or bacon butties waiting for us the minute we walked through the door. No one to hug them or to squeal with excitement about them visiting. There'd be no Cassie.

"Who's that in your garden?" Ma asked as we drove up the drive. "Told you before you should have those big electric gates."

I held back a sigh of frustration. "Alex my gardener. And I told you before, Cassie hated the idea of them, said it made us look like Billy big bollocks."

The rush of air from Ma's mouth almost had me slamming on the brakes.

I knew what she was going to say but thank fuck she didn't.

Instead, she said, "It'd be safer for you."

I tended to agree or would have if I didn't live in such a quiet cul-de-sac and the other houses were owned by people probably equally as rich as I was. They'd worked for their millions though, not written a few hit songs. I had a neurosurgeon on one side, a celebrity photographer opposite and a Judge three doors down. I also had a single mum next door which was fucking odd. I'd assumed that she was married but Alex had told me earlier that she was on her own and he'd been employed by the person who owned the house. I didn't ask anything else, for one I didn't really care, and two, it had been time to go and pick up Ma and Belle.

"I'll think about it," I said, just to shut her up really, but she was right.

"The snowdrops look lovely," Belle said leaning between the two front seats of my Range Rover. "Cassie always loved them."

I nodded, my gaze following Belle's as it struck me it didn't hurt to talk about her with my sister.

"She always said it was the start of life coming back to the garden when the snowdrops came out," I said, memories echoing in my words.

Belle's hand moved to touch my bicep, but she quickly snatched it away. She couldn't stand to touch me she was so angry. The guilt at pushing her away reared its ugly head again Why had I been so stupid? My sister would have helped me so much if I had just let her.

"Come on then," Ma blustered, unclipping her belt. "I'm ready for some lunch. It's hours since I had my cornflakes."

"She still refusing to buy anything off the train trolley?" I turned to Belle and laughed.

"Yep." My sister's reply was short and curt.

"She still taking her own flask of tea too?" I powered on, hoping to break down Belle's barriers. Let her see that I still loved her and that I'd just needed to be alone.

"And that's because their tea and coffee is awful," Ma answered back. "Now let's get inside."

When she flung her door open and practically jumped out of the car, Belle sighed.

"She's nervous," she said quietly as we watched Ma stretch her arms up over her head. "She's scared of what it'll be like without them." She turned to me. "Don't be hard on her. She took it really bad."

"And I didn't?" My brows disappeared up under my overgrown fringe.

"Of course, you did but no one has any clue how you feel, seeing as we've barely heard from you for a year. All I'm saying is she didn't cope so well." She looked back to Ma who was now talking to Alex. "You've no idea how happy she is that you've finally let her visit."

"Didn't have much choice."

Bella laughed emptily and turned back to me. "I know but sometimes, Beau, she needs us as much as we hate to admit need her."

I opened my mouth to speak but she shook her head. "We'll talk later. We need to eat."

***

The atmosphere in the house was a little strained, one reason being that none of us knew what to say about the Cassie and Bobby sized big and gaping hole. I didn't know how to be a host on my own and my mum and sister didn't know what to say about that fact. We skirted around the issue, so I just showed them to their rooms and left them to get themselves settled.

Thankfully, I'd mentioned to Di about them coming and she'd made sure that everything was set for them, clean sheets, fresh towels in their bathrooms and even flowers on each dressing table. I hadn't even realised she'd brought them into the house that was how much notice I took of anyone.

"Where's Ma?" I asked Belle as she wandered into the kitchen. "I'm going to make some lunch."

She took a step back. "You are?"

"Yeah, I can make a sandwich." I pulled some slices of bread from the packet and started to butter them. The simple task of feeding my family saw a feeling of longing overcome me, and I had to inhale to stop myself from shouting at the world to fuck off. After taking a couple of deep breaths, I asked, "Ham okay?"

"Fine. I'll make some tea."

I looked up and smiled but Belle didn't return it. The atmosphere was decidedly frosty as she stared at me for a couple of seconds before moving to the cupboard to get the mugs out. Water was added to the kettle, and it was switched on; all in silence. It wasn't us, we used to be able to talk about anything and everything.

"You still have sugar?"

"Yes please." I nodded.

"Okay."

I put down the knife and manoeuvred around Belle to get the ham. Her cheek twitched and she quickly dropped her gaze.

"Belle," I sighed and grabbed her hand. "Talk to me."

"Oh, so now you want to talk. What about?" she asked, as she pulled her hand away and leaned back against the kitchen counter, crossing her arms firmly over her chest.

"Who was the guy that dumped you? What happened?"

"Oh okay," she huffed. "Only I thought we might start with how you've been, seeing as we haven't spoken for a year." Her nostrils flared and I didn't think I'd ever seen her looking so angry.

"Talk to me now," I urged.

Belle opened her mouth, but nothing came out and when I said her name, she shook her head.

"Unbelievable," she eventually muttered.

"Belle please tell me what you're feeling, what you're thinking."

"What I'm thinking Beau, is that this is horrible. Them not being here. I don't know if I'm even supposed to say that to you, but how could I when you damn well shut me out. Have you any idea how painful it was for us? We felt like we'd lost you too."

My stomach clenched at her words.

"I'm sorry." I leaned my forearms onto the counter next to her and looked at her through my hair. "You're right it is horrible without them, and I just couldn't cope. I was a fucking mess."

"I could have been here with you," she yelled and poked me in the shoulder. "I wanted to be here, to try and help you get through each day." She poked me again. "It hurt thinking of you doing this on your own. It hurt that you couldn't just text me once and say I'm not okay Belle, I need you. It hurt because you're my brother, Cassie was my friend, and I loved that little boy so fucking much," she gasped, tears now streaming down her face. "All I wanted was to help you, to hug you and to tell you it wouldn't get better but it would get easier. You just shut yourself away."

"I know and I'm sorry. I just couldn't, Belle. I only spoke to Ma to stop her coming over."

"Why? Why the hell wouldn't you want her here? She's your mother, annoying as she may be, she loves you and would give her life for you, for us. Yet you couldn't even afford her the courtesy of a two-minute phone call every other week so that we both knew that you were holding on." She drew in a breath and swiped at the wetness on her cheeks. "I couldn't tell anyone how you were doing because I had no fucking clue. Apart from all that, *I* needed you too. I need a hug from you so often that it was painful."

My eyes closed as her words reverberated around my chest. I'd been selfish in my grief, but I couldn't handle it any other way.

Dropping my head, I groaned. "Everything just seems pointless without them, Belle. Plus, I just couldn't deal with everyone else's grief on top of my own."

"I'm not going to say I know how you feel," she replied. "Because I really don't. I can't ever imagine how you feel. I do know how I felt though. Like my guts had been ripped out. Not just because I wouldn't ever see them again but because I knew you wouldn't either. All I wanted to do was to hug you and sit with you while you cried and yelled. I didn't want to tell you how to feel. All I wanted to do was to be your sister."

"And for me to be your brother," I responded, turning my head so I was facing her.

She shrugged and gave me a tight smile. "I love you, you know that, but sometimes you can be selfish, and it makes me angry. You can't always take, Beau, sometimes you have to give as well. Even when you're in pain."

"I'm sorry. I should have been there for you and for whatever reason it was that you needed a hug."

She snatched up some kitchen paper and wiped her eyes and nose, still not looking at me. It made my stomach hurt to think I might have ruined my relationship with my sister on top of everything else.

"Tell me now," I said, pulling on her hand. "Let me give you that hug now."

She made me wait for a couple of minutes, each one resulting in a crack forming in my heart. Finally, she was ready to speak.

"His name was Daniel and he cheated on me right after he'd asked me to move in with him. Which," she said, raising an eyebrow, "wouldn't be so bad if he hadn't also got me pregnant."

"What?" I rounded on her and pushed off the counter to take her in my arms. To give her that hug she so badly needed. "Shit, Belle. I'm so fucking sorry. What happened?"

"Well, he was a real cliché," Belle replied, her voice cracking. "I found a couple of receipts, for a hotel and fancy lunch in Birmingham on a day he was supposed to be working. I put two and two together and he didn't deny it when I asked him. He said he'd met her on a course last year before we met; she contacted him to say she was going to be there on business for the day. One thing led to another, and they booked a hotel for the afternoon."

"And the baby," I whispered, glancing over my shoulder towards the doorway.

"Ma knows," she replied, resting her chin on my chest to look up at me. "And I lost it. I don't know whether it was the shock of finding out, or just the fact it wasn't meant to be. Two days after I took back what stuff I had at his place I started cramping and," she shrugged her shoulders, "that was that."

"Fuck," I groaned against her hair. "I didn't know. I…"

"Well you wouldn't. Would you?" Her tone was still a little terse, but she hugged me anyway.

"Please can we get back to normal now?" I asked. "As normal as we can be anyway."

She nodded, pulled away and then looked up at me as she pulled a band from her wrist. "You need to get this cut; I can't see your face." She combed her fingers through my hair and pulled it up into the band. Taking a further step back she looked me up and down and smiled. "You suit a man bun, *and* you won't get hair in Ma's sandwich."

I put my hand up to feel it and smiled. "Thanks."

"You need to look after yourself, Beau."

I sighed and pulled her back into a hug. Now I'd held her again I didn't want to let go. I now knew what I'd been missing.

"Like I said," I sighed. "There doesn't seem much point."

My arms tightened around her slim body as my hand ran down her long brown waves. "God, when did *your* hair get so long?"

"When I couldn't be arsed to book an appointment with the hairdresser. Seems we both had the same idea Mr Man Bun."

"Yeah, but like you said, I wear it well."

We both laughed and held each other a little tighter.

"I'll still kill him for you if that's what you want?" I offered.

"Nope. It's fine. His sister told me the other woman went ballistic when she found out he had a girlfriend. Let it be known on social media what a twat he was." She sighed heavily. "It just really hurt, Beau. I loved him and he told me he loved me too. He even said he was excited about the baby."

"Does he know you lost it?"

"I called him and told him and then he tried to come and see me at the hospital. He cried and said he was sorry and asked for another chance."

"I hope you told him to fuck off," I growled.

"I did and Ma finished the job."

We both laughed, knowing exactly how she'd have got rid of him—a good swipe with her handbag if I knew my ma.

"You okay?" I asked, hesitantly. "For the future I mean."

She nodded. "It was just one of those things, but nothing to say it would ever happen again."

"That's good. Kids, they're a fucking joy you know." My chest constricted and I had to swallow back the lump in my throat for fear it would erupt into a howl of pain.

Belle's cheek burrowed closer to my chest, and I heard her whimper.

"I miss them so fucking much, Belle. Every day gets harder, not easier."

"I know," she whispered. "I know."

We stood like that for what seemed like hours but was only minutes until the hurricane of our mother blasted into the room.

"I have no idea who made that bed, but they have no clue what a damn hospital corner is. Cassie used to make them—." She broke off and Belle and

I both turned to her. "What's going on with you two?"

"I'm just getting a cuddle from my brother," Belle said, breath soft and whispering.

"Oh." Ma coughed, stared at us for a few seconds and then stepped closer. "Are we getting any lunch today or what?"

Belle and I pulled apart, both laughing quietly. She might not have been soft and slushy but out mother certainly knew how to put things into perspective. Why let hunger get in the way of a little thing like grief.

eight

Simone

By the time that Alex finished up in the garden, dusk was setting in and the wind had risen. Playing in the garden was out of the question.

"Tomorrow you can," I explained to Ethan getting no understanding of whether he was upset or not. "It's too late now. You'll have to have a bath soon. Okay?"

He simply nodded and ran off to the sofa, picked up his book and settled down to read. Watching him, I saw a smile tilt at his lips as he looked down at the colourful pictures and words that he was mouthing silently—his version of reading aloud.

He seemed happy enough, but I was more than aware that he needed some friends. Not talking though was a real issue. No kid liked to play with someone who was silent all the time—Ethan had been called weird by more than one of his classmates at his old school. Not that he cared, he did tell me that much on a day when he found his words.

"I don't mind, Mummy. I like being different." Then he'd given me a

huge smile and a hug.

I had no idea why he wouldn't speak. Three different therapists didn't know why he didn't speak. He could, but hardly ever had. Professionals had told me that he was well developed mentally and educationally, hadn't suffered any trauma and loved life, he just didn't like talking, except to me.

There were days when I wanted to scream at him that I didn't care that he was happy, I wasn't. Him being silent broke me and made me feel inadequate. I was a bad mother who must have done something wrong. Then I would look at his beautiful smile and quickly come out of my meltdown. All I wanted was for Ethan to be content and he was. The loneliness my son not speaking created though was the worst part about it. I talked to him, but often got no response, maybe a smile or a nod of the head. That was never enough though to stop me feeling alone. That was when the guilt settled heavily in my stomach. He was only five-years old and I shouldn't put that responsibility onto him.

Leaving Ethan to his reading, I tried to stave off the need to change him and decided to bake some biscuits instead. I wasn't a great cook, but biscuits I could do. Ethan loved double chocolate-chip, so the ingredients were a staple of my cupboard.

After turning on the radio, I got to work and was just mixing the batter together when Ethan came running into the kitchen.

"Mummy." Ethan's sweet normally quiet voice was louder than usual. "Mummy come quickly."

"Ethan, what's wrong?" I rushed to him and crouched to his height.

"There's water Mummy. It's coming through the ceiling."

"Oh shit." I raced passed him into the lounge and he was right, water was dripping down the walls. It was a slow flow, not gushing, but enough that panic started to set in.

"What do we do, Mummy?"

I looked down to see Ethan had followed me and was staring at the same spot as I was.

"Okay, sweetheart. I need you to go and sit in the kitchen while I try and sort this out. Okay?"

He nodded and with his book under his arm, ran back off. I moved quickly to the cupboard under the stairs where the fuses were, knowing that the first thing I should do would be to cut off the power. Each room was labelled as was the mains, so I decided it best to cut the whole lot. I had no idea where the water was coming from so better to be safe. As soon as I did, the house went into semi darkness. The evenings were getting lighter, but the clocks still hadn't gone forward.

I ran back to the lounge only to see the water was coming faster. "Bugger," I hissed as the fancy wallpaper that was not my choice started to curl at the edges.

Running into the kitchen, I expected to find Ethan sitting quietly at the table, but he had a stool at the sink and was turning on the taps.

"What are you doing?" I asked, going to his side.

"It was on YouTube." He nodded to my iPad on the table. "It said to run the water and put a bucket under the leak."

Scrubbing a hand over his head, I sighed. "Clever boy. What would I do without you?"

"You need to turn the water off too," he announced, nodding sagely. "It's not under the sink though, Mummy. I looked."

Glancing down, I could see he had. The cupboard doors were open, and all my cleaning products had been knocked over.

"Where the hell would it be?" I asked, mostly to myself.

"I don't know," a tiny voice said. "What shall we do?"

Hugging Ethan to me, I stupidly looked around the kitchen for the stopcock. Ethan then pulled on my tee shirt.

"The man next door might know, Mummy."

My stomach dropped because he was right, he might. That however, meant I was going to have to face Beau Bradley again. It could take me ages to find the stopcock, so I knew I'd just have to go around there and ask, no matter how much I didn't want to.

"Okay, come on get your coat and we'll go and ask him."

"Do I need my shoes?" He looked down at the X-Men slippers on his feet.

"No, baby. Just get your coat, we won't be long."

He rushed off to get his coat, while I scanned under the sink, just in case, but he was right, there was no stopcock there. Which meant I had to go and ask my famous neighbour.

Five minutes later, and hesitantly, I knocked on his door. Twiddling my fingers and glancing down at Ethan, I was surprised when it opened almost immediately, and I was met with brown eyes the exact replica of Beau's. The girl, who had to be some relation, looked around my age and had the most beautiful smile.

"Hi." She frowned as she looked at me. "Everything okay?"

"Oh, erm, hi," I spluttered, taken aback by how much she sounded like him too. "I was wondering if Mr Bradley was home." I pulled Ethan's hand up. The bizarre thought in my head that showing I had a little boy might make me look less like a crazy fan. "We live next door and if he's got a minute…"

"Oh, okay." She grinned down at Ethan. "Love your slippers."

He looked at them and then back up to the girl and smiled and I had a feeling he'd used all his words for the day.

"You want to step in?" she asked. "I'll go and get Beau."

"Honestly, it's fine." I shook my head and then looked in the direction of my house. "I don't want to bother him, but I really need to ask him something. We've got a leak, with water pouring into the lounge and I have no idea where the stopcock is. I was wondering if he knew. Our houses are pretty similar, so it was just a hope really."

Her face fell and she opened the door wider. "Oh, God. Come in, come in." She moved two paces into the hall. "Beau! Beau!"

"Please don't disturb him if he's busy," I said, pulling Ethan in front of me and wrapping my arms around his chest.

"Honestly, it's fine. We were only going to watch some telly. Beau!"

The long-limbed, rock star immediately appeared in the hallway. He had a mug in one hand and bag of crisps in the other and his hair had been pulled up into a sexy man bun. "What's wrong?" He then saw me and pulled to a halt. "Oh, hello again."

"Hi," I replied, swallowing. "I'm so sorry to bother you, I just have a quick question."

It was almost imperceptible, but I most definitely saw his nostrils flare and his chin jut out. I took a step, about to turn Ethan around and walk out, when the girl spoke.

"They've got a leak. Water is flooding into the lounge and they have no idea where the stopcock is. Do you know?"

Beau's face softened and his shoulders dropped. "The garage," he responded. "Well, ours is anyway. I'm guessing yours will be too as it was the same contractor that built both houses."

I sighed with relief. "Thank you, I hadn't a clue otherwise I wouldn't have bothered you. Okay, we'll get out of your hair. Thanks again."

"Wait," the girl said. "Let us come and help."

"God no," I looked at Beau. "We'll be fine, honestly."

"No way." She turned to Beau. "We'd be happy to, wouldn't we?"

"No!" I cried at the same time as Beau said, "Erm."

"There's no way we'd let you deal with that on your own." She bent to look at Ethan. "How would you like to stay here with our mum while we help yours?"

I was about to turn down the offer when I saw her grin widely. I looked down to see Ethan was nodding.

"Excellent." She held out her hand and then looked up at me. "That is okay. She's really friendly, I promise."

Beau snorted and my gaze shot to his, eyes widening.

"Belle's right, she is."

So, the pretty, friendly girl was his sister, Belle. That explained the matching eyes.

"That's really kind of you, but I don't want to spoil your evening. Come on, Ethan."

"Please, let us. Oh, I'm Belle by the way, Beau's sister." She held out her hand.

We shook and she smiled, and I knew by the determination in her eyes that she was going to insist that they come back to the house. Beau on the other hand looked like he wanted to bolt a thousand miles away.

I glanced between them. "If you could just help me to find the stopcock that would be great. And your mum doesn't need to take care of Ethan. I couldn't put her out."

"You won't be. She's watching TV but," Belle said touching Ethan's shoulder, "I know she'd love to watch the X Men film with you."

Ethan looked up at me, his eyes actually pleading seeing as we didn't have Sky. Freeview all the way in our house.

"Okay." I sighed. "But as soon as I've got the water off, a plumber on the way, I'll come back and get you."

He nodded and stepped away from me. This was how I knew my boy was fine and not weird like the other kids said. He didn't speak but he wasn't shy. He liked people.

"Come on," Belle said, holding out her hand for him. "You come with me. Beau you go with... sorry, I don't even know your name."

"Simone," I replied on a cough. "Simmy."

Beau shifted at the side of us, and we both whipped our gaze to him. Belle had been so welcoming and friendly it had almost made me forget I was in the presence of a great rock star.

"I'm so sorry about this," I said, clutching a hand to my throat. "I didn't expect—"

"It's fine. It might be too tight for you anyway." He turned to Belle and handed over his mug and then stuffed the bag of crisps inside it. "You don't need to come over, it won't take me long."

Belle shook her head. "It's fine. I'll be there in a few. Which side."

Beau pointed behind him. "Twenty-two, right?"

"Yes, twenty-two."

"Come on then," he sighed. "Let's go."

He then strode passed me seemingly determined to get his good deed over and done with.

nine

Beau

Simone practically ran along side of me as I marched toward her house. I wouldn't have left her stranded but I also didn't really want to be there. The sooner I turned her stopcock off the better.

"I'm so sorry to have dragged you out of the house," she said breathlessly as we walked up her driveway. "I'm sure I'll be able to turn it off."

"It's fine." I didn't want to make conversation so widened my stride.

When we reached the garage, I stopped and looked down at Simone. She pointed the small remote control which was attached to her keys and slowly the garage door started to fold up on itself. As soon as I could, I stooped under it and went into the garage. It was clean and tidy. No crap hanging around like there was in mine, so much that I couldn't get my car in. Simone had a pale blue Fiat 500 that took a small amount of the space, but they were huge double garages, so the rest of the space was wasted. There wasn't even a kid's bike in there, just three taped up cardboard boxes in the corner.

"Mine's over at the back," I said, moving to where there was a system of pipes and two stop cocks. "The blue is for the main house, the red for the outside."

"Oh God," she sighed. "I should have thought it'd be in here."

"It's not so easy when you're in a panic." I didn't look at her and reached for the stop cock. "Yeah, it's a bit tight."

I grunted as I wrapped both hands around it and tried to turn it. When it only moved a fraction, I wiped my hands on my jeans, took a hold of it again and tried once more. This time it turned more easily, until it finally did a full three-sixty.

"Thank you so much," Simone said at my side. "And so sorry for interrupting your evening."

When I turned to her, I was surprised to see tears were welling in her eyes.

"It's no problem," I replied, trying to sound friendlier than before. "Didn't take long."

"I'd better go and see what the damage is." She shoved her hands into the long, quilted coat that she was wearing, and I suddenly realised how small she was. She barely reached my shoulder, even with the huge amount of hair piled on top of her head. Her features were tiny, and I was pretty sure her wrists would have been in danger of snapping if she'd tried to turn the water off herself.

"I'll come with you," I replied before I could even think about what I was saying. "You might need some help."

Simone let out a small gasp and shook her head—the bun on top wobbling precariously. "No, you go back. I'll be fine. I'll check it out and then come and get Ethan. I swear I won't leave it too long."

I opened my mouth to say it was fine, when Belle appeared with the sun setting behind her.

"You found it." She walked forward and flashed Simone a smile.

"Yes." Simone glanced up at me and then back to Belle. "It was a bit difficult but B... erm, he managed it."

"We were just going to check out the damage," I replied and walked toward my sister.

"Honestly it's fine." Simone went to grab my arm but thought better of it and shoved her hand back into her pocket. "You've done enough."

"No," Belle said, zipping up her jacket. "We're here to help. Please Simmy just show us the way."

I heard, Simone, or should I say *Simmy*, gasp quietly and wondered, not for the first time, how my sister found talking to people so damn easy for someone so lacking in confidence. I just didn't speak to people because I was a miserable bastard deep down, always had been. When Cassie had been alive, I'd learned to deal but since she'd gone, I wasn't sure I'd care if I never spoke to another human being ever again. Belle though, she was a fucking angel with everyone. It was no wonder she got treated like shit by most of the men she went out with. My little sister was just too bloody nice for her own good.

"Seriously," a small, tentative voice beside me said. "I'll be fine. As long as your mum is still okay with Ethan."

Belle grinned. "She's loving it. Having a little kid around." I made a noise from the back of my throat and Belle looked stricken, like I'd just punched her. Her wide eyes sought mine and she placed a hand over her heart.

I coughed. "Come on lead the way and we'll check the damage." My tone was low, and Simone eyed me warily. I nodded toward the house and she finally passed me and then out of the garage. Belle hung back and when I reached her, she grabbed my forearm.

"Beau I'm sorry, that was really insensitive."

I shook my head. "It's fine, Belle. Now come on and let's see what she's facing."

"Beau?"

"Belle," I snapped without breaking stride. "Leave it. I said it was fine."

Once we reached Simone's lounge it was clear that the fifteen minutes or, so that she'd been away, things had got worse. She was looking at part of the ceiling plaster hanging down with her hands pressed against her cheeks.

"Oh shit," she gasped. "It was just the water when I left. What the hell happened."

I looked up at it and cast my semi-professional eye over it—I'd worked for a local builder before the band made it, both Ronnie and I had.

"Looks like the plastering might have been too thin."

Simone looked at me and frowned. "Oh."

"Beau worked for a builder for a while," Belle explained.

"Oh," Simone repeated and turned back to the mess in front of her. "Looks like I'm going to need a plasterer, a plumber and a decorator then."

"Yeah, looks like it," I added and took a step forward. "Maybe a new rug too." The cream rug's thick fur was sodden.

"I don't care about that thing," she sighed. "I didn't like it anyway."

I had to agree it looked like some sort of dead hairy animal laying on her floor and the thought crossed my mind why on earth she'd bought it in the first place. When I looked back over my shoulder, Simone's eyes were filled with tears again and she looked totally lost as to what to do next.

"I'll make a few calls for you," I offered. "We use a maintenance company that employ all the different trades."

"Would you really?" she asked, practically sagging with relief. "That would be amazing. I'm not from around here so have no idea who to call. You know, who's good or likely to rip me off."

"Your insurance will pay though. Won't they Beau?" Belle asked.

"Should do. You're insured right?"

Simone's face went pale, and I suddenly had visions of not only calling the trades but fucking paying for it as well. Then she nodded and I felt a small pump of relief in my chest because for some reason I knew she couldn't have afforded the repairs. I guessed the mortgage on the house probably took every penny she had.

"I'll need to check with the landlord."

Well, that was a surprise. What the fuck was she doing renting a house this size for her and her boy? Cassie, Bobby, and I had rattled around in ours, which was a similar size, but we'd been planning on having more kids—it was going to be our forever house.

I rubbed my breastbone and closed my eyes against the images that were desperate to haunt me.

"Do you have a partner?" Belle asked, sounding concerned.

My eyes opened to see Simone shaking her head. "No. It's just me and Ethan. Always has been. Well, I have a brother, but he lives in London."

Belle's gaze snapped to mine, and my shoulders sagged.

"I'll get the trades sorted for you. You get in touch with the landlord to find out about the insurance."

"No, honestly, you've done enough," Simone protested.

"He doesn't mind."

Since when Belle had started reading my fucking mind?

"No." I sighed. "I don't mind. The numbers are in my office, so I'll need to go back."

Belle nodded. "Okay, how about you go back and ring whoever, Simmy and I will start to clean up and then maybe you could—"

When Belle didn't say anything else, I shrugged. "Maybe I could?"

"Nope, nothing. It's fine."

I widened my eyes and leaned closer to her, silently urging my sister to answer the question. She ignored me and turned back to Simone.

"You get started and I'll go and get Ethan for you."

Simone blew out a deep breath and looked up at the ceiling. "I can't thank you enough for this." She looked back at Belle. "You've both been so kind."

"That's what neighbours are for."

Yeah, I thought. Easy for you to say when you're not the fucking neighbour.

***

Half an hour later and I'd called the maintenance company and they'd assured me a plumber would be there within twenty minutes. I'd stressed how it had to be the usual level of non-disclosure because although Simone was my neighbour, she was also an attractive woman, and I didn't want people putting two and two together and coming up with front page news. I knew I could rely on them though, especially as they knew I'd ruin their business otherwise.

After I'd made the calls and told them to hold off any bills until we knew who was paying, I holed myself up in my office. Belle, my ma, and Ethan were all in the lounge talking about the film they were watching—well Ma and Belle were, Ethan was silently smiling and taking it all in.

I'd been in there over an hour, playing Patience on my computer when there was a knock at the door. Before I'd even had a chance to tell whoever it was to come in, the door opened.

"Any chance you can take Ethan back?" Belle asked, fiddling with her bracelet.

"Thought you were." I carried on playing, choosing to ignore the plea in her tone.

"It's just that he's fallen asleep, and I can't pick him up."

My stomach turned. That would mean carrying him. That was not somewhere I was ready to go. I couldn't carry my own son, why the hell would I want to carry someone else's?

"You'll have to wake him then." I pushed my chair back and stood up sharply, almost knocking it over.

"Beau, please."

I finally looked at her and could see by the anguish in her eyes she knew how hard it would be for me. Yet she still asked.

"Nope. Not a fucking chance." I went to move past her, but she caught my arm.

"He's just a child, Beau."

"He's not my child, so go get his damn mother." I stormed out of the office and headed for the stairs only for *my* damn mother to hijack my escape.

"You won't take him back?" she asked, her arms folded over her chest.

"No, Ma, I won't. Go and get his mum." I put a foot on the bottom stair.

"He doesn't talk," she said. "Lovely little kid but doesn't say a word."

I paused and turned my head to her. "And?"

"Just saying. He smiles, he laughs, and he understands every word you say but all he does is nod or shake his head."

"Why are you telling me?" I shrugged. "He's my neighbour's kid, that's all. He's shy, so what?"

"I know that, and no way is he shy. It's more than that. He has issues with speaking."

I shrugged. Call me a twat, but I couldn't give two shits what issues he had.

"I'm just telling you so that you realise you're not the only one who's got problems in this world. Makes you wonder why he doesn't speak."

"You're telling me that him not speaking trumps me losing my whole fucking world, is that it?" I growled and clenched my hands into fists.

"Don't be ridiculous." Ma's hazel eyes narrowed on me and she straightened herself to her full five feet four. "No one will ever know the pain that you're feeling but maybe you can show some kindliness to someone else who's having problems."

"I've sorted a plumber, decorator and plasterer for her. Want me to pay as well, is that it?"

A bony finger pointed in my face. "No and don't use the f word to me. I brought you up better than that."

I sighed heavily and dropped my gaze to my feet. "I'm sorry, Ma, but please don't ask me to carry that boy around there and please don't tell me I need to be kind to someone to help *me* get through *my* damn nightmare. I won't ever get through it. It'll be with me every day of my life."

"Not what I was saying," she replied with a shake of her head. "I just want you to consider how you doing this for her tonight might have helped her more than you will ever understand. Her boy not speaking might be as painful for her as you losing your family is to you. He's here and alive and seems happy but as a mother I know that must gut her. Everything is relative, Beau and who are we to say how she feels about her son being mute?"

This was a conversation I was never going to win. My Ma thought she knew how to heal everyone whether it be with harsh words, gentle actions or just pure belligerence, and according to her she was never wrong. Sighing I turned to walk back into the lounge to wake Ethan when there was a knock on the door.

Ma stood to one side as if ordering me to be the one to open it. When I did Simone stood there, still in her long coat.

"You come for Ethan?" I asked.

She nodded. "Yeah. Thanks so much. The plumber was great."

"What did he say?" Ma asked and pushed alongside me. "Sylvie, Beau's mum."

"Oh hi, Mrs Bradley. Thank you for having Ethan." Simone smiled and then sighed again. "He told me to keep the electrics off. Said I need to get an electrician to check them out. He had a quick look and there's a few wires under the boards that look really wet."

"Oh no, we can't have that." Ma tutted. "Come on in love and you and Ethan stay here tonight. You can't be at home with no water or electricity, can she Beau?"

Another battle I wasn't going to win. And as if I'd say no with the woman standing there.

"Yeah sure."

Simone put a hand to her throat and looked at me through one eye. "Are you sure. I've put you to so much trouble already. I do admit, I don't feel very safe over there. No electrics means no alarm."

"It's fine," I replied, understanding why she'd feel insecure. "You want to go and get your stuff."

Ma nudged me. "Maybe you should go with her."

I thought my jaw and teeth were going to break I was grinding so hard. She just couldn't help interfering and trying to heal me. Didn't she realise I didn't fucking want to. I wanted to feel the pain of losing my family for the rest of my life.

Thank God for my sister. "I'll go with you." She appeared beside me. "Ma's right, you shouldn't be in a house without electricity or water. Did you contact your landlord by the way?" she asked as she moved through the doorway.

Simone nodded and I couldn't help but notice how she bit her lip and looked uncomfortable.

"Yes. He's going to pay rather than go through the insurance."

Seemed stupid to me but it was his property.

"Okay, we won't be long," Belle said.

"Is Ethan okay?' Simone asked, looking between me and Ma.

"He's fine, love," Ma replied. "Fast asleep on the sofa. I'll get Beau to take him up to the spare room."

My breath caught and I wanted to run. Why could she not just leave me alone?

"It's fine I—"

"Don't be silly," Ma butted in. "Now go and get your things."

Not daring myself to speak to her for fear of saying something I'd regret, as soon as the door closed, I stalked into the lounge. If I had to take the kid up to bed, I would, but that would be the last thing I'd do to help. I wanted to be left alone. I didn't want to be anyone's saviour, least of all my damn neighbour's.

As I pushed open the door, I found Ethan sitting up, rubbing at his eyes and yawning. He was a cute kid and none of it was his fault, but it still didn't mean I wanted to be in the room with him.

"Hey," I said quietly. "You're awake."

He didn't answer but nodded with a sleepy smile and I recalled what Ma had said—he didn't speak.

"I'll take you up to bed. You and your mum are staying here tonight. That okay?'

He nodded again and I held out my hand. Shuffling to the edge of the sofa, he dropped his feet to the floor and stood up. A tiny hand crept into mine and when I felt the warm, soft skin of his pudgy little fingers, I had to hold my breath to stop me from crying out in pain.

"Oh, you're awake," Ma said and crouched in front of Ethan. "Beau will take you up to bed and your mum will be here soon. Okay?"

Ethan nodded again as I gently pulled him away and into the hallway. As we reached the bottom stair he yawned again and even though my heart was cracking and my soul blistering with pain, I picked him up.

Fighting to keep my breaths steady, when two arms went around my neck, I felt my knees buckle and had to reach out a hand for the bannister. Then a tiny voice spoke.

"Thank you, for helping my mummy, Mr Bradley. You're very kind."

It was then I thought I might die from my grief.

ten

Simone

"So, it's just you and Ethan then?" Belle asked as we walked up to Beau's front door with two bags. "Oh, and your brother."

"Yeah, just the two of us in the house," I said flashing her a smile. "This is really kind of Beau to do this. You've all been really kind in fact."

Belle shrugged. "That's what neighbours are for. To be honest, I think it'll do him good to think about something else for a little while."

"I heard about his family. He must be devastated."

Belle blew through pursed lips. "We all are. Bobby was just the most amazing little boy, and Cassie…" She paused and drew in a ragged breath. "God, it's so hard to think we won't ever see them again. I have no idea how Beau has managed to keep going."

"That must have been a terrible worry for you and your mum." I could imagine the dark days he suffered must have swamped and suffocated him. Grief was the worst possible emotion. All-encompassing and never-ending.

"Especially as he wouldn't see us for ages," Belle replied. "If it wasn't for Di his cleaner, we wouldn't have known whether he was alive or dead. Not in the beginning. Even the boys from the band couldn't get him to talk. Eventually he started to text us but it's not the same." She laughed but it was quiet and empty. "This is the first time I've seen him since the funeral, and I feel so selfish because that hurt almost as much as losing them."

"You're here now and maybe that shows he's slowly making progress."

"Yes, maybe. Okay," she said brightly. "Let's see which room he's put you in."

As Belle opened the door, I felt my stomach flip. How the hell had I gone to spending the night in Beau Bradley's spare room? It was ridiculous. Up until a couple of days ago I hadn't even known he was my neighbour.

Moving into the house, I spent a little time to look around at the surroundings that I'd not been interested in before. The house was pretty much like mine, but even in the hall I could sense it was, or at least had been, much more of a home. On the wall opposite to the front door was a huge black and white canvas of a child who I assumed was Beau's son. He had his back to the camera, blond curls translucent in the sunlight and he was looking out over a field of long grass. It was simple but so beautiful and I wondered how Beau could stand for it to stay on the wall. My heart cracked for him as I thought about how I'd be if I lost Ethan. It didn't bare thinking about, and I instantly wanted to pull him into my arms to be sure he was safe.

My gaze lingered on a side table where there were two glass candle sticks next to a matching glass bowl, the colour of the bluest sky shading into white clouds. Inside it was a set of bangles and it was as if they'd been pulled off the wrist of whoever had worn them the minute that they'd come through the door. There was also a small toy car and a packet of tissues, all discarded as if it were only yesterday that they'd been placed there. Next to it was what took my breath, a framed photograph of a beautiful blonde woman holding a little boy whose head was back as he laughed raucously. It was gorgeous.

Everything in this house must have been a constant reminder to Beau and I understood why he was so closed off. There was not only grief but memories all around him of a life once lived that he'd never get back.

"Oh hey," Belle said, and I looked up to see Beau padding down the stairs.

"I've put you in the back bedroom. The large one with the en suite. Ethan is already asleep. I won't set the alarm sensors inside in case he wakes in the night."

I blinked rapidly. "Oh, okay."

"Bobby used to set it off all the time, so…" he tailed off and glanced at a wide-eyed Belle who was chewing on her thumbnail.

"T-thanks," I stammered. "And sorry again for being a pain."

Beau nodded and moved past me without any further comment as Belle and I watched him. He took long strides across the large hallway and disappeared into the room that in my house I used as Ethan's playroom. When the door clicked shut, Belle sighed heavily.

"I'll take you up."

"It's fine. I know which one he means, it's pretty much a replica of my house."

"You sure?"

"Yes, I'm fine. I'm shattered so I'll probably just go to bed," I replied not caring that it was still fairly early, and I hadn't eaten dinner. I held out my hand for Ethan's backpack that she was carrying. "Thanks again."

"No problem. Sleep well."

Smiling I moved up the stairs to find my boy and hug him tight.

***

I woke with a start as Ethan moved beside me. We were sharing a bed and although it was huge, we'd both felt the need to cuddle up to each other. He was sound asleep and star-fishing with quiet little snores. Now that I was awake the heat in the room was stifling. I'd opened the window a small way when I'd gone up to bed, but now the air was cloying, and I felt a bead of sweat trickle between my breasts which were covered in fleece cotton pyjamas. Slipping the duvet off me, I swung my legs out of the bed and lowered my feet to the floor.

Standing, I held my breath as Ethan moved again, but when he didn't stir any further, I tiptoed across the room. If Beau's kitchen was anything like mine it would be nice and cool and the best place for me. Quietly as I could, I made my way across the landing and down the stairs. Then I crept across the tiled floor of the hallway and through the door that led to the kitchen. When I adjusted to the darkness, I almost screamed when I saw a figure sitting at the island, hunched over a mug.

"Shit," I hissed and cutting off my scream as I realised that it was Beau. "I didn't expect to find anyone in here."

"Couldn't sleep." His voice was deep and rough.

"Me neither. Sorry."

"Can you do me a favour?" he asked, dropping his forehead to his hand. "Can you stop apologising."

He sounded a little irritated and I wondered if I should just turn around and go back to bed. That however would mean going back to the heat of the bedroom and the kitchen was much less stifling, even if Beau Bradley was in it.

"It's difficult for me to accept help," I replied. "And I also don't want to feel like I'm creating a fuss or that I expected you to do all this for me and Ethan."

"Yeah, well, like Belle said, you couldn't sleep over there without electricity and water." As my eyes became more adjusted to the darkness, I saw him look down at his mug. "You want a warm milk, or hot chocolate?"

My stomach could have done with something, so I moved over to the pan that was still on the stove. When I peered inside, I saw that there was still some milk in there.

"You might need to add more, or there's probably enough for a small one." Beau stood up and went to one of the cupboards. He then opened it and pulled out a mug and passed it to me. As I turned the heat back on the milk, I expected him to leave, but he went back to his stool and watched the pan.

"How come you live in that massive house?" he asked.

Surprised, I startled a little and almost spilled the liquid as I poured it into my mug. I took the time it took to put cold water into the empty pan and move over to the stool opposite of him, to decide on my response. It wasn't like it was a huge secret. I was also conscious that he probably didn't actually care and that I didn't like to tell anyone my business. He was being polite, which was magnanimous of him considering I had encroached on his privacy—both by staying over and interrupting his late-night solace.

"I needed a place to live, and I know the owner." It wasn't a lie, but it wasn't the whole truth either.

"But why that place. It's huge?" He picked up his mug and drank and in the dim light I could sense he was waiting expectantly.

"He lets me have it cheaper than I would pay for a two-bed apartment." Beau nodded slowly. "Good man to know."

"Yep," I ground out. "Although I tend to deal with his assistant, Vanessa." "Oh right."

What that meant I had no clue, but it sounded a little judgemental if I was being honest. I wouldn't say that though. He was not only doing me a favour, but I was also a coward who hated confrontation. We sat in silence both looking down at our mugs and my body was beginning to tighten with the tension.

"I guess I should get back up to bed," I said after a few minutes, feeling more uncomfortable by the second.

"Don't feel you have to," Beau replied. "If you can't sleep you don't want to wake Ethan. I know what kids are like if they don't get their sleep."

He cleared his throat and then looked up at me. Even in the darkness of the night the pain was unmistakable on his face. His eyes were empty almost and his lips were turned down, heavy under the weight of grief. It had been a year from what I remembered, and he still looked like he'd only just heard the news. I wasn't surprised. How the hell did you get over something like that.

"I can't imagine what you're going through," I blurted out feeling the need to acknowledge it in some way, without giving the usual platitudes.

Beau looked up and blinked slowly.

"It's something you're never going to get over so how do you even get through each hour never mind each day?"

"Well, that's not what I'm used to hearing?" He shrugged and took another sip of his drink. "Usually everyone can't wait to tell me how it'll get better one day."

I shook my head. "I doubt that. Not sure I would. Losing your son is horrendous, but also you wife too." I blew out a breath. "One day you might wake up and feel less of the pain, but it'll still be there."

A small whisper of a smile ghosted against Beau's lips and instantly some of the tightness in my body began to ease. I'd spoken what I thought was the truth but even so it may well have been something he didn't want to hear.

"I wish everyone was as honest as you," he replied. "Because I agree, this is not something that is going to go away. Even when I'm fifty, sixty, or maybe ninety, I know I'll still miss them. Still have this dull ache in my soul."

"You lost your music too. There must be some element of grief there."

"I can't even contemplate music now. It means nothing to me. I have about as much passion for it as I do that dirty pan." He nodded to the sink where I'd left the pan of water. "Honestly, I feel like that about most things and most people. There's nothing left in here."

He patted his chest against the white t-shirt that he wore. His hair was still tied up on top of his head and it looked like he'd trimmed his beard since I'd seen him a few hours before. It was tidier and a littler shorter. There was no doubt he was handsome, but I could see without joy in his life it had marred his features and dimmed the light in his eyes.

"Maybe one day you'll let people back in." I shrugged. "Or maybe not. I guess the main thing is just putting one foot in front of the other each day."

"Two weeks ago, I barely got out of bed, so perhaps you're right." Beau leaned his elbow on the black granite and then rested his head in his hand. "Mind if I ask you something?"

My heart sped up, scared of what he might want to know. I'd grown used to not having to tell anyone my business—no one really cared except for Marcus, and he'd instantly believed in the story that I'd told him five years ago that Ethan was the product of a one-night stand.

"Go on," I said, offering a smile that felt taut and uncomfortable.

"Where's Ethan's dad? Is he on the scene?"

I swallowed and poked a finger at the skin forming on my milk. I pushed it to one side and then took a sip, killing time. It never occurred to me to tell him to mind his own. Keep his nose out. That's what I'd done at Ethan's last school when one of the mums at the gate had asked the same question. I'd told her it wasn't something that I wanted to discuss. She'd given me a look as though I'd told her I was a murderer and then turned her back on me. I stood away from them after that, not caring that they all called me stuck up. That's why I'd wanted to move, too many people prying into my business and not liking it when I refused to give them the gory details. Plus, I hated the school and the fact that they saw Ethan as some sort of freak. I didn't want the house, but I had no choice.

"He's not on the scene," I replied once I put my mug down. "It was a one-off."

"He doesn't give you any money for Ethan?" He shifted on his stool and his jaw tensed.

How did I answer that without lying? I *could* lie, he was only my neighbour after all but something about him made me think he'd know. I also didn't want him to lose any respect for me—should he have any. I imagined I was just a pain in his arse. If it wasn't my son pushing through his hedge, it was me inflicting myself on him.

"He doesn't acknowledge Ethan in any way, but he provides for him." I kept it short and truthful, hoping that was enough for Beau's sudden interest.

Beau nodded and sat upright. "That's good. Nothing worse than a man who won't provide for his kids. Way I see it, doesn't matter what the circumstances are, it takes two to make a baby, so both should be responsible for raising it."

If he knew what those circumstances were, well he might not necessarily be on my side. I knew what they seemed like, but it just wasn't what people always jumped to the conclusion of.

"Was it him who helped you get next door?" He ran a hand down his face. "Sorry, that sounds bloody condescending, assuming you can't afford it yourself."

"He knows the owner."

Again, another half-truth.

"Do you work?"

I blinked wondering what the hell had suddenly made him so talkative. He'd barely been able to utter a whole sentence earlier yet now he was practically interviewing me.

"I design and maintain websites. I wanted to be a graphic designer but when Ethan came along, I had to leave uni. When I found myself at home with a baby, I decided to do some online courses to get myself a career I could do from home."

"Wow," he said quietly. "That must have been hard work."

"It was but Ethan was a good baby, so it wasn't so bad." I didn't add that I didn't need the money but did it for my own sanity.

Beau let out a yawn, and that weird thing happened where it becomes contagious, and I yawned too.

"I think maybe we could both sleep now," I said, getting up from my stool. I picked up our mugs, which were empty and took them over to the sink. When I started to run the hot water, a hand came over and turned off the tap.

"Don't worry about it," Beau said as he snatched his hand back and took two steps away. "Get yourself to bed, you've had a pretty stressful night."

"It's the least I can do."

He shook his head. "Seriously, leave it."

When I looked at him the shadows were back and I knew our chat was over. I also had the feeling he'd be back to being shut down in the morning. I had no clue what had prompted him to talk so freely to me, but it was gone now.

"Okay, well thanks again for everything you've done tonight. Ethan and I really appreciate it."

He nodded once and leaned back against the countertop, his hands gripping the edges like he was free-climbing a cliff. I gave him a small smile and then went back to bed.

As I slipped between the sheets, Ethan stirred momentarily but soon settled again. As I lay in the dark thinking about the conversation I'd just had with Beau, I couldn't help but wonder if anyone would ever bring him back to life.

eleven

Beau

Waking alone was something I'd never got used to. Not since Cassie had stayed over at my flat on our third date and then never went back to the house that she shared with three mates. When we were on tour, I fucking hated it and usually the first thing I did was facetime Cassie and lay my phone on the pillow next to me. The lads used to take the piss out of me; call me a tart, but I didn't care. I missed her and Bobby.

Looking up at my bedroom ceiling, my throat prickled, and my stomach turned as I wished more than anything I could facetime her now.

Blowing out a breath, I sat up and looked at the mess on the bed. There was my notebook, a couple of pens and a few screwed up pieces of paper. No idea why, but when I'd finally gone back upstairs to bed as the morning light peeked up on the horizon, I'd felt the need to write a song.

The idea had hit me like a punch right between my eyes. Almost caused me to black out I was so damn shocked. I hadn't even thought about music since the day my life theoretically ended. Yet at that moment the need to put a pen to paper and write down my emotions overwhelmed me. Like someone had a pully chain on my heart and was dragging it up from the depths that it fallen to. As it got higher my fingertips tingled and my mouth watered at the idea of writing a song.

If I'd thought it was going to be easy, I was wrong. The number of discarded pieces of paper stood testament to that. Inside the notebook though there was a verse and a chorus and that was so much more than I'd been capable of for the last year. The first line had been the hardest because I knew what I wanted to say, but I was out of practice. I hadn't written down my raw emotions for so long it was hard to be brave enough again. I put my pen to paper, making the stroke of the first letter, but each time I tried to carry on I was scared it would cause my heart to give up. It must have been eight or nine times that I attempted it until finally I took a deep breath and gritted my teeth.

How do I survive the prison of emptiness? How does my heart continue without you?

After that the words flowed and I only stopped because my tears were blotting the ink and it was getting difficult to see anything.

Now though, looking down at the notebook, I had no desire to carry on with it. I had no fucking clue where the inspiration had come from in the early hours of the morning. Whatever it was had disappeared.

When I heard footsteps on the landing, I stopped thinking about the song and remembered that I wasn't alone. I had visitors and they included my neighbour. The woman who'd I'd practically interrogated over a cup of hot milk. I had no clue why I'd felt the need, or where my voice had come from. Talking wasn't my strongest point lately. Maybe it was the cover of the darkness that made it easier, I had no clue.

I leaned across to my phone and was surprised to see it was only a little after eight. I was sure I hadn't fallen asleep until about five, yet I felt like I'd had a lot more than three hours kip. Maybe letting out the words had rested me in some way—but what did I know?

With a sigh I got out of bed and quickly showered. I wondered if maybe I could get myself some coffee and lock myself in my office before anyone else surfaced—although the footsteps earlier told me that someone was awake. I just hope they weren't in the kitchen; I wasn't in the mood for talking.

Once dressed, I slipped out of my room and down the stairs, creeping across the hallway towards the kitchen. Slowly I pushed the door open and peeked inside, it was empty, thank God. Then out of nowhere my ma's voice called out and I felt like I'd been shot in the head by a sniper.

"Oh good, you're up. Simmy made breakfast."

Almost stumbling, I turned to see Ma right behind me. She was smiling but it wasn't exactly friendly, more amused maniac.

I opened my mouth to make an excuse of why I didn't want to eat anything, but she pushed me inside and announced our arrival.

"He's up. We can start now."

Simone popped up from behind the island and gave me a hesitant smile. "Oh morning. I was just looking for a toaster."

My guts rolled. "I don't have one," I bit out.

My head filled with images of me ripping it away from the countertop and smashing it over and over against the wall and the floor. I hadn't stopped until it was just scattered pieces of broken and buckled black metal.

"Oh, okay. No problem, I'll use the grill in the oven." She moved over and pulled a rack out at the same time as stirring something in a pan. "If you want to sit down in the dining room, I'll bring it all in."

Frowning I looked at Ma and shook my head. She glared at me and took hold of my elbow.

"You go and sit down, I'll help Simmy."

"I don—."

"Go on," she said, her tone quiet and commanding. "Simmy's gone to a lot of trouble."

She might have done but I didn't ask her to, and I certainly didn't ask her to set up the fucking dining room table like she lived here. I took a breath and scrubbed a hand across my mouth. "Ma."

"No, Beau," she whispered. "She's been up for ages, even went to get stuff, seeing as she didn't want to use what was yours. The poor girl just wants to thank us, thank you, for the help."

Simone clattered plates behind us and when I looked over my shoulder,

I could see she'd starting to dish everything up. I didn't know if I could sit and eat with them all. It wasn't just Simone and her kid; it was my ma and Belle too. It wasn't happy families. We weren't all going to chat about our day. Why the hell would we? In any case it was my wife's place to set that dining table not some fucking woman from next door who I barely knew.

Huffing like a teenager, I stormed into the dining room, already determined that I'd hate whatever she put in front of me to eat. When I walked in Belle was sitting next to Simone's boy and chatting away to him about something. I had no idea what but did hear the word Dragon. Ethan didn't say anything but smiled and nodded.

I dragged out a chair on the opposite side of the table and sat down.

"Oh, morning," Belle said, her attention momentarily on me.

I grunted a response and then waited, looking sulkily out of the window. After a couple of minutes, the door pushed open, and Ma and Simone came in each carrying plates of food. Simone had two down one arm, carrying them like a proper waitress. Plates were placed in front of us, and I must admit my stomach groaned with appreciation. It was a full English, including what looked like perfectly cooked fried bread. I couldn't remember the last time I'd had fried bread that looked that good—Cassie either drowned it in oil or burned it. The times we'd laughed about the fact she couldn't manage to cook a full English. Everything else she was pretty good at, but a cooked breakfast wasn't her forte.

"This looks lovely, Simmy." Belle grinned as she reached for the ketchup.

"You didn't need to go and buy the food though," Ma added. "There's plenty of stuff in the fridge."

My grip on my knife and fork tightened. I hated that she was talking to Simone like it was all perfectly normal. I wasn't precious about my food, or about anything I owned particularly, but the idea of Ma offering it to her made me want to tell her to get on a train and fuck off back home.

"I'll just go and get the toast," Simone replied.

Toast. I hated it. Irrational maybe but it was damn toast that had ripped my life apart.

A couple of minutes later she was back with a plate full of it. She placed it in the middle of the table and sat down next to Ethan.

"You need me to cut your sausage?" she asked as he took a bite out of it, the whole thing speared on the end of his fork.

Ethan shook his head and took another bite. He then smiled up at his mum and she gently cupped his face. I was sure everyone must have heard my heart crack open.

"Thinking about it," Ma said as she cut her bacon, "you should have just used what was in your fridge, it might still be okay, but it won't last much longer without being refrigerated."

"I don't have much in there." She dropped her head and cleared her throat.

It struck me that she was petite and slim, tiny almost, yet was tucking into her breakfast. Maybe she didn't eat much because she couldn't afford it. Ethan looked healthy enough so what if she gave him all the food? When I looked at everything on the table I wondered if it buying it had skint her. There was fresh orange, bacon, sausage, egg, beans, tomato, mushrooms, fried bread, there were even some of those pastries with chocolate in them.

"You didn't have to buy all of this," I muttered spearing a mushroom and popping it into my mouth.

"It's the least I could do after you all helped me. I just went to the little Tesco Metro at the top of the main road. It was quite a nice walk. There was hardly anyone around."

"What time did you go?" I asked, letting my cutlery fall to the plate.

"About sevenish." She peaked up at me and chewed on her lip.

"That's got to be almost a two-mile walk. You shouldn't have gone there on your own at that time in the morning. Anything could have happened."

"Beau," Ma warned.

"I'm just saying." My brows raised as I looked at her, trying to give my own warning to leave me alone and go home back to Leicester.

"I was fine," Simone insisted.

We continued to eat. Me and Ethan in silence while Belle, Ma and Simone chatted about the weather and whole load of other shit. I watched Ethan as he ate up all his breakfast. He listened and smiled when he was spoken to but didn't utter a word. I wondered why he'd spoken to me the night before. Like Ma said he wasn't shy, but he certainly wasn't talking much today.

We'd almost finished eating when Simone's phone buzzed with a text. She fished it out of her pocket and looked at it.

"Oh, it's my plumber. He's just pulling up at the house."

"You go," Belle replied. "We'll clear up the dishes."

Simone smiled and stood up. "If that's okay, thank you. Okay, Ethan. Quickly get your shoes on."

"No," Ma said, waving her away. "He can stay here. You may need to stay another night anyway."

I drew in a breath and Simone's head swivelled my way. "No," she said, looking at me. "We should be able to go back home tonight. The electrician is coming today too."

"Well, whatever," Ma said, standing up and stacking the dishes. "Ethan is fine here for now."

"Only if you're sure."

"Of course," Ma replied and pushed Simone out of the door.

As she disappeared, Belle and Ma started to take the plates into the kitchen. Ethan continued to sit there, smiling, and showing his cute, straight white teeth that were still like baby teeth. This, it was all too much.

"See you later, Ethan."

As I left, he said nothing and that was fine with me.

***

I'd been in my office for probably forty minutes when the door was opened and a little hand appeared, clutching the wood. Next a foot appeared, followed by a leg and then the rest of Ethan moved inside.

"Hi Ethan."

He smiled and held up his book. I had a horrible feeling that he wanted me to read to him but then he went and sat on the leather sofa. He pushed back until only his feet were hanging off the end of the cushion and then opened his book and started to read. He mouthed the words but made no sound. Occasionally his shoulders moved up and down and his smile grew bigger but still silence. I couldn't take my eyes off him. No matter how much I tried to go back to playing on my computer all I wanted to do was watch him. Now and then I managed a few seconds of moving playing cards around the screen, but it wasn't long before my attention was back on Ethan. He had a little habit of poking his tongue out and lifting his brows at certain points and I guessed that was when he got to a good part. Despite myself I couldn't help but smile at him. The sun shone brightly through the window and bounced off my computer screen. There was a brightness in the room, and it finally felt like Spring had arrived. I drew in a breath at the realisation I'd been thinking of something positive for once.

"You okay, buddy?" I asked.

Ethan looked up and with a huge grin nodded.

"What is it you're reading?"

He held up his book, *The Boy Who Grew Dragons*. It wasn't one I'd heard of but then I hadn't looked at many kid's books for a while. Ethan jumped down from the sofa and skipped towards me and held it out. Cautiously, I took it from him and flicked through it. It was a proper book, not just a kid's picture book with sparse lines of text, but a full-on story book.

"You can read this?" I asked.

Ethan nodded but his attention was no longer on me but my ancient acoustic guitar over in the corner. It was an old one, not full size, but the first that I'd ever had. It barely held a tune any longer, no matter how much I retuned or restrung it. It'd been a cheap one that I'd saved up for when I was about fourteen. I did a paper round back when people still had newspapers delivered, and I cleaned cars and mowed lawns. It was only about sixty quid, but it took me an age to save for it and every day I cycled past the music shop hoping that it hadn't gone. It'd been in the window so long the front of it had faded but I didn't care.

When a strange note bounced around the room, I saw that Ethan was pulling his little fingers over the strings. His eyes were wide and expectant as he did it again and when the weird sound came out, his little face shone. His mouth dropped and he blinked rapidly as he took a breath.

"Think you'd like to learn how to play?" I asked, getting off my chair and slowly walking towards him.

Ethan didn't look at me but strummed again, giving me his answer. I crouched down and gently took his hand, placing his middle two fingers to play an E minor—a sad chord of course, and then I strummed the strings to produce a sound so much better than that he'd played before.

"That's an E," I said, flexing my hand as it felt like electricity was sparking through my fingers.

Ethan nodded and gently pushed my hand away and strummed it. As he was standing sideways on, the sound wasn't quite the same and he frowned.

"Sit on the sofa."

He ran back to it and practically jumped on, perching himself on the edge. I sat next to him and placed the guitar between us, the neck in front of Ethan's little body, it still too big even though it wasn't full size. Without me saying anything he positioned his two fingers exactly where I'd placed them before. I strummed and when he smiled, I knew he was happy with the noise he'd made. For the next ten minutes or so we repeated it over and over until he began to fidget.

"Want me to show you another chord?" I asked.

He bounced in his seat and so I put my arm around him and moved his hand. This time I added a third finger to play C. While Ethan held the strings down, I strummed, and he grinned at the sound. We'd almost mastered it when the door opened, and Belle appeared.

"Oh God," she gasped.

The lump in my throat almost choked me as I saw her eyes dart between me and Ethan. This didn't mean anything; I was only teaching the kid a couple of chords.

"I was looking for you, Ethan," she almost whispered. "Your mum says it's okay for you to go home. I'll walk you round."

She looked at me again and I saw her jaw tremble. I couldn't stand to see her get emotional, it made my skin itch, like what I was doing was somehow momentous and I didn't want it to be. I wanted this to be nothing special. Nothing for me or anyone else to get excited about. I stood and took the guitar back to the other side of the room, resting it on its stand.

"You'd better get going," I said without turning to look at them.

"Yep," Belle said clearing her throat. "Let's go shall we."

I let out a long breath, closing my eyes as I heard them leave, until I felt a tug on my t-shirt. I looked down, surprised to see Ethan.

"I thought you'd gone."

"Thank you, Mr Beau," his small voice said. "And I'm sorry you're sad."

He then hugged my leg, ran a hand down the neck of my guitar and then ran out of the room.

twelve

Beau

My scalp was prickling as I looked at my phone. The boys would be arriving for dinner any minute all thanks to my interfering mother. It wasn't just them being around that had me on edge, she'd also invited Simone and Ethan. Ethan was a great kid. Didn't speak much, but after they'd stayed that night, we'd got into a routine of him coming around most days. The first time he'd come in for his ball and saw me so waved, when I waved back, I saw him standing on tiptoes looking in and behind me, so I guessed he was looking to see if I had my guitar in the kitchen with me. I didn't but went out as asked him if he wanted to come in and play guitar. I'd never seen a kid drop a ball and run inside so fast. Belle texted Simone for me to check it was okay and that had become our routine.

It was only for an hour, but he was loving me teaching him. Okay, so we'd only done the intro of *The Seven Nation Army*, but I'd tried to do more chords with him, and it wasn't happening. Ethan had tiny little hands and doing chords meant I had to help him, and well… putting an arm around him and moving my fingers over the top of his was starting to make my chest burn, so strumming was as far as we'd got. It kept my mind occupied though and distracted me from the shit in my life; mainly my Ma trying to get me to interact with people.

As I paced my bedroom, I heard noise in the next room where Belle had been sleeping. I guessed she was finishing off getting ready. If I had it in me, I'd give her shit about doing her makeup and hair and wearing a nice dress, but I couldn't be arsed. I barely had the energy to breathe most days, so giving my sister shit about her crush on Elliot was the last thing I wanted to be doing. I'd always known she'd had one, from the first time I took him home to meet Ma. Belle had gone red and shy and could barely look him in the eye. Over the years it had seemed to have dimmed a bit, but Elliot was a pretty, little bastard, so there was no doubt that the makeup, curls in the hair and new dress she'd bought when she'd gone shopping with Simone was for his benefit.

When I heard her bedroom door click shut, I knew I should think about changing out of my Blondie t-shirt into the pale blue shirt Ma had washed and ironed for me. Why, she'd done that, I had no idea. The boys had seen me looking far worse, not including those times since I'd lost Cassie and Bobby. Damn, in the early days of groupies, pre finding the love of my life, Ronnie and Joey once locked me out of our hotel room wearing nothing but a sock on my dick, so I was sure they wouldn't care if I wore a ratty old band tee for dinner. If I thought about it there was one explanation for Ma insisting that I wear a 'nice shirt'; Simone was coming for dinner too. Well, she could get that thought out of her head. Whether it was just me finding a 'neighbour I could rely on' or not.

Sighing heavily, I pulled off my t-shirt, and threw it into the washing basket. The egg stain down the front did mean it was long past needing to be washed and it was easier to do that than have Ma on my case for the remaining two days of her visit. Fastening the last button, I heard the doorbell ring, and I blew out, puffing my cheeks.

"Great," I groaned with a huge hint of sarcasm. "My friends are here."

I ran my fingers through my hair, scrubbed a hand down my face and then went down to greet them.

When I reached the bottom step, my heart inexplicably jumped to my throat. Ronnie was on in haunches in my hallway, and he was talking to Ethan. I didn't know whether it was because Ethan was grinning from ear to ear that I felt weird, or because Ronnie had found a best friend replacement for my son. I watched for at least a minute as he chatted easily to Ethan, seemingly not bothered by the fact that Ethan didn't talk back. He was relaxed and easy, not finding it awkward like I had at first. Then, Ethan saw me and when his grin grew bigger as he waved to me. Even though we were only a couple of feet away from each other, my lungs felt like a balloon that had the air let out. Oxygen rushed out raggedly and the tension in my shoulders disappeared.

"Hey, Ethan." I waved back and smiled.

Ronnie swivelled around on his heels and then stood. "Beau."

"Ronnie. You made it then?"

He grinned and winked. "Wouldn't want to let you down. I know how much you've been looking forward to tonight."

"Yeah, well, you know Sylvie. She likes to interfere in my life wherever possible."

Ethan looked up, his head going back and forth as we spoke. I took the last step and moved closer to ruffle his hair. Don't ask me why but I felt like I needed to lay some sort of claim on him with Ronnie. That made me feel like a prick. He was my neighbour's kid, what the fuck was going on in my brain?

Ronnie nodded at Ethan. "So, Sylvie tells me that you're teaching Ethan here to play guitar." I nodded and Ronnie shook his head. "Gotta say you really should leave it to the professionals, Beau. I mean Elliot would be better at a push, but I'm pretty sure Ethan would pick up bass pretty quick."

'We're good thanks," I stated the idea of Ronnie or Elliot teaching Ethan giving me a knot in my stomach. I looked down at Ethan. "I thought you might come over today, buddy. Were you busy?"

He nodded and rolled his eyes and I guessed it had something to do with his mum. He then reached for my hand and smiled. When tiny fingers wrapped around three of my large, calloused ones, I heard Ronnie draw in a breath. I looked over at him and saw that his eyes were shining.

"Ronnie," I warned.

"I just… shit," he hissed. "I'm sorry, it's just—"

"Ronnie, don't." I cleared my throat and looked down at Ethan. "Let's go and get something to eat."

Ethan nodded and pulled on my hand to lead me to where everyone else was waiting to study me and decide how much of a headcase I still was.

As we walked into the lounge, I freed myself of Ethan's hold. Ronnie had been bad enough, but I certainly didn't need Elliot getting all weepy on me because I held a little kid's hand. It didn't matter though because he and Joey were talking to Simone, who it had to be said looked petrified. She was wary around me, and she'd stayed in my house for a night so fuck knew how she must be feeling meeting Elliot and Joey, Elliot especially. He had a magnetism about him that drove women wild. Yes, I got most of the attention being the lead singer, but it was of the flashing tits and slipping me phone numbers variety. Elliot was the one that women wanted to settle down with. The one they thought would be romantic and loving, the one they wanted to take care of. Joey and Ronnie's attention was much like my own, except they took advantage of the bare tits and phone numbers.

I noted that my Ma and Belle weren't around and guessed that they were in the kitchen finishing off the preparations for dinner. I'd suggested that we ask Di to do it, but Ma was insistent. It wouldn't be anything fancy, probably sausage and mash, or Ma's meat and potato pie, because she was a great believer in keeping all us boys grounded and reminding us of where we came from.

As I watched Simone clutch her wine glass and look up at Elliot, Ethan joined her and pushed himself close to her body. His head came just about to her waist and her free hand instinctively went to ruffle his hair. The action made my stomach jolt. It was the sort of thing Cassie would do with Bobby and I missed it. I missed little things like that almost as much as I missed them.

Ronnie stepped past me and clapped his hands together as he approached them.

"Okay," he said, pushing in between Elliot and Joey. "You must be Ethan's mum." He offered his hand out to Simone.

"Hi," she replied with a hesitant smile. "Yes. I'm Simone, good to meet you."

"You live next door, right?" Simone looked down at Ethan quizzically and Ronnie touched her elbow. "It was Sylvie who told me when she answered the door."

Shit, Ronnie had spent a few minutes in Ethan's company and already understood his lack of speech and how surprised Simone was that he might have spoken to the man-child of our band. Grief really did make you a self-centred prick didn't it. It had taken me a while to get a handle on the kid. As for Simone, my longest conversation with her had been the night she'd stayed, and we'd drunk hot milk in the kitchen. Since then, every conversation had consisted of three words at most. Even when she'd dropped Ethan off while she went shopping with Belle, all she'd said had been, 'hi,' and 'thanks so much,' when she'd picked him up.

"You lived there long?" Ronnie continued.

"Just a few months." Simone glanced over at the door and then back to Ronnie. "I rent it from a family friend."

The family friend was news to me, but it did explain why it was so cheap for her to rent, and yet I still got the impression money wasn't in abundance for her. As I contemplated that, Elliot pushed up alongside me.

"I hear you're giving guitar lessons?' he said with a grin.

"Yeah, and don't bother telling me that you or Ronnie would be better suited."

He held his hands up in surrender. "Wasn't going to. According to his mum you're great with him."

"Don't, Elliot." I ran a hand through my hair and walked away from him. I was not in the mood for an Elliot Andrews life coaching session.

When I reached the kitchen Ma was plating up sausages while Belle mashed up potato. She waved the masher at me and pulled a face that said, 'you always get out of everything'. I'd seen the same expression many times when we were kids. Feeling like a spare part, I turned on my heels but only got as far as the door.

"Beau, stir the gravy, I don't want it getting lumpy."

I rolled my eyes. "I should have stayed in there, it's slightly less shit than in here."

"Stop being a bloody baby," Ma grunted. "Those people in there are your friends and they came all this way to see you."

"Yeah, like it wasn't you making them come," I muttered like a stroppy teenager.

"Shut your cake hole and stir." Came her response as she then moved next to me to pick up the pan of peas.

***

As he shovelled a forkful of peas into his mouth, Ethan looked up at me through his thick lashes. I glanced at Simone and then Ma and opened my mouth which was full of mashed potato. Ethan's shoulders moved up and down as he giggled silently. I then forked a sausage and put it into my mouth like I was smoking a cigar.

"I can see you," Simone whispered leaning closer to me. She was in the chair next to mine—where Ma had insisted that she sit. "You're not really teaching my son good manners."

I dropped the sausage back onto my plate and turned my head to her. "Sorry."

She smiled. "It's fine. It's good to see him laughing."

"He always seems like a happy kid." I looked back to Ethan who was now concentrating on cutting his sausage with the help of Joey.

"Oh, he is," Simone said with a sigh. "He just doesn't have many friends to laugh with."

"Why not." I frowned, a little aggrieved for the kid.

Simone paused and then leaned closer. "Other kids think he's weird because he doesn't speak."

"Well other kids are dicks," I grunted. "To be fair to him, I think he's got the right idea. Talking is shit."

She snorted a quiet laugh and when my gaze shot to her, she slapped a hand over her mouth.

"What?" I said with a shrug. "It's true. I fucking hate talking to other people. Don't tell me you haven't noticed?"

Her eyes went down to her plate as she cut into a sausage. "I did have an inkling."

"You don't talk so much yourself. Oh," I said nudging her with my elbow. "Except to say sorry."

"Oh yes. I forgot you don't like that word."

"Don't mind it," I replied, scooping up some mash. "You just say it a lot." It was then that I looked up and saw that everyone, except for Ethan, were looking at us. Elliot even had his fork paused in mid-air about to go into his mouth. "What?"

"Nothing," Ronnie said, shaking his head. "Nothing at all."

Joey cleared his throat. Belle chewed on her lip. Elliot stuffed the food into his mouth. While Ma preened like she'd just solved the world's debt. As for Ronnie he opened and closed his mouth a few times. Me? Well, I pushed my plate away and mumbled something about having a headache and left the table.

thirteen

Simone

When Beau got up from the table the room went silent; all eyes on me. I had no idea why. Okay, so we'd been talking quietly but it wasn't like we were arranging a date or anything. Worried, I sat back in my seat. What if I'd said something that I shouldn't have?

I thought back through the conversation and there'd been nothing that I could think of that would send him running from the table. Elliot cleared his throat, and it was like someone had flicked on a switch. The conversation around the table started again.

"What is it you do again?" he asked. He glanced at Belle. "Belle started to tell me but got called into the kitchen."

I looked at Belle and saw her cheeks pink. When Elliot put his eyes anywhere except on her, I had a feeling that something was going on there. My heart did a little star jump at the thought of it. Over the last week of getting to know Belle I'd come to realise that she was a lovely person. She cared about people not only in her job but throughout her whole life. Beau being the top of her list. She deserved some happiness after what happened with her ex-boyfriend. When she'd told me all about it over coffee while we went shopping, tears had crawled down her face. She talked about her miscarriage and how it had made her feel and I felt so sorry for her. Which was why if something did happen between her and Elliot it would be amazing. I didn't know him of course, but he always came across as a good guy in interviews. Plus, he was extremely lovely to look at and they would make a beautiful looking couple.

"I design websites," I replied. "In fact, I designed a fan site for Warrior Creek last year."

He dropped his knife and fork to his plate, looking surprised. "For our fan club?"

"No. A fan site. It's a group of girls that are crazy about the band. You should see some of the fanfiction that they write about you."

He leaned his elbows on the table and grinned. "No way. What's it all about?"

I blushed and pushed my plate away. "They kind of ship you and Beau," I replied with a grimace.

Belle snorted and my gaze shot to her. "Sorry," she replied. "I couldn't help but hear. Please tell me that they have a shipping name."

"A what?" Elliot exclaimed as he moved in his chair to look at her.

"A shipping name. It's a name that fans give two people who they want to be in a couple," Belle explained. She then turned to me. "They do have one, don't they?"

I giggled and nodded. "Yes. It's Beuliot."

Both Belle and I burst into laughter, but Elliot looked at us totally perplexed. He had no clue what we were talking about.

"What the hell does Beuliot mean?" he asked.

"That's the shipping name." Belle bit the side of her lip trying to not smile. "They mix the two names together."

"And Beuliot is the best that they could come up?" I shrugged and Elliot shook his head. "And they want me and Beau to be a couple?"

I nodded. I had to admit some of the stories written about them were hot. It wasn't surprising seeing as they were both extremely good looking and sexy guys.

"Does Beau know about this sort of stuff?" Elliot asked Belle.

She shrugged. "No idea. Cassie did. We used to laugh about it." She looked wistfully at a photograph of Cassie, Beau and Bobby that was on a shelf by the window.

"I bet she had a real good laugh at that," Elliot sighed. Then without any warning, he reached for Belle's hand and squeezed it. She looked up at him through her lashes and it was when he licked his bottom lip that I knew I'd been right about them. There was a definite attraction there.

"Do they write any about me and Ronnie?" Joey asked. "Because I've got to be honest. I'm not really down with being left with the ugly one."

Everyone laughed except for Ronnie who threw Joey a dirty look and protested, "I have appeared in the top one hundred sexiest men poll you know."

"Yeah, after me, Elliot and Beau," Joey replied. "Like I said you're the ugly one."

"What the hell are you talking about?" Sylvie asked, looking up from cutting Ethan's second sausage. "It all sounds like a foreign language to me."

I smiled and mouthed a thank you to her for helping Ethan. She waved me away and then turned to Joey. "And stop being mean to Ronnie."

"I'm not," he said. "Just stating a fact, Sylvie."

"I wouldn't want to be shipped with you anyway," Ronnie grumbled.

"I'm still lost." Sylvia shrugged. "Do they want to send you off in some sort of container together."

The boys laughed and Belle rolled her eyes.

"No Ma. I'll explain later."

"You don't need to bother, I'm not that interested." Sylvie's concentration went back to her food, pretty much dismissing us.

Elliot sighed and when everyone also went back to eating their food, he leaned closer to me. "I just want to say that I think Ethan is helping Beau."

I blinked rapidly. "Ethan is?" I'd been under the impression that Beau begrudged every minute he spent with Ethan, but Sylvie was encouraging it.

"Yeah," Elliot replied. He coughed deep and low and scrubbed a hand over his mouth. "After Cassie and Bobby, he went within himself."

"Belle told me," I filled in. "It's totally understandable. He must be devastated."

Elliot nodded. "He is. Some days I don't know whether he'll ever come out the other side. Spending time with Ethan though, well I think it's helped to distract him."

"I don't know about that. I think it's more Sylvie and Belle's idea than Beau's." I glanced over at Ethan who had cleaned his plate. He might not speak but he certainly could eat.

"Sylvie told me that Beau was looking for him yesterday. He kept going to the window to check if he'd come through the hedge."

My eyes widened in surprise. "Really?"

"Apparently so." He looked down at the table and took in a deep breath. "It devastated all of us. I don't know if you know but we were all Bobby's godfathers and Cassie was my best friend from primary school."

My heart pinched as I considered how the loss of Beau's family had affected all of them. Not only had they both died but it had also changed their friend; broken him possibly beyond repair.

"It's an awful thing that happened," I replied. "I have no clue how you're all managing to cope."

"We didn't at first but we're getting there. That was why we ended the band. We just couldn't imagine carrying on. Our hearts were too shattered, and Beau was not in the right headspace at all."

"And now?" I asked, sensing that it was a decision that had been regretted in time.

Elliot smiled. "Well, there you have the million-dollar question."

He didn't say anything else, and I didn't expect him to. He'd only known me for a couple of hours. For all Elliot knew, I could go straight to the press with whatever he told me. Not that I ever would, but Elliot was right to be cautious.

"Right," Sylvie said as she got up from the table. "I'll go and sort pudding. One of you boys go and get my son and tell him if he's got a headache to take a pill."

As Elliot got up to do her bidding, I had a feeling that Beau would be okay with his mum helping him along. She seemed a determined woman and now that determination would bring her son back to life.

fourteen

Beau

When the door to my study opened, I half expected it to be Ethan come looking for me to play guitar. The other half expected Elliot, and that half was right. He stood in the doorway grinning, one hand on the door the other on the wall.

"Get your dirty mitts off my wall," I grumbled.

"Pudding is ready soon and your mum said I had to come and get you." He took a step inside and bent to strum a finger down the strings of the guitar on the sofa. "Is that the one you're using to teach Ethan."

The fact that he was questioning me about it pissed me off. I didn't want to talk to him about me teaching Ethan and was annoyed that my ma had told them. Elliot knew me too well.

"And no point being a grouch about it. If you don't tell me, I'll ask your mum and you know she'll embellish everything." He picked up the guitar and fiddled with the tuning keys and then running his fingers over the strings again. "You always were shit at tuning."

"There was nothing wrong with it," I replied, turning off my game of Solitaire, knowing that I wouldn't be finishing it. "You're just an interfering twat."

He played the first few bars of Smoke on the Water. "Did you start with this?" His smile was easy, and I envied him. I knew he was gutted about Cassie and Bobby, yet he was still able to feel a level of happiness throughout each day.

"Nope. *'The Seven Nation Army'*."

Elliot nodded as he then moved into playing the opening riff of Black Dog and even on my crappy old acoustic, he made it sound fucking amazing.

"Christ you piss me off sometimes."

Still playing he looked at me and grinned. "Listen, I can't hold a note like you, so all's equal." He put the guitar down. "How's he doing?"

I shrugged. "Okay. He's only doing the basics, but he seems to enjoy it."

"What about you? Are *you* enjoying it?" When I rolled my eyes, he moved over to the shelf that held our Brit award for Best Band. He picked it up, rubbed it on his t-shirt and then put it back. "You need to ask Di to polish that a bit more."

Elliot ever the frigging perfectionist. It was perfectly clean, and Di would be offended if anyone thought otherwise. Ronnie and I had a Brit award each, Elliot had the Grammy seeing as he wrote the song that won it and Joey had the two framed platinum albums on his wall. Anyone would think we broke up the band because we each had a souvenir of our success and didn't need any more awards.

"How did Ali take the no about the interview?" I asked, surprising myself at bringing it up because normally I'd avoid any conversation to do with the band.

Elliot scratched at his stomach and shrugged. "She expected it. She thinks we're mad for saying no, but she understands."

I opened my mouth to tell him that she was mad for thinking I'd even consider it, but he disarmed me by laughing out loud.

"What the fuck is wrong with you?" I asked, getting out of my seat.

"Just something Ali said."

"What?"

"Just that when I told you what she said that you'd pull that face you pull when you hate something."

"What fucking face?"

"The one according to Ali that looks like you're trying to let out a fart without shitting yourself." His shoulders shook as he continued to laugh. "I never thought of what it was like before but now she's said that I totally see it."

"Wow, you're such a pair of comedians," I grouched, but couldn't stop the smile twitching at my lips. "If you'd ever sharted you'd understand why I wouldn't want to do it again."

Elliot's eyebrows rose. "Fuck off, you've sharted before?"

I shrugged. "I was nine and had a stomach bug. It was not pretty let me tell you."

His laughter was surprisingly good to listen to and for the first time since my world had collapsed, I felt myself wanting to join in with someone else's joy. Chuckling quietly, I scratched the back of my neck.

"What's Ma made for pudding?"

"She didn't say," Elliot replied on what sounded like a contented sigh. "Just that I had to come and find you and make you take a pill if you still had a headache."

"I promise you, once she's on that train tomorrow afternoon, that's the only pill I'll need." I walked over to him and reaching behind him moved my Brit a little to the left. "Stop moving my shit."

"And you think I'm an anally attentive twat." He rolled his eyes and then turned to leave. "I think you should know though; I think your mum is planning on staying a bit longer."

"What the fuck!"

***

Simone and Ethan had gone home straight after she'd helped clear up the dishes. I think Ethan wanted to stay and play with his new friend, Ronnie, but he was dead on his feet and his eyes were drooping closed when he didn't think anyone was watching. As soon as Simone told him it was time to go though, he went without any argument. Not even a frown or stamping of feet. Bobby would have thrown a real wobbler.

Ethan was a good kid and I had to admit it felt odd seeing him giving everyone high fives as they left. When they all hugged Simone, it became decidedly weirder. It was as if we ate dinner together regularly and it hadn't been the first time that they'd met my neighbour. Not one of them even questioned why she and Ethan were there, which made me wonder if Ma had planned it all along. I bet she hadn't asked Simone on the spur of the moment that afternoon when she'd popped over with some crappy romance books for Belle.

Now, it was nine o'clock and Ma had already gone to bed. Nicely timed because as she said goodnight, she had dropped it in that she and Belle were staying for a few more days. I was guessing that she thought I'd have forgotten by the morning. I doubted that I'd bother to argue with her either way. I wouldn't win and even though I hated to admit it, there'd been something good about having her and Belle around. The house didn't feel so empty and cold that was for sure.

"What are your plans for the next few days then?" Elliot asked Belle. His voice croaked and I could hear the nervousness in it. I didn't know why he just didn't ask her out. I wasn't the sort of brother who would forbid it. I'd always known he'd fancied her. Even when she was fifteen my little sister was a stunner and eighteen-year-old Elliot couldn't hide the fact that he thought she was. At that time, I had told him to stay away from her. Only because I didn't want them to hit it off and then my little sister to be hanging around with us. I wouldn't have wanted her to see what I got up to without Ma there supervising me. I certainly wouldn't have wanted her to see me getting my dick wet at any given opportunity. Besides which, she had to be in for ten at night so Elliot would either have had to take her home and miss out on gigs and partying or let her go home on her own. I'd have kicked the shit out of him for that. So, no, I didn't encourage their mutual attraction. As we got older though and we all started to act a bit more like mature adults, I often told him to give her a call. He wouldn't though. He always said the timing wasn't right, or he was too bus. When he did finally get his arse into gear about three years ago, Belle had a boyfriend who she seemed to really like. He didn't last long but by then El had met Katie Delaney. She was a popstar from New Zealand who was based in the UK. We met her at a party that her record company held for the release of her second album and she and Elliot hit it off. So much so they moved in together within a month. And then she moved out two months later. Cassie took it upon herself to find out what had gone wrong, but Elliot wouldn't even tell her. He just said it was between them and they were still friends. Funny though, we'd seen Katie a couple of times since and she could barely look at Elliot and vice versa. All we knew was Elliot had been hurt but refused to lay the blame at Katie's door.

Now he was looking at my little sister like she was a cold drink in the middle of a dessert.

"Not sure," Belle replied, also sounding nervous. "I had planned to sort out a flat if I'd been home, so I might do that but online instead."

Elliot's face darkened. "Your mum told us about your ex."

I gave a short laugh. "Sylvie is a real little chatty Cathy isn't she."

Belle groaned. "She even told a woman on the train, on the way here. Delighted in telling her that we were having a few days with her son so her daughter could get over a bad break up with a shite of a cheating man."

Ronnie gasped. "She never did?"

"She did." Belle sighed and then looked back to Elliot who looked a lot tenser than his usual laidback demeanour. "Yeah, I think I'll definitely be checking for flats online."

"Well think about looking around here," I said. "Wouldn't hurt you to get away from Leicester."

"Ma would throw a fit at that."

I shrugged.

Elliot's lips thinned and he sighed too. "Wherever you decide, if you need any help then let me know."

Joey looked at me and raised his eyebrows while I gave him a double thumbs up and mouthed an unenthusiastic 'yay'. He laughed and mumbled something about me being a miserable fucker.

"What about you?" Ronnie directed to me. "What are your plans?"

I frowned. "I don't have any." I hadn't had any for over a year so why the hell would he think I'd have some now.

"Just thought you might, seeing as Sylvie will be around. Take the opportunity to get out of her way."

I ghosted a smile as I understood what he was getting at. "Maybe I'll look for a flat too. That way if she turns up on my doorstep again, I can go and live there for the week."

I'd been totally serious, but everyone burst out laughing and when Ronnie and Joey started to banter off the back of it, I couldn't help but feel lighter.

fifteen

Simone

After the leak everything was almost back to normal in the house. The lounge had been completely redecorated, because, according to Vanessa, a touch up wouldn't do. The electrics had been checked and all pipes were sound and secure. It was a big relief and I hoped that it meant I didn't have to deal with Vanessa more than was absolutely necessary.

Other changes had also come about because of that night; Ethan and Beau had become best buddies. The day after we'd stayed next door, Ethan obsessed over watching guitar tutorials online, which since he didn't have a guitar seemed a little pointless. However, after going to get his ball, which I'm pretty sure he threw over on purpose, Beau had kindly offered to teach him to play. What worried me was that Beau didn't really want him there and every time that Ethan went over, I battled with myself to go and drag him back. He was currently there and today had been longer than the usual hour and a half, because after guitar lessons Sylvie always gave him juice and a biscuit. Deciding he'd probably outstayed his welcome, I decided to go round. As I had my hand on the handle of the back door, my phone pinged a text. I read it and my heart clattered against my breastbone.

Belle: Ethan's going to stay here for a bit longer than usual. I'll make sure he gets back safely when he's ready if that's okay with you.

Worry coursed through. What if Ethan didn't talk and maybe Belle and Sylvie thought he was being rude? I probably should have said something the night we'd stayed at the house, but it didn't even occur to me.

Simone: If you're okay having him there. If he doesn't speak, he's not being rude he...

What did I say? He...what? It wasn't that he was shy or mute, he simply chose not to speak but would saying that might sound strange.

"Shit," I groaned. "I should have told them." I went back to my phone and finished typing before hitting send.

...chooses when he wants to talk and it's just not very often.

I got a pretty much immediate response, one which shocked me.

Belle: It's fine he's still with Beau playing guitar and he doesn't speak much either ☺

I almost dropped my phone as I read the words. Playing guitar with Beau? What if Beau was playing with him under duress. I didn't want Ethan being a pest, so I tapped at my phone.

Simone: Is that okay? I mean he isn't being a nuisance, is he? I can come and get him if he is.

Waiting for Belle's reply, I strummed my fingernails against the screen of my phone and stared out of the window. My gaze was on the hedge in the garden, half expecting Ethan to push back through, or maybe Beau to be dragging him back. There was nothing though and no response from Belle and I wondered if I should go around there.

I was almost to the door when my bell rang. I pulled it open expecting to see a grim-faced Beau, but Belle was there smiling widely.

"I thought I might as well come around as text you," she said. "It's probably just as quick."

"Come in," I said, gesturing and leading her into the lounge.

"Wow, nice wallpaper." She looked around and then back to me. "Didn't realise you were going to have the whole room redecorated."

I sighed. "Neither did I. The man who owns the property insisted." I hadn't wanted it doing but Vanessa had at least let me pick the grey and rose gold wallpaper and a new pale grey rug to replace the big ugly cream one that had been down. We could talk about my new décor later, once I'd got around the fact that my son was playing guitar with Beau Bradley of Warrior Creek.

"So, is Ethan being a nuisance, because I'm so sorry if he is. You know Beau doesn't have to do these lessons with him. He can stop now if it's getting too much."

"He's perfectly fine." Belle smiled. "Don't forget it was all Beau's idea. He was the one who saw him in the garden and invited him in. I can't say Ethan's mastered the art just yet, but he seems to be enjoying himself."

"And Beau isn't wishing he hadn't bothered asking?"

"No. In fact." She sighed. "It's the chirpiest I've seen him since we got here."

I chewed at my lip and glanced out into the garden my eyes drawn to the place in the hedge that Ethan used.

"He doesn't really talk much," I said.

"You said in your text, but we kind of gathered as much when you stayed."

My gaze went back to Belle who was smiling gently. "He's not mute or disabled or anything like that."

"God no, we didn't think he was." She frowned and reached out to rub at my arm. "Ma worked with kids years ago, she was a youth leader, so she spotted pretty quickly that he just doesn't like talking."

I sighed and felt my shoulders drop. "Most people just think he's weird. He struggles to make friends because of it. I'm just hoping his new school will be better."

"When does he start?"

"After Easter. They don't have a place until then so I'm home schooling him at the moment." I shrugged. "I'm not very good at it, I've got to be honest. I think I have less concentration than he does. As soon as I can see he might be struggling with an answer, I move on to another subject. At least he's getting decent music lessons."

Belle laughed. "I wouldn't worry too much. I'm sure he'll be fine. He seems really bright."

"He is." I pointed to the sofa. "Sit down and I'll get you a drink."

"I'll sit but I'm fine for a drink, thanks."

We both sank into chairs, and it was silent for a few moments making me feel a little uncomfortable. I had no clue what to talk to her about. For all Belle's kindness over my leak and that she seemed lovely, I barely knew her. In any other circumstance, I doubted that we'd ever cross paths; her brother was a Rockstar for God's sake.

"I'm sorry if Beau comes across a bit gruff," Belle interjected into the silence. "Especially at breakfast when you'd gone to all that trouble."

Her eyes lowered to her hands which were twisting in her lap. Again I wondered how as a family they'd all managed to handle such a tragedy.

"Were you close to them?" I asked. "Your sister-in-law and nephew."

Belle blew out a breath, her cheeks puffing. "Everyone loved Cassie, she was beautiful and funny, and so good for Beau. Don't get me wrong they weren't the perfect couple. Both are stubborn, Cassie probably more than Beau, which led to some big arguments. She kept him grounded though and her favourite phrase was 'get out from up your own arsehole, Bradley." We both laughed quietly, and Belle followed hers with a huge sigh. "As for Bobby, God he was a gorgeous boy. All blond curls and giggles. He adored Beau but Beau spoiled him like you wouldn't believe."

She swallowed and sucked in her bottom lip. The pain she was feeling was clear and I couldn't imagine it.

"You must all be in so much pain. If that was Ethan, God I don't think…" I trailed off unable to put into words the agony that I'd feel.

"It was the worst time of our lives," Belle continued, her eyes closing on the painful memories. "Ma was the one who told me. She could hardly breathe she was crying so much. I'd never seen her like that before, it was heart-breaking. She adored them both, but Bobby was her shining light. The one who had her heart." She smiled and looked at me, her head tilted on one side. "You know that thing people say, about someone being a better grandparent than they ever were a parent, well that's Ma. She was the one who taught him how to tie his own laces during a two-week stay here one Christmas. The one before they… well," she sighed and wiped her hands on her thighs. "Anyway, like I said, today is the best I've seen Beau in a long time, which isn't difficult seeing as this is the first that I've seen of him in a year."

"I know I've only been here three months," I replied. "But I haven't seen anything of him at all. Not that it's the kind of street where everyone mingles and chats over the garden fence."

Belle screwed up her nose. "It is a bit stuffy isn't it. A year or so back Cassie wanted to throw a street party for VE day or something, I can't remember exactly what it was for, but she was so excited about it. She sent out letters to everyone inviting them to a planning party at the house, but only one person turned up. The investment banker who lived here before you went but it turned out that all he wanted was Beau's autograph."

I winced, imagining how Beau would take that.

"Cassie kicked him out and told him she'd manage without his frozen vol au vents as a contribution."

I giggled. "Did the party go ahead?"

"No, Beau made her realise they were a bunch of, in his words, 'miserable tossers', and she decided not to bother."

We both smiled and silence fell again, as if we were getting lost in our own thoughts. When I started to fidget in my chair, Belle turned to me.

"Do you fancy going out for lunch or something while I'm here?"

I blinked and sat back in my seat a little surprised. I didn't have many friends. In fact, I didn't have any. Old schoolfriends had all gone off to Uni and lost touch, and I hadn't been at Uni myself long enough to make new friends. I definitely didn't want to be friends with Mum's whose kids though my son was a weirdo.

"That would be lovely," I replied.

"Ma would look after Ethan for you. Let you have some you time."

I laughed softly. "I could do with some adult time; I don't know about me time."

"There really is just you and Ethan then?"

"Hmm, apart from my brother Marcus, but he lives in London."

"Is that where you're from?"

My scalp prickled and a shiver ran over me. I hated talking about myself, but I'd found that keeping quiet just made people more interested.

"No, we're originally from Manchester, but Marcus and I both went to university in London, and he decided to stay." I coughed. "We lost both our parents. Mum of a heart attack when I was sixteen and Dad took his own life three years later."

"Oh my God, Simmy, that's awful." Belle put a hand to her throat. "How the hell did *you* cope with that?"

I shrugged. "It was hard but I figured he wanted to be with Mum more so who was I to judge."

Thoughts of my dad always made me angry. I hated him for doing that to me, to us, and I hated myself for being the reason he had. Marcus always thought Dad wanted to be with Mum, that's what Dad's note had said, but I'd thought differently for a long time. Now I probably had to agree with my brother, especially after seeing how losing his wife had affected Beau.

"God, even so," Belle sighed.

"Life is full of tragedy, Belle," I replied. "And we just have to deal with it as best we can."

She nodded. "Yes, you do. I just wish Beau would start to deal with his. I wish he'd listen to Elliot a bit more."

When I looked at her, I noticed a slight blush to her cheeks but wasn't surprised. Elliot Andrews was gorgeous and enough to make any girl get hot and bothered just by thinking about him.

"It's good he's got friends looking out for him," I offered.

"Yeah, it is. They've been brilliant and to me and Ma." Her colour rose again and then she pushed up from the sofa. "Anyway, I'd better go. I'll bring Ethan back when he's ready and maybe you can have a think about which day that you'd like to go shopping. I just can't do Friday as Ma is insisting the boys come over for dinner before we leave on Sunday."

There was that colour again.

"Yes, yes, I will. Thank you, I'm looking forward to it. And don't hesitate to bring Ethan back if he's being a nuisance."

Belle moved in to hug me and even though my body stiffened, it felt okay. I was glad to have a friend, even if it was just for a short time.

sixteen

Simone

I t wasn't long after Belle left, that I heard footsteps in the hall. I wondered if maybe I'd left the door open, and Belle had come back having forgotten something. Even so, I wasn't sure how I felt about her just wandering in. Walking into the hallway, my whole body was in danger of collapsing in on itself when I saw who it was that had entered my home. Stumbling backward a step, I grabbed hold of the doorframe to steady myself. Air whooshed through my ears and my legs wobbled like they were boneless.

"Simone." His voice was severe and condescending as his eyes raked over me, disdain masking his sharp features.

"W-w-what are you doing here?" I stammered, pushing the words through the fear forming in my throat.

"It's my house." He turned his head and looked around, taking in the surroundings of what was supposed to be my refuge, my safe place. "Would say I like what you've done with the place but it's not like you've had any input. Remind me to speak to Vanessa though," he sighed. "She really needs to improve her design skills. This is so suburban and middle class."

It was plain white with hints of black in the console table and the coat stand, nothing suburban or middle class about it? It wasn't his choice though, not opulent or garish enough for him.

"What do you want, Richard?" I asked trying to steady my breathing. "You can't just let yourself in."

He cocked his head to one side and smoothed down his tie. "You did hear what I said about it being my house? The fact that you also don't pay rent means you have no say in the matter, Simone."

"I told you I would. I also told you I'd find my own place when I moved. You were the one who insisted I came here."

"Not sure how you'd have managed to find *your own place*," he sneered. "When you have little or no money. What is it you do again? Make pretty little pictures online?"

"Design websites and maybe if I'd been able to finish my degree, I'd have a better job." I wanted to yell at him that it was his fault that I hadn't but knew better. Richard never took the blame for anything, and his venom and cruelty weren't worth trying to make him see what he'd done.

"Plenty of other women have kids and do a degree, but then you're not like other women are you?"

He licked his thick, bottom lip as his eyes looked up and down my body and the bile climbed higher in my guts. I knew if I didn't get him out of the house soon, I'd puke all over his awful black patent loafers and shiny grey suit that made him look like a second-rate gangster. When he took a step closer to me the stench of his citrusy aftershave hit my nostrils and the back of my throat. Memories of him, that smell, flooded back and an involuntary squawk of panic escaped from me. Richard smirked, fully aware of how he affected me, and he had no care. He loved the power he had over me. He relished it, craved it and I hated him for it. I hated myself at giving him that control. Self-loathing was an emotion I was more than aware of.

"Anyway, you couldn't afford even a fraction of what I'd want for rent on this place," Richard continued. "And it's the deal we agreed on. The deal that you signed, Poppet. Don't forget that. No rent and I leave to your own devices."

The nickname he used for me was hateful and I wanted to spit it back at him. I wasn't his Poppet. I wasn't his anything except his plaything. He was the cat, and I was the mouse that he batted in the air and toyed with.

"Yet you're here now," I replied, quaking on the inside.

Without warning, Richard pushed past me into the lounge and as his arm brushed mine, I thought I might pass out. That or turn to stone. Closing my eyes, I prayed that someone would come and rouse me from the nightmare. Then I thought about Ethan coming home and the panic increased ten-fold. There was no way I wanted Richard here with Ethan around. It was bad enough the monster was in my life; he didn't need to be in my son's life too.

Swinging around and pulling in a bracing breath, I took a step into the lounge and watched his back. He was standing in front of the wall that had been redecorated and looking up at the ceiling.

"I want you to leave," I said, false confidence lacing my tone.

"This leak was most unfortunate." He completely ignored me. "And who the fuck did you get to repair it? No one on our list that's for sure. You're lucky I agreed to pay."

"Richard." More insistent now, my voice an octave higher. "I want you to leave."

Before I could do anything, he was on me, backing me up against the wall with his palm flat against my breastbone. Dark grey eyes turned molten as he sneered and spat out his words.

"Don't test me." A finger moved between my eyes and spittle landed on my cheeks. "This is my house and I choose who does the work on it, not you. Never again ring Vanessa and tell her you have someone and then ask if I am paying. I don't fucking care what you think you have on me. If you do anything to anger me again I'll make your life a misery. I know what will break you and don't think for one minute I won't do it."

Cruel and controlling. A monster.

The wetness on my face was no longer just from his venom but my tears too. He did know what would end me and the mere thought that he did know scared me as much as the act. He could end my life and not by stopping my heart from beating.

"Anything else happens in this house you call Vanessa first," he hissed his mouth so close to mine that I could taste his breath. "You don't own it, you're merely the tenant, remember that. You don't and you know what I'll do."

My lungs held still as I silently prayed for him to leave. When his hand then clutched at my breast and squeezed it, my organs felt like they were going to fold in on themselves. They burned with the pressure of keeping me still as Richard watched with beady eyes. After a few seconds, which felt like hours, he dropped his hand and sneered at me before taking a step back.

"Remember what I said... *Poppet.*"

Then he was gone but I could still feel his hand on me. Still smell his aftershave. Still see his shiny slip-on shoes and hear his vicious tone. It was too much, and my legs finally gave way as I slid down the wall and collapsed into a crumpled heap.

seventeen

Beau

Throttling my ma was top of my list for the evening's entertainment. She was bossy as fuck and irritatingly nosey. Pointing out that I was twenty-six and in my own home didn't appear to make much difference, she still made me go over to Simone's and invite her over for dinner. What did I have to say to get her to understand that I didn't want her over at my house more than was absolutely necessary? I liked the woman, and her kid was great, but that was it and I didn't want to think about what Ma was cooking up. I might have woken up from my coma of pain and grief, but it didn't mean that I was fighting fit and ready to move on. I loved my wife; I was *in* love with my wife and that didn't change just because she was fucking dead. Sylvie Bradley didn't understand that though. No, as far as she was concerned Simone was single, I was single so why not fuck each other and live happily ever after.

Feeling manipulated and wanting to run, I knocked on Simone's door. As I moved my hand away, I noticed it was ajar, so pushed it open wider.

"Simone," I called, her name wrestling with my tongue. "You there?"

I knocked again, a little harder and louder this time and when there was still no answer, I took a step inside. She'd added a coat rack and a tall, thin hall table since I'd last been there, when she'd had the leak. It was still devoid of anything though—no life or presence of it being a home. I knew she rented the place but there was no stamp of who she was or who Ethan was. It weirdly made my heart sink. Letting out a breath, I hitched it when I heard a noise. It was crying, a sound that I'd been used to over the last eighteen months. It had become the soundtrack of my life.

"Simone, are you okay?" Tentatively I walked toward where the noise was coming from. I got to the lounge and looked around the door. "Shit."

She was on the floor, huddled into a ball, holding her knees against her chest with both arms wrapped around them. Her cries were pained and laced with something else, something I didn't understand. Grief was the sound I was used to, and this was different.

"Simone, are you okay?" I fell to my knees and without even thinking about it, wrapped my arms around her and pulled her to me. When the feel of her against me, the physical contact, didn't repulse me, my chest cracked open a little bit. The guilt started to creep through but when she let out another sob, I knew this had to be about her.

"Hey, come on," I cajoled. "Tell me what's going on. What's happened?"

"He was here," she cried. "He was here, Beau. He let himself in."

Fear now hit me and sent my blood cold. "Who did? What did they do to you?" Urgently I scoured her body for signs of her being hurt, of being violated. Her clothes were still intact and there were no scratches or bruises, but someone had scared her witless. "Simone. Who was it. What did they do?"

Shifting to my arse, I lifted her so that she was leaning against me and wrapped an arm around her slim shoulders. She buried her face against my chest and drew in a shuddering breath.

"Take a breath and tell me," I said as softly as I could.

"R-r-richard was here."

"Richard?" I queried.

She nodded and as her gaze met mine, she began to sob again. Taking her with me, I pushed to my feet. After months in bed and no gym time, I wasn't as strong as I used to be so just about held on to her as I carried her to the sofa and deposited her on it. Dropping to my haunches in front of her, I took both of Simone's hands in mine and shook them gently, urging her to look at me.

"Did this Richard guy touch you inappropriately?" I asked, trying to keep the tremor of nervous anticipation from my voice.

She nodded and the urge to punch something was great. I tried to push to my feet, but Simone held on tight.

"Please don't go."

"He... I need to... fuck, Simone." I pulled her closer again and looked over her head toward the door. I wanted to run out of it, find the fucker and punch him. She was a tiny little thing, and he had no right touching her, scaring her. No man had that right. "Who is Richard?" I asked when after minutes of soothing her Simone's shaking was finally subsiding.

Simone pulled away from me and sniffed. She looked up at me with her dark eyes still brimming with tears and pulled the sleeve of her jumper over her hand and lifted it to wipe under her eyes and then her nose. Blowing out a breath she placed her palms down on the sofa, bracing herself.

"Richard is Ethan's dad."

If she'd smacked me around the head with a pan, I don't think I would have felt as floored. I knew he had a dad, of course I did, but he was my little buddy and the thought that his dad was suddenly back on the scene made me feel weird... jealous. Then I looked at Simone still clearly petrified by whatever had happened and felt a total prick.

"How did he hurt you?"

My hands clenched into fists as her fingers trembled over the top of her jumper, over her boob. People say you see red mist when you're really mad, but I never believed it until that moment. Fury pulsed through my body, and I don't think I'd ever wanted to pummel someone in the face so much.

"Did he... did he touch you anywhere else?"

She shook her head. "He said things to me," she whispered. "Told me that I need to remember whose house this is."

I knew she couldn't have afforded to rent this house. I knew that there was something odd about just her and Ethan living in this big house. Now I knew.

"So, he bought this house for you and Ethan?"

She shook her head while biting her lip. "No. He already had it but lets us live here rent free. I wanted to move, and we ended up here."

"That's his contribution to Ethan's life?"

"Pretty much. Ethan doesn't even know him. Richard has only seen him twice, once after he was born, and the other time was when we moved in here. He came around to tell me what the rules were to us living here. Our last place I chose it, and I paid the rent, but this time he made me come here because he knew I was desperate. I should have been stronger and told people to keep out of my business. I wasn't and now he controls me even more." She dropped her head to her hands and groaned. "I hate him, Beau. I wish I'd never met him."

Something didn't add up. Simone seemed like a sensible, bright woman, so why the fuck would she get mixed up with a bloke who would scare her and touch her where she didn't want to be touched?

"I have to ask." I placed a hand on her thigh and then quickly pulled it away. She didn't want more unwanted attention and to be honest touching her weirded me out. I knew she'd been in my arms earlier, but that felt different somehow. "Why did you get involved with such a creep in the first place?"

She shook her head. "I have no idea. Although, I didn't not really. Not how you think. Not how *he* makes everyone think."

"How was it then?" I shifted and edged back from her. She suddenly felt too close.

"I worked for him," Simone replied, messing with the cuff of her sleeved. "It was an internship at his IT company. Not the job I wanted. I wanted to get right into the designing of websites or coding, but I was given the job of his PA. I thought it might at least help me to get to the area that I wanted to work in." She huffed out a humourless laugh. "Now, I know why he wanted me working beside him every day."

Closing my eyes, I inhaled before I spoke. "He groomed you?"

"Nope, it was worse than that. He didn't feel the need to ease me into it."

My eyes flashed open, and I saw it written all over her face. She was staring into space with eyes dead of emotion.

"He fucking raped you?" I asked, incredulously. This time I did stand and moving to the door, punched it hard. Thank God the fucker had chosen cheap shit because a fist shaped hole appeared. Turning around I looked for something to throw or annihilate but when I saw Simone edge back into the corner of the sofa and lift a cushion in front of her as a barrier, I stopped. She was scared of *me* now and that made my chest hurt. Drawing in a calming breath, I dropped my hands to my knees and bent over. I counted to ten, took another breath and then repeated the counting.

"Beau?" Simone askes hesitantly. "Please don't get upset. It was a long time ago and I'm fine now."

I stood upright and stared at her wide eyed. *"You're fine."* I pointed at her. "You don't look *fucking fine*, Simone. And what the hell is he doing even coming near you? Why isn't he locked up?"

"I've learned to live with it and besides I have—"

Her words stopped abruptly, and she slapped a hand to her mouth. My eyes narrowed wondering what she was going to say that was worse than the fact that the arsehole raped her.

"Go on, Simone. Tell me what you were going to say."

"It doesn't matter."

Then like a dick I realised. "Shit, that's when you got pregnant with Ethan. He fucking raped you and got you pregnant. Living here is his damn apology for that? Next you'll tell me that it was your first time!" I knew I was yelling at her, but I couldn't help it, there was so much anger inside of me for what he'd done. "What's he doing out of prison already?"

Simone dropped her gaze and fiddled with the edging on the seat cushion.

"No way," I blasted, gripping my hair and stamping my foot like I'd seen Bobby do occasionally. "Do not tell me that he hasn't done time for raping you."

"You don't understand, I was—"

"You were fucking raped. I understand that much, Simone. What I don't get is that he didn't go down for it. What are you telling me? Did he hire some sleazy celebrity lawyer to get him off or something?"

The shake of her head was almost imperceptible, but I was looking for it and when I saw it, I thought my anger might jettison me into orbit. The need to smash up the place was real. I could practically smell the blood on my knuckles and the scent of splintered wood. It was different than the anger I'd felt at the death of Cassie and Bobby. That one had been laced with grief; this was pure, demonic rage.

"You have no idea what he's capable of, Beau," Simone protested.

"Rape. Rape is what he's capable of, Simone."

"He made me feel like it was my fault." She pushed up from the sofa and stalked towards me. "I'd have dinner with him, or sit and eat my lunch with him, we were friends. Well, he was more like a father figure to me, he obviously had different ideas. He made everyone think I threw myself at him. That I wanted him for his money."

"Even if you did, rape is rape. That doesn't make what happened to you your fault."

"I know, but I was nineteen, alone and pregnant. He was very persuasive." Simone wrapped her arms around her waist and waited for me to speak. When I didn't, she continued. "He asked me to work late. It had only been ten minutes after we started work that he tried it on. He couldn't believe I wasn't interested. He called me a prick tease. Afterwards he threatened me."

Now I had words. "Threatened you with what, Simone? Because rape wasn't enough of a threat? This is fucking unbelievable. What the hell can he have said or done that would make you decide not to call the police on him? Did you not think that you had a duty to other women?"

Her face crumpled and I felt all sorts of shit for making her feel like that. I couldn't take it back though. It was how I felt. She had a responsibility to all the other women that he'd probably gone on to abuse.

"I do, I do. I know that, but I couldn't think about them. I had to think about my brother."

"Your brother?" I asked. "What the hell does your brother have to do with it? Did he hurt him too?"

"No, but he said he would." She swallowed. "My dad died, and Marcus was all I had. He's a teacher and Richard threatened to tell everyone that he was a paedophile."

Snorting out a humourless laugh, I shook my head. "You could have gone to the police before he had a chance to do anything to him. And you kind of have to have proof for that sort of accusation."

Simone moved over to a bookcase and pulled out three or four books to reveal one of those clear plastic files with a black press stud on the front. She snatched it from the back of the shelf and practically threw it at me. I almost dropped it but caught it at the last second.

"What's this?" I asked.

"Open it, but you need to know it's all lies manufactured by Richard." I opened the file. "He told me when he gave me the file."

Skimming through the pages I could see there were a series of emails that were supposedly a conversation between Marcus and a girl. As I read them it was clear that the girl was only young, mentioning that she was only thirteen years of age. It was about him wanting to cuddle and kiss her when they met up.

"He threatened to send it to the police. That and much worse." Simone pinched the bridge of her nose and turned away from me. "He told me he could make any lie stick if he wanted to. Marcus is a primary school teacher, Beau. It would have been easy for people to believe him. Even if he was proved innocent, do you think anyone would still want him teaching their kids? That sort of crap sticks. It would have ruined him."

I thrust the papers back inside the file and dropped it to the floor.

"There were pictures too, pictures that Marcus was supposed to have on his computer. I burned those." Simone wavered and reached out a hand, so I rushed forward to hold her up before she dropped to the floor.

"I've got you." With my hands under her arms, I guided her back to the sofa.

When we both sat down, she looked at me with tear filled eyes. "You only saw the rear view of the guy, but he could easily have been my brother. The same hair colouring, the same physique. Marcus is kind of tall and skinny. In the picture he was talking to a young girl." She placed a hand against her stomach. "It could have been perfectly innocent but those coupled with the emails would have ruined Marcus' life."

"But the police would have needed evidence from the girl and if she didn't exist—"

"You don't understand. He said he could easily put something on

Marcus' computer that would see him locked away for years."

"Fucking hell," I groaned. "What a piece of work."

Simone nodded. "All that though, Beau, is nothing to what he threatened to do if I so much as breathed a word of what had happened."

"W-what?" I stammered.

"He said if he got sent down, he'd see to it that I ended up dead and Ethan would be given to some not particularly nice people." It was then that Simone broke down again. Sobs wracked her body. When I pulled her against me guilt hit me again because this time, even with all this shit going on I was enjoying taking care of someone again—taking care of her.

eighteen

Beau

I tried my hardest to get Simone to come over for dinner, but she was adamant she wanted Ethan to come home and they'd eat there. The need to be alone was something I understood well, but her being like that also made me realise what I'd put my family and friends through. As far as I was concerned, she was better off with people around her. Okay, so maybe I wasn't always the best company but, on this occasion, I wanted to help her.

"You okay?" Belle asked, putting down the magazine she'd been flicking through.

I ran a hand through my hair, making a mental note to get it cut, and sighed. "Worried about Simone."

She hadn't told me I could tell Belle or Ma about what had happened, but I wanted help to know how to handle it. Plus, I thought it would be good for someone in the house to know what was going on in case Richard came back and I wasn't around—like I went anywhere.

"Why are you worried about Simmy?"

The use of Simone's nickname by my sister and Ma still made me feel angry. It was totally irrational, but it felt like they'd replaced Cassie too easily with *Simmy*.

When I didn't answer, Belle moved to the edge of her seat. "Tell me Beau. What's going on with her because you looked really concerned?"

"It's fucking horrendous, Belle, what she's gone through." I told her all about Richard and what he'd done to Simone, and the threats that he'd made. Belle listened with her mouth dropping wider and wider with each thing I told her. By the end she was white with fury, her fingers twisting together.

"What a bastard," she gasped. "She won't report him though. There's no way she'll risk turning her brother's life upside down or losing Ethan."

"Do you think I should speak to Maxwell my solicitor about it?" Leaning my forearms on my thighs, I dropped my head and stared down at the floor. It was a real shit show that Simone was living, and I wanted to help her, I just had no clue how.

Belle took my hand in hers and tugged on it. "Beau the best thing you can do for Simone is to be her friend. She won't do anything to bring this guy to justice, there's too much at stake for her. If you speak to a solicitor and she finds out she might be worried that you're going to report him, then she'll never confide in you again."

"But the bastard needs to be charged, Belle."

She nodded. "I agree but imagine how much pressure she must have been under the last five years keeping it to herself. She's had no one to support her, no one to share it with. Don't take that away from her."

"You're saying go with the flow. Listen when she wants to talk but do fucking nothing about the rapist that has a key to her house?" My heart was going faster than a speeding train at the thought of letting the bastard get away with what he'd done.

"That's exactly what I'm saying," Belle said softly. "Listen, I'll let Simmy tell me about what happened but I'm here or on the other end of the phone if you need someone to sound off to. Okay?"

I nodded and smiled.

"Right, I'm going to bed. I'm knackered." She stood and bent forward to kiss my cheek.

"Night Belle, see you in the morning."

She rubbed a hand through my hair. "And book a haircut big brother."

I smiled and watched her leave the room wishing I hadn't pushed her out for the last year. Belle was the sort of person who would have told me the truth, not what she thought I wanted to hear like most people. She was exactly who I'd needed to help me through my grief, and I hadn't given her a chance. I decided that I wasn't doing that to Simone. I'd be a friend if she needed me to be—that I could manage. Being her friend was what Cassie would have been and she'd want me to be too.

> **Beau: Hey Simone. Just checking you're okay. I got your number from Belle when you went shopping in case Ethan needed you.**

Placing my phone face down on the arm of the chair, I wasn't sure whether I'd get a response. It was gone eleven and she was probably asleep. Besides, I hadn't texted her to strike up a text conversation. I only wanted her to know I was there for her. That was why I jumped when my phone shrilled with the sound of a parrot—fucking Ronnie had been messing with my phone again.

> **Simone: I'm fine thanks. It's amazing what a long, hot bath and an episode of Outlander can do for your mood**
>
> **Beau: I have no clue what that is but I'm guessing it's some girly shit that my sister would watch**

> **Simone: Well it was Belle who persuaded me to watch it. The hot Scotsmen in kilts was the deciding factor**

I started to laugh. This had been the most relaxed we'd ever been with each other, and Simone had certainly never joked around before.

Beau: I can't compete with a man in a kilt, so I'll say goodnight. Remember though I'm here if you need me. If he comes back call me straight away. Oh and stop stressing about Ethan coming over for guitar lessons. Tell him to come over at about ten in the morning.

Simone: Are you sure? Don't you have other stuff to do?

I rolled my eyes. What the hell else did I have to do on a daily basis?

Beau: Honestly it's fine and don't forget to call me if he turns up again!

Simone: I will and thank you for supporting me today. You're a good person

Scratching at the scruff at my chin I smiled because that meant a lot. Cassie would have been proud of me and that was all that mattered.

nineteen

Simone

Since Richard had come into the house uninvited, I'd taken extra precautions by slipping the door chain on, even when I was home and keeping the door into the garage and to the garden locked with the key in the door. I hadn't even allowed Ethan to play in the garden and the poor kid was going a little stir crazy. He'd been allowed next door to practice his guitar with Beau, but I'd taken him, and Beau had brought him back, no pushing through the hedge for now.

Every day had been a struggle to get through without breaking down in tears. I thought that I'd got through the nightmare of what Richard had done to me, but it seemed that I hadn't. Every knock on the door had me breaking out in a cold sweat. In fact, yesterday when Beau had called unexpectedly to collect Ethan on his way back from a jog, to save me having to go over. I'd opened the door with a knife in my hand so wound up I hadn't even registered Beau in shorts and a running vest. When I told him that the knife made me feel better protected, I thought he was going to burst a blood vessel. Ten minutes later Belle appeared with a bottle of wine and orders from Beau to keep me company. I'd told her everything about Richard and while she acted surprised, I had a feeling that she already knew the details. It was the sympathy in her eyes as soon as she walked through the door and the fact that although she appeared to be surprised, she didn't jump to her feet and demand that I go to the police. That's how I knew that Beau had already told her.

Thinking of Beau, I looked at the clock and noticed that it was almost time to take Ethan round to see him.

"Ethan, get your shoes on," I called from the lounge door. He looked up at me and smiled before closing his book and putting it to one side.

Grinning back, I moved towards the coat rack to get his jacket because Beau had started to take him into the garden for a quick game of football. Just as I reached for it there was a knock on my front door, and I froze. The only thing I could hear was my heart thudding, whooshing in my ears like I was plummeting underwater while I struggled to reach the surface. Before I had time to think the door sounded again, this time though it was accompanied with Beau's voice.

"Sim, it's me."

Sim? When the hell had I become Sim to him?

"You in there?"

I moved to the door and pulled it open. "He's just getting his sho—" The sight of Beau with two guys in black cargo pants and t-shirts with a white logo of D&B Security, had me taking a step back. Had he organised security men to stay with me?

"W-what's going on?" I asked, looking from Beau to the two guys.

"Dan and Ben are here with their team to upgrade your security system." I looked down the driveway to see there were three black vans with D&B on the side. Beau stood to one side and held an arm out and Dan, or Ben, stepped forward and held out their hand.

"Miss Addison. I'm Ben Chancellor, Mr Bradley has asked us to upgrade your security system with our Home Secure Smart System. We—"

"Beau," I said, interrupting him. "I can't afford to upgrade and Richard—"

It was then his turn to stop me. "I don't care about Richard and I'm paying." He moved past Ben and ushered me inside. "Don't argue with me. This is happening." He leaned a little closer to my ear and I tried not to feel affected by the way his breath whispered against my skin. "I don't want to be threatened with a knife every time that I knock on the door. He even tries to threaten you over this then I mean it Sim, I'll fucking end him. I don't give a shit who he thinks he is or what he can do. Let him try and ruin me, I've nothing left for him to take so…"

I gasped. "Beau."

He grabbed the back of his neck and breathed out heavily. "Besides which he probably has all the codes to your current alarm."

"God, do you think so?"

"Stands to reason," he grunted as he moved away from me. "His house, his alarm system. He'll know the code. Okay guys," he called over his shoulder. "Come on in. Ethan, buddy, you ready to roll?"

I watched on as Beau took charge and for once I didn't feel like I had the whole weight of the world on my shoulders.

**

A few hours later and my home was safer than the Bank of England. There were new locks on the doors with fingerprint recognition, a video panel at each exit door, and a lock on my bedroom door as well as panic buttons in each room that were connected to the police. I even had an app on my phone so I could activate or deactivate it when I wasn't home, or if I was. I could even turn the lights on with it. Thank God I had some semblance of knowledge of technology because when Dan went through it with me, I had to write notes. After a couple of practice runs though, I was confident that I had it. There was some serious kit that had been installed in my home and all I was missing was a panic room.

Now the guys had all gone and I was on my way around to Beau's with a cake that I'd baked for him. There was no way I'd ever be able to afford to pay him back for what he'd done for me. It wasn't just the security system; it was the fact that he'd given me my peace of mind back in my own home. Well, okay it was Richard's house, but my home and at least now it felt like a safe haven.

When I knocked on the door Sylvie answered it with a pile of clothes in her arms. She looked a little flustered and blew up at her fringe.

"Come in, me duck," she rushed out and I smiled at the colloquial phrase of her hometown. "I'm just packing up ready for the off tomorrow."

My heart sank a little as I thought about Belle and Sylvie leaving, particularly Belle. It finally felt like I had a friend.

"That's a shame that you're going home. I brought you this." I held out the chocolate cake.

"Ooh lovely. We'll have some for pudding tonight and I'll take some home with me. Anyway, must get on. Beau is in his office with Ethan."

"Okay, thanks. I'll put this in the kitchen and then go and collect him."

Sylvie bustled away towards the stairs, and I walked to the kitchen. I was surprised to see Beau there. He was running the cold water tap and had two glasses with orange cordial waiting to be filled.

"Hi." I smiled at him and placed the cake on the counter.

"Hey. You okay?" He went back to filling the glasses. "We've built up a bit of thirst."

"Oh, okay." I was a little surprised. I didn't think playing guitar at Ethan's level would make you thirsty. "The cake's a bit of a thank you by the way. I mean it's a miniscule fraction of the thanks that I owe you for the security system but... well, I'll find a way to pay you back. I could ask Vanessa, Richard's—"

"Nope," Beau said before knocking back half of one of the drinks. "Don't want anything from that bastard. I just want you to be safe so just let's say it's my good deed for the year." He picked up the other glass and started to pad across the kitchen in bare feet. "You want to see something?"

I scratched my neck and shrugged. "Um, yeah, I guess so."

He nodded his head to indicate for me to follow him. When we got outside his office, the door was slightly ajar and from inside I could hear music, real music. Okay it was a little clumsy, but it was most definitely music that my son was playing on the guitar.

"Do you know what it is?" Beau whispered.

I cocked my head on one side and listened again and smiled. "*Seven Nation Army?*" I queried.

Beau nodded with a grin. "He's doing really well."

He pushed the door open wider with his foot and I followed him in. As we entered the room, Beau stood to one side so that I could take it all in. Ethan was perched on the edge of the sofa with a guitar and strumming. His little tongue was poking out of the side of his mouth, and he was nodding his head with each time his tiny fingers went down the strings. My heart was beating in time with the music, and I felt that it was doubling in size with the amount of pride I had for my little boy. When he finished, I gasped and looked to Beau who was still holding the glasses but looking on Ethan with as much pride as I knew I was. When Ethan looked over at us and smiled, I began to clap wildly. Beau put the glasses on the desk, and he joined in too and it took everything in me not to hug him.

"Ethan that was so good," I gushed.

"Well done, buddy. You got all the way through."

Ethan's spine went straight, and his shoulders went back as he looked over at us and then floored me.

"Can I do it again please. I think I made a mistake."

I saw Beau's mouth move as he replied but heard nothing. All I could focus on was the fact that Ethan had spoken to Beau. There'd been no shyness in his tone, just joy and confidence. He'd spoken. He'd formed words to someone other than me. Suddenly I owed Beau Bradley a whole lot more than money for a security system. I was pretty sure I owed him my heart.

twenty

Beau

When I woke up with the early morning light creeping through the curtains, everything came crashing down on me. The emptiness, the grief, the loneliness, and the loss. Some days are better than others, today wasn't one of them.

Maybe it was the fact that I knew I was alone in the house. Maybe it was because it was Thursday and they died on a Thursday. Or maybe it was just the fact that rain fell outside the window in depressing sheets. Who knew? Blackness smothered me tight, that much I did know. It must have been bad because I was even considering calling my ma and asking her to come back, and she'd only been back home for two days, plus we hadn't exactly left on the best of terms. What I also knew was I should have sent Ethan home the minute he knocked on the lounge window to tell me that he'd arrived for his lesson.

As soon as I saw him, I dropped my head and slowly walked over to the patio door.

"Hey, Ethan."

He didn't answer but just smiled up at me with the youthful expectation of someone who had no idea how shit life could be. Simone had obviously shielded him from the crap that she'd had to endure. Apart from his desire not to speak, he was a well-rounded, happy kid. To him learning to play guitar with the miserable bastard next door was great, the most amazing thing in his little life. To me it was probably saving my life on days like today, days when I woke up wishing I hadn't.

"Okay," I said as Ethan settled on the little stool that I'd got for him. "We'll try some more chords today."

Eagerly he picked up the guitar and grinned up at me like I'd offered him the moon. Distractedly I thought about getting him a kid's guitar, maybe in a few weeks when I knew it wasn't a fad with him. I didn't think Simone could afford one even if she did live in the rapist's house for free. Then that thought added to my black mood—Simone not reporting the man who'd raped her. Truth, it disappointed me—she disappointed me. At least today she did, yesterday I'd understood as I might do tomorrow. That was how illogical the depression of my life made me. That was why I'd spend almost a year alone, but no one would fucking listen.

After about twenty minutes of trying the same two chords over and over, Ethan was smoothly moving from one chord to another. I found myself looking at the time on my phone though, wishing it was time for him to go so I could go back to bed.

"My little boy Bobby used to like to play the drums sometimes," I announced, surprising even myself. I had no idea why I'd felt the need to share that with a five-year-old kid. "His favourite was the guitar though. Probably because his best friend. My friend Ronnie, plays guitar."

Ethan looked at me a little confused. Of course he had no idea that I was in a band, a famous band. He saw me as Mr Beau the man next door.

"I'm in a band. Sorry, I *was* in a band," I explained. "And Ronnie who plays guitar in the band was Bobby's best friend."

Ethan nodded and swung his little legs down to the floor. He padded over to my desk and climbed onto the chair before shaking the mouse of my computer.

He wanted to watch me.

"Warrior Creek," I told him.

His head went down, his tongue poked out of the side of his mouth and his fingers tapped slowly on the keys. I moved behind him and when I saw that he was on YouTube, I typed in the word Warrior for him. He was a bright kid though and with a little help sounding it out he had no problem with the word, Creek. There was a list of songs from various gigs and a few music videos that we'd done—all of which we'd all hated doing, well except for Joey who loved acting out a part, hence going into acting.

Ethan looked up at me and grinned.

"That one," I said, pointing at the live performance of *Stella* at a Berlin gig.

Ethan clicked on it and the music blasted out. As I hit the first note on the anthemic song, Ethan's eyes lit up. I felt a surge of pride as his little hands curled into small fists and his head bobbed in time to the music. Then when I took a break and Elliot stepped up to play a riff, I thought the kid was going to combust. He started to bounce up and down in his seat and seemed to be holding his breath as he watched with rapt attention.

"Breathe buddy," I said, placing a hand on top of his head.

He looked up at me and there it was in his eyes. He'd fallen in love with Warrior Creek, with music, with Elliot, with lead guitar; he was gone. When his head turned back to the screen and he mouthed the word, 'wow', I even managed a small smile.

That moment should have been the one to give me a new perspective. The one defining moment that dragged me from the misery and gave me my love of music back. It wasn't and I should have known that the day would turn to shit.

It started when ten minutes in to watching videos of us, Ethan picked the worst one he could have. One of our first hits, back when we were still signed to our original label, *Welcome to the Sunshine*, was our first time doing a music video. It was a cheap production on a low budget, but it was my favourite because Cassie was in it. She was doing a bit of modelling at the time and when Elliot said he had a mate who'd be great in it, we all thought it was some lad who he'd drunkenly offered a part to in exchange for a six-pack of lager. When Cassie turned up though, I thought I was going to end up impaling something with my cock. The minute she ran in cursing that 'the fucking bus was late and some twat on there had the worst farts', I knew I was in love. Luck would have it she was playing my love interest. Me being a cocky git, slipped her my tongue in during a kissing scene. It could have gone either way but when she whispered in my ear, 'hope your cock is as good as your tongue', I knew I'd done the right thing. We had a date that night and then two more dates later she stayed the night and never went home.

When the part where she sashayed on screen loomed, I couldn't watch. I had photos of her all around the house, but I couldn't bring myself to watch her on video. I couldn't bear to see her living and breathing thinking that she had years of life left when she actually only had six more very short ones. She was nineteen, gorgeous, vibrant and sexy, and on limited time.

"Ethan shut it off now," I snapped. "That's enough. If you don't want to play damn guitar then I don't know what you're doing here."

Ethan looked up at me with wide eyes. He was surprised but didn't seem scared by me raising my voice. He turned and quickly closed down the video and then shuffled out of the seat, dangling his legs until his feet hit the floor.

"Just go home Ethan and don't come tomorrow."

I knew I was being a bastard to the poor kid, but I couldn't help it. He'd reminded me of what my beautiful wife should have been, what she could have been.

He grabbed my fingers in his tiny hand and tried to drag me back to the guitar, but I wouldn't budge, no matter how hard he tried.

"Ethan, go home now!"

It was then that his bottom lip began to tremble, and tears formed against his lashes. I was the lowest form of human being. I'd made the sweetest little kid cry. Hating myself for it I shook my head and let out a shaky breath. Before I could do anything else, two tiny arms wrapped around my legs and a tiny voice spoke.

"I'm sorry I made you sad, Mr Beau."

God, what the hell had I done? What sort of person was I?

"Ethan," I shuddered his name with a shaky breath.

It was too late, he let go of me and then ran out of the room, leaving me feeling more alone than I ever had before.

twenty-one

Simone

Ethan rushed through the door and it was more than obvious that he was upset. He tried to get past me so that I didn't see or ask questions, but that was never going to happen. I'm his mum and know when things aren't right with him.

"Ethan?" I managed to grab hold of his hand before he escaped me. "What's wrong?"

He looked up at me and his beautiful eyes brimmed with unshed tears as he shook his head. No way was there nothing wrong and it obviously had something to do with Beau. That was where he'd been for the last hour or so. What or who else could it be?

"Did something happen when you were next door, baby?" I knelt in front of him and took a gentle hold of both his shoulders. "Ethan, please tell me. If you don't want to speak, that's fine I'll ask you and you can nod or shake your head. Or I could go next door and ask Beau."

Ethan's head shook so fast his cheeks wobbled. He definitely didn't want me to go next door. If he wasn't willing to tell me though then I didn't care, I'd get to the bottom of it somehow because at that moment my heart felt as though it was in my throat.

"Please, Ethan. Something is upsetting you and I need to know what it is."

He dropped his chin to his chest and looked up at me from under his lashes. His bottom lip was jutting out and his hands were firmly behind his back; the closest he ever came to a tantrum.

"Okay," I sighed, getting to my feet. "I'll go and see Beau."

"No." His voice was loud and clear and there was even a stamp of his foot with it. When I looked, tears silently slipped down his cheeks and his tiny nostrils flared.

"What on earth happened?" I asked, pulling him into my side.

He didn't have to say anything because there was sharp rap on the glass of the back door. I swung my head around even though I knew who it would be. No one could get around the back unless they could scale a seven-foot gate. It could only be Beau having scrambled through the hole in the hedge.

"Stay there," I said to Ethan as I turned to the door. When I pulled it open, Beau looked as upset as Ethan. His eyes were red, and he had his hands at the back of his head.

"Sim," he breathed out. "I'm so sorry. I just… damn I…" He looked over my shoulder to where Ethan was standing. "Ethan buddy, I'm so sorry."

I heard his footsteps and then felt his little body push next to me. His hand slipped into mine and he looked up at Beau and smiled.

"It's okay, Mr Beau."

Beau's face crumpled and he dropped forward, resting his hands on his thighs. He lifted his head to look at Ethan.

"Beau, Ethan, just call me Beau."

"I think you'd better come in." I took a step back, taking Ethan with me. As Beau straightened to his full height, he looked at me warily. "I have no idea what happened, Beau. I'd appreciate you telling me, please."

He nodded and stepped inside. "T-thanks."

I tugged on Ethan's hand to get him to look at me instead of Beau. It took a couple of goes but his gaze eventually met mine.

"Go on upstairs and play while I speak to Beau."

Ethan looked like he might shake his head again, but I widened my eyes and gave him the mum look. I didn't need to use it often, but I'd still perfected it. He nodded and turned to Beau and pushed against him and wrapped his little arms around Beau's legs. Beau's chest shuddered as he pulled Ethan's head closer against his body.

"I'll see you soon for some more lessons, okay." Beau's voice was quiet and unsure but when Ethan nodded, he let out a long exhale. "Now, get yourself upstairs and play while I speak to your mum."

Ethan pulled free and ran away, just about avoiding the mop and bucket of water that I'd abandoned in the middle of the kitchen. Once I heard his footsteps on the stairs, I pulled a stool out at the island and nodded to the other one, indicating for Beau to sit too.

"Okay, so what happened?" I was torn between feeling sorry for Beau and wanting to punch him in the face for upsetting Ethan. I didn't know the full story though, plus he looked as upset as Ethan did.

"I don't know." He shrugged one shoulder. "I woke up feeling shit and in a bad mood."

"And you took that mood out on Ethan?"

I'd never been a confident person. Always hated conflict, avoided it wherever possible. After Richard I became even more insular, and if it hadn't been for having to take care of Ethan, I was pretty sure that I'd have become a recluse, living in a flat of cactus plants and macrame potholders. That was why I was surprised that I was willing to confront Beau. I supposed that was one of the consequences of motherhood—you would do anything to protect your child.

"Why did Ethan come rushing back here in tears, Beau?"

His shoulders stooped and he looked as broken as he had a month before when I'd first met him. He'd seemed to be making progress, but now, sitting at my kitchen island, he looked terrible and on the point of breaking.

"He wanted to watch the band, so he put some YouTube videos on."

"Watching yourself when you were in the band made you mad at him?" I asked, sitting back on the stool and raising my eyebrow.

Beau shook his head. "N-no. Well kind of. It was one particular video. The one Cassie starred in for us." He scrubbed a hand down his face. "It was six years before she died, Sim. She looked so damn beautiful and vibrant, and it was just too much." He looked up at me, eyes ringed with shadows and regret. His gaze pleaded for me to forgive him as the once confident rock star worried his bottom lip. "I snapped at Ethan to turn it off and told him to go home. I regretted the words as they came out of my mouth, but I couldn't help myself. It was like I was on the outside of my body looking on. Something took over my brain and made my mouth work in a way that I didn't want it to."

"And then he left?"

Beau shook his head. "No, not straight away."

"What did you do, Beau?" I whispered my heart back in my throat.

"Nothing. He… shit…" He took a deep breath. "He said he was sorry for making me sad and then he left."

I watched, my hand pressed against my chest, my heart thudding hard, as Beau let the tears fall. They were tears that I knew were for himself and Ethan in equal measure. Watching his wife living and breathing on the screen must have been devastating. It would have been like she was there, but he couldn't touch her, close to him yet miles away. The pain must have been indescribable.

"I'm sorry you had to go through that Beau," I said, placing my warm hand over his cold one. "It must have been awful, but Ethan is just a little boy. He wouldn't know what it meant to you to see your wife on the screen. He has no clue that your heart is shattered and that there's a constant ache in your chest. Or that every day is a battle for you to put one foot in front of the other without screaming your lungs out with the pain of it all. You know that because you're living it, I know that because I see you and I'm a grown up that's suffered misery of my own. He hasn't though. He's five years of age and has known nothing but love and happiness, despite how he came to be here. Even the kids who don't want to be his friends, or the parents that look at him like he's weird don't affect him, but you Beau, you made him cry."

"Fuck," he groaned and pulled away from under my touch and covered his eyes. "I messed it up so much. I'm so fucking sorry, Sim."

He dropped his hands to between his thighs and looked down at them and as much as I wanted to comfort him, I also wanted him to feel remorse.

Ethan was my baby, and I would protect him with my life. Beau had betrayed the trust that Ethan had built in him.

"I won't give him lessons anymore," he whispered. "I'll hook you up with someone good and they can take over."

I shook my head even though he wasn't looking at me. "Ethan would hate having lessons with someone else, but I do think you need a break. Just until you're feeling..." I paused trying to find the right words because he would never feel *better* about things. "When you're feeling calmer and there's less noise in your head. Just a few days. Maybe a week or two."

Beau finally looked up and nodded. "Okay. Whatever you think."

"I'll explain to Ethan that you're not feeling well at the moment."

Beau stood up from the stool and his head bobbed again. He moved to walk past me and gave his forearm a squeeze.

"I am sorry," he said, looking down at my hand.

"I know."

As the door clicked shut, I watched Beau walk slowly across the garden, his shoulders stooped, his hands shoved deep in his pockets. As he started to push through the hole in the hedge, he glanced back to the house. To me, still sitting at the kitchen counter it seemed as though sorrow engulfed him.

Once he disappeared, I sighed heavily and went to find Ethan to let him know that Beau Bradley wouldn't be teaching him guitar for a little while. And that was a sentence that I'd never imagined I'd ever have to say.

twenty-two

Beau

In the eight days since I'd seen Ethan, I'd realised Simone had been right. I'd needed it to clear my head, to try to get to a better place. A place where every small thing didn't bring me to my knees.

When I returned home from apologising to them both, I reverted to type and went to bed. I stayed there for two days. It would have longer if hunger hadn't gnawed at my stomach. Once I was up and had eaten, I forced myself not to go back. Di came in cleaned and changed my sheets and pretty much forced me to go and take a shower. After that I did feel a little bit better. I still wanted to tell the world to fuck off, but the skies were now more grey than black.

Every day after that I sat in the lounge and waited for a little boy to push through the hedge, but he never came. I even went out into the garden and checked to make sure his entrance hadn't overgrown, even though I knew Alex had cut it back as I'd asked. Each day got longer as my fingers itched to pick up a guitar, but I just couldn't, not without Ethan there. It seemed wrong to play without him and I treated it as some sort of self-punishment for upsetting him.

Elliot had called me twice, followed by Ronnie and Joey but I didn't answer any of their calls. I was fully expecting a surprise visit until I remembered that Joey was in LA doing some promo for his Netflix gig and Ronnie was sunning himself in Mexico with two of his mates. That didn't explain why Elliot hadn't turned up though. He was usually in my shit at any given opportunity, but not this time. It was weird because where I'd normally tell him to keep out of my business now I kind of wished he would turn up, even if it was just so I could tell him to keep out of my business.

When the light outside started to fade, I thought that it was probably going to turn to nine days of not seeing Ethan. It was almost half past seven and I was sure that Simone would have him in bed, or at least ready for it. That was why I jumped out of my seat with my heart beating its own drum solo when I saw his little body pushing through into the garden. Rushing to the patio door I wasn't sure why I felt so anxious, so nervous. I'd performed in front of thousands, but this kid and the thought of talking to him again made me want to puke. My stomach was turning over like an industrial washing machine.

At first his steps were tentative but as soon as he saw me, he picked up pace and began to run towards me. I was out and crouching down before he even reached the patio and was ready for him to run into my arms.

"I'm so sorry, Ethan," I whispered against his hair.

"It's okay." His voice was a whisper, and it was the best thing I'd heard in over a year.

His little arms wrapped around my neck and clung on tight as we both squeezed with relief.

"I didn't mean to upset you. I was sad but not because of anything you'd done," I reiterated as I hugged him even tighter. "And when I get sad, I just want to be on my own."

"But I don't want you to be alone and sad."

My heart stuttered at his words, I held my breath, trying to hold back the tidal wave of sobs that pushed against my chest. This little boy had chipped away at the blackness around my heart and had loosened the hold that grief had on it. The crippling pain was still there but had lessened since knowing Ethan. It didn't escape me that he was a similar age to Bobby and that subconsciously he'd become a replacement, a crutch to help me through each day. Yet they were so different, so how could he be? He was quiet, unassuming, and not at all like my loud, brash, attention loving son. Maybe when he died, he took a piece of my heart and Ethan had filled it, it was just a different shaped piece.

"Sometimes I need to be alone, Ethan," I explained, gently loosening my hold on him. "But that doesn't mean I'm angry with you. Okay?"

I held him away from me and made sure that he saw the truth in my eyes. When he gave me a single nod, I let out a long breath of relief. Then I realised that he had come to me, and I wasn't sure whether Simone was even aware that he had.

"Does your mum know you're here?" I asked, giving him a look that said don't tell me lies. It was a look I'd perfected with my high-spirited three-year-old. He nodded that she knew and looked over to the hole in the hedge. "Okay, let's go and see her."

I stood to full height, took his tiny hand in mine, and let him lead me to his mum.

When he reached up for the back door handle, I felt that tumble in my stomach again. Whatever else grief had done it had turned me into a damn pussy—I was scared of facing the tiny little woman who lived next door—what was that all about?

With trepidation, I stepped in behind Ethan.

"Hey," Simone said as soon as we walked through the door. She was standing at the kitchen island, obviously waiting for either both of us, or maybe just Ethan to return. "He insisted that he come alone, so I waited at the hedge until I knew that you were home."

And to make sure I didn't upset him again, I thought. Nodding, I cleared my throat. "Yeah, you know me, I don't get out much." I gave an empty laugh and laid my hand on Ethan's head.

"He wanted to come yesterday, but I thought it best to leave it one more day." She rubbed two fingers on the quartz countertop, studying it like it was the most interesting thing in the world. Her gaze was tentative as her eyes flicked between me and the interesting non-existent mark on the countertop.

"Are you okay?"

"Yeah," I breathed out. "It's been a long eight days, but you were right. I needed it."

She nodded and moved to the kettle and flicked it on. "Tea?"

"Tea would be good."

I watched as Simone moved around the kitchen, padding around in bare feet wearing black leggings and an oversized cream jumper. With her dark hair piled on top of her head, it struck me how pretty she was. Fresh faced and wearing little or no make-up that I could see, she had a peachy complexion which made her look much younger than her age. Seeing as she'd told me that she was nineteen when she had Ethan, twenty-four was still young. The fact that I was even looking at her as a woman and not just Simone, made me sway on my feet. I was a man. I wasn't dead from the waist down, but since Cassie, I'd barely looked at another woman. I'd still appreciated the opposite sex, but my wife was all I needed and the only person I truly saw. Watching Simone though reminded me that I was a man with natural instincts and when she swiped a whisp of hair from her cheek, something stirred inside me.

"How's your week been?" The words were the first that came into my head. Anything to distract me from silently appreciating my neighbour.

Leaning back against the counter, Simone nodded. "Yeah good. It's been fun getting used to the alarm. I just about managed to stop it going off a couple of days ago. We were seconds away from having the police, fire brigade and probably a SWAT team landing on us."

I laughed and shit it felt good. "What happened?"

Her gaze went to Ethan. "Someone decided to rush back for their plastic dinosaur just after I set the alarm."

Biting down on my lip, I raised my eyebrows at Ethan who was grinning. "Apart from that though, you've got the hang of it?" I asked. "You're using the video panel before you open the door, right?"

Simone rolled her eyes. "Yes, Beau, I've been using the video panel. Although, the only person who's visited was the delivery man with my new hard drive."

I shrugged. "I won't even pretend to know what the hell you're talking about. As long as you're being safe that's the main thing."

And it was, I hated the idea that Richard might get to her again. It made me want to punch another door. Talking of which, I looked over to the one that I had put a hole into.

"I'll get someone to come and repair that," I said, nodding to it. "I meant to say before, but well, with one thing and another."

"God, you know I've never thought about it. I walk past it every day and it doesn't register that it's even there."

"Well, I'll still get it fixed. It's my responsibility and we don't want anyone—"

"Ethan, do you want to go and get your pyjamas on."

I'd forgotten that he was there, because as usual he was so quiet. She didn't want me to talk about Richard in front of him and I should have realised. I was bloody clueless. However, there was something that I wanted to say before he disappeared up to bed.

"Before you do," I said. "Can I ask something?"

"Me or Ethan?" Simone asked.

"Both of you, but I'm probably doing the wrong thing and you'll probably get mad at me again." I smiled, hoping to bring some lightness to the situation.

Simone shrugged. "Probably."

There was that fun between us again and I realised how much I'd missed it. How a strange little friendship has snuck up on us.

"Go on then, ask," she sighed.

Looking down at Ethan, I took a deep breath and once again wondered how the fuck my neighbours managed to make me feel like such a nervous wreck half the time.

"I'd like to buy Ethan a guitar of his own."

"No, Beau," Simone immediately responded. "Honestly you don't have to do that he's okay borrowing yours. Unless of course you don't want him to."

I shook my head and held up a hand. "No, honestly I don't have a problem at all, but it's not full size and it's still way too big for him. I thought it would be good if he had a kid's size one. It'd help him a lot more." Looking down at Ethan I found an amazing and huge, captivating smile on his face. It lit up the room and thawed my bitter old heart a little bit more.

"There's a shop I know in the city, they have some great guitars for kids. Actually, there's have a whole range of instruments for them. In fact, Joey got…" I trailed off thinking about what it was Joey got—a kid's drum set for Bobby.

I don't know if Simone knew where my thoughts had strayed, but she saved me by saying, "It's a great idea," as she turned to put teabags into a couple of mugs that were already on the side and then poured in the boiled water. With the water safely in the mugs she turned and added, "I'll buy it though. I don't expect you to."

"No, no way," I insisted. "It's my treat, honestly. I suggested it."

Simone turned back and handed me the mug of tea.

"That's never brewed properly." I laughed and reached around her for the spoon. "And you put the milk in first, that's not right in any sense."

She raised her eyebrows. "Don't be ungrateful Mr Rock Star otherwise in future you can make your own."

The breath rushed from my lungs as a memory of another woman, in another kitchen hit me.

"You're so ungrateful Mr Rock Star, make your own flipping tea next time."

"Whatever, Cassie my darling, whatever."

I slapped her arse and pulled her in for a kiss… a kiss that led to kitchen counter sex.

"You okay?"

I scrubbed a hand down my face. "Yes, just remembered something I was supposed to call Elliot about. Anyway, I was thinking that maybe we could go tomorrow."

"If you're sure." She looked down at Ethan. "Would you like that?"

Ethan nodded and looked up at me with pure joy in his eyes.

"That's really kind of you, Beau." Simone's eyes glistened and it struck me that no one ever did anything for her or for Ethan. No wonder my ma had taken her under her wing.

"The only problem is," I replied, wincing. "It'll have to be in the evening.

When the shop is officially closed. You know, because of fans and all that." I also didn't want to be photographed with Simone and for gossip to start. "Will that be okay, as it might mean Ethan's bedtime is a bit late?" I looked at Ethan whose eyes were wide with anticipation. He looked at his mum and seemed to be holding his breath.

Simone laughed and ruffled his hair. "Okay. But I'm paying for it."

"No, you're not. But," I replied, "you can buy the burgers on the way home."

Ethan was practically jumping on the spot. A new guitar, late bedtime and a burger had created a combustible pressure of excitement. It was barely anything compared to the sort of things that Bobby got as the son of a celebrity. A burger was nothing to him, it was our regular Saturday treat. As for the guitar, well Bobby had a half drum kit, an electric guitar and a stage in his bedroom with a working mic. I spoiled him, I knew I did and Cassie always told me so. He was my baby though, my son, the light of my life and I would give him everything I had if he'd asked for it. Cassie would have bollocked me, but I'd have done it anyway.

"Okay," Simone conceded. "Burgers are on me. Now you, young man," she looked down at Ethan, "need to get upstairs and get ready for bed."

"Night, Ethan." I smiled down at him, but he tugged on my shirt.

I bent down as that seemed to be what he wanted me to do. When I was level with him, he surprised me by kissing my cheek. Then he whispered, "Thank you."

Before I had a chance to reply, he darted out of the kitchen.

"Wow," Simone said, her voice quiet and a little awestruck. "Apart from me you're the only person he talks to. Not even Marcus."

My chest swelled. To think I'd helped him to have the confidence to talk was an awesome feeling. Some good had come after the crap in my life.

"I think we've helped each other," I replied.

"I think you have." She gave me a soft smile. "Now drink your tea because I think it's probably stewed, never mind brewed."

Giving my drink one last stir, I threw the spoon into the sink and then took a sip. She was wrong, it was just right.

twenty-three

Simone

Ethan was more excited than I had ever seen him. If he wasn't bouncing around, he was standing on his bed looking through the window for Beau's Range Rover coming up the drive. When Beau finally appeared, Ethan scrambled off the bed and shot down the stairs to wait in the hall. We'd had the conversation about opening the front door and the fact that he couldn't, even if he knew who was on the other side.

I joined Ethan in the hall and to appease Beau, I pressed the button on the video intercom.

"Hey," I said as the image of Beau came into focus. I had to admit he took my breath away. Although he had a baseball cap pulled down low, it wasn't difficult to see how handsome he was. He'd been handsome before but over the last few weeks he'd put a little bit of weight on, and it suited him. His eyes were less sunk and brighter, and his broad shoulders didn't look like they might break with the heavy grief that he was carrying.

"You both ready?" he asked, rubbing his hands together and looking around rather than at the camera.

"Yes, two minutes."

When I clicked on the button and turned to Ethan, he was already at the door, wearing his coat with his hand on the handle. He really was desperate to go, and my heart felt full because while he'd always been a happy boy, I'd never seen him *this* happy. I picked my jacket from the coat stand and opened the door. Before it was open fully, Ethan was out and running past Beau to his car.

"Someone's eager." Beau grinned at me and then looked back to Ethan who already had the door open. "Hang on Ethan. Let me give you a lift up." Beau jogged over to him and lifted Ethan under the arms to place him safely in the shiny black vehicle.

When I reached them, Beau opened the passenger door and waved for me to get in before moving away. There was something different about him today. He seemed much brighter, there was a lightness to his step, and it almost seemed like he was enjoying life. I knew that couldn't be the case, not carrying the heavy weight of tragedy that he was, but at least he didn't look like he wanted to curl up and shut himself off from the world.

Pleased for him feeling some release, I got in and buckled up almost as excited as the little boy in the back seat. Then when Beau whipped off his baseball cap and placed it on the dash, my excitement changed to something else. He'd had his hair cut. Beau with a man bun was gorgeous, but Beau with hair cut short at the sides and longer on top with a little light stubble on his chin and cheeks, was magnificent.

"Okay?" he asked, rousing me from my staring. I nodded, unable to say anything. "Right, let's go and buy a guitar."

***

Along the length of the huge bay window was the name of the shop, Foxy Freddie Music. It was a little weathered and the paint was peeling on some of the lettering, but the window underneath more than made up for it. Brightly coloured guitars were displayed, three either side of a huge royal blue and gold drum kit and in front was an array of other instruments like maracas, tambourines, and a shiny black and silver flute. It was busy but it was exhilarating, and I could see why on the way over Beau had mentioned it was one of his favourite places.

"You're going to love in here," Beau said ruffling Ethan's hair.

Ethan looked up at him and grabbing Beau's hand dragged him to the door. As we approached it, it was pulled open and tall man with long grey hair and a beard just as long and grey appeared.

"Beau, my man," he greeted. "Come on in quick before someone in the pub over the road spots you."

We were in a side street in the city centre and apart from the pub there were two boarded up shops, a café which was closed with a stretch of waste ground next it. It was deserted but the pub did appear to be busy. The lights were all on and music was blaring.

"It's a rock pub," Beau explained. "There's not many left since the city went trendy to cater for the vegans and the poets."

I laughed because while I hadn't been into Manchester much since I'd been back, I knew it was much more diverse than that.

"He's a rock snob," Freddie said and held out his hand. "Freddie Dixon, love. You must be Simone, Beau's neighbour."

I nodded and shook his hand. "Yes I am. Lovely to meet you."

He ushered us inside and once we were in and the door slammed and locked, Freddie turned to Ethan and stooped down to his height.

"And you are the guest of honour, Ethan." Freddie got a shy smile and a nod in response. "Excellent. Now, how about you and Beau have a look around and when you see something you like let me know and I'll get it down for you to try."

I lifted my eyes to where Freddie was indicating for Ethan to look and was amazed at the all the different shapes, colours and types of guitars that were hanging from the wall. They covered the whole expanse from the front to the back of the shop. There appeared to be four of each one, all different sizes and when I glanced over at Beau he seemed to be in as much awe as Ethan. His shining eyes and wide-open mouth were pretty much a replica of my son's.

"I think they're overawed," I whispered to Freddie.

"It gets him every time he comes in," Freddie said leading me towards the back of the shop which smelled like a mixture of old paper and wood.

"He's a great guitarist, but not as good as Elliot and Ronnie, they just have the edge, but no one can sing like Beau though."

I had to agree. For a rock star Beau had a beautiful soulful voice that reached every part of you. For me Warrior Creek's ballads were their best music because they were what showcased Beau's voice.

"Come, sit here, love." Freddie pulled out a black leather look desk chair that had seen better days. The fake leather was peeling and, in some places, had been covered in strips of thick black tape. "If I know Beau, they'll be ages. Ethan doesn't have to get up for school tomorrow, does he?"

"No, not really. I'm schooling him at home at the moment, phonics, the basics, that sort of thing. Albeit a little unsuccessfully." I grimaced. "He's got a place to start after Easter."

"I'm sure you're doing a great job." Freddie shifted a pile of music magazines from a stool and plonked down on it, next to me. "You see that," he said, nodding toward what looked like a huge shower cubicle.

"What is it?" I asked.

"Sound booth. That's where Beau recorded his vocals for their first release." Freddie grinned proudly and winked.

"*Ever Since*," I said, proud of myself that I knew which song it was.

"That's the one. They'd just come to Manchester, and they were in here because Elliot wanted a new guitar, which was also used on that track I should add. They were looking around when Beau said he'd got an idea on how to deliver the song they'd written that morning and so went in there and did it."

"So you've known them since the beginning then?" I asked.

"I have. Oh look." He paused and pointed to where Beau and Ethan were studying a guitar and Ethan was nodding and bouncing up and down. "Seems we may have a winner." Freddie got up and went over to them and exchanged a few words with Beau, before taking the guitar down and giving it to Beau. Freddie then collected another stool from near to the books of music on display, placed it down and patted it. Ethan, with his wide- eyed stare on the guitar in Beau's hands, sat down. He adjusted himself and then Beau passed the guitar to him. Ethan took it gently, treating it with care like it was delicate and fragile, and looked up at Beau. When Beau crouched down in front of Ethan, Freddie moved away and came back to me.

"He's got good taste that lad of yours."

"It's not really expensive, is it?" I knew that Beau had insisted on buying it for him, but I didn't want him to spend hundreds of pounds on a guitar that Ethan would probably outgrow soon.

Freddie smirked. "It's a Baby Taylor Koa acoustic, the most expensive half size that I stock."

"Oh God, really. Are we talking a couple of hundred?"

Freddie pointed upwards and I groaned dropping my head into my hands. "I can't let Beau pay that much. I thought it might be about fifty or sixty pounds. Do you have anything for fifty or sixty pounds?"

"I do," Freddie replied. "But I don't think Beau would be down with buying one for that much. That's a great guitar and will last him until he's about eight or nine, depending on how fast her grows."

I bit my lip and looked over to where Beau was animatedly talking to Ethan who was strumming the guitar made of a beautiful reddish-brown wood.

"I'll see if I can persuade them to look at something else," Freddie said and got up again to re-join Ethan and Beau.

I watched as he pointed to another gorgeous looking guitar dark blue with touches of black around the edges, and then another which was painted with the Union Jack, but each time Beau shook his head and pointed back to the one that Ethan was playing. I groaned and wondered how on earth I could pay Beau back. Freddie looked over and shrugged and Beau spotting him walked over to me.

"What's wrong?" he asked, sitting on the stool that Freddie had vacated.

"It's too much, Beau. Freddie said it's hundreds of pounds and I can't ask you to pay for that, but I can't afford it either. What's wrong with the navy blue one?"

"It's shit compared to the one he's chosen. And I don't want you to pay. It was my idea so I'm buying it." He looked at me as if I'd come from another planet. He had no idea what my issue was with him spending hundreds of pounds on a guitar that would only last Ethan a handful of years. "You said that you were buying the burgers anyway."

"It's hardly the equivalent, is it?" I protested, glancing anxiously at Ethan who now had Freddie moving his little fingers for him as his other hand strummed.

"Sim, please let me do this." I turned back quickly. He sounded defeated while he'd been so upbeat earlier. "I need to do this."

Inhaling slowly, I nodded and instantly his shoulders relaxed, and a small smile twitched at his lips.

"I *am* buying the burgers though," I replied.

He saluted me and then got up and went back to Freddie and Ethan.

***

"Stop picking on me," I protested as I drove Beau's Range Rover home. "I can't help it if I've never driven anything this big before."

Beau laughed and leaned forward to grip the dashboard as I took a bend in the road. He'd insisted that I drive it through the burger drive-thru just in case he was recognised. I hadn't wanted to, but he was adamant. I got that he didn't want there to be pictures of us together which could be misconstrued, but the baseball cap and sunglasses to go to Freddie's shop and then in the car were a bit much. It was important to him though, so after a quick run through of the controls in the yard behind Freddie's shop, I drove. Admittedly, I'd scraped a bollard manoeuvring out of the drive-thru, but when Beau checked it when we pulled over to eat our food, he said it wasn't as bad as it had sounded.

"Seriously though, Sim," Beau groaned. "I think you need a refresher course. If you actually passed your test."

At that very moment the gears made a grinding sound as I changed down to take another corner. Beau held his hands up and laughed. "Enough said."

Keeping my eyes on the road, I slapped my hand out and connected with his chest. He made an 'oof' sound followed by a chuckle and then silence fell for the rest of the journey. The banter had stopped but it still felt easy in the confines of the car. It was nice to think we'd created a friendship of sorts. It felt so comfortable that when I turned into Beau's driveway, I was disappointed that the evening was over.

"He's well away," Beau said looking into the back seat as I turned off the engine.

I shifted in my seat to look at Ethan. He was fast asleep with his tiny little hand gripping the handle of his new guitar case. My heart swelled at the sight, and I knew I would never, ever love anyone or anything as much as him. I was wondering whether Beau would carry him home for me when Ethan stirred and slowly opened his eyes. He rubbed a hand against his nose and then smacked his lips a couple of times. Beau and I both giggled and Ethan smiled, albeit sleepily.

"Hey, you," I said, gently rubbing his knee. "We're home."

He looked outside the window and nodded.

"You think you could say thank you to Beau?" I asked, ever hopeful.

Ethan unstrapped his belt and clambered down from his booster seat. As he did, it struck me that Beau's wife and son had died in a car accident, and I had no clue how he'd felt about driving. I'd argued that I didn't want to drive his car but maybe he'd driven all he could and needed a break.

As Ethan pushed between the two front seats to hug Beau around the neck, I stared at him trying to see how he really felt. Had the joking about my driving and not feeling safe really been a joke or was he truly scared. When Ethan let him go and went back to his seat, Beau looked and me and frowned. "What's wrong?" he asked, glancing between Ethan and me.

"You drove," I whispered.

"Well, yeah." He looked confused and I didn't blame him. I wasn't making much sense.

"Were you okay. Should I have driven there too? God, I'm sorry I should have asked."

He scratched his head and studied me and then after a few seconds I saw the lightbulb moment.

"No. Honestly no," he insisted. "I was fine. It was fine."

"Are you sure?" I felt sick that he'd probably hated every single moment in the car and all I'd done was complain about having to drive his stupidly big car.

"Yes." He nodded his head vigorously. "It's not a trigger, I promise."

I reached for his hand and as soon as there was skin on skin, I wanted to pull back. I couldn't though, I'd committed to it and taking my hand away from his then would have simply made it awkward.

"I-I-I am sorry if it is," I replied and gave his hand a quick squeeze before pulling away and mine into my lap.

Beau swallowed. "Nope, it's fine."

Turning my head to look in the back, I mentally chastised myself at acting like an idiot and then plastered on a smile for Ethan.

"Okay, let's get you home."

Ethan then opened his mouth and spoke. "I want to put my guitar with Beau's."

"W-what," I stammered, shocked that he'd talked in front of, to, Beau *again*.

"I want to put my guitar with Beau's. In his office place," he repeated, voice quiet.

I turned to Beau who didn't seem in the least bit shocked. He smiled and reached to give Ethan a fist bump.

"Okay then, kiddo, let's go so Mummy can get you into bed." He looked at the clock on the dashboard. "It's almost nine, way past your bedtime, I'll bet."

Ethan grinned and nodded and started to reach for the door handle.

"Hang on," Beau said. "Let me help you out."

Perplexed that Ethan had spoken so freely in front of Beau, I sat back in my seat and watched them. As Beau got out, he ducked his head back in. "You want a cuppa?" He asked, his smile shining dimly in the dark night air. "I'm guessing you might want to discuss what's just happened."

"I guess so."

"Come one then and I'll stick the kettle on."

With that he gave me his back and disappeared with Ethan clutching his guitar in one hand and Beau with the other.

twenty-four

Beau

I had no idea what had made me invite Simone in for a cuppa. She'd been willing to go home, and I could easily have persuaded Ethan to let me take his guitar into the house. It'd been a good night though. I felt almost normal. Playing guitar and chatting with Freddie had been like old times and then when we went for a burger it didn't feel odd. I'd enjoyed it, and the joking around with Simone about her shit driving—and she was shit at driving.

Turning on the light in the kitchen, I was relieved that it was warm. Too many nights I'd sat in there in the darkness and the cold, to the point that when the house wasn't warm it brought back memories of misery. The fact I was thinking of my misery as a memory made me stall a little. I was no longer quantifying it as the here and now, at least not every hour of every day. Now some of the crippling grief was a memory

Not wanting to think what that might mean I went over to kettle and flicked it on and then turned to Simone who was taking Ethan's coat off. They were grinning at each other as they tried to remove it without Ethan give up his firm hold on his guitar. They started to giggle and suddenly it felt warmer in the kitchen than just because of the underfloor heating. Finally, it was off, and she hung it off the back of one of the chairs at the kitchen table.

"Do you need any help?" I asked Ethan as he rushed past me towards the hallway. He shook his head. "Put it on the spare stand next to mine." Another quick nod and he was gone.

Simone watched as she removed her own jacket and when he was gone, she blew out a breath.

"I can't believe how much he speaks to you." She shook her head. "I've never known him to talk this often."

I shrugged. "Maybe he feels sorry for me. We all know if I could I'd happily speak less than he does."

Simone's brow furrowed. "No, I don't think it's that. I think he actually likes you."

"And that's so difficult to believe." I smirked, wondering whether she'd agree.

She shrugged and smiled and there it was again that easy, carefree banter.

"Fancy a wine instead?" I asked as the kettle clicked off. "It's not like you've got to drive badly home, is it?"

**

Simone drained her glass and I picked up the bottle to refill it, only to find that we'd emptied that too. I could have opened another but that would feel like it was more than two neighbours chatting. There was no way I could be ready for anything like that. It would still feel like cheating and my heart was in bad enough disrepair as it was. Maybe Simone read my mind or maybe she was just ready to go home, but she pushed her glass away and sighed.

"I'd better get Ethan home. It's gone ten and he'll be a nightmare to get up in the morning."

She stood and picked up both the empty glasses and the bottle and took them to the sink. I watched as she moved around my kitchen with ease, remembering where everything was from when she stayed over. She knew where the washing up liquid was, she knew that the recycling bin was next to the sink and once she'd washed the glasses she knew where the tea towel was to dry them. Whereas that made my skin itch before, now it didn't bother me. Definite progress.

"Right, I'll go and get Ethan for you," I said, pushing up from the table.

"Thank you." She smiled as she placed the glasses back in the cupboard.

When I got into the hallway, I realised that the strumming we'd heard in the background of our conversation about Simone's crap taste in music over the last hour had stopped. The door was ajar, so I pushed it further open and peeped around it. As I suspected Ethan was fast asleep, hugging his guitar. That he cherished it so much already, pulled at something in my chest. I knew I wasn't a guitarist, yet I felt like I'd passed something onto him. A love of something special and magical because that was what making music was, magical. There it went again, my head blown that I'd thought of making music as magical. I'd barely even listened since Cassie and Bobby died, never mind considered it as something amazing.

Pushing the thought aside, I moved into the room and gently prised Ethan's arm from around the neck of his guitar. No wonder he was keeping a firm hold of it, it was a fucking beautiful instrument, especially for his first one. I'd felt proud when he'd picked it out from the hundreds in the shop. He had no idea it was the most expensive one that Freddie had in stock; all Ethan knew was that he liked it. When he sat down and put it in his arms, he loved it and I knew nothing else would do for either of us. Even when Freddie tried to show us something on the cheaper end of his stock, neither of us were budging on our choice.

As I moved the guitar, I felt Simone's presence in the room. "Want me to carry him home for you," I whispered without looking at her.

"I'll wake him," she replied. "It's fine."

I turned and saw she was gazing down at him, the love she had for him obvious in her smile and shining eyes.

"Honestly, I don't mind."

I didn't mind. I'd done it before, and it no longer felt wrong. He was my little buddy and it felt good.

"Thank you."

As I picked him up, Simone moved forward draped his coat over him. "I'll go first and get the door unlocked. Are you able to get through the gap in the hedge with him?"

"Yeah, no problem," I replied, shifting Ethan so that he was draped over my shoulder. As soon as I did his arms came around my neck and he snuggled closer.

"Are you okay?" Simone asked as my feet faltered.

"Yep, all good." My voice tightened, but I continued to move out of the room regardless.

By the time we got to their back door everything felt easy again and when I took him upstairs and laid him on his bed fully clothed and then pulled the duvet over him, it didn't occur to me not to kiss his forehead. A simple act that I'd done every night for Bobby, but once more the pain I'd expected was just a dull ache in the dark recesses of my chest. I left the door open to his room and met Simone on the landing. She looked around me.

"He didn't even stir," she said.

I shook my head. "No, he's well away."

She stood to one side to let me pass. "Thanks again Beau, for everything. I honestly can't thank you enough."

I waved her away. "Honestly, I loved it. I was amazing to see the pleasure he got from it." Then without thinking, I turned and pulled her to me and hugged her tight, both my arms wrapping around her. She didn't push me away, or ask me to get off, but she didn't exactly hug me back either.

Feeling a real dick, I quickly let her go and took two strides to get to the top of the stairs.

"Night," I muttered. "And don't forget to come and lock up and set the alarm."

"I won't," she replied but I wasn't taking much notice as I had to get out of there. I needed to be a distance from her because to my shock and disgust, it hadn't felt wrong.

By the time I got up to my bedroom I'd gone back and forth between thinking I was a shit for disrespecting Cassie by hugging Simone and a wanker for disrespecting Simone for thinking it was wrong to hug her. I don't think I'd ever been so confused about anything in my life. My head felt like it was full of mush and my thoughts were trapped in it, fighting to separate themselves from each other.

Going to the window to pull the blinds I noticed that there was a light on in the bedroom that was the equivalent to mine. It was the largest bedroom with an en suite so I figured it was Simone's room. With the blinds half down, I stood and watched. Not sure what I was watching, or why, but I couldn't drag myself away. Nervous anticipation bubbled in my stomach, but I had no idea what it was I thought was going to happen. When the main light went off next door, I sprang back like someone had jumped out at me. My heart was thumping as I moved away from the window, worried that I might be seen.

"You fucking idiot," I muttered to myself as I moved back to the window and pulled the cord on the blind, letting it drop. As it thudded to the bottom of the sill, a light cast through it. Lifting the blind again, I felt my body relax when I saw that there was now a lamp on. With my eyes still pinned to the house next door, I pulled out my phone and tapped at the screen.

Me: Thanks for the burger and the wild ride home.

Once I'd sent off the text, I let my forehead drop to the cool glass and waited. There was no movement, although I wasn't sure why I expected there to be. I was sure she hadn't been waiting for my text or thought that I'd be at the window watching like a creeper, but I watched anyway. As I exhaled the window fogged and memories of me and Bobby breathing on windows and drawing faces came into my head. I smiled as I recalled Cassie chasing us around the house for dirtying the glass that Di had just cleaned. It was a good memory, and I was surprised not to feel a knot in my stomach.

Simone: I don't know what you mean. I'm a great driver! Burgers were the least I could do after what you did for Ethan tonight. He's sleeping with a smile on his face... and next time I need to drive we'll go in my Fiat...and by the way, I meant to say, nice haircut.

Stepping backwards, with my eyes still on the window, I moved to the bed and sat down on the edge. Not sure what to do, whether to text her back or not, I placed my mobile on the mattress next to me and then stared at my bare feet.

"Fuck it."

I picked up my phone and tapped out another message.

Me: No way am I getting in that thing. Maybe I'll give you some driving lessons. Thanks, it was about time, I was beginning to look like the Beast—yeah, I love Disney! Anyway, night, Sim, sleep well x

I sent it before I could second guess why I'd put a kiss on the end or used the name Sim which I'd decided I was more comfortable with than Simmy. At least that was what I was telling myself was the reason for using it instead of whatever everyone else called her. I waited a couple of minutes to see if she texted back, but there was nothing and when I looked across at her room, the light was off. With a little relief I got up and closed the blinds deciding to go to bed with a little less acid than usual in my stomach.

As I came out of the bathroom having cleaned my teeth, my phone started to ring. It had to be close to eleven-thirty so it could only be on the guys Everyone else I knew would have been tucked up in bed. I was right, it was Elliot.

"Elliot to what do I owe the fucking pleasure at half eleven at night?"

"Sorry Princess, were you getting your beauty sleep?"

"Just about to. Spill it then, what do you want me to do now?"

Elliot chuckled on the other end of the line. "Nothing. Well, I do but nothing you'll hate. Well, you will hate it but maybe not as much as some of the stuff I might ask you to do."

"Now I wish I'd put my phone on silent," I muttered, pulling back the duvet and throwing one of my pillows to one side. "Okay, what is it?"

"I'm having a birthday party, seeing as it's my birthday next week."

I rolled my eyes and dropped back onto the mattress. "I do remember. You don't have to remind me. You'll get your usual bottle of expensive as fuck whisky that you won't drink and just put in that cabinet with the rest that are gathering dust."

"You don't have to get me anything," he protested. "It's fine."

I knew what he was really trying to say; don't put yourself through that hell if you don't need to. That was because Cassie was normally the one who did the present thing. She sourced him something unusual every year and I just signed the card.

"You'll get your whisky, Elliot. What about this party you're having then?"

"I know you won't but I'm inviting you anyway."

"Why invite me if you know I won't come?" I asked, pulling the duvet over me.

He didn't answer immediately, but I could hear rustling and then he sighed. "Because I invited Belle and I couldn't invite her and not you."

"About fucking time," I grunted.

"What is?" he asked.

"You and my sister. It's about time you got your acts together and hooked up." Finally, it seemed he'd grown some bollocks.

"It's not like that."

The twat was definitely lying. I could hear it in his voice. I couldn't remember a time when he didn't want her.

"I call bullshit, but I'll let you think you've got away with a lie. Why else would you call her out of the blue to ask her to a party?"

"It isn't out of the blue," he sighed "I've been helping her to find a flat, like I promised."

My heart jumped. "Why didn't she ask me?"

"Because I said I would and I called her," he responded, sounding agitated. "So do you want to come to the party?"

"Yeah, I think I will."

I'm not sure who was more surprised, Elliot who squeaked out a 'what', or me who felt a bit pukey at what I'd just agreed to. Then if I hadn't been lying down, I'd have fallen over because of what came out of my mouth next.

"Can I bring someone?"

"Uh, yeah," he replied hesitantly. He made a clicking sound and then asked, "Do I know them?"

He knew the answer to that, and he damn well knew that he did.

"Who the fuck do you think I could possibly have been spending any time with? I didn't actually join Tinder. That was a joke you know."

"Okay, okay." Elliot sighed. "I'm guessing it's Simone."

"Well you guessed correctly. Now if that's it, I need my beauty sleep. Oh, and before you start ringing around and spreading the news, we're just friends, me and Simone."

"I know," he protested. "I didn't say anything."

"Yeah, well I could hear that tiny brain of yours working and it needs fucking oiling, it's too noisy."

"You're just friends. Okay I get it."

I pinched the bridge of my nose and once again wished I'd had my phone on silent.

"You know what, El—"

"Beau, I get it, I do and I'm glad you've got a friend."

I curled my lip and dropped my mouth open not able to believe what I was hearing.

"Did you grow a pair of tits?" I finally asked.

"What the fuck are you talking about?"

"You're glad I've got a friend," I repeated sarcastically.

"You know what," Elliot said sounding exhausted by the whole conversation, "I'm going to go. Party starts at mine at half four. It's a barbeque you don't need to bring anything except yourself, your *friend* and my bottle of whisky."

I couldn't help but smile at the arsey little fucker.

"Understood."

"Oh, and Beau," he added. "Call Sylvie and apologise for calling her an interfering old bat on the day that she left."

I rolled my bottom lip over my teeth. She'd been giving me a lecture about what a great girl Simone was on the journey to the railway station—all the damn way.

"Who snitched?" I asked. "My sister who you're *just* helping to find a flat?"

"Call your mum, Beau and I'll see you on the twenty-third"

Then he was gone like he hadn't stopped me from getting my beauty sleep or had pushed my buttons about Simone.

twenty-five

Simone

"Hey, Marcus," I said answering my phone a few days after our visit to the guitar shop. I closed my eyes thankful to hear from him. I'd been trying him for a couple of days without any luck and my fears told me that Richard had done something. "Are you okay?"

"Hiya. Yeah, I'm good. What about you?"

He did sound okay so I'd been worrying for nothing, hopefully. "Great, we're great. I was worried about you though. I've been calling you and left messages."

He made a strange noise from the back of his throat. "Yeah, about that. I'm sorry but I've been busy."

He sounded off. Not like he was scared or anything, but like he was keeping something from me.

"What's going on?" I asked, chewing on the edge of my thumbnail. "You sound funny."

He sighed and then groaned. "I didn't want to tell you this because it's new, but as you've asked. I've met someone."

I squealed and jumped up from the stool at the kitchen island. "Oh my God, really? What's her name?" Just because we weren't close it didn't mean I wasn't excited for him.

There was silence at the end of the line, so I looked down at the phone to check it was still on.

"Marcus. You still there?"

"Yep." His answer was clipped.

"What?" I asked. "What did I say wrong?"

"Assuming the person that I met was a '*she*'," he ground out, venom lacing his voice.

I flopped back down onto my seat, the air leaving my lungs in a rush. It wasn't a problem but what hurt was his attitude, the iciness in his tone. I'd had no idea, so that's what I responded with.

"You never told me that you were gay?"

He let out an empty laugh. "You never told me that you were straight."

He was right I hadn't, but then we hadn't told each other much about anything. I was never really interested in his life and vice versa. Our five-year age gap had seemed like a chasm when were younger.

"That's different and you know it is," I protested.

"Maybe, but the point is it wasn't a big deal. I've known since I was about eleven that I didn't like girls. It wasn't as if I could bring a boy home to dad was it." He sighed and after a short pause said, "I'm sorry, Simmy, I didn't mean to be a knob about it. I guess I hate myself for hiding it for so long. You're right I should have told you."

I placed my hand on my heart and took a deep breath. I knew we weren't as close as a lot of brothers and sisters, considering we only had each other, but I should have known something like that. "I wish you hadn't had to hide who you really are Marcus."

"Here I don't, Simmy."

"Yet you never in all these years told me." I felt the tears well and my throat became scratchy. "Because you thought I'd judge you?"

"God no," he replied. "It just didn't seem something you would want to talk about. You've been distant for so long; I mean you can just about stand me hugging you."

Nausea overcame me as I heard the words and was reminded of why I was that way. Richard had taken so much from me and not just that night, he taken my brother from me too. How could I tell Marcus though? How could I tell Marcus that I was that way because he forgot to pick me up from work when he promised and that night I was raped and got pregnant. I took a deep breath and swiped at the tears on my face. How could I say that in some way I blamed him for what Richard did to me or that I put up with Richard's shit because I was scared of what he would do to Marcus. There was no way that I could say that all the roads of my brokenness led to him, my brother. I couldn't. The only thing that I could do was to choose to move on.

"Okay," I said taking a deep breath. "What's his name? Tell me all about him."

"His name is Lee and he's pretty amazing actually…"

***

After talking to Marcus, I heaved a sigh of relief that our call had ended better than it started. I knew now that he'd been seeing Lee for a month and that they met at the gym. I also knew that I had to try and let the blame go and welcome him back as my brother. I couldn't keep him at arm's length any longer and maybe one day I would tell him the truth about Ethan's father. As I put my phone into my back pocket it occurred to me that I hadn't told him about Beau. Not that there was much to say, but I was sure he'd be interested to know that he was my neighbour. Maybe that would be a conversation for the next time we spoke. Now though, I had dinner to get ready for Ethan. It was when I stood up that I heard the scream.

Ethan!

Careering into the lounge I yelled his name as I saw him lying on the floor. There was a stool toppled over, his arm was at a strange angle and Ethan was crying.

"Oh baby, what happened?" I dropped down to the floor and looked at his arm while running a hand through his hair.

His eyes went to bookcase, and I knew what it was he was trying to get. The iPad to watch guitar tutorials. I scanned his body to check what the best option was.

"Can you stand up?" I asked, one hand hovering over his arm while the other went under his armpit to help him stand. As soon as he tried to sit up though he yelped out.

"Okay." I shushed him and helped him to lay back down. "I'm going to have to take you to the hospital, it'll be quicker than an ambulance, but you have to get up."

"It hurts."

"I know." I surveyed him again wondering how the hell to get him up and to the car. There was only one thing for it. I pulled my phone from my pocket and tapped onto Beau's contact details. He answered on one ring.

"Hey, Sim."

"Beau can you get round here quick? And bring your car."

"On my way," he rushed out and the line went dead.

He must have been able to tell from the tone of my voice that it was urgent. As I looked back down at Ethan, I realised that Beau wouldn't be able to get in. I'd locked up already.

"I'm just going to let Beau in," I told Ethan. He nodded and let me go without any complaint.

As I got to the front door, I heard the banging. I quickly unlocked it with my thumb on the keypad and Beau practically fell in.

"What's happened?" His shaky hands came to my shoulders as he looked me up and down. "Has that fucker been here."

"No," I replied pulling away from him "It's Ethan, he's fallen, and I think he's broken his arm. I can't pick him up and an ambulance will take ages." I ran into the lounge confident that Beau was right behind me.

As soon as we were in the lounge, Beau moved past me and dropped down next to Ethan.

"Hey, buddy," he said soothingly. "What happened."

"I fell," his tiny voice said.

"So I see. Good job it's not your strumming arm, now that would be a disaster."

Ethan managed a small smile and when Beau deftly but gently lifted him he made no sound at all. He moved quicky through the house and to the front door standing back so that I could unlock it with my thumbprint after grabbing my bag from the coat rack. We rushed outside and Beau's Range Rover was parked on my driveway with the driver's door open and the engine running.

I rushed to open the back door and Beau moved towards it but paused.

"I'll drive. You get in the back with Ethan."

Thankful not to have to drive the huge beast of a car again, I got in and shuffled along to sit behind the driver's seat. Beau then ducked inside and gently placed Ethan in my arms. He groaned a couple of times as I tried to get him in the right position, but when Beau appeared with a rolled-up coat and placed it under Ethan's injured arm, we were ready to go.

"Okay?" he asked. When I nodded, he closed the door and ran around to the driver's side. He jumped in and within seconds we were screeching out of the drive.

twenty-six

Beau

As we pulled up at the hospital, I could hear Simone singing softly to Ethan. She had a sweet voice and it reminded me of how Cass used to sing to Bobby when he was a tiny baby. As he got older, she handed the singing duties to me, but Bobby always liked it when Cassie joined in with me—it was a great memory.

"If you help me out, I think he can walk," Simone said, bringing me back to the present. "Then you go, we'll get a taxi back."

"No way." I frowned at her in the rear-view mirror. "I'm not leaving you."

"But what if you get recognised. Can you imagine what people would say if you got caught on camera?"

I took a beat and then shook my head. "I'm not leaving you." Stretching over to the passenger side I opened the glove compartment and pulled out the baseball cap and glasses that I'd worn the night we'd gone to buy Ethan's guitar. "Right, you wait there, and I'll come and take Ethan from you."

I jumped out of the car and went to the back door, and with some manoeuvring got Ethan from her arms into mine. We then rushed off into the A&E department where we were directed to the children's department. While Simone booked Ethan in, I found a couple of seats and sat down, still holding onto Ethan.

"You doing okay, Buddy?" I asked, dipping my head down to his.

He nodded and snuggled closer to my chest. Warmth and contentment spread through me as his tiny fingers gripped my t-shirt and everything felt weirdly normal despite the unusual circumstances.

"They'll try and get someone to see him as soon as possible," Simone said, letting out an uneven sigh as she plonked down onto the chair next to mine. "The receptionist said that we're lucky as they're not too busy."

"That's good." I felt Ethan's brow which thankfully wasn't hot or clammy. "So what exactly happened?"

She rolled her eyes. "He was trying to get the iPad so he could watch some more guitar videos on YouTube. He'd already had it for a while earlier, so I'd put it away."

I thought back to Bobby and how he loved to watch stuff on my iPad. It was usually cats or dogs on skateboards or driving lawn mowers, but I never restricted the time he was allowed to use it—Cassie did, but as usual I spoiled him.

I whispered close to Ethan's ear. "You don't need to watch videos anyway I can show you everything you need to know." I tickled his side and earned myself a little giggle which caused Simone's shoulders to sag in relief.

Good to their word, it wasn't long before Ethan's name was being called. Ethan however was now whimpering with the prolonged pain, so I carried him to the bay that the doctor asked us to go to. When I laid him gently down on the bed, Ethan winced.

"The doctor is going to check you out now. Okay?"

He nodded to me and then turned his head to seek out Simone. She gave him a beautiful soft smile and reached out for his hand on his good arm.

"I'll wait outside," I said to her.

"You can stay, Dad."

The doctor's words hit me like a brick in the face. It didn't sound right.

He was wrong. I wasn't anybody's dad and the reality of it made me feel sick. My stomach turned and my chest felt like it might cave in.

Simone gasped and when my eyes met hers all I could see was sympathy. I knew it was because she cared, but I couldn't take it. Not because I didn't think I deserved it, any thoughts I'd had of it being my fault were fading. Yes, I'd made a mistake which had led to the accident, but I wasn't to blame though for the snow or the ice or the fact that the local council didn't think it was necessary to grit the lane leading into the village. The reason that I couldn't stand the sympathy in Simone's eyes was because it made it all true. I really had lost my wife and my son and people felt sorry for me, the lead singer of Warrior Creek, the twenty-six-year-old man with millions in the bank and the world at his feet.

"I have to go," I blurted out. "Be a brave boy, Ethan."

Within minutes the hospital was in my rear-view mirror.

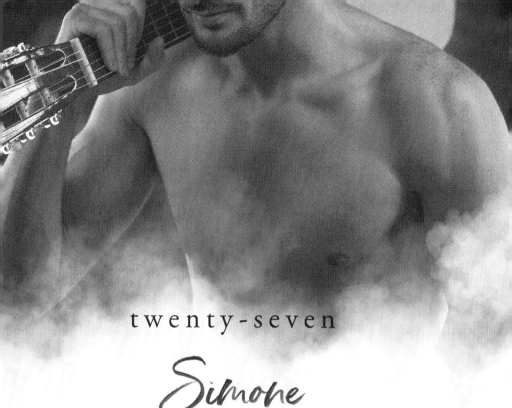

twenty-seven

Simone

After a few hours of examinations, x-rays and having a plaster cast, we were finally ready to go home. Ethan had perked up as soon as he'd seen the bright blue cast that he had and evidently didn't think it was going to be so bad, because as he whispered to me it wasn't his strumming arm.

Thinking of him playing guitar made me think of Beau and especially the torment in his eyes when the doctor had assumed that he was Ethan's dad. I totally understood why he'd had to go. It must have been awful for someone to call him the name that he'd never hear ever again from the mouth of his beautiful son. I knew that I'd have been broken and distraught. That was why I didn't blame him for running.

"Do you have a taxi number please?" I asked the receptionist as Ethan tugged on my hand.

"There's a taxi rank love," she replied, reaching for a lollipop out of a jar. "Can he have one?"

I nodded. "Yes, sure."

"There you go," she said reaching it out to Ethan. "For being a brave boy. Now, if you go out of the double doors, turn left and then first right it's there by the entrance to the physio centre."

"Thank you." I smiled and hoping that the taxi driver took cards, walked away with Ethan waving and smiling around his lollipop.

"Right," I said as we got outside. "Hold my hand and we'll go and find a taxi."

"Sim."

The call was loud and clear, and it was Beau. When I turned around my heart crashed against my rib cage because he looked so lost and as I moved towards him, I could see that his eyes were rimmed with red. His hair was messed up like he'd run his hands through it a thousand times and his shoulders had the stoop of grief once again. Glancing around to check no one had spotted him, I rushed to his side.

"Your hat. What if someone recognises you?"

He shrugged. "There's no one about and so what, I'm just helping my neighbour out."

He took a step back and it was obvious despite his words he didn't want anyone snapping a picture of us standing close or looking like we were more than friends.

Were we friends?

He'd just said he was helping a neighbour. Was that all I was and if that was the case why did that make me feel like I'd been punched in the stomach?

"You didn't have to wait," I said, clearing my throat. "We were going to get a taxi."

"It's fine," was all he said as he turned to go to his car.

When we reached it and he opened up the doors, he finally acknowledged Ethan.

"Blue plaster hey? It looks cool."

Ethan grinned and with a little help from Beau hopped up into the back seat. The booster seat was back in, and I wondered if Beau had gone home especially for it, or it had been in the boot the whole time. It really didn't matter but it helped to busy my mind with the trivialities so that I didn't have to think about anything else. One thing I did think though was that it was probably best if I got in the back with Ethan. I wasn't sure how comfortable he'd feel sitting up front with me, seeing as he could barely look me in the eye.

When I did jump in with Ethan, Beau didn't say anything, so I supposed it had been the right choice, and as we made the journey home in silence, I knew it was.

We'd gone back to being just neighbours. He'd gone back to being lost in his grief.

"Here you go." Beau finally said as we pulled up outside my house. He turned and smiled at Ethan. "You get a good night's sleep and I'll see you soon for your guitar lesson, okay?"

Ethan nodded and with a quick wave unbuckled himself, opened the door and jumped out.

"Thank you so much," I added as I opened my own door. "And for staying it was really kind of you."

"No probs," he replied and then looked down to mess around with one of the dials on his dashboard.

"Okay. See you soon… maybe." I got out and could have slapped myself for adding the 'maybe' on the end. It made me sound like a spoiled child. It made me sound like I cared that he was being off with me. Obviously, I did care. I cared that he was upset but now I'd made it sound like it was all about me.

As I closed the front door behind me and locked up the house, I wished I could replay the last few minutes. In fact the last few hours so that Ethan hadn't broken his arm, or that Beau hadn't had his heart broken again.

***

As I gently closed the door on Ethan's room after checking on him, I felt my phone buzzing in my sweatpants' pocket. It was almost eleven, and I was absolutely shattered so decided whoever it was could wait because I was going to bed. Wearily I carried on to my room and got into my pyjamas, cleaned my teeth, and finally put my phone to charge. As I plugged it in the screen lit up and I saw the text had been from Beau. Surprised, I stared down at it, having been convinced that we had taken a backward step in our friendship, as had he in his recovery.

Beau: Are you okay to talk?

I had no idea what to do. Of course I was okay to talk, but if I went back and said that I was, then I knew what would happen. He'd tell me that we couldn't be friends, only neighbours and that would hurt. I barely had anyone in my life except for Marcus and Ethan and having Beau as a friend had allowed a chink of light in. I'd felt safer knowing that he was only feet away from helping me if I needed him, and it wasn't just the physical help that I was grateful for. Being alone in the house with a little boy who hardly ever spoke was suffocating. The loneliness made me want to scream at times and made me think stupid things like maybe Richard could help out. Then I'd remember he was a rapist, and I would never allow my son to live with him. That's what your own company did to you. It made you think stupid things. It made you overthink. It made you wonder how bad a person you were if no one wanted to spend time with you.

Beau had eased all of that, first by bringing his sister into my life and second by him being willing to listen and to talk. If we went back to being just neighbours, I would be desperately alone again with my fears and my thoughts. So, if I ignored his text message, I could postpone the talk and for one more night I would have a friend.

"God, I'm pathetic," I groaned as I flicked the screen off on my phone and got into bed.

I pulled the duvet up to my chin just as a text buzzed again.

Beau: Please, Sim. I can see your light is still on.

My eyes opened wider as I looked at my lamp and then the window, not sure how Beau knew which my room was. Pushing up in bed, I looked down at the text message again. Would he be so adamant to speak to me if all he wanted to do was say, 'please don't come around anymore'? Would he have called me Sim in the text? There were so many questions buzzing around in my head and I knew the only way to deal with them was to speak to Beau and listen to what he had to say.

"Hey," I said when he answered after two rings.

"Hey."

Then there was silence and I wondered whether I should just end the call and save myself the embarrassment. Yet, he'd been the one who'd asked to talk.

"You wanted to talk."

"Yeah, I do," he replied. When he let out a deep breath, I knew he was struggling to find the words.

"Beau, it's fine. I understand how hard that was for you at the hospital and I also understand that you're grieving and want to be alone to deal with it. I get why you left, and we don't have to be friends; we can just be neighbours. Like I said, I understand."

"No," he immediately responded. "I don't think you do understand. I don't think you can imagine how I feel about being friends with you."

I chewed on my lip not sure what to say. Not sure I wanted to know how he felt because it scared me to think it would be something that would hurt.

"Tell me." How could I ever be natural with him if I was always wondering.

"It's, it's h-hard," he uttered, stumbling over the words. "I like being more than your neighbour. I like being your friend, but I hate it too. I hate it because…"

I waited for him to continue, to tell me what was upsetting him about our friendship. When the silence continued, I took a deep breath and opened my mouth, but Beau beat me to it.

"I hate it because I feel guilty that I enjoy your company. I like you and you make me feel lighter than I have done in so damn long, Sim." His voice broke and if I could have reached through the phone and gathered him into a hug I would have. I hated hugging but for him I would have.

"Beau."

"No, let me finish." Another long exhale. "Cassie was never the jealous type. She always trusted me, and I never once betrayed that trust. She didn't mind if I had female friends, or whether I was photographed standing next to other women that the press would spin some shit lie about it. She knew that I would never ever do anything to risk our family. She would have liked you. She would have encouraged me to teach Ethan guitar. She'd have invited you round for coffee, and she'd have made a friend of you. I also know that she'd want you to be my friend and to help me to deal with all this.

"The thing about Cassie was, she was the most beautiful and generous soul. She really didn't deserve to be the one to die. If anyone had to die, then it should have been me. I should have been the one who went out in the car that day to get fucking bread. I should have told her to stay home with Bobby and I'd go and get it. I didn't though and I can't change that."

This time his breath was shaky and the pause a little longer. I slid down under the duvet and turned onto my side, waiting until he was ready.

"If that had been me, she would have coped with it all so much better than I have. She was so damn capable. She really didn't need me." He let out a quiet laugh, one that was vacant of humour and joy and then continued. "We went to a film premier once and the film was about a woman who was dying and how she spent the last few months of her life putting her house in order and trying to find someone who would look after her husband and kids once she'd gone. It turned out that person was her daughters' teacher. But the plot doesn't matter, what does matter is that as we drove home Cassie made me promise if that was ever us that I'd move on. That one day I'd look for someone else."

My heart began thudding like there was a marching band inside my chest. It was so hard I could feel it in my throat, so loud that I could hear it in my ears. My stomach churned and I wondered if I wanted to hear what he was leading up to. Or what if he didn't say what I thought he was going to? Would I be disappointed? It hadn't struck me before, but what if it was possible?

"I told her that it wasn't go to happen," he continued, breaking my thoughts. "That she was stuck with me, but she went on and on until I agreed. I was lying though because there was no way I could ever move on from her. So, to lose her and Bobby in one go, it just… fuck… it didn't just break my heart, it annihilated it."

I startled, amazed at the stupid thoughts that I'd just had. There was no way he would ever think of us as anything more than friends? We were barely that if truth be told. He was a famous rock star, and I was just a single mother with enough baggage to fill the hold of a passenger plane. Why would it even cross my mind that we could be anything else? His speech though, his words about moving on and what Cassie would have wanted for him, they'd stupidly ignited surprise, a small flickering flame in my lonely heart and a stupid, idiotic thought in my head.

"Beau," I whispered. "What happened today was hard for you and you have to deal with your grief in your way. Not how your friends tell you to, or what Cassie wanted you to do. You're the one living it, and you have to live it how you see fit."

There was rustling on the other end of the line and then a pained groan. "It's so hard though, Sim."

I smiled at the use of his nickname for me, and if I was honest with myself, I was glad that the idea of us was idiotic. He was good company, becoming a good friend, great with Ethan too and that was so much better than not having him in my life because we tried something impossible.

"I know it is. I lost my dad when I was nineteen," I told him. "He committed suicide."

Beau gasped. "God, Sim, I'm so sorry."

"For a while I believed it was my fault."

"*Your fault?*" he exclaimed. "Why would you think that?"

"Because it was just after I told him I was pregnant. In my dad's eyes being nineteen, single and pregnant was not good. He was ashamed."

"You never told him, did you?" Beau stated.

"Nope." I turned to lie on my back and looked up, the night shadow dancing on the ceiling. "I told myself it would kill him. Ironic, hey."

"God. Do you know how damn strong you are?" Beau asked and I was surprised at the reverence in his tone.

"I'm not," I replied. "I'm weak and afraid, but I now know that my dad killing himself wasn't my fault. After my mum died, he lost himself in his grief and he couldn't stand to live without her any longer." I remembered those times of his crying for hours and not getting out of bed like they were yesterday, and I didn't want that for Beau. "You see, although I'm telling you to get through your grief in the best way you know how, I'm also asking you not to lose yourself in it either. Never forget what Cassie wanted for you, even if it's not something that at this moment you can comprehend. Don't drown in your sadness until you forget the reasons for breathing."

"What if my reasons for breathing are gone?" he asked so quietly I almost missed it.

"What if they haven't?" I replied. "What if they are your mum and sister, your friends? Your music, your future."

"I have thought about it you know."

"What?" I asked, knowing with a cold spindle of fear along my spine that I already knew the answer.

"Killing myself. I figured it was better to be here missing them, remembering them rather than me dying and there being nothing afterwards. Because if there is nothing, no *other side*, then I won't have those memories." He laughed. "Twisted logic hey."

"No," I sighed. "Not at all. Perfectly logical."

"You know, Sim," he retorted. "You're a good friend."

Of that I was glad and when a few minutes later we started a conversation about my lack of taste in music, I forgot any other idiotic ideas that I might have. When we finally ended the call, both yawning at two in the morning, I turned off my lamp thinking that maybe I had gone some way to save my friend's life.

twenty-eight

Beau

Waking up feeling groggy, it took me a couple of minutes to remember that I hadn't been drinking the night before. The memory of my late-night call with Simone came back and although I'd let a few things off my chest, there was still something weighing heavy in my soul.

Brushing it aside, determined to try and move forward, I got up and quickly got dressed. For some reason I felt the need to see Simone to make sure we really were okay. I knew she understood why I'd left the hospital. I knew that she felt sympathy for me, but she wasn't stupid, and I was fully aware that she knew I'd been about to end our friendship before it had even begun.

What I was sure she didn't know was why.

I was petrified of the things that I was feeling. How I felt lighter. How I felt more able to cope. How when I drove away from that hospital the one person that I wanted to talk to about it was her.

She didn't know those things and never would because I didn't think that

I'd ever be ready to admit them to myself.

When I knocked on the back door of her house, it was hesitant. Yet again my tiny little neighbour had turned me into a quivering wreck. When the door pulled open and she met me with a huge smile, I was glad I'd had the bollocks to go and see her.

"Hello," she said looking surprised to see me. "Were you expecting Ethan this morning?"

I shook my head. "Not today. I guessed he'd need to let his arm rest for a couple of days. No, I just thought I'd pop round, see if you need anything."

She moved into the kitchen, and I followed her in. There was a smell of baking and proper coffee and on the side was a tray of cake mixture ready to go into the oven.

"You've been busy." I looked around. "And that coffee smells awesome."

"You want one?" she asked, taking a mug from the drainer. "I thought it was a must seeing as I only got four hours sleep."

"Oh shit." I grimaced. "Sorry, I shouldn't have kept you talking last night."

"It's fine. Ethan never wakes before seven-thirty, so when he crawled into my bed at six complaining that his arm ached, there was no way either he or I were going to get any more sleep."

"Is he suffering?" I asked as I watched her pour out some coffee from a cafetiere on the kitchen island.

"He was, but I've given him Calpol and he's having a little nap."

I glanced at the clock on the cooker and was surprised that it was almost midday. Unlike Simone, I'd had the luxury of a lie in. The reason why I'd had that luxury, I glossed over. Today was going to be about moving forwards with my life.

"You should have taken one as well," I suggested.

"I've had too much coffee." She laughed and then rolled her eyes, handing me the mug. "I had it to keep me awake at nine this morning and then kept drinking it. I'm on my fourth one and think I might have overdosed. You may have to get me into rehab if I carry on."

"God, you don't want to go down that road." I took a sip of the coffee, and I was right, it was awesome. "Joey tried it once, but it was a complete failure."

When Simone gasped, I realised what I'd said. I was so completely at ease with her I'd divulged something we'd all done everything to keep out of the media. There had been paper talk about Joey having an addiction, but nothing confirmed—well now I'd just confirmed it.

"Should you have really said that?" Simone asked, biting at the corner of her bottom lip.

"Probably not." I grimaced and scratched the back of my neck. "You likely to tell anyone?"

"God no." She slapped a hand over her heart. "I would never."

I laughed and placed a hand on her shoulder. "I know that. I was joking."

"Seriously, Beau. I wouldn't say anything but please don't tell me."

"Sim don't be daft. I trust you not to say anything." I frowned.

"If anything about it ever came out, I'd hate to think you might consider it was me." She shook her head slowly, her eyes wide and wary. "No, don't tell me."

"Why on earth would I think that?"

"Because who knows what Richard might use against me if he ever felt the need." She chewed on the corner of her bottom lip, and it was evident that the bastard still worried her. It wasn't just about locks and video panels to keep him out. He was in her head too.

"If it makes you feel better then I won't say anything, but that's the only reason, because I trust you. Remember that."

"You barely know me," she replied, her voice unsure.

She was right I didn't but even so, I did trust her. I'd taken her into my home, I'd spilled my guts and I'd introduced her to my family and friends. Yet, it was only a couple of months since I'd first set eyes on her. Now I was going to prove it even more so.

"Okay," I said, stepping back and leaning against the island. "The other reason I came round was to ask if you'd like to go to Elliot's birthday party with me."

"Me?" she asked taking a step back.

"Yeah. Belle's going so I thought you might like to catch up with her." That wasn't why I was asking her. I wanted her to go but using Belle as a reason seemed… I don't know, more acceptable.

"Well, I don't know." She sat down at one of the island stools and looked up at me. "Are you sure Elliot wouldn't mind me going?"

"I told him that I was going to ask you," I replied, pulling out the stool next to her. "It's a barbeque in the afternoon, so we could take Ethan too."

She jerked her head back. "Ethan?"

"Yeah. I'm pretty sure El's sister will be there with her kids. We're a bit past the wild and debauched parties these days."

Simone laughed and hearing it made me smile. She had a nice laugh, soft and giggly, and I hadn't heard enough laughter in the last year or so. I realised that it made *me* feel better hearing it.

"I don't," she replied. "I won't really know anyone, and you know Ethan being the way he is."

"He doesn't talk much," I responded taking a sip of coffee. "Nothing wrong with that."

"Some people think differently." She sighed heavily and leaned forward, resting her chin on her hand. "You know even his therapist used the word *normal*."

"What?"

"Hmm. She said that if he was normal, he might have better chance of making friends. You can imagine what I thought of that," she hissed. "We didn't stay and that was our first and final session."

"Did you get another therapist?"

"No. I know he can talk. I know he's bright. He just picks and chooses who and when he uses words. I mean look at him with you, he talks loads to you."

I smiled, feeling a certain amount of pride that he did.

"There's nothing physically wrong with him," Simone continued. "Nothing has mentally scared him into not talking. He simply chooses not to."

"Yeah, well, like I said," I replied, lifting my mug. "I personally think he's got the right idea."

The smile that Simone gave to me was full of gratitude and wondered how much she'd had to shoulder alone. Not to tell her family about Richard and how she came to get pregnant with Ethan wasn't something I necessarily agreed with, but it was her life, her choice. It must have been hard though making those decisions alone.

"Listen," I said. "If you want, I could ask Di my cleaner to babysit Ethan. If you'd like to go but prefer not to take him."

"Oh, I don't know." I could see the mechanics of her brain working.

"She's worked for us for years and before she was our cleaner, she worked for a friend of mine. He was the one who recommended her as he and his family were moving to Cornwall. She often looked after his three kids, so I know she's sound. I understand though if you don't like the idea."

"I'm sure she's lovely, but can I think about it?"

I nodded. "Of course. But you'll come to the party?"

She paused for a moment and then letting out a breath, bobbed her head. "Okay."

The amount of pleasure that single head bob brought to me was a surprise. My heart picked up pace and I felt the turn of nervous excitement in my stomach. Not sure how to handle it I drank some more of my coffee.

"How are fee—" Simone started but was interrupted by the ringing of her mobile. As it rang and vibrated on the island's countertop, she looked down at it. "Shit, it's Vanessa."

"Who's Vanessa?" I asked, leaning closer.

Simone's face was panic stricken as the phone continued to rattle around. "Richard's assistant," she replied barely above a whisper.

I reached for her phone, but she quickly slammed her hand down on top of mine.

"No. I have to speak to her. I'm just worried what it's about."

"Could it be Ethan's arm?"

"He wouldn't care."

The phone's ring seemed to be more insistent and with each second that past, Simone seemed to be getting more agitated.

"Answer it," I told her. "But be assertive. Don't let her give you any shit."

She nodded, not looking convincing, and snatched up the phone.

"Vanessa," she said.

I shook her arm and mouthed silently for her to put it on loudspeaker, because if that bastard came on the line, I wanted to hear what the twisted prick had to say.

Simone pressed the screen, and I heard a clipped accent ask, "What is going on with your alarm, Miss Addison?"

"What do you mean?" Simone asked, her eyes darting in my direction.

"The alarm company can't connect to it, so Mr Richard has asked that I find out from you what the problem is."

Simone swallowed and when she grabbed my hand, I almost jumped out of my seat. She looked to me for guidance and when I gave her a reassuring nod, she took a deep breath and replied.

"I've upgraded," she said, pulling her shoulders back and lifting her head high. "It's not at Richard's expense so he doesn't need to worry. It'll protect his property better so there's no need to worry about it."

It was obvious that the Vanessa woman was shocked because there was a pause before she said, "Fine, I'll let Mr Richard know."

When she ended the call what struck me was the amount of pride I had in Simone and the fact that I suddenly had an urge to kiss her pink, full lips.

twenty-nine

Beau

As I waited outside Simone's house leaning against my car, I had no idea whether I'd done the right thing agreeing to go to Elliot's party, let alone taking her with me. I wasn't sure what people would think, seeing us arrive together. I'd spoken to Belle, and she'd told me to stop being a dick head about it. Simone was our friend and my neighbour and that was all there was to it. She'd also told me that El's sister Lucy was taking her kids so Ethan would have company. My sister seemed to know an awful lot about the arrangements, which made me think that she was talking to Elliot about a fuck of a lot more than him helping to find her a flat, like she'd told me.

When the front door opened, Ethan was the first out, smiling and waving as he ran to me.

"Hey, Ethan," I greeted him, opening the rear passenger door. "How's the arm?"

He lifted it and grinned. There was my signature pride of place with a musical note next to it. I wondered if when the plaster was taken off, if whoever removed it recognised my signature whether they'd keep it, or maybe flog it. That wasn't my huge ego talking either. I'd known someone search my bloody bin for anything with my moniker. We weren't even that famous then and had been living in a flat above a pub in the city centre. I remember we'd howled laughing because he'd found Joey's but thrust it back at me when I'd told him it wasn't mine or Elliot's. I think Joey still hadn't got over it.

While I recalled the memory, Ethan heaved himself up into the back seat and was scrambling into his booster seat. Abstractedly it occurred to me the booster spent more time in my car more than it was Simone's.

"Want me to help with the seat belt?" I asked.

He shook his head and with all the independence of a five-year old kid, struggled to fasten himself in. I watched carefully and when I was satisfied that he'd managed it, I turned back to face the house.

As I did Simone appeared in the open doorway and she took my breath away, she looked so fucking pretty. Cassie had been model beautiful, tall, leggy with long blonde hair that made her look like she'd be at home surfing in California. She wasn't aware of just how gorgeous she was and was at her happiest in sweats and her ratty old Muppets t-shirt. God, she'd been one hell of a woman and I missed her so fucking much. Then my mind focused on Simone again and my heart was still beating at double time. She was wearing a lemon coloured short-sleeved dress with tiny flowers on it, and on her feet were white Converse. She had a denim jacket in her arms and her hair was in a high ponytail, which swished from side to side as she walked towards me carrying a blue gift bag.

She was the epitome of pretty and cute and she was making me feel things that I'd been sure I'd never feel again. I was attracted to her. I had to finally admit it. I plain and simple fancied her. But I loved my wife. I loved Cassie. It was a mantra that I wouldn't allow myself to forget.

"You look nice," I said as she reached me.

There was a slight blush to her cheeks as she looked down at the stones on the driveway. "Thanks," she said so quietly it was almost a whisper.

"Let's get this over with then," I joked and started to go around the front of the car, but Simone stopped me.

"Beau, if you don't want to do this, or you'd prefer to go alone, I'd totally get it."

"No," I protested moving back to stand close to her. "I want to go, but I admit I feel nervous about it. I haven't been out socially since… well, for over a year. And I wouldn't have asked if I didn't want you there."

Her hand cupped my elbow and the contact felt good. "All you have to do is say the word and we can leave. Okay?"

I nodded, grateful that she had my back. "Okay, Sim, and thank you."

We both got in the car and set off with, I think, both of us feeling nervous.

"You heard anything else from you know who?" I asked, glancing at Ethan through the rear-view mirror. It had been a week since the call that I'd been a party to, but I'd only seen Simone a couple of times when Ethan had been round for his guitar lessons. Other than that, she'd been busy with work, creating a website for a vegan food company. As for me, I'd written a song. It wasn't the deep, meaningful stuff that I knew would be cathartic, but it lightened the darkness a little bit.

"No, I haven't," Simone answered to my question. "Doesn't mean I won't though."

When I saw her hands tremble, I felt the anger surging inside of me. "I wish you'd go to the police, Sim. It might at least scare him off even if they can't do anything."

"I can't. He's evil and I don't know what he'll do," she said quietly. "Before I moved to this house, I was thinking of going to live in Spain and made a few enquiries. I knew a guy who ran an IT company. Within days I had Social Services knocking on my door because they'd been told that I had a drug addict living with me who was a danger to Ethan. As soon as they came in, they both could see it was obvious that I didn't. It was a one bedroomed flat and I slept in the lounge which was so tiny I could barely fit a sofa and a chair in there, never mind another human being."

"And he knew you were living like that?" I asked, my fingers tightening around the steering wheel, wishing it was Richard's bloody neck. "He's a fucker."

Too late I remembered that Ethan was in the back seat. When he giggled, I glanced at Simone whose face looked something like that picture called

The Scream. Eyes and mouth wide open with horror. I couldn't help but laugh at how shocked she was and yet was on the way to a rock star's party with her son.

The laugh built in my stomach and rumbled up through my chest and out of my mouth. Ethan joined in and the sound of his giggles made me laugh even louder.

"It's not funny," she protested, but there was a lightness to her tone. When I glanced over, she had rolled her lips and was obviously trying not to laugh. "And how does he know it's a swear word," she whispered to me.

I looked at Ethan again, he was rolling around clutching his side and God it was great to see. A little boy who found the word fucker so hilarious that he was practically wetting himself. I'd missed that sort of laughter.

"No idea," I replied, "but I hope you've brought a spare pair of undies for him."

With that the laughter from the back tripled in its volume.

***

Pulling up in front of Elliot's huge square-shaped house with it's walls of glass, the nerves kicked in. When I turned the engine off, I looked up at the house which was slightly elevated and had steps up to it. As the soft skin of Simone's hand covered mine, I felt my heart pick up speed.

I love my wife. It's nerves.

As quickly as she placed it there it was gone.

I love my wife, but I miss your touch.

"You don't want to go home?" she asked.

I shook my head and then turned a smile to her. "Nope. Let's do it."

As we walked up to the gate where two of our usual security were standing, I started to feel a little easier. Jed and Tank had been with us for years and were more like old friends.

"Hey guys." I moved in for the usual handshake backslap and finally understood how much I'd missed people. "How you doing?"

"Good man," Jed a huge Jamaican guy with the whitest teeth I'd ever seen replied. "Missed you." He slapped my shoulder.

"Yeah," Tank, the eighteen stone of pure muscle, ex wrestler added. "And sorry about Cassie and Bobby. We didn't get chance to talk at the funeral, but it was a sad loss for everyone. They were both amazing."

I nodded and leaned in for another backslap. "Yeah, it's been hard. Anyway," I said, holding out a hand to Simone and Ethan. "This is Simone and Ethan. Simone's my neighbour and is friends with Belle and I'm teaching my little buddy here how to play guitar."

"No way," Jed cried and stooped down to Ethan's level, which was a long drop for him. "You need to ask Elliot or Ronnie, man. Beau here, he's the one with the voice. Can he even play guitar?"

Ethan grinned and reached up for my hand as he nodded enthusiastically. Jed shrugged and went back to his full height.

"Okay then, if you say so." He then started to laugh, a rich, deep baritone of a laugh that made you want to join in.

"Enough of taking the pee out of my guitar skills," I replied. "Let's get in and get something to eat and drink."

As I stood aside to let Simone past, she smiled at both men and said hello quietly.

"Lovely to meet you, Simone," Tank answered. "And Ethan if you want to know any wrestling moves, you come and see me once that plaster is off."

Simone and I both laughed as Ethan's eyes lit up with the prospect. We then walked in together and there was that feeling of normality once again.

thirty

Simone

Elliot's house was amazing from the outside. All cream rendering and glass so it looked like three boxes interlinked. As for his garden, I felt like I'd walked into an award-winning show piece. Everything had clean lines and edges with box hedges and tall trees in huge pots. There was a large seating area of a u-shaped rattan sofa with lime green cushions and purple throw pillows and opposite that what looked like a dance area with flashing lights and a DJ deck under a pergola with a sliding roof. Beyond that was what seemed like miles of lawn with a path down the middle which was covered in arches of white roses. Halfway down was another seating area, the same u-shaped sofa but this had purple cushions and lime green throw pillows. Then right at the end I could see some kids bouncing up and down on a sunken trampoline, with what looked like a miniature swinging pirate ship next to it.

"Wow," I muttered to Beau as he led me towards Elliot. "This garden is amazing. The house too."

"I know. He designed the garden himself," Beau replied with pride. "He was going to do some designs for us, but then…" He trailed off and scrubbed a hand down his face and then looked down at Ethan. "Hey, you see the trampoline up there, do you fancy having a go. That's okay, isn't it?"

"Yes of course," I replied. "It's sunken so I doubt he'll do much more damage. Maybe no acrobatics though Ethan, okay?"

He grinned and nodded, running off towards the end of the vast garden leaving Beau and I watching after him as if we were both his parents.

"Sorry," Beau said, nudging me with his elbow. "I should have asked first. Lydia and Poppy will take care of him."

"They're Elliot's nieces, is that right?"

"Yeah. Poppy is four I think." He screwed up his face in contemplation. "And Lydia is seven. She'll mother him and Poppy will have him digging for worms."

"Well he seems okay." I bit at my thumbnail watching as he approached the girls. I wondered how they'd be with the fact he didn't speak but within seconds the taller of the two had an arm around Ethan's should and was leading him onto the trampoline where they proceeded with gentle bouncing.

"Looks like you were right about her mothering him."

"Told you," he said with a laugh. "So, you like El's house then?"

"I do, it's beautiful." I smiled. "You know I've always wanted to live in a big house like this, but maybe a Tuscan mansion would be more my style. You know those with a huge family kitchen that fits comfy sofa's in and one of those central stairways that has a balconied landing."

Beau didn't answer and when I looked up his whole demeanour had stiffened. I looked to see two men approaching us, one of whom seemed to be more than a little drunk.

"What's wrong?" I asked.

"Gill Roberts, he's a session musician and I fucking hate him, but Elliot thinks he's okay for some reason. I'd prefer to kick him in the bollocks," he growled but then nudged me.

"What?"

"Thank fuck for that."

I looked to see the two men had been diverted from our direction by a beautiful tall woman in a bright red trouser suit. She had auburn hair that streamed down her back and the most amazing gold boots.

"Who's that?" I asked. "She's gorgeous."

"That's Caitlin Monroe."

The name rang a bell and after a few seconds it struck me. "The reclusive artist?" I whisper hissed, my eyes still pinned to the gorgeous woman chatting animatedly. "She doesn't look like a recluse."

"She isn't really." Beau chuckled. "But the idea that she is sells paintings. She goes out in disguise a lot. She's a big friend of Elliot's, so as you can see, we mix in very different circles at times. Elliot used to love the celebrity shit, whereas I only ever wanted a cup of tea and my bed after a show."

"He doesn't like it now then?"

"Nah, not so much. He met a lot of these people when we first started and then after about two years he stopped going out to parties and joined me for the cup of tea. Not sure why, people like Caitlin stuck around and unfortunately Gill, but a lot of his other so-called mates dropped off when he wasn't picking up the bill."

"God," I replied. "People can be horrible can't they?"

"That's one word for them," Beau replied with a laugh. "I'd call them something else entirely and it begins with a c."

"Ugh, that's a horrible word." I slapped a hand against his stomach.

"No it isn't, it's the perfect word for some of the people in our industry. Elliot will agree."

"Elliot will agree with what?" Elliot asked as we reached him.

"That the c word is awful," I said as the same time as Beau said, "That the c word is awesome."

Elliot grinned and pointed at me. "I'm with Beau, sorry, Simmy." He then leaned in and kissed my cheek. "I'm really glad that you came."

I held out the gift bag between us. "This is for you."

"You didn't have to." Elliot seemed surprised as he took the bag from me. "My birthday isn't until tomorrow, but can I open it now?"

"You big child," Beau said.

"Well I notice you haven't got a gift with you." Elliot narrowed his eyes on Beau as he put his hand inside the bag.

"I should point out that Ethan chose them." I winced hoping that it wasn't too cheesy, but Ethan had been adamant about what he wanted to get.

As he ripped the paper off his eyes kept finding mine and the kindness in them made me feel much more at ease. I'd been nervous about coming, not just because I hardly ever went anywhere, but I had no idea whether it would be full of famous people or not.

"Ah that's brilliant," Elliot cried as he ripped off the paper and dropped it into the bag. "Just what I wanted."

I had no idea why, but Ethan had picked a doorplate with the name Elliot on it and a pencil with a rubber on the end, the pencil also having Elliot on it.

"I bet you haven't already got either of those, have you?" I asked.

"I love them and I'm going to put the name plate on my office door."

He leaned forward with his arms out for a hug and immediately my whole body stiffened. Before he had chance, Beau poked him on the shoulder.

"What the hell is Gill Roberts doing here?"

When Elliot turned to Beau, I almost collapsed with the relief. I could hug Belle and Sylvie, and I could just about handle Beau, but everyone else made me feel uncomfortable. I wondered if Beau had seen how I'd reacted and stepped in to help.

"He's okay," Elliot replied, rolling his eyes. "You just hate him because of that time when we were in Michigan."

"Of course I do. He smacked my wife's arse and told her where to find him when she'd had enough of me." Beau grumbled as he shoved his hands into his pockets. "He's a tit."

Elliot laughed and when I looked at Beau whose lips were twitching. It was nice to think he could finally laugh about his wife. He was getting a little better each day.

"Whatever," Elliot said. "Now, where's Ethan so I can thank him?"

Beau pointed up the garden where Elliot's nieces and Ethan were now running around. It was then that I saw Joey and Ronnie approaching. It was nice to see them, but I'd realised that these men were huggers, and I was a little on edge.

"Hey," Ronnie said his bright blue eyes sparkling. "Great to see you both." He kissed my cheek and again I heaved a sigh of relief. When Joey then leaned in, I thought I might freak out, but once again Beau saved me.

He stepped between us and pulled Joey in for a man hug.

"Where's Ethan?" Ronnie asked.

"He's playing with the girls," Elliot replied. "I'm just going up there to thank him for my present."

"Ah what did you get?" Ronnie asked with all the excitement of a young kid as he followed Elliot in the direction of the children.

"Looks like Ronnie's got a new best friend," Joey said laughing.

I felt Beau stiffen beside me and knew he must be thinking of the other best friend that Ronnie used to have.

"What time is Belle coming?" I asked to try and help Beau move away from the dark place.

"She wasn't sure what time train she was getting," he replied, shifting from foot to foot. "So she's going to text me when she's half an hour away and I'll nip up to the station."

"It'll be lovely to see her." I smiled at Beau and when he smiled back it appeared that the memories might not have been swamping him as I'd feared.

"Right," he said, flicking Joey's ear. "I'm going to get us some drinks. You stay and keep Simone company. I'll be right back. Wine or beer, Sim?"

"I think I'll have a beer, thanks."

"Usual, Joe?"

Joey nodded and as Beau walked away, he turned to me. "Right tell me word for word what Beau said when he saw that Gill Roberts was here."

***

"That's about time as well," Ronnie said as he settled down next to me on the rattan sofa. He nodded over to Belle who was chatting to Elliot and looking particularly cosy. She arrived about an hour ago, turning up in a taxi which pissed Beau off for about five minutes.

"Have they liked each other for a while then?" I asked, taking a sip of beer.

"Like forever. At first Beau didn't like the idea, but that was more about Belle hanging around with us than her and El being together. Then we thought Elliot might finally be getting his act together about three years ago, but he arsed about for too long and Belle met someone who she really liked.

When that ended after a few months I think she hoped that it might happen then, but the timing was crap again."

"Why what happened?"

"You heard of Katie Delaney, the popstar from New Zealand. She made her name on TikTok or one of those other shit social media things. Well, she was in the picture by then."

"Yes, I know her. She had a couple of hits but then disappeared." I looked over at Elliot and pictured him with the tiny blonde who sang cheesy pop songs. He was much better suited to Belle.

"Yeah, he was all in with her, even talked about maybe proposing and then one day he just announced it was over. Wouldn't tell anyone what happened, just that it was amicable. Which is pretty strange considering when they saw each other after that they could barely look at each other."

"Poor Elliot," I whispered, surprised again that I'd been told some quite private stuff. They obviously trusted me and that made me feel special, like I did have friends after all.

"Maybe this time is the right time," Ronnie sighed and took a drink from his own bottle of beer. "You seem to have become good friends with Belle, has she said anything to you about it?"

I shook my head. "Only that he was helping her to look for a flat. We tend to talk about girly stuff whenever we chat. It's just nice to have a friend," I explained, my tongue loosening with the beer. "I don't have many."

"You've got Beau and us." Ronnie grinned and tapped my bottle with his.

"I get the feeling you'd all rather be my son's friend than mine."

"No, that's just not true," he joked, nudging me with his shoulder. "He is good fun though."

Silence fell as we both watched everyone around and then Ronnie cleared his throat.

"How's he really doing?"

I looked at him and followed his gaze which was on Beau who was playing darts with Joey. I wasn't sure that I was qualified to answer. I hardly knew him, any of them, so I could only answer with my personal experiences of the rock star.

"He's brilliant with Ethan. Admittedly, we had a little bump in the road a couple of weeks back." I told Ronnie all about them watching the music video that Cassie had starred in. As I explained how Beau reacted, Ronnie closed his eyes on what I guessed was his own grief.

"I can't imagine what he's been through," Ronnie finally said. "We lost them too, but they were Beau's life, his future. The fact that he's even here today is a miracle."

"I'm pretty sure it was a hard decision for him, but maybe not as hard as it might have been a few months ago." I watched as Beau laughed at something Joey said. He looked healthy and light, there was less darkness dragging him down than there had been when I first met him. The handsome man who was rich and famous and who'd become my friend all because of my son. It was difficult to believe. "Can I ask you something, Ronnie?"

"Yeah, sure."

"How come you've all been so nice to me and told me stuff that I could so easily go to the press about?" It troubled me because no one had ever been nice to me for no reason before. Richard only gave me a job so that he could groom me and then take what he wanted from me.

Ronnie gave me a soft smile and leaned his shoulder against mine.

"Because we've been in this business long enough to know who to trust and who not to trust."

"I know but you don't know me. This could all be an act."

Ronnie shook his head. "Nah, you're too honest and kind. Besides, it's because of you we've got our friend back."

As his words swirled around my brain, Beau let out a roar of laughter and when I looked over our gazes locked. It was then I knew that I wanted more than friendship with him, and I'd been kidding myself all along to think otherwise.

thirty-one

Beau

Looking over the rim of my glass of orange at Simone sitting on a secluded bench under a cream-coloured sail thing, I could see that she was a little tipsy. It was pretty funny seeing as she was normally so quiet and maybe a little strait-laced at times, yet Ronnie told me that she'd told him a really filthy joke. Something to do about a woman, a tattoo and being numbed—and that was all he'd say as Ethan was standing next to me. She didn't seem too unsteady on her feet or anything like that, but I'd been keeping an eye on her. I knew she wouldn't want to get wasted in front of Ethan, but she must have a lightweight because as far as I knew she'd only had a couple of bottles of beer.

"Hey you."

I turned to see Ali, our manager grinning at me with her arms open wide.

"Ali." I bundled her into a hug, and it occurred to me at that moment how much I'd missed her. "Is Ingrid with you?"

"No, she's got a photoshoot in Prague." Ingrid, Ali's partner was a fashion photographer, a job which took her all over the world. When we were touring, she tried to fit jobs in and around our schedule, so she was always with Ali. "I've just got back from Edinburgh looking at a band we might sign."

"Any good?"

She shrugged. "They have potential, but they need a year touring the student union bars first."

Ali knew her stuff, so she was probably right. She'd never steered us wrong anyway.

"You look good," she said, cupping my face. "Not drinking either."

I looked down at my glass. "I haven't given up, but I'm driving."

"I thought you'd be staying so you could all jam into the early morning." She laughed and shook her head. "Remember that time you went to that actor's party and ended up jamming."

"Fuck yeah," I recalled. "And that music producer from Holland told us if we practiced more, we could be quite good."

"And you'd won the Grammy the week before?"

"Yeah, and he gave us the card of a guy who did performance coaching."

We both laughed and it felt good.

"Anyway," I said, once our laughing had died down. "When are you going to ask me about the interview?"

Ali shook her head. "I'm not. You told El no. I respect that."

I jerked my head back a little surprised. Ali was one of the most tenacious people I knew. If she wanted something she usually got it.

"Whatever you might think, Beau everything I did was only ever for the good of Warrior Creek. You as people were my main priority, sod what the record company or the management company said they wanted. I just happened to think that some of those requirements were good for the four of you." She reached on her tiptoes and kissed my cheek. "Right, I should go and find Elliot and get myself a drink. You seen him anywhere?"

"Nope," I grinned. "But my sister is missing too."

"About bloody time." She rolled her eyes and turned to leave.

"Ali," I called, making her look back over her shoulder. "Send me the details of the interview and I'll see how I feel about it."

She turned back and placed a hand against her chest. "Are you sure?"

"I can't promise anything but taking a look won't hurt."

She gave me the brightest smile and then went to find our host, who I was pretty sure was feeling my sister up somewhere in his house.

As I watched Ali go, I noticed that the guy who'd been with Gill Roberts was sitting a little too close to Simone. Not only that but he was passing her a huge glass of wine.

"Ethan's now collecting worms with Lydia and Poppy." It was Ronnie back after playing football with Ethan and one of Elliot's cousin's boys. "It seems that my footie skills aren't as interesting as slimy wiggly things."

"Yeah okay," I replied distractedly.

The guy was leaning into Simone, who although she was laughing looked a bit uncomfortable. She took a large swig of her wine and the guy appeared to be urging her to knock it back in one go, the stupid prick.

"I've always thought I was quite good at—"

"The little fucker." I didn't hear anything else that Ronnie had to say because Simone's glass was being filled again and the guy had his other arm around her. "Not happening, dick piece."

Discarding my glass on the grass, I stormed over to where the two of them were sitting. My mind was reeling with what I wanted to do to *him* for putting Sim in that position. It was obvious what his fucking game was, and I was to blame because I shouldn't have left her alone. As soon as Ronnie left her, I should have gone back to her instead of standing off to one side and watching her like a creep.

"Get your fucking hands off her," I growled at the guy as I grabbed his jacket and pulled him up from the seat.

Simone's eyes were heavy as she looked up at me and there was no way she was that drunk on two beers and a glass of wine.

"Who the fuck do you think you are?" the guy slurred, rocking on his feet. "She's quite happy in my company, aren't you, darling?" He leaned forward, putting his face into Simone's and she reared backwards.

"Beau."

My name sounded like a desperate plea on her lips, and it hit me right in the chest. Dropping to my knees in front of her, I took hold of her face in my hands and looked into her eyes. She'd definitely been given something. I'd seen Joey high enough times to know.

"What the fuck did you give her?" I yelled at the guy, who like a fucking idiot was still hanging around. If he'd had sense he'd have pissed off. As he didn't, I jumped up and with one punch had him on the ground.

"Beau, I don't feel well."

I dropped back down in front of her and took her hands in mine. "Do you think you can walk. You need to drink some water." With sweat prickling on my forehead, I looked over my shoulder, frantically looking for help. "*Ronnie. Ronnie.*"

He looked over, mid conversation with a girl I knew he'd shagged once or twice a couple of years before and immediately recognised that something was wrong. He sprinted over and went to the floor next to me.

"What's wrong? Something to do with that guy passed out?" He looked down at the bastard on the floor.

"He's not passed out," I growled. "I fucking punched him. I think he's given Sim something."

"What!" Ronnie moved closer and looked into Simone's eyes. He was more adept at spotting someone high than even I was, seeing as he always seemed to be the one who had to bail Joey out of situations. "Fuck. We need to get her to a hospital."

"No, no. Ethan. No hospital." Simone tried to lift her arms to push us away, but it was as if they were lead weights or something, but they wouldn't move. Breathing heavily, she moaned again. "Beau, Richard."

"Shit," I muttered. She didn't want to go to hospital in case Richard found out. "She won't leave Ethan," I said to him. "You think we can sort it?"

Ronnie looked at me and let out a breath recalling the numerous times we'd 'sorted' Joey. "Yeah, probably. We could do with finding out what he gave her. My guess is he's roofied her with something."

"What's going on?" I looked up to see Elliot. He was clutching a bottle of water, obviously having reached the point where he knew he'd had enough—that was El, always the sensible one.

"Give me the water," I snapped and held out my hand, making a grabbing motion.

"Why? What's wrong?" He handed over the water and peered around me. "Shit, is she okay?"

"No, we think that dick there on the ground gave her something," Ronnie replied as I cajoled Simone to drink some water.

"Who the fuck is he?" I demanded, my eyes on Simone.

"He's a mate of Gill's, don't know his name," Elliot said from behind me.

"Well, you should do. It's your damn party, El. If that twat has hurt her…" I couldn't bear to think of what might have happened if I hadn't been watching. It made me sick to my stomach and as Simone lolled to one side, missing the bottle that I was holding to her mouth, panic gripped my heart and squeezed it like a rag. "Sim, sweetheart, try and drink some more okay."

She nodded but her eyes were practically closed, and it was quite clear all she wanted to do was sleep.

"What the hell has he given her?" Ronnie said.

"Get that fucker up and get him to tell us," I spat out.

At that moment Gill Roberts appeared and if I hadn't been feeding water to Simone, I'd have put him out too.

"Did Brad pass out?" he asked with a laugh.

"Gill, you need to tell us what gear he brought with him," Elliot said, calm, collected and far too politely for my liking.

"Get your fucking dickhead of a mate awake," I hissed. "And get him to tell us what he gave to her."

"He wouldn't, he's—" Gill started.

"He would and he did." I turned my head to look up at him. "Get him awake, Gill before I do. And believe me the only reason I haven't called the coppers at this point is out of courtesy to Elliot and her because she won't want them involved."

Gill to his credit turned and looked at his mate with disgust, kicking him in his side.

"Brad, get up you piece of shit. *Now*."

Brad stirred and brought his hand up to feel his jaw where I'd landed the punch. It was already starting to bruise which didn't surprise me as my hand was throbbing.

"I'll fucking sue you," he groaned, pulling himself into a sitting position.

"Shut up," Gill barked. "What the hell did you give her?" He pointed at Simone; his words spat out in fury.

"Look, I think we need to call the police," Ronnie said, moving close to look at Simone's eyes. "And I'd feel better if she went to hospital."

"No," she groaned. "Please no. Richard. Beau, Richard, Ethan."

"Okay, sweetheart," I said softly. "We won't, I promise."

"Beau I—"

"No, Ron, she doesn't want to." I stared at him and gave a small, almost imperceptible shake of my head to indicate I couldn't tell him then, but I would."

"What have you given her?" Elliot ground out. "Because if Beau doesn't kick you in the fucking bollocks, I will."

Apparent that she wasn't going to drink any more water, I put the bottle down and cupped her face. "You think you can walk?" I asked her.

Simone's eyes closed and her head bobbed away from my touch as she passed out.

"I'm taking her home. Ron can you just hold her a second." He got up onto the bench next to her and then put his arms around her. As soon as I was sure he had her, I stood and turned to Elliot. "Can you get Ethan for me. Give me a few minutes to get her into my car and then bring him."

"Yeah, sure. I think he's with Belle and the other kids. Last I saw they were inside doing some drawing." He turned and ran off up the garden towards the house.

"One last chance," I said getting into Brad's face. "Tell me what you slipped her, or I'll pummel your face until even you fucking mother doesn't recognise you."

"Tell him," Gill hissed.

"Okay, okay. It's jusa sedative. Over counter one," he said, slurring his words, drunk from alcohol and my punch.

I leaned down and grabbed his shirt, pulling him inches from my face. "You're a fucking piece of shit and I will make sure you pay for this one way or the other." I then threw him back to the ground and spun around to see Ali coming towards us. The relief was immense because Ali always knew what to do. She always sorted our shit out and it struck me how sometimes we totally undervalued her.

"Ali," I groaned. "He's fucking slipped her a sedative." The idea of what might have happened had I not seen it, rose to the forefront of my mind and I could practically taste the need to kick shit out of him.

"Okay," Ali said pushing past me to kneel in front of Simone. "Let's get her into the house and make her be sick. Ronnie run and tell Elliot not to get Ethan to the car just yet. Get Belle to keep him occupied." She turned to me. "Beau take her upstairs through the side door so you don't bump into Ethan and I'll come up with some salt water. Gill," she said her voice icy. "Get that wanker away from here and if you ever want to work in the music industry again you need to kick people like him to the curb. And you, you bastard, if I hear or see from you even in the distance, or you go with a hundred feet of anyone here today, I will personally see to it that your life is ruined beyond repair. Drake!" she yelled and another security guard who who I didn't know appeared. "Make sure that these two men leave Elliot's property, immediately."

"Will do, Miss Bennet. Come on," he commanded and hitched a thumb at Gill.

"Get up," Gill said as he dragged Brad to his feet. "I'm sorry, Beau. I had no clue he was like that."

I didn't acknowledge him; all I could do was focus on Simone whose head had lolled forward onto Ali's shoulder. She looked so small and vulnerable, and I wanted to kill Richard, Brad and all predatory men like them with my own bare hands. How dare they take what they want or manipulate a woman into giving them that without permission. A woman shouldn't have to say no, she should be given the option to say yes.

With my blood boiling, I bent, put my arms under Simone, and lifted her. Her arm fell to the side and her head lolled onto my chest and if I couldn't see her chest rising and falling, I would have thought she was dead. I'd seen that once and there was no way I wanted to go through that pain ever again.

thirty-two

Simone

The quiet voice whispering in my ear seemed familiar, and I wasn't in my bed but that felt familiar too. Everything felt fuzzy though. My head. My skin. Even the voice saying my name again sounded like they were talking through cotton wool. Slowly I opened my eyes to see who it was that was talking to me.

"B-Beau?"

"Hey, time to drink some water, sweetheart." His voice was soft and soothing, and it brought a smile to my face.

"You're here." I tried to lift my hand to touch his face, but my arm felt heavy and impossible to move. "I really like you; did you know that?"

He laughed softly and his rough fingertips brushed my hair to one side. "I didn't know that no."

I sighed heavily and snuggled closer to his body. "Hmm, well I do. A lot, but I'll tell you about it later."

"Okay, drink this first and then you can go back to sleep."

I felt a straw at my lips and sucked up. The cool water hit my tongue and it felt so good.

"Right, back to sleep now."

"What time is it?"

"Half past three in the morning," his soothing, soft voice said.

I remembered being at a party and Ethan playing with two little girls. "Ethan?" I asked, trying to push up, but was stopped by a firm hand on my shoulder.

"He's tucked up in bed, fast asleep and has been since nine last night."

"Oh no, that's way past his bedtime. He'll want to sleep in in the morning," I groaned, my eyes feeling heavy again.

"That's no problem. It's Sunday tomorrow, so we can all just chill out. Now go to sleep."

"Okay. Night, night, Beau."

"Night sweetheart."

***

As I opened my eyes, I thought that my head might explode with the pain from the effort. It felt like there was someone inside it thumping away at my skull, the bit between my eyes, with a hammer. My mouth was dry, and I was absolutely roasting. I needed to wee too. When I tried to push up though, I couldn't move, mainly because there was a heavy arm across my chest and strong, denim clad leg entwined with my bare one.

Then it struck me. I was in a t-shirt that was far too big for me, but I didn't remember getting undressed, plus there was someone in the bed with me. A bed with navy blue bedding, not peacock green like mine at home. I looked around the room and recognised it as the one I'd stayed in when my house was flooded. This was Beau's spare room in his house.

Then another thought struck me, that someone was Beau. I didn't even have to look at his face. I could smell him. That gorgeous, familiar scent of his.

"Beau," I said cautiously as I poked at his arm that was over my chest. "Beau, are you awake?"

He made a growling noise and muttered something about it not being time and then snuggled closer to me. My heart sped up and my hands started to shake and not because I was afraid of his touch or the fact that he had me pinned down. This was nothing like the last time that I was pinned down, this was… nice. This made me have butterflies. My hands were shaking because of what this could mean if I let myself think about it. Because I wanted to touch him.

"Shit." He was suddenly wide awake and pushing himself up. "What time is it. I forgot your water."

"What happened?" I asked, disjointed images of the night before flitting in front of my eyes. "Actually, I think I need to go to the bathroom first. Can you—"

"God, yes, sorry." He moved his leg and then dropped his feet to the floor. "I'll tell you everything when you get back."

Practically running to the small bathroom, I looked down at the band t-shirt and wondered if he'd put me in it. When I realised that I at least had my underwear on there wasn't a much dread pooling in my stomach. The thought of Beau undressing me though did strange things to me. My nipples involuntarily hardened, and something happened between my legs that made me feel sexy and dirty all at the same time. As I closed the door, I wondered why my attraction to Beau had suddenly become up front and centre when I had been doing so well at denying it.

When I opened the door and walked back into the bedroom, Beau didn't help my sudden onslaught of sexual tension. He was sitting on the bed looking at his phone, back against the grey fabric headboard and his legs out in front of him, ankles crossed and feet bare. I had to take a deep breath before I approached him to try and centre myself and stop myself from jumping on him. What had happened I had no clue. I could hardly remember the previous night which I knew was probably through alcohol, but I'd woken up feeling hungover and sex hungry for the man I could never have.

"That's better," I said as stood at the side of the bed.

Beau looked up from his phone and smiled softly. "I think we'd better talk about last night."

I chewed on my lip and contemplated whether to get back on the bed and sit next to him or take the small armchair in the corner. When he shifted himself up the bed and then moved to the right, I figured that he'd made my mind up for me.

Edging myself onto the bed, it occurred to me that my legs were bare, so I lifted the duvet and covered them up. What happened with Richard had resulted in me hiding myself for a long time. Wearing long skirts or jeans and full-length sleeves or baggy tops became the norm for me, but after a while I started to feel more comfortable in my own skin and started to wear clothes a little less like those for a seventy-year-old woman. Now I wasn't scared to let a man see my body, but I was nervous about Beau seeing it.

"What happened?" I asked. "I remember drinking a couple of bottles of beer and then some man called Brett or Brad or something like that offering me a glass of wine. After that I have no clue."

Beau's nostrils flared as he breathed out and his grip on his phone tightened.

"He slipped you a sedative."

As he said the words, my blood ran cold and the hairs on my arms stood on end.

"No," I gasped.

"I was watching you and I didn't like the way he was trying force you to drink the wine he'd given to you. By the time I got over to you, which was seconds, you'd gone from tipsy to flat out drunk, to the point you were already almost comatose." He drew in a shaky breath and grabbed my hand. "I was so fucking scared, Sim."

"He was going to… Oh my God."

Tears started to crawl down my cheeks making sticky paths until they dropped and landed on Beau's t-shirt that I was wearing. If Beau hadn't been nearby, the idea of what might have happened was too terrifying to contemplate.

"Why me?" I whispered. "Why would he want to do that to me? Do I have something about me that makes men think it's okay to do that sort of thing? Do I look like a victim, Beau? Do I throw off some sort of aura that says I can be abused without consequence?" Twisting my fingers together, the tears came faster, and my cold body started to shake uncontrollably. Beau pulled me against him, wrapping me in his warmth and security.

"No. No you don't, so don't even think that. It was on him," he said, kissing the side of my head. "It was all on him, him and men like Richard, who don't give a shit about anything more their own wants. There is nothing that shows you as a victim, he was a predator, that's it pure and simple."

"Ethan." I try to pull away from him, but he won't let me. "Did Ethan see anything?" I cry, panic stricken.

"No, nothing. He thinks you ate something dodgy. Ali gave you some salt water to make you be sick and we thought you'd finished at Elliot's but on the way home you were sick in a bucket."

"A bucket?" I asked through my tears.

"Elliot thought it safer to take one. Ethan sat up front with me and you sat in the back with Belle."

"Belle's here." Another image flashed through the foggy memories of the night before. "She went to the party but she's staying here at your house for a few days."

He nodded and squeezed my hand. "Yeah, she is. She's the one who got your clothes off, seeing as you puked again when we were walking you through the hall. This time it went all over you."

Mortified, I slapped a hand against my mouth. "Oh my God, I'm so sorry. I'll pay for any damage or a cleaner or—"

"Sim," he soothed with a smile. "It's fine. It was just a bit of puke. It's tiled floors, it cleaned up."

"What about Ethan?"

"He slept with Belle last night in one of the other spare rooms. We didn't want him to be alone if he woke up in the night, so hope that's okay. Elliot wanted us all to stay there, but I wanted to get you home. I thought you'd prefer it."

I nodded and swiped at the wet on my cheeks. "Thank you, so much. I don't know what I'd have done without you these last couple of months."

"It's fine." Beau's eyes went to mine and locked into place, rendering me speechless and unwilling or unable to move even an inch. His hand came to cup my cheek and his touch instantly set me on fire. My blood heated up and everything below my waist came to life for the first time in years. "I was so scared, Sim. I thought that I'd lost you."

"Beau, I—"

I had no idea what I was going to say and didn't even need to think about it because his mouth was on mine. His tongue urged me to open and when I did, I became lost in the urgency of the kiss. Beau's hands in my hair and his chest rubbing against mine were everything. He kissed like he'd been put on earth to do that and only that. It was hard when it needed to be, soft when I wanted it to be and earth-shattering as it brought me back to life.

"Hey, are you awake yet?"

The sound of Belle's voice broke the spell. All the pieces of my heart that were being put together like a jigsaw, fell apart and drifted away because as we pulled apart and distanced ourselves from each other, I saw the regret on Beau's face.

thirty-three

Beau

When I walked into the kitchen after having taken a shower, I expected to see a smirk on my sister's face. An 'I told you she was amazing' grin. She didn't, busy cooking breakfast; stirring beans on the hotplate while toast cooked in the new toaster that I'd asked Di to get for me.

"Cheesy baked beans on toast," she explained. "Ethan's request. He's in your office practicing."

I nodded and looked down at the pile of mail that had been delivered. Flicking through the mainly manila-coloured envelopes.

"Was he okay through the night?" I asked.

"Yes, he slept like a log. He's a little heater as well." Belle laughed as she turned down the beans. "He cuddled up to me and was roasting."

"He wasn't upset though, about Sim?"

Something twinkled in Belle's eyes, but I chose to ignore it. I couldn't go there, not yet. The kiss had been enough to send me over the edge. As soon as Belle came into the room to check we were awake and ready for breakfast, Sim and I pulled apart and hadn't looked at each other or spoken a word to each other in the whole thirty minutes since then.

The moment that we separated my first thought had been, 'I love my wife, what the fuck am I doing?'. My second thought had been, 'I love my wife, but she isn't coming back but this beautiful woman in front of me is here. She's real and she's alive and she's maked *me* feel alive.'

For a long time, the thought of being with another woman, finding another woman attractive, touching her, being with her and wanting her sexually had filled me with dread. There was no way I could even fathom it. It wasn't possible. Over the last couple of months though, particularly the last one, that dread had turned to guilt. How could I betray my wife like that? I loved her, would always love her. The idea that I found someone attractive made me feel like the biggest bastard on the planet.

Then I kissed Simone. After weeks of denying she was anything more than my neighbour, I given in to the feelings buried deep and took her mouth with mine. I'd wanted to taste her. I'd wanted to do more. I'd practically felt the life creeping through my veins and heating up my body. Another twenty seconds and I'd have had her underneath me and begging her to let me more to her than her neighbour.

And that was why I felt fucking guilty because I didn't feel bad about it. I enjoyed it and I wanted to do it again.

"Is Simone coming down for breakfast, or is she going back to sleep?" Belle asked.

"She's coming down, I think. I'm not sure." I studied an envelope far longer than necessary to avoid making eye contact with my sister. She wasn't stupid and she'd see that things had changed within me.

"Maybe I'll give her a shout," Belle said and in my peripheral vision I could see she was setting plates out.

"She'll come down when she's ready," I snapped.

Why I was being a shit about it I had no idea, other than if she came down and looked at me like I was another fucking bastard man who'd tried to take from her, I might lose it. When the door opened and Simone shuffled unsteadily into the kitchen, I didn't see regret or hate. So much worse, I saw rejection.

My chest hurt as I took a deep breath and closed my eyes. I hated that I'd become the sort of person who could make her feel like that. I hated that she would think that I'd push her away after she'd been the one to bring me back to life. Was that how everyone saw me? Was that what grief had done to me? Opening my eyes, I smiled and hoped it was enough.

"Hey," I said, taking a step towards her. "Do you want to sit down?"

"God, Simmy," Belle said before Sim could answer. "You look so pale." She moved to her and pulled her into a hug. I noticed that as opposed to usual, Sim didn't pull back or freeze and I was glad she had my sister. "It was so scary."

"Belle," I said, placing a hand on the small of her back. "Let her sit down."

"God, yes, sorry."

She pulled away and as she did Sim's eyes met mine. I hoped that what she saw in them wasn't remorse because I would never regret her, no matter what. After a few seconds of drinking each other in, Sim moved, and my hand instinctively went to hers.

"I'm not sure I should have got out of bed," she said quietly. "I felt okay at first, and in the shower, but now I don't feel so good." She was wearing a pair of Belle's jeans and a hoodie of mine, and it drowned her, making her look even smaller and frailer than she already was.

"Why don't you go back to bed," I suggested, guiding her to one of the stools. When she didn't have the strength to heave herself up onto it, I put my hands under her arms and lifted her. Our gazes met again, this time hers was shy and I was sure mine was full of heat from having my hands on her. I looked away because that was the last thing she needed after what she'd gone through. My kiss had been the last thing she'd needed, but I'd been a fucker of enough to take it anyway.

"I should get Ethan home," she eventually said.

I looked at her and tried to neutralise my gaze, now in knots on how to be with her.

"He's fine here. Belle has made him cheesy beans on toast and then I'll do some practice with him on his new guitar. He's in there now trying to play chords with his broken arm."

Simone laughed quietly and grabbed a hold of the island. "Not very successfully by the sound of it, I'm afraid."

"Well Beau will sort him out," Belle added. "He's right, go back up to bed for a while."

I waited, the silence seeming endless until she eventually said, "Okay, if you don't mind."

And I didn't because the thought of her not being where I couldn't keep an eye on her made my stomach churn with fear.

***

Ethan and I had practiced for an hour before I could see his arm was starting to ache. I placed him in front of the TV with Belle and left them watching Harry Potter. I checked on Sim, and she was fast asleep on top of the bed, so I got a duvet from another spare room and placed it over her. She'd stirred momentarily, making me jump because I was just staring at her and wondering what the hell we were going to do. How were we going to navigate my grief and the ups and downs it created in my mood?

Knowing the answer wouldn't be simple, I closed the door and left her sleeping, taking out my phone to call Elliot. By the time I'd made it to my bedroom, he answered.

"Beau how is she today?" he asked straight off the bat. "I've been trying her but getting no reply."

"She's sleeping because she still a bit unsteady. How did you get her number anyway?" Something I hadn't felt for a while poked at me—it was green, and it was jealousy.

"Ronnie gave it to me."

"How did he get it?" I demanded, realising I was sounding a bit too invested in Simone. Not that I wasn't but we had things to sort out before my mates knew that.

"You know Ronnie, he befriends everyone," Elliot replied, and I could hear amusement in the fucker's tone.

"Yeah, well, he can fuck off," I muttered.

"Something I'm missing?"

"Yes, actually there is."

"Go on," Elliot said, sounding excited at the prospect of gossip.

"Your fucking brains for inviting Gill Roberts and his fucking twat of a rapist friend."

Elliot made a strange noise, a cross between a gasp and a groan; like he'd been shot or something and was shocked by it.

"I didn't know Gill was going to bring him and I'll forever be sorry for that. Gill's not like that, he's an alright guy."

"Oh yeah definitely if he hangs around with people like that. I just wish that I could damn well report him." I pinched the bridge of my nose and thought about who else he might be slipping drugs to. It didn't sit well with me, but Simone was adamant that if Richard found out he'd do anything possible to hurt her.

"Why can't you? I'll do it right now; you've just got to say the word."

"Simone doesn't want it," I replied.

"But he could do it again," he protested, echoing my own thoughts.

"I know, but I have to respect her wishes. She has her reasons and it's to do with Ethan's sperm donor."

"What?"

"El, I can't," I sighed. "It's her story to tell."

"You seem to have got closer recently," he said, his voice quiet and thoughtful. "You like her don't you, more than just a friend."

I paused not sure how to answer but when I thought about the moment we'd had and how scared I'd been the night before, I realised it was pointless denying it.

"Yes, I like her, more than just as a neighbour or friend, but I want you to keep it to yourself, El."

"Why?" he asked. "Are you not sure about your feelings?"

"Am I sure I like her, then yes, but am I sure I can be the best person for her, then no. I still have grief deep in my bones, Elliot." My voice cracked and there was the exact reason why Sim and I still have a lot to steer through.

"I won't tell anyone but remember that we're all here for you. And remember that—"

"Don't even think about saying it's what Cassie would want because that doesn't help me come to terms with this, El."

"I wasn't," he argued, but I was pretty sure he was lying. "I was going to say remember that before you have sex for the first time go and have a wank first, so you don't embarrass yourself."

"And with that you can fuck right off, Elliot." I ended the call, enough was enough, but at least I was smiling.

"Beau." Her soft voice came from the doorway and when I turned around the missed heartbeat of a new attraction told me everything I wanted to know.

"I thought you were sleeping," I said and walked to her, stopping inches away. "How are you feeling?"

"The headache has gone."

Her smile was small and wary and even though she was washed out with barely any colour to her cheeks, she looked beautiful, and I wanted so much to be the right person for her. I reached up and tucked her hair behind her ear and wondered whether it was the right time to talk about our kiss and what it might mean. As I opened my mouth to talk, I stopped, I could hear singing.

"Can you hear that?" It sounded like it was in my room, but I had no idea where from.

"That sounds like Ethan," Simone gasped.

We both went to the door to check if he was on the landing. I went back into the bedroom where it was much clearer.

"It's definitely in here, Sim."

She came back in, and I looked around the room. It was then that I spotted the baby monitor plugged in down by the side of Cassie's dressing table which still had her bottles of perfume and a bright pink lipstick that she loved. I rushed over and picked it up, turning up the volume. It then came through clearly, every lyric and every note delivered perfectly. Ethan was singing Bob Marley's Three Little Birds, the song that we'd been practicing earlier. His voice wasn't small or timid and his joy of singing shone through. I knew because it was the same joy I used to hear in my own voice. When he finished and we heard Belle clapping and telling him how amazing he was, my fingers found Simone's and entwined in them and when I heard her sniffling, I let my tears flow too. I thought that I was ready but standing there with our hands joined together, my thoughts had been of Cassie and Bobby and how this could have been such a different memory if only life wasn't so fucking cruel.

thirty-four

Simone

L ooking down at our entwined hands, I took in a breath at exactly the same time that Beau pulled away. And there it was, the dismissal of what had happened that I'd been expecting. My cheeks flamed as he took a step back and scratched the back of his neck.

"Wow, that was flipping awesome," he said, unable to look me in the eye.

"Yes, it was. I'm so proud of him." I looked down at the floor and rubbed one bare foot over the top of the other. "I'm going to get him home and bathed then spend the rest of the day chilling in front of the telly."

"Yep, okay. No worries. As long as you feel okay."

I nodded but had nothing to say. I couldn't believe how quickly his mood bloody changed. One minute he's looking at me all dreamily and doing the classic hot leading man thing by tucking my hair behind my ear, and the next... The next he's pulling away from me and can barely look me in the eye. I get that everything is hard for him, but I'd been drugged by some slimeball, was still dealing with my past because I couldn't afford to live anywhere except in a house owned by the first slimeball to ruin my life.

"Yep, I'm perfectly fine thanks. And thanks again for last night, for saving me and sorting things out." I gave him a stupid little wave and turned to walk away.

I was halfway down the stairs when I heard my name called. Turning a part of me hoped that he'd seen sense and was going to ask me to stay and to talk about what happened that morning. Beau was leaning over the glass surrounding the galleried landing and holding up a blue hoody that I recognised was Ethan's.

"This was on the bedroom door handle," he called down.

I held up my arms, not wanting to be any closer to him. Beau paused and then when he realised that I wasn't moving he threw it down to me.

"Tell Ethan I'm really proud of him," he called.

I wanted to say don't be a stupid coward and come down and tell him yourself, but I was quiet little Simone Addison who wouldn't say boo to a goose. The woman who didn't let people in but had let a stupid rock star sneak past the walls she'd put up and was now feeling like shit again. I didn't say, *come down and tell him yourself.* I said, "Will do." And then I sloped away wishing I could turn back the clock and stop Ethan from kicking his ball next door.

After saying goodbye to Belle and saying that we'd see each other soon, I walked Ethan back home. I couldn't help the tears from flowing as the feelings of loneliness began suffocating me once again. I'd come so close to having someone who cared about me, who wanted to protect me and now that feeling of belonging was even further away than ever.

With Ethan splashing around in the bath, his plastered arm in a plastic bag, I took the opportunity of him being happy to see if he'd talk to me.

"I heard you singing earlier," I said, soaping his back with the sponge.

He looked up at me and smiled and then went back to splashing his boat around in the soapy water. My chest deflated but I needed to push through because I couldn't end the day with another low. I needed a high to balance out the last twenty-four hours.

"Do you prefer singing to talking?" I asked.

He nodded again and when he crashed his toy boat into the wave he made, I assumed that was it, but then he took a big breath.

"I like it," he said quietly.

"Why?" I asked, my heart beating faster in case it was something that I'd done or said. Everything I'd done over the last five years had been to make sure that Ethan had a normal life and never felt like he was missing out by not having a dad. What if in the middle of all that I'd been the cause of him not wanting to speak.

"I like it better than talking." He shrugged and then gave his full interest back to the water.

It was too much. I felt like my chest had been ripped open and my heart wrenched out and ripped to pieces.

"E-Ethan," I stammered, placing a hand on his back. "Are you sad, baby?"

He looked up at me and frowned and then shook his head. "No. I'm happy, Mummy. I'm really happy." He gave me the brightest smile and then shook me. "Are you happy, Mummy?"

I blinked back the tears that were threatening to fall and nodded, swallowing hard. "Of course, I am. You make me very happy."

"I think you are now," he said, causing me to rear back.

"What do you mean now?" I asked, sitting back on my thighs.

"Since you made friends with Beau and Belle," he replied matter of fact. "You smile more."

God this boy slayed me, and I hoped that I gave him everything that he needed. He had a beautiful soul and so what if it was just him and me, we would be perfectly fine.

"Okay," I said, flicking water at him to make him giggle. "Five more minutes and then we'll get you dry."

He nodded and I no longer had his attention. While he played for a little longer, I took my phone out of my pocket and checked a couple of emails about websites that I was building and then had a quick check to see if Belle had emailed me a link about a website for vintage clothing. She hadn't, but there was a text from her brother. Part of me wanted to delete it before I even read it, but I was too inquisitive.

Beau: Sim I'm so sorry for earlier. For the kiss and then what happened later...

Turning my back to Ethan, I drew in a breath and let the tears start as I read the rest of the text.

...I wish I was ready to move on because if I was it would be with you. I hope that we can still be friends, but I totally understand if you want me to keep my distance, for a while at least. Beau x

Large wet drops landed on my screen as I fought to keep my emotions in check. Ethan thought I was happy and that's what he needed to believe. He was too young to have the responsibility of my happiness on his shoulders. Beau was a big part of his life, a part that he loved, and I couldn't take that away from him. I tapped away at the screen.

Me: Don't be silly, it's fine. We were both lacking in sleep and had been through a lot of emotion. And yes, we can still be friends. Simone xx

I sent it and then turned off my phone before giving my attention back to the one person who never let me down; my son.

thirty-five

Beau

Being friends with Simone fucking sucked. Everything over the last three weeks had sucked. Guitar lessons with Ethan had sucked because his arm was giving him problems, if it wasn't aching it was itching, and he was becoming frustrated that we hadn't moved on to more complicated chords. He'd also started school a week ago which meant he was often too tired to come round in the week.

The loneliness had got so bad, I'd even considered inviting Ma to stay again. In the last three weeks Belle had finally found a flat, with Elliot's help, and it wasn't a surprise that it was closer to his place than mine. I'd spoken to Ma about Belle coming to Manchester and the only thing that helped her to accept it was that she'd be near to Elliot. Fuck the fact that I might need some company.

I had made use of my time by writing a couple of songs and looking at the proposal that Ali sent about the magazine interview. It was well planned and with a good hook of Warrior Creek over the years. The only thing I wanted vetoed was talking about Cassie and Bobby's death. I was happy to talk about everything else because they, especially Cassie, were part of our journey. Their death wasn't. It may have been the catalyst for the end of Warrior Creek, but it wasn't necessary to go over it again in a music magazine. I wasn't naïve enough to think it couldn't be mentioned in the article somewhere, but I was going to ask for it to be a simple end note, a sympathetic obituary. The rest of the guys seemed excited by it, so I guessed that we were good to go as soon as I said yes.

All that though didn't make the alone time any easier, especially knowing that Sim was only next door. She might have been miles away though for the time we'd spent in each other's company. So much for staying friends, but whose fault was that?

I was going stir crazy which was why I'd invited to guys over to watch the last footy match of the season. The weather was surprisingly warm for May, but I'd decided not to BBQ and had asked Di to cook us one of her Shepherd's pies. Truth—I couldn't stand the thought that Sim might be in her garden and hear us and not come through to say hello. Knowing she was avoiding me was hard and I didn't want the guys to see that too.

When I heard the doorbell, I was more excited to see them than ever before. I'd missed them seeing as Joey had been back in the US rehearsing the Netflix show he was doing. Elliot had been busy doing God knew what, but I had an idea it might have been my sister. The only one I'd seen had been Ronnie and that had been when Ethan was at the house, so Ronnie had taken over the lesson for that day.

"God something smells nice," Joey said as he pushed in after I'd barely opened the door. "I'm starving, all I've eaten for the last two weeks is shit location food."

"I thought those location food carts were good." Ronnie grinned and patted my cheek as he followed Joey. "I hope Di made whatever we're eating and not you."

"Well I wouldn't want to poison you, would I?" I smiled at Elliot who was last in. "No key?"

"I told you the key is only for interventions from now on." He patted my back and then followed the other two through to the kitchen.

***

Sitting around the table, chatting, after eating until we were all stuffed, felt almost like the standard day in the life of Warrior Creek. We'd even talked about Cassie and Bobby without me flying off the handle or falling into a chasm of despair. There was still that sense that things had changed, but the change was starting to feel normal. Yes, I found that heart breaking and was desperate to make sure that none of the guys forgot that there had been a before, but I also knew that I was ready for the after.

"You start shooting next week, is that right?" I asked Joey, passing him another can of coke.

"Yeah, it's going to be full on for six weeks." He groaned. "I mean I'm excited about the role and everything, but it's fucking hard work."

"Don't you get a sex scene in this one though?" Ronnie asked excitedly.

I threw my serviette at him. "Why are you such a child? Anyone would think you didn't have sex, had never had sex."

"But has he though?" Joey asked, laughing.

"I had sex only two nights ago, if you must know."

"Really," I said, leaning forward as if I was interested. "What was her name? Made in Taiwan."

We all laughed, even Ronnie.

"Her name was Kerry, and she was gorgeous. I met her on a photo shoot." Ronnie had a partnership with Epiphone who had created a Ronnie Dwyer series of guitars. They were pretty good because Ronnie had been adamant that he wasn't just putting his name to any old shit for marketing purposes. It meant that he got to go to a load of photoshoots where there were plenty of models hanging around.

"You seeing her again?" Elliot asked with his eyebrows raised, seeing as he knew the answer.

"Nope. Besides she lives with her parents and grandmother, who I should add caught me naked having a piss at four in the morning."

"Four in the morning?" Joey cried. "You need to get that checked out mate. If you're pissing at four in the morning there's something wrong, that or you've got the bladder of a fifty-year-old."

"What, you reckon he's lied about his age all these years?" Elliot gasped.

"He does look kind of old." I peered at Ronnie. "Yep, definitely signs of wrinkles and I'm betting that's why he has his pubes waxed, because they're grey."

"Oh, you're all so bloody funny aren't you," he complained, but I could see a smile around the lip of his beer bottle as he took a swig.

Everyone looked relaxed and I knew they'd taken their lead from me. It was good to smile again.

"Has Belle got her move date sorted?" Elliot asked.

I smiled at the sudden change in topic and the fact that he was trying to look like he wasn't that bothered, or that he didn't know. Of course he knew. He spoke to my sister more than I did.

"You tell me," I replied. "You're the one who's been helping her."

He shifted in his seat and looked a bit uncomfortable, which made me chuckle. He was always in everyone else's business being a do-gooder. Now he could get a taste of what we all had to put up with.

"I just recommended a few places."

"Yeah, all close to your house. How weird is that?" I winked at him.

"You're a fucker Bradley," he replied but I knew he didn't really care. It took more than that to upset Elliot Andrews.

That was the thing he might always be in your business, but he did it for all the right reasons. He never got offended and if he did, he had it out with you and then it was forgotten. He was an all-round great bloke, and I couldn't have wished for anyone better for Belle. I just hoped that they didn't fuck it up somehow and make life difficult for everyone.

"What about you?" Joey asked, twirling his can around. "What's happening with Simone?"

"Nothing's happening with Simone," I replied, a little too defensively.

"You were pretty cut up about what happened at El's party. And don't tell me you were just being a good friend. I thought you were going to fucking kill that twat who roofied her."

"Talking of which," I said, pointedly changing the subject. "You found out anymore, El?"

He shook his head and his demeanour changed. Suddenly he was sitting stiffly in his chair, and I knew he was grinding his teeth because his jaw was set hard, and it was pulsing.

"Like I told you, Gill doesn't know him that well. Just that he's met him on the studio circuit. He's a percussionist and appeared on Devil's Daughter's last album."

"Well he won't be appearing on anyone else's," I growled. "Not if I have anything to do with it."

"I still think Simmy should have gone to the police," Joey offered.

"It's complicated and to do with Ethan's dad, but like I told Elliot, it's not my story to tell."

My head then jolted forward as Ronnie slapped me around the back of it.

"What the fuck is that for?" I asked, rubbing it.

"Because you're an idiot," he replied. "Simmy is lovely, gorgeous and you obviously care about her but are being a prick about the whole thing. Cassie would—."

"Don't even think about it." I pointed a finger at him as my blood started to heat up. "Not one word."

Ronnie shook his head. "No, I'm not going to keep quiet. Cassie would love you to meet someone like Simmy. Someone kind and generous with her time."

"How the hell do you know she's kind and generous with her time." My heart felt heavy, weighing down my chest. In the three weeks since I'd seen her, had Ronnie been getting to know her and taking my place as the person she confided in?"

"And that is why you're a selfish prick as well as an idiot." Joey and Elliot both grinned, because surprise surprise they agreed with him, of course they fucking did. "You're ignoring her, but you hate the idea that I might not be." He grinned at me, and I'd never wanted to throat punch someone as much as I did at that moment.

"I know she's kind and generous with her time because who else would spend hours trawling the internet to find me a supplier of the port that my auntie Mo drank five years ago and loved but could never find it because it was a special import. Yeah, Simmy did and that's exactly the sort of thing that Cassie would have done." He then slammed his bottle on the table and almost pushing his chair over stood up. "You can clear the table by yourself you, fucker, I'm going to watch the footy. You two coming or staying in here with Mr bloody Twat Face?"

With grins, Joey and Elliot stood up and nodded at me, telling me silently to take notice of what our bandmate was saying. They would be right too because Ronnie rarely lost his temper. He was the sweet, puppy dog one of us who loved everyone and wanted everyone to love him.

As the noise of the football crept through from the lounge, I sat at the kitchen table alone, and looked through the window. I'd told myself for the last twenty-two days that if the ball was in the garden, then that was a sign to put things right with Sim. But, just like the last twenty-one days there was no ball. Without that sign I didn't think I could put things right, but if I didn't try, I knew I'd regret it for the rest of my life. Maybe just not today.

thirty-six

Simone

Tapping my foot and biting my thumbnail, I waited nervously for Ethan to appear at the school gates. It had been like this every afternoon for the last three weeks, even though things appeared to have been going well for him. He'd made a couple of friends who didn't think he was weird because he didn't speak. One was a little girl called Hattie who seemed to like bossing him around, so Ethan not speaking wasn't a problem for her newly developing organisational skills. The other was a little boy called Charlie who his mum told me was also very quiet, so he didn't mind Ethan not speaking either.

When the end of day bell finally rang out, I stood on tiptoe, looking over the heads of other mum's, I waited in anticipation for Ethan to appear. When I saw he was with his teacher Miss Trent, my breathing spiked. She was smiling though, relaxing I went down to the flats of my feet and wiped my hands on my jeans.

"Is everything okay?" I asked as she approached me. I reached out for Ethan's hand and pulled him to me.

"Absolutely fine. I just wanted to let you know that Ethan has had a great day and has joined the choir."

My eyes went wide as I looked down at him and then back up to Miss Trent. "The choir?"

She nodded. "Yes, he has a beautiful singing voice. Also," she said, smiling down at Ethan, "he did really well with his numeracy today and buddied up with Callum."

"You did?" I rubbed a hand over Ethan's head as he looked up at me and smiled. "Thank you, Miss Trent, I really appreciate you letting me know."

She gave me a knowing smile which said, 'I told you he'd be fine', and then walked back into school. As we drove home even the thought of Beau and what had happened couldn't dampen my spirits. Ethan was thriving at his school and that was all that mattered. There'd be plenty of time for my life once he was older.

I'd been so determined about that thought, that when we drove up the driveway, when I first saw Beau leaning against the wall, hands in jeans' pockets I didn't falter. My heart didn't skip a beat, I didn't get butterflies, I didn't second guess why he was there. When we stopped though and he smiled at me, everything hit me like a wrecking ball.

My heart missed three or four beats, the butterflies in my stomach were not only flying but loop the looping and I couldn't help but hope that he was there for me. To tell me that he was wrong and that our kiss had meant something. That us linking our fingers together and feeling the same emotions as we listened to Ethan sing had had an impact on his heart too.

Before I could say anything, Ethan had unbuckled himself, opened the door, and was running to Beau. He practically threw himself at the tall, sexy, rock star and wrapped his arms around his long legs. Taking a deep breath, I got out of the car, watching them intently as Beau asked about Ethan's day and said it was great when Ethan simply nodded and grinned. God, how I wished that my son had been gifted with a man like Beau in his life. Maybe he wouldn't have been silent so often, maybe he would have wanted people to hear his voice. I considered how well he'd picked up the guitar and wondered at his potential if only... I stopped myself. If only was a phrase that I'd always vowed I'd never use where Ethan was concerned. I'd always considered that using *if only* about Ethan would mean that he wasn't enough, but that wasn't true he was everything.

As I approached them, Beau smiled again and once again my stomach went on a roller coaster ride. Ethan looked up at me and I knew he was ready for a snack.

"Biscuit?" I asked. He nodded and grinned, running to the house. "Would you like to come in?"

I didn't look at Beau as I asked him, instead I rooted around in my bag for my keys which were perfectly visible. My face was burning, I could feel it as I second guessed asking him to come inside, but I couldn't exactly say, 'oh sorry, I changed my mind'.

Acting like a full-grown adult I pulled out my keys and led the way to the house.

As I let us in, disarming the alarm, I could feel the heat of Beau behind me, his presence filling the space of the vast hallway and I wished I could go back to being unaffected by him. It was so much easier thinking that we were just friends, and I was simply the friendly woman next door who was an ear for her widowed neighbour.

"Take these into the lounge and watch some TV," I said to Ethan handing him a biscuit and a cup of milk. "I'll be in soon."

I thought that he might want to stay in the kitchen seeing as Beau was there, but I could see that he was tired and as soon as he'd finished his milk, he'd nap for half an hour. Thankfully it didn't stop him sleeping at night.

"Tea?" I asked, still not having given Beau eye contact.

"Please, and don't forget to let it brew." He gave a little chuckle, but it sounded forced, and my heart sunk a little further.

"So, how's your week been?" My tone was bright as I determined to get us back on track.

"Not bad. The boys game round for something to eat and to watch the footy, so that was good. Ronnie tells me you found his auntie Mo some drink that she'd been after."

I turned and was shocked to see Beau looked as nervous as I felt. His hands were linked together at the back of his neck and there was a pulse underneath his right eye. This calmed me a little bit, glad that I wasn't the only one affected by what had happened. Determine again to move forwards, I grinned and gave him full eye contact.

"I did, he'd been trying to find some for a while for her. I love searching the web for stuff, it's my favourite hobby."

"Really?" he said letting his hands drop. "Don't you get frustrated if you can't find what you're looking for?"

"God no. That's all the fun." I turned back to finish making his cup of tea and then handed it to him. He took a sip and gave me the most beautiful smile and my insides went to mush as I opened my mouth again without thinking. "Would you like to stay for dinner?"

**

As we finished our dinner, I was surprised at how comfortable it had been. There'd been no awkward silences and lots of laughter and it felt like we were back to being friends again. Beau told me all about the interview that he was thinking of doing and we talked about Belle and Elliot and what her moving to Manchester might mean for them. Then, when we'd finished, Beau cleared the table and put everything in the dishwasher while I took Ethan to get ready for bed before he watched some TV and I read to him.

"I'll read to Ethan if you like," Beau said as we sat at opposite ends of the sofa watching the end of Dinosaur Train.

Ethan's head shot around, and his eyes were like saucers as he nodded enthusiastically.

"You don't mind?"

"No, I'd love to."

Ethan too excited to wait, stood up and ran out of the room.

"I'll make us another cup of tea then," I offered. "Unless you'd like a beer or something?"

"Tea is good, Sim," Beau replied. "I'll make sure it's just one story, don't worry." He then followed Ethan up the stairs.

Walking into the kitchen, I remembered that I hadn't opened my post, so picked it up from the island where it was still sitting. Flicking through there was a lot of junk mail, a couple of bills and then a white envelope with Rogers & Rogers Solicitors printed on it. Ripping at the thick paper I felt sick wondering what it could be. I wasn't the sort of person lucky enough to have been named in someone's will, so it was a scary thought that a solicitor had contacted me. When I read the neatly typed document, I found out I'd been right to be scared.

Richard was filing for custody of Ethan because he'd found out I'd taken him to a party where I'd taken drugs. The date of Elliot's party was noted in the letter as well as his address including the time that we'd left and the fact that I'd had to be carried to the car.

It felt like my guts had been ripped out as the pain overtook me and my whole body started to shake. The blood which flowed through my veins had turned ice cold and every breath I took was laboured as I stood on the floor. Clutching the letter and reading it over and over again, I sobbed, unable to understand how he could be so cruel.

"Ethan's just on the toilet," Beau said as he marched into the kitchen. "Fuck, Sim, what the hell's wrong."

I couldn't speak. I could barely breathe. I shoved the letter at Beau as he dropped to his knees next to me. He skimmed it, threw it to one side and then pulled me into his lap.

"Hey, hey, come on, it's going to be okay. We're going to sort this." He sounded like he meant it, but he couldn't promise. He shouldn't promise because he had no idea what Richard was capable of.

"H-h-he'll do it B-Beau," I stammered between sobs. "He'll take m-my b-baby."

Beau took my face in his hands and pulled it closer to his. "No, he won't, I won't let him. Ethan stays here and I'll make sure of it."

He then wrapped me in his arms and rocked me as my whole world fell apart.

thirty-seven

Beau

"**G**ive me the worst-case scenario, Maxwell." I was talking off the record to my personal solicitor, desperately trying to get some good news for Sim.

"If we can prove that Miss Addison didn't take the drugs freely that will obviously help her case. However, it won't stop the custody hearing. Only the boy's father can do that. I'm guessing this is simply his first shot and if he really wants custody, he will have other incidents that he hasn't yet disclosed."

I closed my eyes and cursed silently. This was not happening. There was no way a rapist should be given custody of Ethan, even joint custody.

"It would have helped if you'd reported it at the time, but now it will look simply an act of desperation."

Blowing out a breath, I wondered if I should tell Maxwell everything, but it was up to Simone.

"Beau," Maxwell said. "Would you like me to represent Miss Addison?"

"Yes," I replied without hesitation. "And all the bills come to me, okay?"

"Sure. I'll call you in the morning when I get into the office. I'll introduce Miss Addison to my paralegal Kate, and she'll arrange a meeting so that she can get every single detail from Miss Addison."

"Thanks, Maxwell," I sighed. "Appreciate it."

Once we ended the call, I took a few minutes to pull myself together. To stop this happening felt totally hopeless, especially if Richard was the type of man that I believed him to be. He was a rapist, I knew that much, and a manipulator and a controller. His freak out over the leak proved that. I was surprised he hadn't been around after I'd had the new alarm fitted. Feeling like I could actually put a positive spin on things, I went back to the lounge where Ethan was sitting on Sim's knee reading. I checked the time on my phone, it was almost nine and Ethan had school in the morning. Not wanting to tread on her toes, but thinking she needed to keep everything as normal as possible, I ruffled Ethan's hair so that he looked up at me.

"Do you think it's time for bed buddy?"

Like the amazing, well-behaved kid that he was, he smiled, kissed Simone, and then jumped off her knee and took hold of my hand.

"I think that means he wants you to take him." Simone managed a watery smile and even though it was probably the shittest moment of her life, she looked beautiful.

"I'll be five minutes," I told her, hoping that she could keep it together for that long.

Pulling back the dinosaur duvet cover on Ethan's bed, I thought about Bobby. I thought about him thousands of times a day, him and Cassie, but they weren't thoughts that prompted as many tears recently. Some did but generally they were accompanied with a smile, which is what I did at that moment. Thinking about Bobby insisting on taking his three feet high blow-up dinosaur to bed with him.

"Comfy?" I asked as Ethan snuggled under the covers. He nodded and I bent down and kissed his head. That was a moment that caused my throat to tickle and my eyes to sting. When I pull the door closed behind me, I had to take a deep breath to stop myself from letting out the cry of a wounded animal.

"How you doing?" I asked as I went back into the lounge.

Sim looked up at me with tear filled eyes. "What am I going to do, Beau?" She poked at the letter next to her on the sofa. "Why the hell is he doing it to me?"

I picked up the piece of paper, folded it and put it on the coffee table. "We'll sort it tomorrow." Sitting down next to her, I did what I felt was the natural and right thing to do. I pulled her into my arms.

"I owe you so much already, Beau," she sniffed against my t-shirt.

"You don't owe me anything," I sighed. "We're friends and friends help each other out. You have no idea how much Ethan has helped me over the last couple of months." I wanted to tell her that she had helped too but it still felt a bit awkward after the kiss that I'd ruined. "I'll speak to the guys' tomorrow and see if between us we can find Gill's friend and get him to fess up."

"I doubt he'll do that," she replied snuggling closer and making my heart rate increase.

"I'll ask Elliot to put some pressure on Gill. Threaten him with his career if necessary."

"No, I don't want you to do that. It wasn't his fault."

As I looked down at Simone, she looked up at me and I frowned. "He took that bastard to the party, so yeah, Sim, it's his fault."

Chewing on her lip she nodded. "I can't let Richard have him, Beau. He won't understand him."

"We'll make sure he doesn't. Maxwell's paralegal, Kate will be in touch to get as many details as possible from you." I paused and thought carefully about my next words, whether I should say them or not, but I knew I had to. "When she does, I think you really need to consider telling her about what he did to you."

She started to shake her head, but I placed my hand on her cheek.

"Don't say no now but think about it overnight. Please."

"Okay."

Breathing a sigh of relief I pulled her to me, kissed her head and realised that I would do anything to help her, and it wasn't even a surprise.

***

Simone is in my kitchen and has just finished her meeting with Kate. She decided to not to tell them about the rape, still petrified that he would hurt her brother. He was in a new relationship with a guy that he liked, and she didn't want Richard doing anything to spoil it. The main reason she couldn't though was because she knew if she did Richard would stop at nothing to get Ethan, and as Maxwell pointed out this might only be a threat. Sadly, I had to agree with her on that point and it made me want to kill him with my own bare hands.

"Maxwell said that Richard's employed the best family lawyer in the UK," she moaned, resting her cheek on her hand. "Never loses a case."

I ran a hand down her hair because touching her was no longer an issue for me. I held her, touched her, and had even lain next to her on the sofa when she'd napped that morning after what I was guessing had been a sleepless night. All I wanted to do was be there for her and help her in any way I could.

"Well, there's always a first time," I replied.

Simone stood and when she did the huge jumper that she was wearing fell to her knees, the sleeves to the end of her fingers. There were dark circles under her eyes and her hair was a mess on top of her head. Yet still she looked beautiful.

"What if he wins, Beau?"

"We will do everything to make sure he doesn't."

With a handful of wool, I pulled her to me and when our chests collided something shifted in the room. The silence wrapped itself around us and when my gaze met Simone's my throat went dry. Her tongue flicked out to wet her bottom lip and all I could think about was taking it into my mouth and sucking on it. There was that little voice though, still whispering that I couldn't, that I shouldn't. It wasn't as loud as it had been, but it was still there. Yet the idea of not kissing her was fucking agonising.

"Sim, this is killing me," I whispered.

"What is?" she asked, her eyes cautious and I didn't blame her considering what I'd put her through already.

"Us. What could be happening. The fact that I can't stop thinking about you."

Wide eyed she let out a quiet gasp. "You can't?"

Shaking my head, I let my finger stroke slowly down her cheek as my eyes drank her in. "Every day you're in my head, but..." Dropping my forehead to hers, I closed my eyes, unable to put into words what I hadn't said or thought already because I was beginning to sound like a broken record to myself.

"Beau." Her breasts rubbed against me as she sighed out my name. "I don't expect anything that you're not ready to give. It hurt to think that you were ready and then pulled back, but only because you didn't tell me what you were feeling. You just made me feel like I wasn't worthy of an explanation. You regretted that kiss and that was that."

"That wasn't what I meant to do," I declared.

"I know." She placed her palm flat against my chest and the warmth from her fingertips sent the best kind of message around my body. "You're still hurting, and I understand that. Cassie was the love of your life, Bobby was your beautiful boy. I'd be shocked if in five years, even ten years' time if you weren't still feeling their loss."

"It does still hurt, so much that some days it's actually a physical pain." I took in a deep breath before I could continue because if I didn't, I wasn't sure that I wouldn't run again. "You know when someone loses a limb, but they say they can still feel it itch afterwards." She nodded. "That's how I feel. I can still sense them in the house. Still hear Bobby or feel Cassie's touch on my back or my head. It's weird and it's scary but it's also the best feeling because they're never coming back."

"I love that you get that," she said with a soft smile. "It must be the most comforting feeling in the world."

"Yeah, but when I'm with you everything is less. The pain, the sense of them and that conflicts me. I don't want to hurt anymore, but I still need to feel them sometimes. Being around you I'm free of the hurt but I don't feel them either. I've still got a lot of stuff to get my head around, so are you happy to go slow?"

Sim nodded and a tear dropped down her cheek to the end of her chin and silently fell and I knew this was killing her too. Not knowing what I needed, what I wanted. I didn't help her at all by being hot and cold with her. I had to decide and stick to it, so what was worse? A life with the odd moments of peace and no Sim, or a life without the gut-wrenching pain, but a sense of guilt because I was leading a life with Sim.

My lips answered for me as they sought out Simone's and kissed her. It was more tentative than the first time. This time I knew that I had something fragile in my hand, her heart, my heart. Slowly my hands moved up and down her back as hers gripped my t-shirt and we got lost in each other in a kiss for our future.

We were so lost that we didn't hear the door open, and Elliot come in. Clearing his throat, he startled us apart.

"Put my fucking key on the table now," I barked.

Simone dropped her head and wiped a touch of her lips with her fingertips. Elliot just grinned like a damn idiot and then pushed past me to pull Simone into a hug. I braced, ready to pull him away, but she didn't stiffen like I expected. Weirdly I felt a small sense of pride that I'd relaxed her to the point that she could finally stand a hug from another man.

"I'm so sorry, Simmy," Elliot said, stooping to look her in the eye. "For everything that's happened. If I'd not had that party."

Simone shook her head. "No, don't be silly. Not one part of this is your fault. It's the man who fathered my son and the man who tried to drug me. This is all on them."

"That's really generous of you to say, but—"

"Elliot, if she says it's not your fault, it's not your fault." I held out my hand. "Now my fucking key because I don't believe this is an intervention."

Elliot laughed and took his keys from his pocket and slipped mine from the fob."

"Why don't you set your alarm?" Sim said. "Then it wouldn't matter who had your key."

"What she said," Elliot agreed, and his hand paused mid-air with my key dangling from it. "Maybe I'll keep it for emergencies."

Too bored with his dicking about, I grabbed the key and pushed it into my pocket.

"Right, now tell me what you're doing here. Have you got news on Brad?"

"No, sorry. Gill says he's gone off the radar since he returned from the States, but I'm betting it's him that told this Richard guy."

"How would he know Richard though?" Simone asked, moving to sit on a stool. The need to move with her was great, but I stayed where I was— nobody liked a fucking clinger.

Elliot shrugged. "No idea sorry. I asked the security guys if they spotted anyone hanging around who looked suspicious, but they didn't."

"Did you use our usual security team?" I asked. "That guy Drake, I've never seen him before."

"Yeah, same team. I know Tank said that they'd got a couple of new guys and Drake was one of them, but I think he said they'd been with them for about six months. I'll check though."

I nodded and looked over at Simone who looked deep in thought. "We'll find out, Sim, don't worry."

She flashed me a smile and then took out her phone. "I'd better go. I need to pick Ethan up from school."

"Okay, I'll see you out."

She said her goodbyes to Elliot and then I followed her to the front door as her car was already parked on my drive, in readiness for the school run. When she stepped outside, I reached for her hand and linked her little finger with mine.

"Shall I call round later?" I whispered, not sure why when there was no one around.

She nodded and smiled. It felt like my chest loosened by another ten percent. I looked over my shoulder and then kissed the top of her head and as she drove away waving to me, I felt that ten percent increase to twenty.

thirty-eight

Beau

When I walked back into the kitchen Elliot was smiling like a fucking kid at the funfair. No, in fact, he looked like my proud parent because I'd just been given the best ever end of term school report.

"What the hell is going on with your face?" I asked.

"Pleased that something good has come out of this shit-show."

"Well don't jump the gun. We're taking it slow because I'm not miraculously relieved of all grief and guilt just yet, mate."

"I know." He nodded. "The fact that you're even willing to go slow though is massive."

Before I knew what was happening, I was in his arms and being hugged, having my back vigorously slapped. Pretty sure I heard a sniff or two as well. I pulled away.

"Alright, alright, stop acting like a baby about it." When I looked at Elliot and saw the joy and relief in his eyes, it hit me how huge this thing between me and Sim was. Not just for me. Everyone was invested in me and in us making each other happy. "Shit, I never thought we'd be having this conversation." My tongue felt thick as I swallowed back the emotion.

"I know."

Elliot gave me a single nod; consent to me moving on from his best friend. Was it moving on though if I still loved her and thought about her every day? Would I ever be free of the shackles of guilt by pursuing something with Simone? How would I ever know unless I tried.

"I can't think about what Cassie would say or think," I said, taking one of the stools at the island. "Because I don't want to regret anything about this. Sim deserves more respect than that."

"I know that too." He smiled and now there was peace in his eyes.

"If I didn't respect her, I know that Cassie would fucking haunt me."

We both laughed because it was true. Cassie was all about the sisterhood and I was sure things would go bump in the night if I didn't do right by Simone at any time.

"Cuppa?" I asked.

"Yeah, why not," Elliot replied and picked up the kettle. "I'll make it."

He busied himself in my kitchen and more normal edged its way into my life; it felt good.

"I hear you spoke to Ali about the interview," Elliot said over his shoulder as he put teabags into two mugs. "Said you asked her to send you the details."

I still hadn't decided about it—well, I had but hadn't told Ali or the guys yet. I supposed it wouldn't hurt to give Elliot some good news for a change.

"Yeah, I'm good to go with it."

He swung around with the milk in his hand. "Yeah?"

"Yeah, I'll call Ali tomorrow. And don't you dare put that fucking milk in first."

He grinned. "Wouldn't dare."

Once the tea was made, Elliot joined me at the island and we both sighed like it was a full stop, a natural end. The idea of it felt right and so I decided that I was going to go all out fucking Santa Claus with him.

"Here." I pushed a memory stick that I'd taken from my pocket and pushed it across the island.

"What's that?" he asked, picking it up and shaking it into his palm.

"Five new songs," I cleared my throat, not sure I would get the words out. "Thought maybe we could perform them as a band again one day."

Elliot's eyes shone and fuck me if he wasn't getting emotional again.

"Will you stop with the damn crying," I protested. "It's like drinking tea with a hormonal teenage girl."

"Don't let a hormonal teenage girl hear you saying that," he replied, looking down at the memory stick. "How come?"

I shrugged. "Ethan, I guess. Teaching him to play guitar and seeing the joy the music gave to him lit a fire within me again."

"I can't wait to listen."

"Don't get too excited, I haven't written anything for ages. It might be— Who the hell is that?"

Loud banging at the door caused us both to push up from our seats and walk to the hallway. It was heavy and insistent and something about it caused my stomach to roil. When I was within reach of the door, I heard Simone shouting my name on the other side. Rushing to open it I wasn't ready to see the state she was in. Mascara was streaked down her cheeks which were deathly pale.

"What the hell?" I asked as she fell into my arms. "Sim, what's wrong? Where's Ethan?" I looked over her shoulder but her car, still running, was empty.

"Simmy, what's happened." Elliot was at my side and thank God he was because I'd lost all function of my feet and my mouth. All I was able to do was hold her and stop her from collapsing to the ground.

"Simone?" Elliot asked, more insistent. "Tell us what's happened. Where's Ethan?"

Simone looked up at me, her face crumpled with a look that I recognised from those first days when I'd looked in the mirror.

"No, no. Fucking no," I cried, gripping her head between my hands and forcing her to look at me. "Tell me."

"R-Richard," she sobbed. "He's taken Ethan. P-p-picked him up from sc-school and t-taken him f-for a burger."

"No fucking way." I felt the colour drain from my face and the relief seep through me that it wasn't my worst nightmare revisited. I took a deep breath to pull myself together because she needed me to be strong. "Come one. Let's get you inside."

Between us Elliot and I practically carried Simone into the lounge where we sat her down on the sofa, both of us either side of her. I gripped her hands in mine while Elliot rubbed her back as slowly and gradually, she calmed down. Her sobs subsided and her breathing returned to its natural rhythm and then finally she was able to tell us what had happened.

"How was he allowed to take him?" I asked after she repeated what she'd told us previously. "The school are fucking idiots."

"No," she said quietly. "They're not. He's down as Ethan's father."

I couldn't say anything, but even so Elliot stared at me wide-eyed anyway, warning me not to. That pissed me off because who was he to tell me how to behave with the woman who I was falling for, who I was involved with.

"You want to make Sim a cup of tea?" I snapped.

"I don't want one." She shook her head and twisted her fingers in mine. "I *had to* Beau, *he* told me that I had to as part of our agreement. He even checked with the school. As for Marcus, he's in London. What happened if I couldn't get there? They wait for two or three hours for Marcus to get here by train? *I literally had no one else in an emergency.*"

"You had me." I threw my hands in the air. "And he couldn't force you to put him down. He didn't need to know."

"Beau," Elliot warned, and I threw him a glare.

"I gave the details months ago. Plus," she sighed looking up at me through her lashes. "The day he started we weren't exactly talking. What was I supposed to do?"

The pain in my chest was all for her and the crap she'd had to deal with because of that bastard. I wished I could take all that away for her, but life wasn't like that. Doing the only thing I was capable of at that moment, I pulled her into my arms and kissed her head. When her phone trilled with a text, the three of us all jumped. Fumbling it, Simone opened the screen and gasped.

"What?" I asked, ready to kill with my bare hands if necessary. She showed me the picture that had come through. It was Ethan and he was smiling at least.

"He says Ethan's having such a good time he's going to take him to the cinema first and then for a burger."

Unable to control the anger that had been boiling inside of me, I pushed up from the sofa and paced towards the patio doors. I looked out to the garden and almost screamed when I saw Ethan's ball there, exactly where he'd left it the day before.

"He has no fucking right to do that," I yelled, turning on my heels to face Simone, whose hand was now in Elliot's. "He can't just take him out for the evening without asking you. You're the one with custody."

Simone shook her head. "We don't have a formal custody agreement," she replied, her voice sad and her shoulders sloped in defeat.

"How come?" Elliot asked.

He could fuck off holding her hand as well. I took my place back at her side and took back possession of her; and don't think I didn't see the way his stupid face softened.

"He's a powerful man," Simone continued. "And I have nothing. He owns the house that I live in and even though I have something on him, I can't use it because he's threatened to ruin my brother if I do."

"Shit," Elliot groaned. "And what you have on him could it ruin *him* if there was no threat to your brother?"

"Yes," she breathed out and then looked Elliot in the eye. "He raped me when I was an intern at his IT company. He told me that I'd led him on and that no one would believe me. He said that if I told anyone at all he'd make sure my brother's life was worth nothing."

"How the hell has he got away with it?" he asked. "Simmy, you have to tell the police all of this. You can't let him have this amount of control over you."

"How can I?" she cried. "Especially now he's starting to use Ethan in his power games. He'll make sure no one believes me and then he'll get custody of my baby and I can't even comprehend that. It would kill me."

"We'd back you up though," I offered. "Tell the police what you told us and how much he scares you."

Her gaze met mine and I knew enough about her already to realise neither of us had got through to her.

"It's five years ago, Beau. You can imagine how it would seem. He'd spin it to make it look like I was just being spiteful."

We fell silent and when I looked at Elliot, I knew he'd come to the same conclusion as I had—she was right.

"What's his surname?" I asked, pulling out my phone. "Let's at least try and find out what we're dealing with."

Simone sighed. "Gregory. Richard Gregory."

The air around us turned thick as Elliot and I looked at each other. Shock and surprise blanketed my friend's features. I was sure that mine were no different.

"You're sure?" I asked, swallowing back the bile.

Simone nodded. "Yes, why?"

I looked at Elliot again, but his face was now pale, no expression, just a blank emptiness. It looked like it was a bigger shock to him than I expected. Taking out my phone I clicked on the internet and keyed in Richard's name to bring up pictures of him.

I turned the screen to Simone. "Is this him?"

She nodded.

"Fuck," I groaned.

"Beau, what is it?" she asked, pulling on my arm.

"Richard Gregory is Dicky Gregory," I replied.

"And?" Simone shrugged.

"He owns Tenfold Music."

"He's your boss," Simone exclaimed.

I nodded, Simone gasped, and Elliot left the room.

thirty-nine

Simone

Watching the shock on Beau's face it felt like I was living in some sort of alternative universe. My neighbour, the man I had developed some sort of a relationship with, was a rock star whose boss was the man who raped me and got me pregnant. Maybe I should offer it as a concept for one of the romance writers who I designed websites for.

"I honestly had no idea," I said, wrapping my arms around myself. "It was his IT company that I worked for. I didn't even know he owned a record company."

Beau scrubbed a hand down his face and groaned. "I never liked the little bastard."

"You've met him then?" Ice ran through my veins as the idea that Beau might have talked to Richard on the day that he'd violated me, or one of those when he was intimidating me with threats to my brother.

"Yeah, a few occasions. He was only an exec at the label when we first joined, but he bought it just over three years ago."

He looked at me and deep brown orbs flecked with whisky tones made me feel safe and secure. I'd not really had anyone since my dad died, and even before he took his own life, he'd been absent. Now though, as Beau took my hand in his, it felt like I was more than a team of one caring for Ethan.

"I think I need to tell Marcus," I announced.

"What?" Beau's brow rose.

"I think I need to tell Marcus," I repeated. "If he knows and is prepared then Richard loses the upper hand."

"He could still use Ethan against you though, if you decide to go to the police."

"I know." I bobbed my head. "And that's why I still can't do it, but my brother needs to know what I've been dealing with for the last five years."

He reached forward and brushed my hair from my face before briefly touching my mouth with his. "I've got to tell you Sim, I think you're making the right decision."

I nodded. "I know that too."

He gave me a beautiful smile which lit up his whole face and I knew in that instant that Cassie must have loved him so damn much.

"Whatever happens between us," he said quietly. "Whatever we become, I'll always be here for you. You're not alone anymore, Sim."

"Thank you," I whispered and doing something I'd never have dreamed I was capable of, I kissed him. It was sweet and it was short, but it meant everything to me.

"I think you should probably eat something," Beau said, standing and pulling me to my feet. "And I need to find out where Elliot went to."

We walked into the kitchen, hand in hand and think both of us were surprised to see Elliot leaning with his forehead against the window, looking out into the garden.

"What's going on, El?" Beau asked, leading me to a stool and nodding for me to sit.

"Nothing, just thinking about Dicky," he replied, talking to the glass. "How we move forward."

"Even though you've split do you still work for him?" I asked.

Elliot turned around and looked at Beau who shrugged. "We officially still have some time on our contract, but I'd be more than happy to pay to get out of it."

"You can't do that." I looked between the two men who usually commanded the attention of thousands of people. "What if you decide to perform again as a band? Tenfold are supposed to be one of the best labels in the world, aren't they?"

Neither of them said anything as Beau started to search through the fridge and Elliot watched him. I got the feeling that Warrior Creek performing together again wasn't as absurd as Beau might want himself to believe.

"I need to go," Elliot said suddenly. "Let me know what happens with Richard and Ethan, okay?"

"Yes sure," I replied, wondering what had upset him. I wondered if it was me being around Beau, after all Cassie had been Elliot's best friend. "Are you okay?"

"Yep, like I said just wondering how we deal with the Dicky thing."

"I've got bacon," Beau said, his head still inside the fridge. "You can stay for a butty if you like."

"Nope. Got to go." And he left.

"Is Elliot okay?" I asked.

Beau turned and placed a packet of bacon and a jar of mayo on the side and looked at the door that Elliot had disappeared through. "Not sure but I've learned over the years that he'll tell me if he isn't. It's probably just what he said, the problems we might have working with Dicky."

"So you are going to perform again." I said, something strange happening in my stomach. Was it excitement or worry?

"I don't know," he said, moving over to stand in front of me. "I'm not averse to it, but I can't work for Dicky, or fucking Richard, whatever his name is, if we do."

"You have to Beau. You know that they're the best and I can't ask you jeopardise anything just because of my history with him."

He eased my knees apart, edging in between them and cupping my face with his hands as he smiled at me.

"You didn't ask."

"You know what I mean. I'm only your neighbour. You barely know me. This is your career."

Beau shook his head and breathed out slowly. "You are so much more than my neighbour and you know that. Okay so it's new, it's just the beginning but I think it could be something good, Sim."

The air changed between us and around us as our gazes stayed locked on each other I licked my bottom lip and our mouths collided. Beau's hands went to my hair, mine to his back, drawing him closer, encouraging him to invade my space. There was nothing slow or cautious about the kiss. It was the sort of kiss I had only ever dreamed of. A kiss that said more than words ever could. My third kiss with this man and it felt so good that if the world ended at that moment, I would have had my moment of pure bliss. Third time is a charm, most definitely.

I let my tongue play with his, exploring, enticing, and encouraging him to do more. And he did. As one of his hands fell to my bottom and pushed me forward on the stool, into the hardness behind the fly of his jeans, I soared. I felt every inch of him exactly where I wanted it to be, even though I was absolutely petrified of what might happen next. It wasn't a fear of him, of a man, touching me again, it was the anxiety of what having sex with Beau might mean. I was already falling for this beautiful, broken man and to share something that intimate with him would only reinforce those feelings; make me fall harder. Make me need him more.

Beau's teeth nipped at my bottom lip and when I dropped my head back with the sheer pleasure of it all, his mouth moved to trace a path up to behind my ear. His hand moved to my side and when his thumb softly tracked the outline of my breast, I felt like I might explode with the need for more. My nipples hardened and every single inch of my body ached for his to cover it. I had nothing to compare the feeling too. I'd been a quiet, insular teenager who had no idea of the pleasure that a man could bring to me. Then my first experience of touching and feeling, being intimate had been soured by someone who didn't deserve what I had to give to him. Being with Beau though, simply kissing him, erased every bad memory I had. When he nibbled on my ear lobe, I thought I might implode.

"Beau," I begged, unsure and inexperienced of what it was I was desperate for.

He groaned from the back of his throat and his fingertips dug into my skin, even as his mouth moved away from mine and his body lurched back creating a void of despondency.

"What's wrong?" I asked, breathing like I'd run up three flights of stairs.

He looked at me and he was no longer the rock star. Now he was the nervous boy, unsure how to take the next step. His eyes searched my face, desperate to look at me but scared to see.

"I don't think I can," he breathed out, his hands still touching and anchored to me. "I'm so fucking scared, Sim. What if I mess up? What if it feels…"

"Different," I whispered, holding his face in my hands. "And it might. It might feel the strangest thing in the world. We might not fit. I will feel unusual. I will not do what you're expecting. It's inevitable."

His face crumpled and his shoulders sagged as the realisation of what this next step would mean. His mind might have said he was ready to move on, but his heart was still lagging behind in the race to the future.

"I feel like I've let you down," he said, his voice cracking. "Again."

"Oh my God, no. No way," I said taking him in my arms and pulling him to my chest. "You have so much that you have to come to terms with. We agreed to take this slow."

Pulling away, Beau dropped his forehead to mine. "Are you sure. I just feel… fuck…I feel nervous." His laugh trembled just like his hands were at my back.

"You're nervous!" I exclaimed. "I'm petrified."

We both laughed together this time and then shared a silence and a peace that caused us both to smile.

"What time is he bringing Ethan back?"

Then the peace was gone and the knot in my stomach reappeared and tightened.

"I don't know, but it's probably best you're not there." I traced his full lips with my finger, wishing that I could taste them once more.

"I'm going to be there," Beau announced. "I'll hide if I have to, but I'm not going home."

Then as if he had planted some sort of listening device on me, my phone buzzed with a text.

Richard: We are five minutes away. He hasn't eaten except popcorn.

I showed it to Beau who looked like he might smash my phone and feed it to Richard if he had the chance.

"He was supposed to be getting him a burger," he hissed, moving away from me to pace the kitchen.

"I know. At least I'll know he's eaten something decent." It was little consolation really, but I had to think of the positives of the situation otherwise I'd be the permanent wreck that I'd been earlier.

"I hate this for you." Beau dropped his head back and groaned. "He's a fucking bastard."

"I know, but I need to get home before he does."

It was then that we heard a car horn and we both stopped and held our breath for a few seconds. When it sounded a second time, I got up and rushed towards Beau's the back door.

"Why can't I just come with you and hide?"

"Please, Beau. If he finds you there it'll just make things worse."

"Okay, but do not show him that you're afraid and if he touches you press the panic button. I'll be there in twenty seconds."

I nodded and as I opened the door, Beau pulled me to him and kissed me quickly and hard. I then sprinted across the lawn and rushing to unlock my back door and disarm the alarm let myself in as I heard the banging on the front door. My heart jumped, one because my baby was back and two because he had Richard with him.

With a confidence that I by no means had, I unlocked the front door and opened it. Richard looked at sleazy and as greasy as he usually did, no longer the kind older man who I thought had taken me under his wing.

"Hey, sweetheart," I greeted Ethan. "Did you have a good time?"

Ethan smiled and nodded but I stiffened when Richard put his hands on his shoulders and commanded, "Use your words, Ethan."

"Why don't you go up and get ready for bed." I smiled at Ethan and took his hand, pulling him towards me. "Then I'll make you something to eat."

Ethan not waiting for me to say anything else, or even pausing to say goodbye to Richard, raced past me and up the stairs, his tiny feet thundering on the polished wood.

"You're too soft with him." Richard glanced around the hallway and stilled when he spotted the video and access control panel. "I'm not sure that school is right for him," he continued, choosing not to mention the state-of-the-art alarm that he hadn't paid for.

"He likes it," I responded, moving closer to the panic button.

"I think boarding school would be a much better fit. I might check some out. I believe that there's a good one in Hampshire that deal with odd children like him."

The desire to punch him was so great that I had to clench my fists at my sides. "He's not going to boarding school and you even try to do that, I swear to God, Richard, I'll go to the police about what you did to me."

His top lip and left eye twitched, my insolence infuriating him. He took a moment to compose himself and then flicked something off the arm of his expensive looking suit jacket.

"As if they'd believe you after all this time," he sneered. "And if there was even a sniff that's what you'd done I'd have the child away from you quicker than you can set this ridiculous alarm." He lifted his nose haughtily in the air. "Don't forget what I'd also do to your brother, just as quickly."

I tried to hold in the gasp, but it was like trying not to flinch when an ice-cold blade pierced your stomach; it was impossible.

"Enjoy your evening, Simone." He slicked his hair back with his hand. "Oh, and what's wrong with his arm?"

He thought he had a right to send my son away to school yet hadn't even been bothered to find out why his arm was in plaster.

"He fell and broke it," I snapped.

He rolled his eyes without comment and then moved out of the house, slamming the door behind him and when I heard his car start, sobbed over the fear that he had instilled in me.

forty

Beau

Point to note, pacing your garden is not conducive with calming the fuck down.

As soon as I'd gone through the door of Simone's kitchen, I'd vowed I'd take a breath and trust that Sim could handle Richard. That lasted until I pushed through the hedge and the pacing started. After about five minutes I even walked along the road and stood at the end of her drive to check if Richard had left. He nearly caught me because I'd taken three strides closer to the house. Luckily, I heard the car engine and bolted back down and up my own drive.

Three minutes later I was back at Simone's front door, banging on it to be let in. I was grateful that Ethan was upstairs because it gave me the opportunity to ask what happened and then kiss her. To say I was proud that she'd stood up to him was an understatement. I only wished I could have been there and punched his lights out. My time would come though, I was determined about that. When we heard Ethan coming down the stairs, I decided it was best to sneak out the back way and leave them to it. He'd had enough excitement for one day and Simone needed time with him.

That meant that I hadn't spent any time with Simone the night before and was why the next morning I watched intently from the bedroom window for her car to return from the school run. As soon as I saw her pull onto her drive I was out of my house and legging it across the garden to her house.

"Hey," she said as she opened the door.

"He get off okay?" I asked, kissing her cheek.

She bit the corner of her lip and then looked at me through one eye.

"What? What did you do?"

"I told school he had a dental appointment so that I can pick him up early. That way Richard can't just take him again."

Following her into the lounge I contemplated what my response should be. It wasn't my place to comment because if things had been different and I'd met her in a club or something, we'd only be at the 'let's have dinner *as well as* drinks' stage, definitely not the 'let me give you advice on how you should bring up your son' stage.

"You're very quiet," Simone said, dropping onto the sofa and pulling her feet up. "Do you think I'm being stupid?"

Any man knows you do not admit that to any woman, never mind the one you're in a fledgling relationship with. My problem had always been I didn't listen or learn.

"I think it's absolutely bloody ridiculous. Why didn't you tell the school what was happening?" I stood in front of her, my arms folded over my chest and quite clearly not giving off the best body language.

"I told them that his father wasn't to take him again without them calling me first," she replied. "I told them he's ill and I don't like Ethan being in the car with him."

"For fuck's sake, Sim," I cried, feeling totally frustrated. "Why didn't you just tell the truth."

"You know why," she protested, scowling at me.

"Don't look at me like that."

"I just don't understand why you don't get that I can't tell anyone what happened."

"Have you told Marcus?" I asked, already knowing the answer.

"I haven't had time." She started to do the thing she did when she was nervous. Biting her bottom lip. Another time in a different environment it would have got me thinking all kinds of stuff. Stuff that I hadn't thought of in over year of not being with a woman. Now it just made me mad at her because she knew exactly what she should have done.

"I'm not judging you, Sim, but last night you told me that you were going to tell your brother."

She shrugged one shoulder. "Well, I didn't have time."

"Ethan goes to bed at seven-thirty, eight at the latest and I know you didn't turn your lamp off until ten-thirty so what did you that meant you couldn't tell him?"

"You were spying on me?" Her brows raised and she dropped her feet to the floor.

"No, of course I bloody wasn't. I went to bed and closed my blinds at the same time as your lamp went out." It really had been a coincidence, but it also sounded creepy especially with Simone's history. "I swear."

"It doesn't matter," she sighed. "I just wish you'd understand how difficult this is."

"Not telling the police, not telling Marcus is making it more difficult though, Sim. Why can't *you* understand that?"

"I'm just your bloody neighbour Beau, why do you care so damn much?"

That floored me. She knew what turmoil I'd gone through to get that point and then had the nerve to say she was just my neighbour.

"I tell you what then," I snapped, "I'll leave you to it. You decide how the fuck you're going to sort this Richard shit out and let me know what you come up with."

"I've been dealing with it on my own for five years, Beau so it's just another day."

I shook my head, deciding that if this relationship was to continue being fledgling and not dead in the water, I needed to go.

"Where are you going?" Simone called after me.

"Home. I'll see you later when we've both calmed down."

Slamming out of her house I'd barely made it across the lawn to the hedge when I felt the pull to go back. The invisible thread that is created when you care for someone was already there. Simone had it attached to her fingertip and was beckoning me back. With three long strides I was at the back door and saw her at the sink as I burst in.

"Never ever refer to yourself as just my damn neighbour." She slammed a mug down on the drainer. "And why the hell did you not lock that door as soon as I left?"

She turned to me her face full of fury and there right on the end of her nose was a big blob of soap suds. As much as I wanted to be angry with her I couldn't. She was so beautiful, so small and so fucking brave.

"What are you laughing at?" she asked.

I reached out my fingertip and wiped the suds off her nose and then held it up in front of her face. She breathed out heavily and then smirked, smacking at my hand.

"I'm so mad at you," she whispered. "You made me shout and I never shout at anyone. I felt terrible."

Wrapping my arms around her I breathed her in. "You should shout more often," I whispered. "Because you have a voice, Sim. A strong voice that should be heard. You shouldn't have to keep silent about what happened to you. I hate that you had to keep that inside and that he carried on beating you with it. Well no more because as well as you being stronger you've now got me, the guys, my ma and Belle all in your corner."

She made a little noise that I knew was her trying not to cry. I was getting used to her sounds, her moves, her little tells and it made me realise how far we'd come in just a few short weeks. As we stood together, entwined in each other's arms, my pocket started to vibrate, and Simone giggled.

"Please don't even think about it," I groaned, kissing her quickly as I pulled out my phone. "It's Elliot. Hey, El."

"I have some info about what happened to Simmy."

She exhaled and looked at me with anxious eyes.

"Just let me put you on speakerphone. Right okay," I said once we could both hear.

He paused and then said. "You're not going to believe this shit. It seems that one of the security guys was told to report back to Dicky about the party."

"Let me guess," I responded. "That guy Drake."

"Actually no." Elliot sighed. "Fucking Tank of all people."

"You're joking." I moved over to Simone's kitchen island, taking her with me and sat on a stool. I opened my thighs and made sure she settled in between them.

"I wish I was," Elliot responded, his tone flat. "It appears that Dicky has been keeping tabs on us for a while."

"So me being there was just a lucky coincidence for him?" Simone considered out loud.

I kissed her forehead and waited for Elliot to continue, but silence echoed down the line.

"El, you okay?"

He cleared his throat. "Yeah, sorry. It's just knowing he's been watching us all this time. I don't know…"

I couldn't say I was surprised about Dicky spying on us. It was typical of record company bosses to make sure their product didn't fuck up and cost them money. Elliot knew this, we'd spoken about it often enough with other bands and artists. My main concern was that it was Tank who'd been his little stoolie. I'd had him in my home, he'd watched wrestling with Bobby.

"If he thought that you were split though," Simone questioned, "why would he still be keeping an eye on you?"

"No idea, maybe he had an inkling we might go again. What do you reckon, El?"

"Listen, I have to go," he said, his words sounding they were stuck in his throat. "I'll call you later in the week." Then he was gone.

"Weird." I threw my phone to one side and looked at Sim. "At least we know now."

"He knows that we're friends though," she replied, looking thoughtful. "What if—"

"Nope. Don't even think it. Nothing that turd can do will hurt me. It does mean that as we're both connected to him, it's going to be tougher than we thought for us to get rid of him."

"We?" She smiled sweetly and a little blush touched her cheeks. "Us?"

I ran my finger down her cheek and nodded. "Absolutely. You mean a lot to me."

"You mean a lot to me too." She shook her head and giggled. "It's such a surprise."

"You're telling me." Looking down on her it struck me that all I wanted to do was to take care of her. Make sure that she no longer had to fight for herself, by herself. The idea of being with her was suddenly easy. The need to be with her was strong. "I'm not feeling nervous anymore, Sim."

She frowned and then suddenly understanding hit her and her eyelashes fluttered as she closed her eyes briefly before looking back up at me. "Are you sure?"

"Never surer."

"I am though," she said laughing. "Nervous."

Watching her my heart thudded, sweat pricked the back of my neck as I considered what might be about to happen.

"I want to be with you, Sim. Now."

She nodded and without saying anything took my hand and led me to her room.

A few minutes later, Simone stood in front of me, her eyes huge and hesitant and chewing her bottom lip. This time it sent me crazy in that different time, different environment, not been with a woman in over a year sort of crazy. It was hot and sexy, and I wanted to do it for her. My carnal thoughts didn't stop my nerves though and lifting my hand, trembling fingers skimmed her cheek and then over her brow as I watched her watching me. I had never felt so nervous. Not even my first time on stage in front of millions of people. Not even my wedding day. As I thought of Cassie looking beautiful in her white lace dress, guilt edged into my consciousness, but I quickly pushed it back. This had to be about me and Simone. This huge step I was taking was about us and if I let any other thoughts and feelings filter through it would spoil something that I knew was going to be beautiful. I knew that because she was beautiful, and she'd made me feel again. She'd reminded me that there was blood in my veins, so to give her every ounce of my attention was the least she deserved.

"Beau," she whispered like it was a question.

I shook my head and cupped the side of her face. "I want this, Simone. I want you, I'm just a bit out of practice." I gave a short self-deprecating laugh. The great Rockstar was scared of touching a girl. It would be laughable if it wasn't so fucking tragic.

"We can go as slow as you want." Simone's eyelashes flickered and pink tinged her cheeks. "Because I have no real experience of what sex should be like. All I know is I want to be with you."

Looking at her beautiful face I saw self-doubt shadow her features. This was huge for both of us, and it made me more determined to try and concentrate on the here and now and not the past.

I let out a slow breath and moved my fingers to the buttons of her shirt. Her chest was heaving as she breathed in and out and I could see her nipples were hard against the fabric. She was a bundle of apprehension and desire, and it made my heart and my dick ache for her even more. Using both hands, I slowly began to unbutton the small black buttons. Each pop of a fastening revealed a slither of silky cream. With each reveal my nerves spiked a little more. I'd had a lot of women before Cassie, but she was meant to be my ultimate and yet here I was, desperate to bury myself in another. The logic of it felt wrong. How could I possibly want another woman when Cassie had been my wife? Yet how could I not when that woman was as beautiful and as strong as Simone?

Once her shirt was undone, I slowly pushed it from her shoulders and scared to look at her, I watched the red plaid fall to the floor. Simone pulled in a ragged breath drawing my attention back to her face and when she gave me a shy smile I leaned in and kissed her. It was gentle, soft, and amazing, as she sucked on my tongue I felt like free falling. For someone so shy and nervous, she kissed wantonly and uninhibited. Her hands threaded through my already messy hair and drew me closer until there was no way she couldn't feel the hard on pushing against my sweats. My hands were still nervously hanging at my sides but when she moaned softly, they instinctively went to her bum, pushing her against me.

"Beau," she whispered, her voice cracking. "Are you sure."

I pulled back and stared down at her knowing that I couldn't imagine anything in that moment that would cause me to stop. Yes, I still felt the fear of what we were about to do. The trepidation of the step I was about to take, that *we* were about to take, but I wanted her badly. I couldn't say that I wanted her more than anything I'd ever wanted in my life. In an ideal romance novel, the kind Carrie used to read, maybe I would do, but wherever Simone and I ended up on our romantic journey there would always be the spectre of death in the background; the deep bone crushing loss I'd felt over my wife and child.

"I'm sure. I want to see what we can be, Sim. I want to move on with my life and I want it to be with you."

Her delicate hand lifted and brushed the hair away from my eyes as hers raked over my face. She flicked her tongue out and breathed out slowly.

"I know she will always be your true love and I know that in an ideal world I would just be your neighbour. The woman with the kid who doesn't speak. The one you and Cassie would discuss over dinner and wonder about, but this isn't an ideal world, Beau."

I rested my forehead to hers and closed my eyes. Her words were true and I felt guilty that she knew that. Maybe I should have lied and told her that she was all I would ever want, but I couldn't deny the times I'd begged whoever was in charge of the world to bring my wife and son back.

"It doesn't matter," she continued. "I understand it, I do, Beau. All I ask is that whatever we become or however long we last you don't lie to me or make it obvious that I'm not your first choice. You don't have to tell me I'm the love of your life because I know that position is already taken, but please don't ever tell me that I'm you're alright for now."

My hands moved up her bare back until they reached her black lace bra. Thin straps stretched over her slim shoulders, shoulders that had carried the heaviest of loads for the last five years. When I looked down at the honesty and bravery in her eyes, I knew that I could love this woman with all my heart. She could become my happy ever after and I would do everything in my power to make sure she never felt second best.

"You're so fucking beautiful," I said as I slipped down the straps of her bra and then brought my lips to the swell of her breast.

Shorter than me by almost a foot, Simone stretched up onto her tiptoes and then dropped her head back to give me access to her neck. My heart was thudding as I dropped open-mouthed kisses on her cool skin, over her collar bone, along her shoulder and then up her neck to below her ear. When she whispered, "I want you," my heartbeat stuttered, and my fingers began to tingle. Images of another person and another time tried to push to the forefront of my mind, but I flashed my eyes open and drank in the beauty of the woman in my arms.

Needing to centre myself, I stopped kissing Simone and held her at arm's length. I put my hand over my shoulder, grabbed a handful of white cotton and dragged my t-shirt over my head. I threw it to the floor and as it landed at my feet, I moved my hands to the button on Simone's jeans.

"You are aware I might blow this totally, literally, by coming in record time?" I gave her a pained expression and popped her button. "I feel like a teenager." I slowly pulled down her zip. "I'm fucking nervous as hell." I pushed her jeans down.

"Whatever you're feeling, I feel the same." She stepped out of her jeans and then reached behind her to unhook her bra. It fell to the floor to reveal creamy, white, perfectly round tits with dark brown nipples that were hard as bullets.

"God, you're perfect," I said reverently. "I want this to be good for you. For both of us."

She kissed the middle of my chest and then stared up at me. "It will be and if it isn't." She shrugged. "We try again until it is."

My muscles twitched and my mouth went dry as I looked at her and decided that she was right. There was no pressure. We had plenty of time to get things right.

Stooping I caught hold of Simone's arse and helped her to climb my body until her legs were wrapped tightly around my waist. Her arms snaked around my neck and with her lips on mine I carried her to the bed, dropping us both onto it as we still clung to each other. Our kisses became heavier and more insistent and with my dick straining against the fabric, Simone's hands went to my sweatpants and pushed them down. When she got them so far, her feet took over the job and she pushed until they were around my ankles, and I was able to toe them off. When small hands went to my arse, I flexed it tight and groaned against her mouth. It wasn't just that it was a woman's touch after so long of being without, it was the fact that it was her touch. The tiny, brave, beauty who had somehow pushed her way into my life and my heart despite my resistance.

"Get your knickers off," I said against her nipple just before I sucked it into my mouth and ran my tongue around it.

Sim's hips lifted and I felt her shimmy her knickers down her legs and then kick them to one side. Once she was free of them, she opened her legs wide allowing me to settle between them. My dick was hard and throbbing and I could easily have slipped into her but the flapping of wings in my gut and nagging doubts stopped me. I continued to kiss her and pushed both of her hands above her head, holding them with one of mine while the other anchored itself to her hip. Simone writhed and moaned beneath me and the insistence of her tongue duelling with mine told me that she no longer had doubts about what we were about to do. Mine were all about me, not her. There was nothing I could ever doubt about her, with her gorgeous, thick, dark hair splayed around her on the pillow. Not even thoughts of Cassie were stopping me, it was all me and my nerves that I might have forgotten how to please a woman—my woman.

Then suddenly, when Simone's teeth went to my jaw and nipped it and her legs tightened around my waist and she whispered, 'Sweetheart', in my ear, and I was woken from a slumber. I was ready and I needed her. Groaning out her name I pushed inside of her and for a moment I stilled, but when Simone lifted her hips to meet mine, I started to pump. Like the true musician I was, I listened for the beat and to a slow sensual rhythm I fucked her. Our bodies rubbed against each other, the friction of skin on skin, heartbeat against heartbeat urging me on until I felt like I was in heaven.

"Sim," I cried as she dug her fingertips into my back. "Fuck."

"So good," she whimpered. "I'm so close."

"Baby." The word was a plea because I felt like I was going to explode with the feelings that were inside of me. Guilt mixed with pleasure mixed with happiness mixed with grief.

Then as if she knew, Simone grabbed my face, forcing me to look at her and whispered, "Let it all go."

Like she'd flicked a switch, I did as she asked and let absolutely everything go.

I came hard. I started to cry. I screamed. I smiled. My heart shattered into a million pieces.

"Sim, baby."

She didn't say anything but kissed me and I had a vague notion that she hadn't reached her own climax. I pulled out and she moaned at the loss of my dick and tried to pull me back, but I was too strong and too determined. I dropped down between her legs and with one long sweep of my tongue against her soaking wet pussy she screamed out her release. Needing to have her close to me, I gathered Simone into my arms and kissed her. Scissoring my fingers and rubbing them against her clit, I prolonged her orgasm and held her shaking body against mine. We had done it. We had taken that next step. We were an us and I didn't know whether to laugh or scream.

forty-one

Simone

The sun dappling on the ceiling of my bedroom created the prettiest of patterns and I'd looked at them for so long I was convinced I could see a rabbit in them. Beau was sleeping after the most amazing, most epic moment in my life. I had no idea that sex could be like that, sensuous, gentle, and passionate. I'd read about it in books and thought about how perfect it would be to experience something like that. My only other experience had been anything but those things. I'd been held down and told I was a cock tease the whole time. He'd also tried to tell me that I was lying to myself and that I really wanted what he was giving to me and that it was always like that. I might have been a virgin, but I wasn't stupid. Sex with Beau though had been perfect, for me anyway.

I'd wanted to ask him if I was okay, did I do it right, was it as good for him, but I couldn't get the words out. They would have only made me seem childish and naïve and I wanted him to think of me as a woman who knew exactly how to please him. He'd been nervous too and when he cried along with a beautiful smile as he came, I knew then how momentous it had been for him to have sex with someone who wasn't Cassie after losing her. As we cuddled his fingers whispered up and down my arms, but he didn't say a word and then finally he fell asleep. It was a deep restful sleep, with his chest moving up and down in a steady rhythm and I didn't want to wake him. I wanted him to rest, and I also didn't want to see the regret in his eyes.

As my gaze drifted to his face, I almost jumped when he shifted beneath me and raised his arms with a yawn. This was it; this was the moment that my perfect little bubble was burst.

He turned his head towards me and looked shocked to see me there. "Hey."

"Hey," I returned, not daring to move an inch to maintain the perfection for as long as possible.

He looked confused as he then turned away, looking at the door that led to my en suite, no doubt planning his escape. As I held my breath, I felt tears form against my eyelashes and I already felt the agony of his leaving, even though I was still in his arms. All of it disappeared though when he turned back to me with the most beautiful smile.

"I forgot where I was for a minute," he said, pulling me closer and kissing the tip of my nose. "How long have we been asleep?"

"You've been asleep for about an hour."

"You didn't sleep?" he asked incredulously. "After I sexed you to the point of exhaustion."

The relief was immense as he laughed and dragged me closer to nuzzle at my neck.

"Fuck I was so nervous," he groaned, then took a nibble of my shoulder.

"I wouldn't have guessed," I sighed as his hand moved down my side to give my bum a squeeze. "Whereas I..."

Beau looked up and pushed my hair from my face. "You were amazing." Brown and whisky stared at me and all I could do was stare back. His penetrating gaze told me so much, yet there were many things that they were hiding from me. I hoped that he would tell me one day but for now I felt happy that the ghosts of the past weren't haunting him.

"You made me feel confident and sexy," I replied, wrapping my arms around him. "Not something I've ever felt before."

His finger traced my brows as he continued to watch me, and the air was electric with anticipation. Only the gentle hum of the heating broke the silence, no words were necessary. When Beau's hand pushed my thighs apart, I knew what he wanted, what *I* wanted and welcomed his fingers inside of me. I more than welcomed his tongue against mine and when he'd worked me up to the point of screaming, I absolutely welcomed him inside of me. This time there were no nerves, no hesitation, this time was pure fucking, and I loved every single, spine-tingling moment. When Beau screamed his release moments after mine, I relished the strength of his hands as they squeezed mine to the point of pain. When he dragged his stubbled chin up my breast to take my mouth in his as he gave one more deep thrust, I loved the sting of it.

I was becoming addicted to him after just a few stolen hours in my bed. I was going to need a regular fix of his manliness, his supreme sexuality, and the way he made me shatter beneath him. Beau Bradley was my drug of choice, and I did not want to ever give it up.

***

"I'm going to be late," I cried as I rushed around searching for my jeans.

Beau handed them to me. "You're not. You've got plenty of time so no speeding or taking chances down the back lane."

"I won't," I replied, pulling up my zip.

"I wish you'd let me take you." His pout disappeared behind his t-shirt as he pulled it over his head. "I could wait round the corner."

"No. If Richard is watching it'll just give him more ammunition." I paused doing the buttons of my shirt. "I'm going to call Marcus later."

"Really?"

"Yeah, you're right I can't keep putting it off."

"Come round for dinner afterwards." He grabbed my belt loops and pulled me flush against his hard, chiselled chest and I didn't think I'd ever been anywhere better. "I'll cook my famous fish fingers, beans and chips."

I rolled my eyes. "Well, how can I resist. I don't think we should tell Ethan about us just yet though."

Beau rested his chin on the top of my head and wrapped his arms tighter around me. "I agree. It'd be too confusing. We'll say you're coming round for him to play his guitar. Then…" he paused and nipped at my earlobe. "I'll walk you both home and when Ethan has gone to bed, we can make out on your sofa like we're fifteen."

I giggled, very much liking that idea.

***

As we drove up to the house, Ethan gave me a confused look seeing as he thought he was going to the dentist.

"I wanted to spend a little more time with you," I whispered like it was a big secret. "Since you started school, I don't get to do that."

He grinned and I was glad I'd done what I'd done even if it was for the wrong reasons. Feeling much brighter about things, because that was what an afternoon of sex did to you, I fixed Ethan a snack and then sat down in the lounge with him.

"How did you enjoy your time with Richard?" I asked, watching as he nibbled his way around the edges of a chocolate biscuit.

Ethan shrugged and then picked up his cup of milk.

"Did you enjoy the film?"

This time he gave me a confused look, giving me his full attention.

"You went to the cinema, didn't you? Richard said he was taking you there."

He shook his head and said quietly, "No, we went to his office, and I had to sit quietly on a chair by the door."

Fury took over as I recalled how hungry Ethan was when he got home and how it was almost six-thirty.

"Did he give you a snack?" I asked, holding tight to the edges of my chair.

Ethan shook his head. "I told him that my tummy hurt, and he told me to shut up."

Inhaling, I counted to ten as I let my breath out slowly. "Okay, baby, well hopefully you don't have to go there again, unless you'd like to, of course."

He shook his head slowly, four times, his eyes wide and cautious. That was it as far as I was concerned. No way would Richard see Ethan again and no way would he continue to use scare tactics.

"Eat your snack. I'm just going to call someone." I pointed at his arm. "And when I come back, I'll scratch it for you."

He smiled and looked relieved seeing as it was now starting to itch beneath the plaster. My mum's old knitting needles had started to come in handy. I went out to the kitchen and stood at the large window which overlooked the garden and dialled Beau's number.

"Hey, miss me already?" he asked brightly on the second ring.

"Something like that." I smiled, not wanting to change the call to something heavy but needed to tell Beau what Ethan had told me. "So I asked Ethan about Richard."

"Right. Okay. What did he say?" There was a quake in Beau's voice and wondered what on earth he thought I might be about to tell him. Whatever it was I knew that he was fully invested in doing whatever was best for Ethan, and that was not Richard.

"He didn't take him to the cinema, he made his sit on a chair by the door in his office while he worked. He didn't even feed him, Beau. He told me that he'd eaten *popcorn*, like that's a healthy dinner. Yet Ethan just told me his tummy hurt because he was hungry and that Richard had told him, and I quote, 'shut up'."

"Fucker," Beau cursed. "You can't let him go there ever again, Sim," he practically begged.

"I'm not. I don't care what he threatens to do."

"Good girl," Beau breathed out. "I'm proud of you. I'll call Maxwell and let him know."

"You don't think I should tackle Richard about what Ethan said?"

"No, Sim. Leave it to Maxwell. It's more good stuff for your case. Now I need to go because I'm creating a masterpiece for dinner."

I laughed. "Are you making fishfingers from scratch, or are you actually peeling potatoes for chips?"

"Eh no, I'm just putting them on a baking tray, but," he replied sounding bright and happy, "I am making sure they're placed in neat lines. That way they cooked right through."

"Okay," I replied shaking my head with amusement. "I'll see you at six."

"You certainly will," he replied. "And I'm counting every minute."

That was when I knew it was time to stand up to Richard once and for all. First, I called my brother and then I called an estate agent. No longer was he going to push me around and getting out of his house was my primary aim.

forty-two

Beau

Walking into a top-class restaurant with the rest of the guys felt strange. It was like we'd never been away, but it was also alien to be with the three of them and be shepherded to a private section because of who we were.

Fame was a funny thing. When you didn't have it, you craved it and when you had it there were times when you wished you were a nobody. A simple man who lived a simple life, who could nip down to the Co-op for a few bottles of beer, or pop into the bookies to place a bet that you hoped would solve all your money problems. Fame afforded you so much but took away a whole lot more.

"Tell me again why I agreed to this meeting," I groaned as heads swivelled on their necks as we walked through the restaurant.

"To listen to what Ali has to say," Elliot replied from behind me. "If you don't like it, then whatever it is, we say no."

"Way to put the pressure on, Elliot," I grumbled. "If *I* don't like it then *we* say no."

"Hey, Beau," Joey called over his shoulder.

"What?" I snapped, wishing I'd cried off and stayed at home so I could spend the evening with Sim.

"Shut the fuck up moaning. *We'll* all listen to Ali, and if *we* don't like what she's going to ask us to do, *we* all say flipping no. *Okay?*"

Ronnie giggled like a toddler on a sugar high and my desire to run out on them tripled. Before I had a chance to even check the exit points though, Ali was standing up from the table and welcoming us. Hugs and kisses all round and because it was Ali and I had a new appreciation of her since Elliot's party, I reciprocated.

"How's Simone?" she immediately asked.

"She's good thanks. It took her a bit to feel less wobbly but she's fine now." Thank God that Ali had thought to make her sick, or it may have taken much longer for Sim to feel more like herself. And it didn't bare thinking about, but it could have been so much worse if I hadn't seen the fucker.

"I hear that you've been spending a bit of time together," Ali's voice dropped almost to a whisper, but it was obvious the others were listening.

My eyes went to Elliot and mouthed, 'big gob'. The fucker laughed and then dropped down onto one of the chairs at the large round table.

"Okay," Joey said rescuing me from a grilling. "What gives, Al? Why are we meeting seeing as we've pretty much agreed to the interview?"

"I said I agreed in principle," I noted. "There's still a lot to discuss."

"Hey, Beau."

"What, Joey?" I ground, narrowing my eyes on him.

"Stop being a miserable twat."

"Okay, Joey," I replied sarcastically and then flipped him off.

"Right children," Ali sighed. "Sit down. I've ordered your drinks and some bread and olives and your usual array of pizzas."

"How did you know we'd want pizzas?" Ronnie asked, helping himself to water.

Ali rolled her eyes. "Ronnie, I was your manager for six years of course I know that you're a bunch of neanderthal who can't see past a thick crust and dough balls."

She wasn't wrong. This restaurant did loads of amazing pastas in beautiful sauces and all of us always went for pizza, every time—Ronnie even had fucking pineapple on his.

"Okay," she said, straightening her cutlery. "The interview, are you doing it or not?"

Each of the guys said yes and then they all looked at me.

"I know you had some reservations, and you also had some stipulations but what are you thinking?"

I took a deep breath. "I originally said yes but didn't want any mention of Cassie or Bobby in the interview. I agreed though to an end note, an obit."

"What are you saying?" Ronnie asked. "You've changed your mind?"

"Nope, not what I'm saying." I looked at Ali. "I'll do the interview and I'm happy to talk about Cassie."

Ali gasped. "Really?"

"Are you sure?" Ronnie asked as he slapped a hand on my shoulder.

"Yes, but only in relation to the band. Her starring in the first video and her getting Tenfold to go and watch us when we were still signed to Hobart Music. They're both pivotal moments for the band and she should be talked about. Other than that, I'm happy to say yes we then got married, but I don't want to say and then she died." My voice cracked on the last word, and I took one step back from the two I'd made forward that day; a step pattern that I took most days. Although now I had Sim the one back was more every other day. "The guy doing the interview can mention it, but I do not want to answer questions about it. The end note still stands."

I took a large swig from the glass of water in front of me and then sat back in my seat, waiting for the questioning to start. There was nothing. No one said a word. They all simply looked at me.

"What?" I asked.

"You're sure about this?" Elliot asked. "You want to do the interview and let Cassie be included." I nodded. "Are *we* allowed to talk about her?"

I'd thought about this long into the night when I couldn't sleep because of the turmoil I was having over my decision. I'd concluded we all deal differently. I didn't want to talk about something that made my chest feel like it was being ripped apart by a pride of lions while my heart still beat strongly. The rest of them though, well they could do whatever helped then to deal.

"If you want to in your personal interviews, I have no problem with that."

That was the set up—four separate interviews and then a group one. It was a great idea, and it was probably going to earn the guy interviewing us a lot of plaudits because we may have 'split' over a year ago, but we were still seen as a hot topic. We'd beaten a path for other young bands who could play actual instruments and could really belt out a rock tune. Many had tried to emulate us over our relatively short six years but had failed. But for a tragedy we would have carried on and been mega because we had already been on the way to world domination.

"Thanks, Beau," Elliot said, his lips drawn into a thin line. "She was the one who persuaded me to start a band in the first place. I think she deserves for people to know that. She was the one who said, 'He's a real knob but you should ask that Beau Bradley lad from Wigston to join the band. I heard him sing, he's pretty good'."

I grinned, recalling the tale that Cassie had told me many times. She hated me originally because I took a different girl home pretty much every night from Mosh, a nightclub we all used to go to. I had no idea she even existed, because she was right, I was a knob. When I met her though, that first time, during the video shoot it was like a bomb had gone off in my chest. Thankfully, I managed to change her mind about me as soon as I slipped my tongue in during *that* kissing scene.

"Okay then," Ali said, leaning on the table. "Now the other thing I want to talk to you about."

We all watched her expectantly and then finally she spoke.

"The label and the management company want you to tour again. One last time to say goodbye to the fans properly. After Joey finishes up filming."

The guy's eyes all lit up and I had to admit there was a tiny spark of excitement brewing in my own stomach. The thought of leaving Sim and Ethan though, I wasn't sure I could do it. I'd only just found her, only just started to feel healed, and now I could be leaving her because how could I say no if the others wanted it? I had the sweaty palms and the buzz on my skin like I used to when we talked about performing. I'd almost forgot what it was like, but I could practically taste the sweat, the excitement and the anticipation of the crowd.

"How long?" I asked.

Everybody's eyes fixed on me while Ali's eyebrows almost disappeared into her hairline."

"Six months," she said tentatively.

"Three," I countered. "Then four months at home and then the other three."

"Did someone swap him?" Ronnie asked.

Joey burst out laughing. "Got to say I'm surprised."

"What about, Simmy?" Elliot asked.

I swallowed. "That's why it can only be three months and I want to do the initial three during the summer so that she can join us if she wants to."

"Wow," Ali said, putting a hand to her chest. "That's some statement you're making there, Beau."

"I know. I want to show her that I'm committed and fucking off around the world for six months hardly does that. I also know that she'll tell me I'm stupid if I say no and that these three will bitch about me like those housewives off the telly."

"What the hell?" Joey groaned.

"What can I say, Sim has shit taste in music and telly programmes."

I grinned thinking about her. We'd been seeing each other, dating, whatever you called it for almost three weeks, and it was already pretty intense. The night before I'd spent my first overnight at hers although getting up at six to sneak back home through the garden hedge was not my idea of fucking romance. I understood though, she didn't want Ethan getting confused. However, I knew what she really meant. She didn't want him to get excited only to be disappointed when I dumped her because of the guilt at moving on. Well, she was wrong. Yes, there were days when I was consumed with guilt, but not as many as she seemed to think. I loved Cassie with all my heart, but she wasn't coming back. Sim however was in the here and now and was everything I wanted in a woman, in a partner.

"I think I can wangle that if timescales allow but I know that they're pretty desperate to get you on the road this year," Ali replied looking me directly in the eye.

"One other thing," I said leaning across the table. "I don't want Dicky Gregory involved in any way. The fact that he owns the record label is bad enough, but he doesn't need to make any decisions regarding the tour. All that is down to Brit Arts, otherwise I'm out."

"Same," Ronnie chimed in.

My eyes immediately went to Elliot who looked decidedly guilty seeing as he was really interested in the tablecloth.

"Can I ask why?" Ali asked.

"Nope," I replied.

"It's personal," Joey responded.

I looked at Elliot again and shook my head. "And again, big gob."

Ali pushed her chair back and tapped on her phone with a long red nail. "Let me go and make a call about the length of the tour first and then we can discuss any other sticking points."

When she went Elliot looked at me and raised a brow. "Well, that was unexpected."

"I know you all want it," I replied and pointed at him. "But I won't forget you've got a big mouth."

"Beau, fuck off," Ronnie said, poking me in the arm. "Of course he's going to tell us. We're family and we were there when Simmy was drugged. She means something to you, so she means something to us. That's how family works."

"Ron's right man," Joey added taking a sip of his water. "We're all going to look out for her."

I opened my mouth to argue that I was perfectly capable of doing that job, but Joey cut me off with a 'Psst' and a palm held up to my face. Elliot laughed and Ronnie shrugged.

"You all do my fucking head in," I grumbled knowing that I was a lucky bastard to have them at all.

forty-three

Simone

"O kay," Beau said, thrusting his hands into his pockets. "I need to talk to you about something.

My stomach lurched as I looked at him shifting from foot to foot. I wasn't going to like what he had to say, and I had a feeling it was probably going to be about him changing his mind about us.

"Just say it, Beau." I swallowed the lump in my throat and took two steps away from him.

"You know we all met Ali last night?"

"Yes." I frowned. Had Ali warned him to stay away from me because of Richard, or had Richard got to him?

"The management team, well, they want us do a farewell tour. Say goodbye to the fans properly."

"Oh." My eyes popped. "Seriously?" That was not what I was expecting him to say and was relieved, excited and worried all at the same time. I was excited for Beau and the boys and for the fans, but selfishly I was worried about what it meant for us.

"Yeah." He reached out his hand for mine and linked our fingers. "What do you think?"

"What do I think?" I asked and placed a palm against my heart that was beating hard and fast.

"Yeah, it kind of affects you too," he replied, stooping to give me a quick touch of his lips to mine. "We're a couple and I'm going to be gone for a while, so yeah it affects you."

"Beau that's silly. We are so new, and this is your career, your life. What I think doesn't matter one little bit, but for the record I think it's amazing and you most definitely have to do it."

"You think?" He stooped so that he could look up at me as I was studying the floor. "We'll be away for a while."

"How long?" I held my inhale a little longer than usual in an attempt to stop me from sounding like I was about to cry. There was no way he was going to know that all I could think of was the nights and days that he would be away from me and around other women.

He led me to the sofa and pulled me down next to him. "I asked for three months during the summer, a four-month break and then the final three months."

"You asked?"

"They wanted us do a six-month stint in one go but I didn't want to leave you for that long."

My mouth dropped as Beau stared at me, waiting for my response.

"You didn't?" I finally managed to get out.

"Of course I didn't," he said softly. "We're just starting out, Sim. I don't want to rob us of the beginning of what we could become."

"But you want to go?"

He nodded and licked his lips, trepidation in his eyes as they darted around, watching my face.

"And I want to be with you too," he sighed and taking my hand in his, rubbed his thumb backwards and forwards over it. "That's why I asked for the first part to be in the summer. I thought maybe you and Ethan could come with us for a while."

"You did?" I whispered trying to blink back the tears that were threatening to fall. "You honestly wanted us there?"

I was pulled onto Beau's lap, facing him with his hand rubbing rhythmically up and down my back. The warmth beat through my t-shirt to my skin and when I looked into his beautiful eyes all I wanted to do was lose myself in him.

"There is a problem though," Beau said softly.

My heart stuttered. "What?"

"We can't do the summer. Joey has a few weeks left of filming and rehearsals will take a couple of months and so we won't go until September and—"

"And Ethan will be back at school then," I responded, disappointment washing over me.

"You could home school him on tour for a couple of months," he suggested.

I shook my head. "I can't, Beau. It will be his full first year in a proper school."

"Isn't that a good time to do it then?" His eyes were bright with excitement at the possibility. "Think of all the things he'll see and experience."

"I don't know, Beau. He's just making friends for the first time, and I think taking him away might spoil that for him. I mean he's at Charlie's house now with two other boys, that's never happened."

He nodded. "Okay. So, thinking that you might say that I asked that we do stints of four weeks and then home for a week. Plus, I'll be home for Christmas which we've agreed will be for two weeks."

"You did that for us?"

"Yes, Sim, I did it for us."

Soft lips took mine in the sweetest of kisses as Beau's arm wrapped tighter around me. If ever I'd felt safer and more cared for than this, I couldn't think of it. Not even by my parents, especially not my dad, the man who was supposed to scare the monsters away.

"I need to tell you something," I said, laying my head on Beau's chest.

"What's that?"

I looked up at him and gave a half smile, not sure how he was going to react. "I've found an apartment. I'm leaving next door."

Beau pushed me away from him and blinked rapidly. "What do you mean? Where?"

"After I spoke to Marcus I—"

"Hang on, you told me he wasn't home."

"He wasn't but he called me back this morning."

He looked hurt but I just hadn't had a chance to tell him. "You wanted to talk about the tour as soon as I got here," I replied. "I was going to tell you. I am telling you now."

"Okay tell me what he said and then we're going back to the bloody apartment subject."

I had to smile at his sulky pout which made him look like a sulking teenager.

"I told him everything that Richard said he would do to him. Making out he was a paedophile, planting stuff on his computer, ruining his life basically."

Strong arms came back around me as Beau sighed heavily. "Did he tell you that you should have said something before?"

I gave a little grunt, recalling how my brother had chastised me for baring the burden on my own. "Yes, he did. He told me that if I'd told him he could have made measures to ensure that Richard's in his words, 'fuck up of a plan', failed."

"Yeah, well I'm with him on that one." He paused when he felt me inhale sharply. "I get why you thought differently. He's a bully and a manipulator and neither me nor your brother have been on the other end of that. I guess it's easy for us to say it was hardly a credible plan."

He was right. When Richard wasn't around, I could be all confident and vow that I wouldn't be intimidated by him again, but once he was in front of me... it was a different matter. The little, quiet, naïve young girl in me believed every word that he said.

"Marcus wants to come over. He wants to visit for the weekend so that we can talk about how to deal with it."

Beau nodded. "Great, I look forward to meeting him. When's he coming?"

"This weekend. He's bringing his boyfriend, Lee."

"Okay, sounds good," Beau said, arching a brow. "Now, about this apartment."

I drew my lips into a thin line and thought about the apartment, well flat, above a bakery in town. A place that I could only just about afford.

"It's above Hudson's Bakery on South Street in town."

Beau shook his head. "That's a flat, Sim, not a fucking apartment. You're not going there."

"I can't stay next door, Beau. He has control over me if I continue living there. I should never have agreed to it in the first place."

"I agree you need to move out but you're not moving into a flat above a shop. How many bedrooms does it have?"

When I told him two, he looked a little disappointed. If I'd said one it would have been more power to his argument that I wasn't moving there. Not that he could stop me. If Beau had given me anything it was a voice and confidence to do and say what I wanted.

"Move in here," he suddenly announced, like it was the most natural thing in the world. "If you want you can have a separate bedroom to me, although expect me to sneak across the landing every night." He winked and he looked so sexy, I almost said yes. "Then in a few months I'll be gone most of the time anyway. It'll be doing me a favour, you taking care of the place."

It was tempting but if I moved in here there would be no way of hiding my relationship with Beau from Richard. Although, I was pretty sure he knew but was biding his time to twist the knife in over it. Besides, we'd only just started being a couple.

"Beau, that's a lovely thought but it's too soon. We are so new and what if you go on tour and realise that you quite like being away from me?"

It was the easiest way I could think of to express my fear that he might find the women on tour too irresistible. When I saw the hurt in his eyes, I knew I hadn't been kidding anyone, least of all Beau.

"You know what it took for me to move on, Simone. Do you really think I'd risk it by having meaningless sex with some groupie?"

"That's not what I said," I lied.

"Not the words maybe, but that's what you meant."

I took a deep breath and knew that the truth was what I had to give to him."

"I'm nothing, Beau. I'm not a model, I don't have anything to my name except for a whole load of baggage. Your boss is the man who is determined to ruin my life and I have no experience sexually." I threw my hands in the air. "Why the hell would you want to stick around when you could have uncomplicated and meaningless?"

I braced expecting Beau to blow with anger, but instead he gave me a beautiful smile and cupped my face with both of his hands.

"You are so much more than you give yourself fucking credit for, Sim. Whatever that bastard has thrown at you you've dealt with it. You haven't folded and sat in a corner and cried. You've done what needed to be done for you and Ethan."

His kiss was surprising but welcome and it lit me up like a touch paper. His lips were soft and his tongue probing as his hands threaded into my hair and quickly heated things up to another level. He wasn't doing it to silence me, he was doing it to make me realise what I was to him. That I *was* much more than I allowed myself to think I was.

"Don't ever," he whispered seductively in my ear, "think that you are inexperienced sexually. You have no idea how much you fucking rock my world in bed. You're adventurous and enthusiastic, not inexperienced, Sim."

Having had his say, Beau went back to kissing me and when his hand slipped inside my leggings and his finger stroked through my wetness, he groaned out his desire.

"So fucking wet."

His voice deep and quiet turned me on more and I felt myself get wetter. As he pushed two fingers inside of me, I rose to my knees to give him better access. Stroking my inner walls sent my body into a frenzy and I ripped my t-shirt off. Beau groaned and his hand moved from my hip and pulled down my bra so he could take my puckered nipple into his mouth. As he sucked in rhythm with his fingers stroking me, it wasn't long before I cascaded into my orgasm. Mewling and moaning as I thrust in time with him.

When I came down from the ecstasy I didn't hesitate. Beau was looking at me reverently as he pulled his fingers from inside of me as I put my hands at the waistband of his sweatpants and pulled them down, urging him to lift his bum so I got better access. As they moved down his hips his beautiful, smooth cock sprung free, rock hard and glistening at the tip.

Shifting so that my head was in his lap, I took him and pulled my mouth up his shaft. When I reached the end, I swirled my tongue around and cupped his balls in my hand. Beau's groan was loud, and it filled me with confidence that I was doing it right. I'd never given a blowjob before and owed everything to the romance novels that I read. They must have been well written because as I licked and pumped at the same time Beau gripped the side of the sofa cushion. My jaw ached a little, but I was determined and continued to lay every trick I'd read about cock sucking on him.

"Sim," he ground out, his hand going to the back of my head and taking hold of my hair. "I'm gonna come."

I knew he was warning me that if I didn't want to taste his cum then I needed to stop. I didn't, I carried on and when the warm liquid hit my tongue, I felt like I was Wonder Woman. He pumped and pumped, and I swallowed, taking everything that he had to give until he flopped back against the sofa loosening his grip on my hair.

He then looked at me through one eye and said, "Are you sure you don't want to move in."

forty-four

Beau

Pressing Simone's fingers to my lips, I gave her a reassuring smile. Marcus was walking up the drive with his boyfriend Lee, who it had to be said was a good-looking bastard. Tall and dark he gave Elliot a run for his money in the best-looking man on the planet stakes.

"Hey, Simmy." Marcus gave her a one-armed hug, which she stiffened into while his other hand came out to me. "Nice to meet you, Beau."

"You too," I replied as I gave him the once over. He looked like Simone but was my height and a slimmer build than me. He smiled at us both, but he was definitely wary if his stiff spine and neck were anything to go by.

"This is Lee," he said standing to one side and letting his boyfriend come closer.

"Hey, lovely to meet you both." He shook both our hands and then took a step back to Marcus' side. "It's really great of you to invite me."

"Don't be silly," Sim said. "Anytime, while I still have the room."

"What do you mean?" Marcus frowned but looked at me as if I was the one responsible for her going to live in a shitty flat above a bakery.

"I'll tell you later," Simone replied. "Come on let's go inside. Leave your bags in the hall and I'll take you up to your room after we've had a cuppa."

Simone led us all into the house and as we walked through the hall to the kitchen, I could hear Marcus and Lee whispering. It pissed me off for some unknown reason, to the point that I shot them a glance over my shoulder.

"Everything okay?" I asked.

Marcus' shoulders sagged and he nodded. "Sorry, it's just all such a shock."

"Yeah well, it's not exactly been a picnic for your sister."

"No, I'm sure." Marcus gave me a tight-lipped smile and I was pretty sure that me and big bro were going to butt heads at some point.

We all sat around Simone's kitchen table while she busied herself making mugs of tea. None of us really said anything apart from the usual, 'did you have a good journey?', 'I really enjoyed your last album', and 'at least the weather is getting warmer'. All highly exciting, so when Simone sat down with a tray of mugs, I heaved a silent sigh of relief and grabbed the most stewed looking one.

"Did you have a good journey?" she asked.

I almost spat my tea out.

"Yeah," Marcus said. "I was just saying to Beau that we had a lovely breakfast on the train."

"Oh nice." Simone smiled and it was obvious to see why she'd had to cope alone for the last five years. There was hardly any bond between them; nothing like me and Belle and I'd practically ignored her for a year.

"I guess we should discuss the Richard thing," Marcus said and glanced at Lee.

"Nothing much to discuss if I'm honest, Marcus," I replied. "He's a twat and I personally think he should be reported to the police. That's been my standpoint right from when I found out and it won't change."

"Even though you knew he'd try and ruin me?" Marcus folded his arms over his chest and glared between me and Sim.

Simone shifted in her seat and looked down at the table. I moved my arm to rest along the back of her chair and lifted my hand to softly draw circles with my thumb on her shoulder.

"Got to be honest, Marcus," I replied giving him a half smile, "you weren't my priority. Sim was."

"Well, she could have been mine too, if she'd told me."

There was a little hint of ice in his tone, and I didn't fucking like it. He had no real idea of what she'd been through trying to protect him. Now she was feeling able to deal with Richard, Marcus was all in, turning up wanting to be the big brother who solves all her problems.

"I was trying to protect you," Simone protested, her fingers gripping her mug so tight I thought she was going to crush it.

I hooked her around the neck with my arm and pulled her closer for a kiss to the cheek and whispered in her ear, "Sim, it's okay. No one's blaming you."

"Marcus," Lee said peering around his boyfriend's shoulder to gain his attention. "Maybe we should forget what Simone did or didn't do, respect her decision and discuss how we sort this out."

Yep, I certainly liked the boyfriend more than the brother.

Marcus blew out a frustrated breath and nodded. "I'm sorry, Lee's right. How do we handle this moving forwards?"

Fuck, he just nailed his coffin. *Moving forwards*, shit he'd be talking about Blue Sky Thinking next.

"Beau's solicitor, Maxwell is dealing with the custody case and he—"

"Hang on." Marcus held up a hand to stop her. "Custody case? You never said anything about a custody case."

Simone poked her tongue out and held it against her top lip and it was the closest I'd seen her to looking pissed off. Even when we'd rowed over Richard she didn't look as mad as she did at that moment.

"Richard is trying to get custody of Ethan," she said slowly and deliberately. "I didn't tell you because I thought I'd put enough stress on you telling you everything else."

"And this solicitor of yours," he said and turned to me, "how confident is he that he can resolve this?"

"Very. He doesn't think Richard wants custody he's just doing it to frighten Sim."

"So even though you're involved you're unable to protect her?"

If Simone had been pissed with Marcus before she now looked like she might kick him in the bollocks and then pluck them out of his throat. My thumb stopped circling and I moved my hand to her waist, anchoring her to the chair because I was afraid for Marcus' tackle.

"Don't you dare," she snapped. "Because Beau has done everything in his power to protect me and we've only been together a short time. Richard is his boss as well so that—"

"For God's sake," he cried. "This just gets worse. Richard who raped you and got you pregnant is *his* boss." When he pointed an accusatory finger at me, I feared for his life, never mind his bollocks.

"Now hang on a minute," I protested, letting go of Simone and leaning on the table. "I had no idea that Richard was the Dicky who owns my record label, so don't point your finger at me."

"Come on guys," Lee cajoled putting a hand on Marcus' forearm. "This is all going to shit and not what we came for. It's certainly not helping Simone."

Marcus dropped his head to his hands and groaned. "You're supposed to make sure she's okay. Not drag her into more crap." He looked up at me with haunted eyes and if I didn't think he was such a twat, I might have felt sorry for him. "He's your damn boss no wonder he's come after her again."

"Now wait a minute, pal—"

"He didn't know," Simone yelled, interrupting me as she slammed a hand down on the table. "And you should be very careful what you say about blame, Marcus."

I wheeled around to look at her and saw my beautiful girlfriend was red with rage. Not only that, but she was shaking. There was much more to that statement than I knew. I made a mental note to ask her later, but Simone was on a roll and didn't leave me hanging.

"That night," she said, breathing heavily, "that night that he raped me I shouldn't have been there. That night, Marcus, *you* were supposed to pick me up because we were going to go to dinner…" Marcus groaned, and my hand grabbed Simone's and enveloped it. "… but you bumped into some friends and forgot about me. Richard saw me sitting there waiting and so said seeing as I was there maybe I wouldn't mind working. That was the night he raped me, so don't look to Beau or anyone else to blame."

I'd had no idea that's how she'd ended up being at work late. I just assumed it was normal for her to work late. My heart thudded and nausea swirled in my gut as once again thoughts of what he did to her flashed through my mind. As for Marcus, how fucking selfish forgetting her like that. If he'd just done what he was supposed to this crap might not have happened to her.

Marcus opened his mouth to speak but Simone held up a hand to silence him and pushed her chair back and stood up. She went over to the bookcase and pulled out a plastic file that I recognised. She walked back to the table and threw it in front of her brother.

"That is what I've been dealing with for five years Marcus. So please don't come here and point your finger or tell me that I've handled it all wrong."

Marcus took everything out of the file and he and Lee read through it. When I heard a strangled groan, I guessed he'd read the email which was supposed to be to the young girl.

"I'm sorry, Simmy I had no idea," Marcus said, his eyes brimming with tears.

"Maybe if you'd spent more than two weekends with me since Dad died, you'd have realised that I was struggling."

"Is this," he took a deep breath, "is this why Ethan doesn't speak?"

Oh boy, this idiot was just the gift that kept on giving.

"You really think she'd let this affect, Ethan?" I asked, shoving the file. "She's an amazing mum who does everything in her power to make sure that little boy has a good life. She even sucked up that bastard taking Ethan after school just so Ethan wouldn't get scared or anxious about it."

"No disrespect but how long have you known my nephew? I'm a teacher and I have also had training to recognise PTSD in kids and Ethan is a prime—"

"You know fucking shit, mate." I was so done with his bloody crap and didn't care if he never spoke to me again for the rest of my life. "There's not a thing wrong with that kid. He doesn't speak because he doesn't want to, and I don't blame him to be honest. Nothing better than your own company at times believe me." I looked at him in such a way that he knew I was referring to him. Call himself an expert, from what I could gather he'd barely tried to figure out his nephew. He hardly knew him. "Did you know he can sing like an angel?" I asked. Marcus shook his head. "Or that he's a natural at guitar? Or that he has the biggest heart? Or that he loves cheesy baked beans on toast? Or that he's become obsessed with Harry Potter? No, I didn't fucking think so."

My chest was heaving as I sat back in my chair and blindly pulled Simone to my side. I would do anything for her and Ethan, even give her brother a few home truths if I had to.

"I think we all need to calm down," Lee said quietly as he gathered the contents of the folder. "Maybe we should go up to our room and unpack our bags, give Simone and Beau a bit of breathing space." He looked at us both and his eyes were practically begging us to forgive Marcus for the shit he'd spouted.

I nodded and Lee's shoulders sagged. He seemed a decent bloke and I was sure Marcus was seen to be by most people, he just hadn't got off on the right foot with me, so maybe some space would help.

As Marcus and Lee stood, Marcus' eyes were fixed to Simone, but she wouldn't look at him, hers were set on watching the table with her hand firmly in mine.

"Will Ethan be back later?" Marcus asked.

I looked at Simone who clearly wasn't going to answer, so I nodded. "Yeah. Sim thought it might be better if he was at a friend's house while we talked."

That was an understatement.

Marcus nodded and cleared his throat. "Well, dinner is on us tonight. I don't know if you go out much, Beau, you know with being recognised, or we can get a takeaway?"

"Yep, no problem. We'll sort it later, but takeaway is probably best because of Ethan's bedtime," I replied. He's had a couple of late nights recently."

Simone didn't utter a word so Marcus nodded and turned to go. Simone then spoke. "It's the room you had last time." Then she went back to silent.

Once I heard their footsteps on the stairs, I pulled her onto my knee and hugged her tightly. She snuggled close and wrapped her arms around my waist.

"That was horrible," she whispered. "I had no idea my brother was such a prick."

I couldn't help but laugh, she hardly ever swore so to hear her saying prick was amusing.

"You dirty mouth little devil." That got me a giggle and I felt myself relax. "I thought you might be mad at me for giving him shit."

"He started it," she muttered sulkily. "Lee seems nice though."

I laughed again. "Yeah, he does." I kissed the top of her head. "You okay?"

"Yep." There was a heavy sigh and then she said, "On Sunday once Marcus and Lee have gone, I'm going to the police."

I drew in a sharp breath and then stilled, not sure that I'd heard right.

"I'm going to report Richard," she reiterated. "And I hope then that's the end of it."

I wanted to agree with her but had a sneaky suspicion that it could just be the start of something else.

forty-five

Simone

The weekend with Marcus and Lee had been a strain to say the least. After the outbursts in the kitchen, we tried to put it behind us but too much had been said. Stuff that if I'd ever had a therapist, they'd have told me to say years before. I hadn't had a therapist though and had tried to deal with it the best way that I knew how.

Ethan had been pleased to see Marcus at least and even managed a quiet hello to him and Lee. I could see that it made Marcus emotional, but I was still too angry to console him. If he'd taken the time over the last five years like Beau had over the last couple of months, Marcus may have got that hello a lot sooner.

On the Saturday Marcus and Lee went into the city to shop and have a few drinks. They didn't get back until early evening and were both pretty tipsy. So, after I cooked a chilli, they passed out on my sofa while Beau and I played Harry Potter Monopoly, a present from Belle, with Ethan. It was almost nine-thirty by the time we finished and as I told Ethan to go and get ready for bed Marcus and Lee woke up and said they were going up too. At least it meant Beau and I had some alone time on the sofa playing teenage babysitters again. Beau having to put his hand over my mouth to keep me quiet as I came was exciting, but it made me realise that I was almost ready to tell Ethan about us so that we could have sleepovers when we moved to the flat.

Then on Sunday morning after what felt like a forced pleasant breakfast, Marcus and Lee got a taxi and left. Beau offered to take them, but I think Marcus knew that Beau would rather scratch his fingers down a chalkboard. Things had most definitely not thawed between them.

All in all, I wasn't disappointed to see my brother go home. We hadn't even decided what to do about Richard which had been the whole point of his visit. He didn't ask me about it again, so I guessed he wouldn't care that I was going to the police. I'd seen a different side to him. Or maybe I'd finally seen him for the selfish man he was and always had been. Beau was right he knew nothing about Ethan and for all his boasting of being a teacher and trained in all sorts of things, he'd never once tried to find out why Ethan didn't speak. He'd tell me that he had, but I knew now he was lying. All that rubbish about Ethan having PTSD, yet Marcus always said to me that he would talk when he was ready. Either way my brother was a liar.

As soon as we'd had lunch on Sunday, I got Beau to drive me to the police station after dropping Ethan off with Belle, who had another Harry Potter film for him to watch. That had gone decidedly better than the conversation with my brother. Beau stayed with me while I told two officers everything that happened. They were kind and considerate and honest that after five years it might be difficult to bring a prosecution without any evidence, but they'd investigate it fully. When one asked for Beau's autograph for his daughter, I did wonder whether that was the only reason they'd been so helpful. It didn't matter though; I'd finally done something about the man who thought he could control my life.

After everything that had been said at the police station, I was shocked to see Richard at my door on Monday lunchtime.

"Shit," I muttered taking a step back from the door. I hoped he hadn't seen me through the glass, but he knocked again and called my name. I was petrified of him, but I wasn't sure whether I should act normal, like I hadn't been to the police and reported him for rape. I tapped on the screen of my phone and brought up Beau's number. He was at Belle's new place putting in a washing machine for her, so he wasn't too far away. About to press dial, I was startled by Richard knocking on the door again. When I looked up, I almost screamed as his face was peering through the frosted glass.

"I can see you, Simone. Why the hell won't you open the door?"

When he took a step back, I went over to the video panel and checked the camera. He didn't look like he was too angry seeing as was flicking through what looked like a magazine and leaning casually against the wall.

I decided that acting normal was the best idea and spoke into the intercom. "What do you want Richard?"

"I'm here to talk about Ethan's boarding school." He held up a glossy brochure and tapped on it.

"I told you, he's not going.".

"You could just look at the fucking brochure, Simone," he growled.

I watched as he smoothed a finger along his eyebrow and then straightened his tie. He didn't look like he'd been visited by the police and if I didn't open the door, he'd more than likely find some other way to make me pay.

"Get Vanessa to post it," I tried, wondering why he had come in person. For the last five years I'd dealt with Vanessa, yet now he wanted to do his own dirty work.

"Simone, open the damn door and take the brochure. I also want the key to the garage. I've lost mine and I have some boxes in there that I need."

He wasn't lying about that. For some reason he had three packing boxes in the corner of the garage, and they'd been there since I moved in, but I had no idea why he'd suddenly want them. I'd just take the brochure hand over the key and then he'd be gone. I went and got the key from the hook in the kitchen and rushed back to the door. I unlocked it with the thumbpad and opened it up a crack, holding the key through. Richard took it and then passed me the brochure, sighing as he did.

"Thank you but it's not necessary," I said and moved to shut the door.

He was too quick for me though and before I had a chance to do anything, he'd pushed his way in.

"Richard, get out," I cried backing away from him and pointing to the door. "I don't want you in here."

"Well seems to me you have no choice, seeing as it's my house." He sneered at me, his eyes so narrow and menacing that a shiver ran all over my body.

Everything in me told me to keep quiet about moving, about going to the police, about my relationship with Beau, about telling Marcus. Richard was manipulative and if he knew about any of those things, I was sure he'd use them against me somehow.

"Please Richard," I said moving away from him. "I'm asking you nicely to leave."

"Ask as nicely as you like," he replied, looking me up and down. "I'm not leaving."

The look in his eyes filled me with fear because I'd seen that look on him once before and I was fully aware of how badly that ended. The way he smirked and sauntered towards me with his hands in his pockets was sinister, as if he'd planned what he was going to do next way before he'd knocked on my door. There was nothing spontaneous about the way he was backing me into a corner, or the way he was eyeing me like I was his prey, and he was about to kill me. He'd known exactly what he was going to do before I'd opened the door to him.

"Richard, you really don't want to do this," I said, my heart racing so fast I thought I might pass out.

"Got away with it once before."

"You won't this time Richard, this time I'd go straight to the police."

A step closer.

"I'd have that kid away from you before you even had a chance to pick up the phone. I have a man on the school right now. Wouldn't it be tragic if he went missing from the school yard?"

"You'd never get away with it. I'd tell everyone it was you. The police would be after you."

"You know what?" he said cocking his head to one side. "I think I fancy a little holiday abroad, make a nice long trip of it. Maybe even move over there."

If I'd have been able to think logically, I would have known what he was threatening was impossible. He was trying to frighten me that was all. Yet I couldn't think logically because all I *could* think was what if he took Ethan and I never saw him ever again.

Richard's head stiffly cocked to the other side as if he was cracking his neck and his hands went to the button of his jacket. He flipped it open and then slipped it from his shoulders. When it slid down his arms, he shook it off, caught it and then threw it to one side.

"I'm sick and tired of you butting heads with me over that kid," he snarled, spittle spraying from the corners of his mouth. "You need to learn to do as your told."

Another step closer.

"I will never let you touch me ever again," I spat back, determined that I would fight for my life.

Richard laughed emptily, his head falling back, and I took the opportunity to run to the panic button by the door. As I pressed it, my head was suddenly pulled back by my hair, and I was dragged away from the door.

"I told you, you're not going anywhere."

Pain seared through my scalp as he pulled tighter and when my legs gave way, I thought I might pass out from the agony. It felt like he'd scalped me with his bare hands. I opened my mouth to scream but nothing came out because there was a huge ball of terror blocking my throat. I reached up to scratch at Richard's hands, his arms, anything and when he cursed out the word bitch, I felt a small sense of confidence that maybe he'd let go. He did but only to grab me and throw me to the floor. My shoulder hit the tiles first and pain seared down through my arm. When I flopped onto my back, tears scorching my cheeks, a kick came to my side, taking my breath away.

"No," I managed to groan out. "Please no."

Richard's face appeared above me, beady brown eyes peering at me with a curled lip of distaste.

"Don't think I don't know you've been fucking the rock star either," he said, his mouth inches from mine. "Because I do. I know everything. I know you're whoring yourself to him and I know you've found yourself a nice little flat that you think will free you of me. Well think again."

My heart sank and he smiled at me like he'd won. Because he had. He knew about Beau and if he let me survive whatever hideous plan that he had for me, I knew that Beau would become a bargaining chip, just like Marcus had been. I wouldn't let that happen though. Beau meant too much to me. I was falling in love with him no matter how much I tried not to and the man who had become my rock wouldn't be ruined by the slimy, hateful excuse for a human being who was currently bending over me and sneering at my pain.

"You know what though," Richard said as his hands went to the button on his trousers. "If Bradley still wants you after this, I've got a cracking little video that you can both watch. You and me, last time, on the floor of my office. Better than a lot of porn that I've seen."

"You bastard," I gasped.

Richard shrugged and standing tall above me, landed another kick. He was the vilest of men, and I hated every single bone in his body. When he unbuttoned his fly and then put his hand to his zip, I vowed that I would kill him the moment that I got the chance. I would never get that opportunity though because he was whirled around by a hand on his shoulder.

Beau threw a punch that sent Richard reeling, smashing into the side table and then stumbling off it back into the path of Beau's fist again. Another punch and then another, until Richard dropped to his knees. His shirt was out of his trousers at the front and there was blood pouring from his nose. His slicked back hair was flopping in front of his pained face, and he was no longer a man that I feared.

"You fucking bastard," Beau hissed as he pulled Richard up by his shirt. "I'll kill you, you vile cunt."

I tried to sit up, struggling with the pain in my shoulder and side. All I could manage was to lean on my elbow and watch as Beau spat in Richard's face.

"Beau," I gasped.

His head shot to me, and it crumpled as he let Richard fall to the floor, gasping and groaning.

"Sim," he whispered and dropped to my side. "Baby are you alright." His large hands gently cupped my face as his eyes took everything in trying to determine if I was okay.

"I'm fine. My shoulder and side hurt, but I'm okay."

"Fuck, I was so damn scared," he said, pulling me against his chest before releasing me to make another check. "Your call came through just as I was leaving Belle's. I had to fucking listen to him the whole way here." His voice broke and tears sprang to his eyes. "I was going as fast as I could, but I didn't think that I'd get here in time."

I reached up and held his face in my hands. "Beau, it's okay. I'm fine. I didn't realise I'd actually called you."

"I kept shouting for you, but you didn't hear me and then I almost cut the call off when I heard you say his name. I kept shouting and shouting but nothing." He finally took a breath. "I was yelling at you not to open the door, not to let him in but you didn't hear me."

Fear and pain shivered through his body as he dragged me closer and held me tight. I clung to him and hung on like he was a life raft, determined not to let go.

When Richard groaned from behind Beau and tried to struggle to his feet, I gasped.

"Beau."

He let me go and stood up and turning to Richard pushed a booted foot against his shoulder.

"You're not going anywhere you fucker."

It was then that I heard the sirens and remembered that I'd managed to reach the panic button. With a little difficulty I was able to get onto my feet and with Beau watching over Richard, I went to open the front door.

Explaining everything to the two officers, it wasn't long before Richard was in cuffs and being put in the back of their squad car. Beau had had the foresight to record the conversation that he'd had to endure as he raced back to me, and I had the bruises on my side to prove what Richard had tried to do.

"How did you get in by the way?" I asked Beau after the detective who'd been to take a statement from me finally left.

He dragged me onto his knee and kissed the side of my head. "You left the back door unlocked, *again*."

I winced. "Sorry, but it was a good job I did really."

"Hmm I suppose so." He studied me, his hand running down my hair and sighed softly. "That ten-minute journey from Belle's was fucking awful. I didn't think I'd make it in time."

"Ten minutes," I berated. "Belle's apartment is at least thirty minutes away. *Beau*."

"I told you. I went as fast as I could."

"You didn't have to go as fast as bloody Lewis Hamilton though."

He inhaled slowly. "For you I did."

It was then that I knew I was no longer alone. I'd never had a partner to help me traverse parenthood, or parents to ask advice from, no one to tell how my day had gone or share the things that happened. Now though, I had my rock, I had Beau and without doubt I was in love with him. I only hoped that his time away didn't take him away from me permanently.

forty-six

Beau

"Well," Maxwell my solicitor said as he settled into the chair in my lounge. "You'll be pleased to know that it was touch and go but The Crown Prosecution have said there's enough evidence for a case against Mr Gregory. The rape charge hinged on your recording in the end Beau. Without it I'm not sure we'd have been able to go for anything else but assault."

Simone and I both heaved a sigh of relief, and I squeezed her hand as it felt like the nightmare was coming to its end.

"Thank God," Sim whispered. "I thought he was going to get off with it, especially the fact he got out on bail two days ago."

"It's going to court, Simone," Maxwell said gravely. "We still have a long way to go. We're going to need more evidence I'm afraid."

"He's still pleading not guilty?" I asked feeling my blood start to heat up. "And what more evidence can you need?"

"Unfortunately, yes. As for the evidence, we'll get to that."

Maxwell opened a manila file which contained a few pieces of paper and pulled one out. He read it and then handed it to Simone.

"That's a copy of your statement and you'll see that there are a couple of things highlighted. The first one being the documentation and photographs that he fabricated about your brother."

"The police don't believe it, do they?" Simone asked, her voice quaking. No matter whether she was at odds with her brother I knew she wouldn't want him to have to suffer an investigation.

"That's what I wanted to tell you. The police did an initial investigation. They talked to your brother and seized his laptop I'm afraid—"

"Oh my God, no," Simone cried.

"It's okay, they didn't find anything, and your brother was extremely cooperative and understood why it had to be done. They questioned him at the station so that no one would find out. That was when he handed his laptop over. All the other things checked out too. The email originated from a PC in the offices of Mr Gregory's IT company but had been pinged around the world a couple of times to hide the IP address, but the police experts know what they're doing."

That all went over my head, but the main thing was that Marcus was free and clear, not that we hadn't expected that. What I did wonder was why Simone's brother hadn't bothered to let her know that he'd been cleared.

"As for the images of him talking with the young girl, the police did a reverse image search and it's a stock image that can be purchased on any of the image sites around. Again, someone in Mr Gregory's IT company did a little photoshopping to make the man look like your brother."

"So that's it, he won't be investigated further?" Simone asked. When Maxwell shook his head, she blew out her cheeks. "Okay, so the other thing you've got highlighted is the video Richard said he had. What did you want to ask me about that?"

This was where I needed her to calm me down, because the idea that the sick bastard had filmed what he did to her made me want to puke. The idea that he might have watched it, relived it, afterwards made me want to stake his balls to the wall with rusty nails. Sensing I was close to erupting, Simone pulled our joined hands to her and then wrapped her other one around them.

"The police can't find it, I'm afraid," Maxwell said with a small wince. "Without it it's your word against his. I think they told you when you first reported him that getting a conviction after five years would be hard."

"But we have my recording," I offered.

"We do, but Mr Gregory is claiming that it was the word rape was never used in his conversation with Simone and he was discussing a consensual sexual encounter that they'd had years before."

"But he kicked shit out of her. Me and the police found him with his fucking flies undone," I protested. "How can that not be enough evidence?"

"To us it is, to most people it will be, but the jury have to believe it beyond reasonable doubt and his barrister will tear that recording and Simone apart. That's why we really need the video."

"But you can't find it," Simone concluded.

Maxwell shook his head. "No. If it exists?"

"You think he was lying about it?" I asked. "Because got to be honest, I do."

"I don't," Simone said, shaking our joined hands. "He was looking me in the eye when he said it. I know he was telling the truth."

"But you have no idea I suppose where it could be?" Maxwell asked. "Or is that a stupid question."

"I haven't worked in his office since that day," she replied, her voice quiet and laced with pain.

"The police have checked his computer but there's nothing on there."

"Have they searched his house, his office at the record company?" I asked. "What does Dicky, Richard, whatever you want to call him say about it?"

"They say they have and can't find it. As for Richard, his defence it that the comment was a joke about videoing the consensual sex that he and Simone had.

Simone and I both sagged because we both knew, deep down, that he would get away with raping her.

"It's a pity we can't go and search his bloody office or his house," I sighed. "Would that Vanessa woman help?"

I looked at Simone, but she didn't respond. She was looking out of the window.

"Hey, Sim," I said pulling my hand away from hers and rubbing her back. "Are you okay?"

"I was just thinking." She looked at me and her eyes were bright, and a thin smile was ghosting her lips. "Richard asked for the key to the garage because he has boxes in there."

"So?"

"Well," she replied, looking between me and Maxwell. "I brushed it off afterwards as his excuse to get me to open the door but what if he wanted them for a reason."

"What boxes?" Maxwell took a paper from the file and read it. "Ah okay the key to the garage he asked for."

"Yes, he said he wanted to get his boxes. I didn't think anything of it after, but at the time I remember thinking why he suddenly wanted them."

"Come on," I said, standing and pulling Simone to her feet. "Let's go."

***

"Nothing but junk," I said as we looked at the contents of the boxes on the floor.

"I was sure." Simone sounded defeated as she dropped her head to my shoulder. "Why would he want to keep all of this anyway?"

"Who knows," Maxwell said and toed a black plastic office stapler.

There was also a paper Hawaiian Lei, one of the cheap sorts that hen parties often wore, various books, some framed pictures, and a pair of brown and dark green men's brogue shoes, which didn't look Dicky's style seeing as he tended to wear shiny slip-ons. There wasn't anything that looked like it might have a video hidden in it.

"There's definitely no DVDs." I crouched down and looked over the stuff again, just to be sure.

"It would be a memory stick," Simone said. "He wouldn't put it on a DVD that'd be too obvious and who uses them anyway, even five years ago."

"There certainly isn't a memory stick among this lot," Maxwell replied. "I think we have to go to plan B and prep you for some intensive questioning by the defence."

Simone didn't reply as she was reaching for the shoes.

"Sim, what are—."

I stopped when she pulled newspaper out of each one and tipped them both up. Onto the concrete floor of the garage fell a bright red memory stick with the logo of Richard's IT company on it.

forty-seven

Beau

As I wrapped the packing tape around the box, I took a deep breath and laid a palm over the top of it. Inside were Bobby's clothes and some of his teddy bears. Now I knew it was time to take that final step of moving on.

When I told Simone what I wanted to do she'd asked me if I was sure. Did I really want to pack up Cassie and Bobby's clothes and send them to charity? I'd paused and that was enough for her to know that I wasn't. That was when she suggested I box them up and store them, either in the garage or maybe at a unit. She suggested that the garage would be better because they'd still be close by, if for any reason I wanted to get them out. Then she said something which made me realise how fucking lucky I was to have her.

"This isn't moving on, Beau," she whispered as the lump grew in the centre of my chest. "All you're doing is singing the last chorus before you start a new song."

The first thing that then came into my head was, 'shit I could fall in love you'. I didn't say it though, instead I nodded and kissed her softly hoping it would convey my thoughts.

Ma had offered to come and help me pack everything up, as had Belle, but it was something I had to do on my own. This had to be *my* last chorus, no one else's.

"Hey," Simone said as she popped her head around the door. "Is that the last one?"

"Yeah," I said. I pushed the packing tape to one side and moved to sit with my back against the wall, my legs bent and my forearms resting on my knees. "Feels a bit weird."

Simone dropped down beside me and rested her head on my shoulder, and it was amazing how much comfort a simple action gave to me.

"It's bound to, but if you want to put everything back then I'll help you."

I reached my hand up so my fingertips could stroke the soft skin of her earlobe and shook my head.

"No, it's time."

It had been sixteen months, two weeks, and three days. Was that time enough? Who the hell knew? Today it felt like it was. I was committed to Sim and Ethan which made it feel like it was. My head and my heart told me it was, so who was I to question that? I knew that the press would probably spin it that I'd forgotten about my wife and son. There may even be people close to me who would think that. I knew though that this was right for me, and Simone.

"Detective Bushnell called," Simone said, edging closer to me and wrapping an arm around my waist.

I twisted my head to look at her, my heart racing, hoping that it was good news.

"And?"

"He's pleading guilty to rape and assault."

The air rushed from my lungs as her words registered. It had been almost two months since Richard had been arrested and the whole time, he'd pleaded his innocence. Two days after he got bail the stupid dick had tried to leave the country though. However, thanks to an eagle-eyed airport official who noticed something strange about his dodgy fake passport, he was soon back inside to wait for his trial.

"I never thought he would," I said, the lump in my throat making it difficult to talk. "I had this shit feeling that he was going to get off with it."

"I know, me too," Simone replied on a breath. "But he won't now."

"It should be for rape, attempted rape *and* assault," I hissed, images of him standing over Sim with his fucking trousers undone still giving me nightmares.

"At least he'll go down, whatever it's for. Thank God I thought of looking in the boxes in the garage for the video."

I kissed her head. "My clever girl," I said softly.

Both myself and Maxwell had doubted it existed, but Sim had been adamant. She said she could see it in his eyes that he was telling the truth. And there it was, just as she knew it would be, on a memory stick. We took it into the house and Maxwell plugged into his laptop and there was a file titled, 'The lovely Simone'. When I saw it, I wanted to be sick so that was as far as I'd let Maxwell go in front of us. We took it to the police and handed it over, at, according to them, the exact time that Richard was being arrested for trying to flee the country—life is full of weird coincidences. It was such a relief when Detective Bushnell came out of her office and pulled Simone into a hug and said, "We've got him."

"I noticed that it's got sold on the sign next door now," Simone added, bringing me back to the present.

"Hmm." I didn't say much else because she knew that I hated her living in the flat she had been in for the last few weeks. "You could have stayed once he was arrested."

She chuckled and gave my waist a little pinch. "It would have been sold at some point and then I might not have been able to get anywhere to live. There isn't much that comes up in the village."

I cleared my throat and Simone laughed again. We'd had numerous discussions about her moving into my house, but she kept saying it was too soon, we were too new. I had a little suspicion it might have also been because this had been Cassie's house, in every sense. She'd found it, she'd loved it and she'd persuaded me that we needed to move here. I'd asked why when although it was spacious, it wasn't particularly modern having been built in the late eighties. We didn't have a pool or a huge garden, or even a home gym, the usual trappings of the rich and famous. She'd said we could add those things if we really wanted to, but there was something about it that was telling her that we needed to be there. Only she knew what that something was because to me it was just a plain, non-descript house that happened to be a good size and on a nice road.

When Simone made a little satisfied sigh as she cuddled closer, I wondered if she was the *something* that had told Cassie we needed to live there. I wasn't sure I believed in Karma and destiny but maybe the universe had been telling my wife that one day I'd need the beautiful tiny woman who lived next door.

"Are you rehearsing later?" Simone asked. "Because if you are can Ethan and I come? He's not stopped going on about wanting to practice with you."

I smiled knowingly because Simone had totally got the wrong end of the stick on that one. Rehearsals were going well for the tour, and we were all almost back to full fitness as regards running around a stage and singing for two hours. The tour started in a week's time, so we really needed to be, hence why we'd ramped up the rehearsals over the last week.

I had to be honest, when Brit Art had suggested an eight-week turnaround to get on the road, I'd thought they were crazy. It wasn't possible, or I didn't think it was, but they'd proved me wrong getting the set, the lighting, the venues all up and ready with a week to spare. Ronnie made a good point that they'd had it ready for months before we even agreed, but it didn't matter if they did. What did matter was giving the fans an amazing farewell tour. And it was going to be farewell but only in the sense of touring. We'd decided to make music together again, but no touring. We weren't old or knackered but if losing Cass and Bobby had taught us anything it was that life was very short. Too short to be spending months away from home living off a tour bus, eating crap and sleeping even crapper. Plus, I'd lost one family who I'd missed a shit ton of time with over the years, and I didn't want that again. If Sim and I were going to go for it and build on what we had, then I wasn't going to make the same mistakes.

"Okay," I said, playfully slapping Simone's thigh. "Let's grab an early dinner and then get over to the rehearsal studio."

"So Ethan and I can come then?" she asked excitedly.

"Yes Sim, you and Ethan can come. But…" I said turning so that I could land my mouth on hers, "don't get excited when the lead singer takes his shirt off, because I've heard he's fucking sexy as anything."

She closed one eye and studied me. "Hmm," she said. "I've heard he's not all that."

"Really." I laughed and taking her arms, moved her so that she was on her back, and I was able to lean over her. "Because I've heard he's awesome."

I kissed her softly and she sighed. "Yeah, he's totally awesome."

"You think maybe you'll let him stick around?" I asked.

She reared back to look at me, her eyes hesitant. "Do you want to stick around?"

"Absolutely I do, you know that in there." I pointed at her heart and then her head. "So stop letting that tell you differently."

Simone smiled and I felt at peace with every decision I'd made. She was who I wanted to make a future with.

forty-eight

Beau

As I watched Simone help Ethan with his food, I could practically feel the sadness seeping from her. We were off on tour in a few days, and I could see it was going to be harder for her than I thought. Shit, it was going to be hard for me. Not seeing her every day—because even though she now lived in the village in a roasting hot flat that stunk of bread rolls, we still saw each other every day and I loved it. Being part of a couple again, doing things together, having someone to share things with, having two people to love and to spoil was the best part of my life. And yes, I did love her. I just hadn't told her yet. I was waiting for the right moment.

To celebrate us going off on tour, Simone had suggested that she cook for everyone at my house. What were we having? Well, there could only be one meal to celebrate the next step for us and that was a full English. Okay, so we were eating it at seven-thirty in the evening, but it had been the first meal we'd ever eaten together so that was what I'd wanted her to cook.

"You okay?" I asked, leaning in, and placing my hand on her thigh.

"Hmm, yeah." She flashed me a smile, but it went nowhere near to her eyes. "You?"

I kissed her softly and felt her body relax. I relaxed. "Okay but can't wait to get you alone later."

She gasped quietly and looked around the table. Luckily, no one was taking any notice. Joey was talking to Ronnie. Belle was making a decent attempt at pretending she wasn't watching Elliot from the corner of her eye, and he was running his finger around the rim of his glass. As for Ethan, he was tucking into his food with a huge grin.

I decided that now was the time for my first surprise for Sim. She'd barely touched her food but everyone else was almost finished. Reaching around the back of her, I gave Ethan a little poke in the shoulder. He turned to me, and I gave my head a nod towards the dining room door. Ethan's eyes went as wide as saucers as he dropped his knife and fork to his plate with a clatter. He jumped down from his chair and ran from the room.

"Ethan," Simone called after him. "Where do you think you're going?"

"It's okay," I said. "I'll go."

When I got into the hall Ethan was already there with his guitar clutched in one hand and mine in the other.

"You ready?" I asked.

He nodded. "Yes," he replied, and my heart filled with pride. He was talking so much more these days. Sometimes we even had to distract him from talking. Whatever had triggered him to give us more of his words I had no clue, but Sim was convinced it was me and the time and effort that I spent with him. It wasn't his Uncle Marcus that was for sure because we hadn't heard from him since his visit.

"Okay, let go." I rubbed my hand over his already tousled hair and let him lead the way.

"What's going on?" Simone asked as I picked up my empty chair and placed it in the middle of the room.

"You'll see." I replied and gave her a wink.

Ethan sat down on the chair, and I stood beside him, throwing my strap over my shoulder.

"No," Ronnie cried. "I told you, Ethan, you need lessons come to me, not the singer."

Ethan giggled, throwing his head back and there was so much joy on his little face it made me feel emotional. The fact that there was laughter in the house, full stop was, ironically, enough to make me cry.

"If you'd like to shut up," I yelled above Ethan and now Ronnie's laughter. "We would like to sing you a song."

Simone gasped and put a hand to her throat. She'd heard Ethan once before singing to Belle. That night when I'd cocked up big style. He'd also joined the choir at school, but they hadn't done any public performances yet, so this would be only the second time she'd listen to his sweet little voice.

"Nice one, Ethan," Elliot cried, and he leaned forward to take Belle's hand in his and rest them on the table.

She smiled at him over her shoulder and immediately she relaxed into her seat. I had no clue what was going on there, but he better not have been messing her around. One sign that he was fucking her over and there'd be no tour because Elliot would be six feet under, and I'd be either on the run or in prison for murder.

"What are you singing?" Joey asked. "Do you need a drummer?"

"No, we don't, Uncle Joey," Ethan said, loud and clear.

It still made us all sit up in surprise when he spoke, but it was fucking awesome. And the fact that the guys were now all honorary uncles made me happier than one word should do. I was now just Beau, not Mr Beau and I had to admit I was kind of jealous that they all got a title, and I didn't.

Maybe one day?

"Let's go, Ethan," I said trying to ignore the faces staring at us.

He nodded and like a champ he started with the opening chords of *'Beneath Your Beautiful'*.

Carefully, with his tongue peeking out between his lips he played, D, E minor, G and A. There was no strumming for the song, it was all chords, and I was so damn proud of how much he'd improved over the last couple of months. Then he repeated the chords and I started to sing. As I sang about the girl being beautiful my gaze was on Sim the whole time. Watching as tears glistened in her eyes which were pinned on me, everything slotted into place. Her, me, Ethan, a future together, it all made more sense than it even had before. My voice broke on a couple of the lyrics, but I continued playing along with Ethan. When we got to the second verse Ethan took over the singing. His voice was quiet but clear and everyone was listening intently so that they could hear every word. It was then that Simone's tears started to flow freely as she watched her son blow everyone's mind. With each word he sang his chord playing got stronger until by the end of the last chorus I had stopped playing and it was only him, Ethan, all on his own. One little boy who'd decided that talking wasn't his thing was now singing to a roomful of people who adored him and was absolutely smashing it.

As soon as he sang the last word and played the final chord, everyone, me included, started clapping and cheering. Ethan's shoulders went back, and it was if he'd grown another foot in the span of one song.

"Ethan. Oh my God," Simone cried amidst sobs and laughter. "That was amazing." She rushed to him and pulled him into an awkward hug with his guitar between them. "I'm so proud of you." She then looked up at me. "Both of you."

When Belle tried to muscle in for a hug, Simone moved to me and as soon as she did, I removed my guitar and put it to one side. I wanted a full body hug, no guitar between us.

"Thank you," she said, walking into my arms. "That was amazing."

I dropped my mouth to hers and kissed her softly with my fingers threaded through her hair. "I have another surprise for you," I whispered when I pulled away.

She frowned. "What?"

I took her hand and led her out of the dining room into my office. As we walked through the door, I saw the tube on top of my desk and felt the nerves kick in. I just hoped that she agreed to what I was going to suggest. I let go of her hand and walked over to the desk, opened the tube and pulled out a blueprint.

"What's that?" Sim asked, taking a step towards me, and nodding at the roll.

I took a big breath and rolled it out on the desk. "This, baby, if you want it, is our future."

She stopped dead still and looked down at the desk. "Is that…Is it…?"

I nodded and tried to weigh up what she was thinking, but her face gave me nothing other than surprise.

"It's a house, Sim."

"But why, why are you showing me?" She did the thing with chewing her lip and I hoped to God she said yes because I now wanted to celebrate by making her come multiple times.

"Because it's our house, Sim. Mine, yours, and Ethan's. If you'll accept it." I took her hand and pulled her closer to the desk. "Come on, take a look at it."

She stared down at the blueprint of the five-bedroomed, Tuscan style mansion with a modern twist. It had a heated pool, cinema room, music room and gym. I'd been sure to ask the architect to include a huge family kitchen with a sitting area and a massive hallway with a central stairway that had a mezzanine landing because... it was for my Sim.

"It looks great," she said but it didn't sound like she really thought so. She looked up at me and must have seen the disappointment on my face. "No, it does but I don't really understand the drawings."

I let out a huge sigh of relief and opened the top drawer of my desk and pulled out a pile of computer-generated images. I passed them to her and watched as she looked intently at each one—pictures of what I hoped was going to be our home and its interior.

"Beau," she gasped, looking at me wide-eyed. "It's beautiful. How did you know?"

I frowned. "You told me," I replied. "At Elliot's party. You said that your dream house was a Tuscan mansion, with the family kitchen and central staircase, so." I shrugged and gave a tentative smile.

I didn't need to be worried because still clutching the pictures, she launched herself at me and started to drop kisses all over my face.

"Oh my God, I love it, I love y—" She stopped and slapped a hand over her mouth.

I grinned and removed her hand to replace it with my lips to kiss her. It was deep and heated and full of promises and dreams.

"I love you too," I whispered against her ear. "Now, please move in here before I leave on tour. I need to know you're safe and not smelling of yeast when I come home to you,"

She burst out laughing and nodded. "Okay."

The happiness I felt was immense. I didn't think I'd ever feel anything even close to bliss ever again, but Simone in my arms and Ethan being loved on by my best friends and my sister was it. Pure fucking bliss.

"We should get back," Simone said after I gave her one more bloody hotter than hell kiss.

"Okay, I suppose." I was more than happy where I was but…

Simone took my hand and led me into the hallway and as we walked past the side table I stopped.

"What's wrong?" she asked.

I looked up at her and saw she was now looking down at the photograph of Cassie and Bobby, the one that I had just been looking at, the one that had stopped me in my tracks. She leaned up on her tiptoes and kissed the corner of my mouth.

"Take your time, I'll get the dessert sorted." She squeezed my arm and moved to walk away, but I grabbed her hand and pulled her back.

"I'll be one second."

"O-okay," she stammered and stood next to me.

I kissed the tips of two of my fingers and then pressed them to the photograph. I drew in a deep breath, let it out slowly and said, "Love you both and always will."

Simone inhaled and when I nodded, she gave me a beautiful smile and let me lead her back to our friends, our future, and to tell her son that we were now a family.

Watching Beau and Simone laugh and cuddle with Ethan, I couldn't help but wish it was me.

"Really?" Ethan had said when Beau told him they were going to be a family. "We're all going to live together?"

"Is that okay?" Beau asked looking more nervous than I'd ever seen him.

Ethan throwing his arms around Beau's thighs was the only response necessary.

"I'm so happy for them," Belle said moving to my side. "I never thought he'd get that ever again."

I gave her a smile and put my arm around her shoulders, kissing the side of her head. I'd loved Belle for as long as I could remember and now that we were together, I should be happier than ever. I wasn't though and it wasn't fair to her. She was beautiful, strong, clever, funny and the best damn sex I'd ever had. There was a darkness creeping into my head though. Things that I wanted to forget had been resurrected and I wasn't sure I could be the person that Belle deserved.

"Are you okay?" she asked. "I'm worried about you."

I cleared my throat and nodded. "Yes," I said. "Everything is fine."

Hear more from Belle & Elliot in 2023
Pre Order The Opening Line

Acknowledgments

The biggest thanks I have for this book is to my friend Donna Wright. When I told her what I wanted to write she was excited as I was. When I told her that I didn't think I could write it she told me that I was being a dick. Needless to say, she won that argument and here we are with what I truly believe is my best book to date. If not my best certainly my favourite.

Donna has been a true cheerleader throughout the process, but she's also told me in only the way that she can when something isn't working and that I need to rewrite it. Not only that she had the unenviable task of looking at hundreds of cover photos with me. When Lou sent over the final cover, I'm not sure who loved it more, me or Donna. Anyway, the point is Donna, thank you for everything. I'd have done it without you, maybe, eventually, but it wouldn't have been as much fun!

There's a whole host of other people I'd also like to acknowledge, so here goes.

Lynn, Sarah, Mandy, Robyn & Janice my beta readers and constant support.

Lou J Stock for another gloriously beautiful cover.

Anna Bloom for your usual no nonsense editing skills. Evident is *the* word for this book lol!!!

Bare Naked Words for your expertise in the promotion of The Last Chorus.

Claire Allmendinger for proofreading what I hope wasn't a total punctuation nightmare for you.

All the ARC readers for taking the time to sign up and agree to review what I hope becomes one of your favourite rock star romance novels.

My Indie ladies, you know who you are!

Finally, and by no means least, you the readers for looking at this book and thinking, '*Isn't she that romcom writer. Oh, maybe I'll see if she's any good at the serious stuff too.*'. I cannot thank you enough for making that decision. This book was written during a time of great sadness and grief for us as we knew we were going to be losing a very close, dear friend. He has now passed away so every word you read is for him and I hope that you know how much I appreciate that.

Love ya millions,
Nikki ♥ x

Warrior Creek Playlist

Available to listen to on Spotify

https://open.spotify.com/playlist/1rBplm7mCw0HN8qVrxDWLW?si=f3c-4c61df7ad4e7a

These songs don't feature in any of the books of Warrior Creek novels but are a great accompaniment to the stories.
The list will continue to grow with each book that is written.

Nikki's Links

If you'd like to know more about me or my books,
then all my links are listed below.

Website:
www.nikkiashtonbooks.co.uk

Instagram
www.instagram.com/nikkiashtonauthor

Facebook
www.facebook.com/nikki.ashton.982

Ashton's Angels Facebook Group
www.facebook.com/groups/1039480929500429

Amazon
viewAuthor.at/NAPage

Printed in Great Britain
by Amazon

79327878R00188

Ahmet Prençi

Anja

Dritan Kiçi

BELBËZIMI
MBAJTJA E GOJËS

PSE NDODH
SI TA KORRIGJOSH

Çfarë duhet të dish dhe
një metodë praktike që ka
ndihmuar mijëra belbëzues
të arrijnë rrjedhshmërinë
në të folur

RL BOOKS

C000131700

BUKË
E KRYPË
E ZEMËR

Receta gatimi dhe shënime të tjera nga Shkodra

RLBOOKS

Nata si e
Dekameronit

tregime e novela

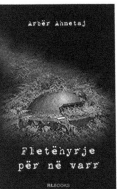

Arbër Ahmetaj

Fletëhyrje
për në varr

RLBOOKS

Haki Stërmilli
Sikur
të isha
djalë

Rishjellë në shqipen e sotme

ANNA KOVE

KAMBANAT
E SË DIELËS

I huaji, ai
kosovari

Arbër
Ahmetaj

roman

RL BOOKS

Ilir Magjistari

Llogari
të mbyllura

tregime

REVISTA
LETRARE

Dritan Kiçi

Zhvillimi i komunikimit
dhe shmangia e belbëzimit
te fëmijët 2-6 vjeç

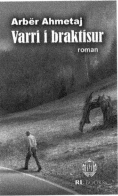

Arbër Ahmetaj
Varri i braktisur

roman

RL BOOKS

Poezia është grua
La poésie est une femme!

SHYHRETE
KURTI-MUSA

Dritan Kiçi

LINDJA
E PERËNDISË
SIME

poezi

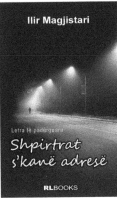

Ilir Magjistari

Letra të padërguara
Shpirtrat
s'kanë adresë

RLBOOKS

Ilir Magjistari

Mos harro
të më puthësh

poezi